Where Earth Meets Sky

ALSO BY ANNIE MURRAY

Birmingham Rose

Birmingham Friends

Birmingham Blitz

Orphan of Angel Street

Poppy Day

The Narrowboat Girl

Chocolate Girls

Water Gypsies

Miss Purdy's Class

Family of Women

ANNIE MURRAY

Where Earth Meets Sky

MACMILLAN

First published 2007 by Macmillan
an imprint of Pan Macmillan Ltd
Pan Macmillan, 20 New Wharf Road, London N1 9RR
Basingstoke and Oxford
Associated companies throughout the world
www.panmacmillan.com

ISBN 978-1-4050-9201-2

1 3 5 7 9 8 6 4 2

A CIP catalogue record for this book is available from
the British Library.

Typeset by SetSystems Ltd, Saffron Walden, Essex
Printed and bound in Great Britain by
Mackays of Chatham plc, Chatham, Kent

Visit **www.panmacmillan.com** to read more about all our books
and to buy them. You will also find features, author interviews and
news of any author events, and you can sign up for e-newsletters
so that you're always first to hear about our new releases.

For Sam, Rachel, Katy and Rose

You're the best.

With lots of love,

Mum

xxxx

My thanks for help in researching this book are due to the National Motor Museum at Beaulieu and Brooklands Museum in Surrey. Also to my mother Jackie Summers for invaluable information, Rajinder Singh for assistance in Ambala and a special thank you to Bill Meyer for the time, expertise and information he shared with me on the way.

'Throughout its history, the car has been a liberator, an agent of freedom. Throughout its history, the car has enabled people to break out of their constraints, to attempt something they could never previously do, to venture somewhere they could never previously go, to support ideas and trends they could never previously endorse.'

L. J. K. Setright

Glossary

anna – 1/16th of a rupee in monetary currency
ayah – nanny
bari hazri – main breakfast
chai – tea (also *char*)
chelo! – go on! get a move on!
chota hazri – 'little breakfast' served around six a.m.
chowkidar – nightwatchman
dal – spiced lentils
dhobi – laundry
dhoti – loose loincloth worn by Hindus
dirzi – tailor
garam chai – hot tea
jhampanis – rickshaw pullers
jao! – go!
limbopani – lemonade
lingam – male fertility symbol (usually Siva's penis)
mali – gardener
pukka – proper, good quality
punkah – fan
punkah-wallah – fan puller
syce – groom
tonga – cart
topi – hat
wallah – man

Chapter One

Birmingham, 1905

'Don't cry over me, Lily, my dear girl! I've had such a very good life – you mustn't grieve.'

'I'm sorry, Mrs Chappell, I can't help it,' Lily sobbed, as she sat beside the dying woman whose motherly kindness she had known during these past, precious years. 'You've been so very good to me!'

She had waited all evening, in an agony of pent-up emotion, for Mrs Chappell's jealous son Horace to allow her to pay her last respects to the woman she loved so much.

'You've been like a daughter, you know that . . .' Mrs Chappell's rasping whisper came to her. The lids flickered over her blue eyes. She was fading fast.

Lily sat in the candlelight beside the big comfortable bed with its silk drapes. She clung desperately to the shrunken hand of this woman into whose household she had arrived as a scullery maid when she was thirteen. In her own grief and loss Maud Chappell had, over the years, grown to depend on Lily as a companion. Mrs Chappell's body had fast become frail with her illness. She did not look any more like the comforting figure who had dressed in pretty, floating clothes, who adored small children, beaming at them with her beautiful, loving eyes. The light of her life was failing and her sons were in the house, waiting. Lily told herself that they were full of pain at losing their mother, that it was their sorrow that made them so harsh, especially Horace, the older brother. They had kept her out of the room all evening, only reluctantly letting her in now it was so late.

'Mother's asking for you,' Horace had said, stiff with resentment. 'You'd better go up.'

Now she was here she sat in dread of them coming to tell her to go again.

'Oh, Mrs Chappell,' she whispered, looking down at the ravaged face, her own tears flowing again. She felt her heart was being torn in two. 'What's going to become of me without you?'

Mrs Chappell was a year off her seventieth birthday, and until her illness had looked younger than her years, with her soft, glowing complexion and cheerful ways. But she was much changed now, months of sickness taking their toll. She lay with her arms straight, outside the covers, her soft brown hair which had so fast turned grey brushed back from her face. She seemed to have slipped far away into sleep, so that Lily thought she might never wake again. But as if a sign had been given, just as the grandfather clock down in the hall was striking eleven with its gentle 'bong', the elderly lady opened her eyes, seeming quite alert, and tried to get up.

'Lily?'

'Yes, dear Mrs Chappell?' Hope surged through her. Perhaps Mrs Chappell was not dying! She seemed so bright suddenly, as if she might sit up and take some broth.

'I'm still at home, then?'

2

'Yes, you are. You're in your own bed.'

'Bring me the picture, please, my dear. Of my Naomi.'

'It's here – right beside you.'

She lifted the silver-framed photograph from its position on the bedside table and turned it so that Mrs Chappell could see the face of her dead daughter. Naomi, a dark-eyed beauty, had died of a cruel brain fever when she was only seventeen. It was the last portrait taken of her, her shoulders wrapped in a lace shawl and the young face, never now to age, smiling radiantly from behind the glass as it had for over twenty years.

Mrs Chappell reached out as if to embrace the portrait, a gentle smile on her lips.

'My darling . . .' she murmured. And her arms dropped back. She had not the strength.

'I think you'd better fetch my boys,' she whispered. But she clutched at Lily's hand to stop her.

'You'll get a good appointment. You're so sweet, so beautiful. You be happy, my dear love. Bless you.'

By the time Lily had fetched Horace and John Chappell up to their mother's room, she was lying on her pretty, embroidered pillows with her eyes closed and a look of utter peace. She had already left them.

'My mother has left you a small bequest, according to our solicitor,' Horace Chappell told her. His voice was icy cold.

Lily stood before him on the Persian rug in Mr Chappell's old study. Horace had not invited her to sit down.

They're kind really, she made herself believe. Mrs

3

Chappell said so. Since Mr Chappell died only three years ago, Mrs Chappell had relied on her sons, Horace and John, for everything. After all, they have looked after their mother, Lily told herself. And don't they both have wives and families who all look happy and well cared for?

These were the families who, at Mrs Chappell's strict instructions that she should be included, she had followed to the funeral: Horace and his wife and three little girls, and John and his wife and twin sons, alike as two peas. None of them had said a word to her or even acknowledged her existence, but of course they were wrapped in grief and she was only a maid. Why would they have any time for her? It was a beautiful June morning with laburnum and lilac in bloom, just the right kind of day for Mrs Chappell's funeral as she was such a sunny person who loved young life and flowers and pretty things around her. Once the funeral was over, though, they were fast making arrangements to clear and sell the house and seemed to be in a great rush to get it all done and dismiss all their mother's employees.

'Can't get shot of us fast enough, can they?' grumbled Cook, who had worked for Mrs Chappell for more than twenty years.

'I suppose they have a lot of business to sort out – they're very busy men,' Lily replied, knowing it was the sort of thing Mrs Chappell would have said because she always tried to see the best in her sons.

'They just want their hands on the money,' Mary, one of the maids, retorted. 'Since Mr C died she's had no say in anything – not with those two vultures in charge. They couldn't wait to get their father out of the way – no, it's no good arguing, Lily. You're just like Mrs C – you'll see black as white to find the best in someone. You're going to have to toughen up your ideas when you go away from here! They ain't all like her, you know.'

Horace, the older brother, had called her into the study. He had his mother's blue eyes, but instead of her embracing warmth, his looked cool and calculating. There were official-looking documents laid neatly across the desk.

'My mother left us a number of instructions regarding you and your future,' he said. He didn't meet her eye. He had always seemed most uncomfortable in her presence. 'Far too sultry, that's your trouble,' Cook once said. 'You provoke him.'

'You are very fortunate.' He held out an envelope. 'Firstly, this contains references to secure your future. You should be able to attain a very good position.' He cleared his throat, grimacing, and, as if it pained him to speak, said, 'My mother has not left you money. She did not think that would be the best thing for your welfare.' Lily watched him, wondering, after what Mary had said, whether Mrs Chappell had had any money to call her own in any case. 'But she has left you a number of items of jewellery, from her personal effects.' He nodded at a small box, inlaid with ivory, on the desk, then looked sternly at her. 'I believe them to be rather valuable. More than generous, I should say, Miss Horne. And this is where we draw a line. I should like to make clear that after this there is nothing else you can take from this family.'

Lily was stung to the core by this remark.

'I never . . .' she stuttered. 'I never took anything that

was wrong or out of place! She wanted me . . .' The last utterance, the miraculous truth of it, brought her to tears.

'That will be all, Miss Horne.'

With the envelope and box in her hands Lily fumbled her way from the room, hardly able to see through her tears. She was dreadfully hurt by his unjust, jealous remarks, and overcome by Mrs Chappell leaving her anything at all. Her heart ached with longing for her friend.

'What did he say?' Cook and the others were all agog to know. They had been told they would each have a turn to be called in.

'She left me some jewellery!' Lily told them with tears running down her cheeks.

'Well what're you blarting about?' Cook demanded. 'You're a rum 'un, you are.'

'She was so kind!' Lily sobbed. Mrs Chappell had been her saviour and friend; she had raised her up from nothing, from her beginnings as an abandoned urchin off the streets. It felt unbearable that she was gone.

Lily went up to her room at the top of the house and sank down on the edge of her bed. She realized she was still holding the box and envelope. She wanted to look inside in private. Opening the lid of the box she smelled a lovely scent of lavender, and what she saw on the base of the velvet box made her weep all the more. Lying in a pale, glowing coil was Mrs Chappell's skein of tiny seed pearls. Maud Chappell had always said to her, 'You should wear pearls, Lily. They would look marvellous on your skin.' She picked them up, feeling their warm, smooth weight, and held them lovingly to her cheek. '*Oh, thank you . . .*' she whispered. Also in the box were a matching pearl bracelet and a beautiful opal brooch in a silver setting. Lily laid them out and looked at them in awe.

Then she remembered the envelope containing her references and she pulled out an expensive piece of notepaper. She could hardly read the warm, praising words through her tears. '. . . kind and sweet-natured . . . staunchly honest, hard-working . . . it would represent the greatest good fortune to employ her . . .'

Overcome, Lily lay on her side and wept heartbrokenly. What tugged so powerfully at her heart in those moments was not the shower of kind words, or the gift of precious jewellery, but the strength of Mrs Chappell's love and kindness, flowing to her from beyond the grave.

Chapter Two

Later, she got up from the bed and poured water from the pitcher to wash her face, sitting to look in the glass tilted over her little white chest of drawers. Her face was blotchy from weeping and her dark eyes stared mournfully back at her. Mrs Chappell's death had taken away all the safety she had found for the last nine years in her employment and friendship, where she had settled into a household where she knew her place and was treated with ever-increasing kindness.

When she was fifteen, by which time Lily had worked for nearly two years on the lowest rung of the ladder, Mrs Chappell stopped her one day as Lily was passing through the hall carrying a heavy coal scuttle, dressed in her black maid's uniform with a white cap and apron. She was pink-cheeked and strong, in good condition from the physical work demanded in the house.

'My goodness!' Mrs Chappell uttered the words in a shocked tone, as if she had just noticed some terrible fault in the domestic scene. 'Wait, child! Stop and look at me!'

Lily paused, heart pounding. Although she had barely ever had anything to do with Mrs Chappell, by then she knew her employer was usually a gentle lady. What had she done so wrong?

'Come a little closer, dear – er, what is your name again?'

'Lilian Horne.' *I'm in for it now*, Lily thought, keeping her eyes lowered, seeing the lower edge of Mrs Chappell's sage-green skirt and her elegant brown shoes on the polished tiles of the hall.

'Do look at me,' Maud Chappell said softly. 'It's quite all right. You've done nothing wrong. Put the coal down, dear – it looks heavy.'

Lily obeyed and looked blushingly up into her employer's face. Mrs Chappell wore her hair swept up and pinned in a wispy, abstracted style which made her look rather artistic and vague. Wisps of it were forever escaping about her round face. In her eyes, Lily saw kindness, and a great yearning.

'Oh, my dear . . .' Mrs Chappell put a hand to her chest and her eyes suddenly filled with tears. 'So like – in a way. Your lovely dark hair, your shape . . . A kind of essence . . . I'm sorry, dear, you must find me very strange. You'll know we lost our daughter Naomi, bless her heart, oh, eleven years ago now! And when I saw you just then, of course you're different, but you have a look of her . . . Why have I never seen it before?' She sighed, wiping her eyes. 'How lovely, to have you in our house . . .'

And she drifted away, lost in emotion. Lily picked up the coal scuttle, confused, but also surprised to find her own eyes full of tears, her own hunger for a mother and for love answering Mrs Chappell's loss and grief.

That was how it began, her ascent in the house. By the time she was seventeen, the age at which Naomi Chappell lost her life, Lily had risen to be a maid of all work, and then, gradually, into personal maid and companion of Maud Chappell, a woman whose personal warmth covered a great inner loneliness. There was no shortage of money as Mr Chappell owned a string of carriage-building works, and the house in Hall Green, a pleasant suburb of Birmingham, was large and beautifully furnished. But with a mostly absent husband, two sons whose lives had long moved away from her into working the world, and a dead daughter, Mrs Chappell had lost a great deal that was dear to her. She adored young life and waited in hope of grandchildren.

'Before my marriage, I was a trained nanny, you see,' she explained to Lily one day in the flower-scented drawing room. 'I lived with some beautiful families – and some of the dear little ones still write to me, now they're older.' Her eyes filled every time she talked about her charges. 'There's not much I don't know about small children.' She gave a sigh then, also. 'I should have liked more of my own, but it was not to be.'

As time passed, she grew to require more and more of Lily's company.

'You're such an intelligent, gentle girl, and so very lovely. I can teach you, you see, if you like. If you learn about looking after small children, and a little elocution to correct that accent, you could have a very promising future.'

Over the last five years, especially with the arrival of her five grandchildren, who she looked after as often as her daughters-in-law would let her, Mrs Chappell had more than made up for Lily's lost education, and had also taught Lily everything she knew about the care of young children: diet and feeding, how to play with and handle them and all their infant needs of warmth and cleanliness, their training and how to remedy their maladies. Over the years Lily learned all sorts: how to soothe a child's temperature with a wet pack, to put an infant with croup in a mustard bath or induce vomiting with ipecacuanha wine, to paint a tincture of iodine on a patch of ringworm, or treat scabies with Balsam of Peru. Mrs Chappell's training of Lily became a labour of love and Lily was an eager student, thriving as much upon affection as education. She taught her to read and write beautifully, and speak in a more genteel manner, flattening out her Birmingham accent.

'You really are turning into quite a young lady!' she said sometimes, watching her with pride. As Lily grew older and entered her twenties, Mrs Chappell didn't want to let her go to another position in the world. She needed her too much herself. And Lily had no wish to go either, from this home where she was loved and valued, after the cruel beginning life had dealt her.

Mrs Chappell never asked much about Lily's past. Lily was grateful, since she could remember so little and what she could remember, about living with the Hornes, she preferred to push from her memory. Maud Chappell asked only a few gentle questions and Lily told her that Mrs Horne had been good to her, which she had, until she died, leaving Lily at the mercy of her drunken husband and cruel daughters. But she did not want to think of them, of the agony and loneliness of that time. And Mrs Chappell simply saw something in her that it suited both of them to develop. The other maids working in the house at that time had been envious and spiteful about Lily's rise up the ranks.

'You're the favourite all right, ain't you?' they'd say. 'What makes you so blooming special, Miss La-di-dah?'

Apart from Cook, those maids had all gone now, and the new ones coming into the house accepted things as they were. Lily enjoyed their company – Mary and Fanny and Joan – and knew she was going to miss them terribly now the household was all to be broken up.

Only Joan, the youngest, was staying in the family, as she was being taken on by Mr John Chappell's wife.

Lily gazed at her own face in the glass now, suddenly deeply confused and frightened. All these years she had had a place. Now she had to go out and face the world alone.

That week, Horace and John Chappell, with the help of the staff who they kept on for the purpose, were clearing the house with great speed. Two of the maids, Mary and Fanny, were paid off immediately, and there were tearful farewells as they left the house for the last time with their modest bags of belongings.

Lily found it heartbreaking, watching her home of so many years being taken to pieces and having no say in the matter. Furniture began to disappear, workmen in overalls came and took away dressers and cupboards, rugs were rolled up and now their feet clumped loudly on the bare floorboards. Mrs Chappell's elegant curtains were taken from the windows in the drawing room. More than once, Lily found Cook weeping into the pastry in the kitchen, and she kept dissolving into tears herself. It wasn't just the house. Although Horace Chappell was unkind, his brother John was a more gentle character, and she was genuinely fond of all their children, whom she had known since they were born. Now she would never see them again!

As her illness progressed, Mrs Chappell had said, 'What you need to do, Lily dear, when I'm gone, is to apply for a position in *The Lady*. You're quite experienced enough to work as a nanny for a family after all I've taught you. You're just the sort of girl a good family would be crying out for.'

12

Remembering Mrs Chappell's advice, she went in search of a copy of *The Lady*, a genteel women's publication in which were advertised posts for nannies and companions. One hot afternoon she sat out on the terrace at the back of the house, half in the shade of a laburnum, and looked at the positions on offer. She drew a ring round two of them. One was for a family by the name of Clutterbuck, who had just had a baby girl and wanted a nanny very quickly. They lived in Dorset. Lily was not absolutely sure where Dorset was but it seemed a possibility. There was another similar in Scotland, but it was a place she always thought of as dreary and cold. But the third advertisement made her heart pick up speed. A nanny was required by a Mrs Susan Fairford, wife of Captain Charles Fairford of the 12th Royal Lancers, stationed at Ambala, India, for their son, aged two. The address to apply to was in Chislehurst in Kent.

Lily looked up from the magazine and stared unseeingly at the rose beds along the side of the house. India! Her head reeled. She was bewildered, afraid and suddenly full of excitement. India was the other side of the world! It was so different she could barely imagine it, except for other pictures she had seen in books of people riding elephants and one she remembered of a huge, waving grove of something called bamboo. But she was already captivated. She already knew she was going to apply for the position and go far away from this place, now all that had kept her here was gone. She had no one now. For a moment she thought about Mrs Horne. She was the only person she had ever called mother – but she was not her mother. Why had Mrs Horne brought her up in her kindly but rough and ready way? What had happened to her real mother and father?

'They did a flit one night, according to the neigh-bours,' Mrs Horne had told her. 'Hadn't been there long, in any case. They said she was dark and pretty like a gypsy, and expecting another child. All I know is, there you were playing in the gutter, all alone in just a little camisole, in the pouring rain. But I don't s'pose you'll ever find out now, bab. Best not think about it.'

Lily knew there was no hope of ever finding out about her origins, and it hurt too much, looking back. She had moved too far from Mrs Horne, from growing up in Sparkbrook. She would start again, clean and fresh, and with sudden resolve she hurried up the now uncarpeted stairs to her attic room, sat at her little table and took the references Horace Chappell had handed her out of their thick envelope.

But looking down at the sheets of paper with her name at the top of Mrs Chappell's glowing reference, that desperate, lost feeling washed through her again. Her name, *LILIAN HORNE*, was written in capital letters at the top in Mrs Chappell's immaculate copper-plate script.

Little Lilian Horne. Whoever was she? Had she not been playing the part of someone else all these years, someone who Mrs Chappell needed her to be, and whose identity she had now taken on herself?

She stood up and went again to the glass on her chest of drawers and her face stared back at her, strong-featured, with her burning dark eyes, her thick, wavy chestnut hair modestly fastened back and her demure, white-frilled blouse at her neck. It was the look of a respectable young woman, one who was now nicely spoken, genteel. Not an abandoned slum child fit only for the workhouse, the way the two Horne girls had made her feel. They'd always made sure she was a cuckoo in the nest, with their cruel tricks, their slaps and scratches.

'*Not Lilian Horne*,' she whispered. 'I'm not a Horne and I never was.'

She sat at her little table and opened its drawer, where she had some writing paper. Beside it in the drawer were three books. The one on top was a book of wildflowers, sketched by a John Waters. For a moment she picked it up and looked at it.

Lily dipped her pen into the bottle of ink, and began, painstakingly, to copy out the references again, well instructed in mimicking Mrs Chappell's elegant hand. At the top of the page, in large letters, she gave her name: *LILY WATERS*.

Chapter Three

'Miss Waters?'

The maid had shown Lily into the parlour of the Chislehurst house to face a small, plump woman with a harassed expression and faded blond hair curling round the edge of a white bonnet. She found herself appraised by pale blue eyes, but somehow the experience was not as frightening as she expected. The house, though a fair size, was shabbier than the one in Hall Green! And she could hear children's voices, squabbling in the background somewhere.

'My name is Mrs Burton,' the woman said, distractedly. 'I am Mrs Fairford's sister. Please, do take a seat.'

She indicated an upright chair with a slightly moth-eaten seat cover, while she perched on another wooden chair nearby, her feet, in their laced brown boots, barely touching the floor. For a moment they both looked at one another. Mrs Burton seemed at a loss. She was obviously not used to the job in hand.

'Well, you're here, anyway.' There was a pause in which Lily wondered what she was supposed to say, but this was followed by, 'You have come all the way from Birmingham, I take it?'

'Yes, I have.'

The woman pressed the tips of her fingers to her forehead as if to gather her thoughts, then said, 'My sister, Mrs Fairford, has asked me to find a nanny for her son, Cosmo – he's just two years old. If my sister was in the country herself, she would be doing the interviews.'

There was another awkward silence in which it occurred to Lily's interviewer that she might peer at the references provided, holding them as far away from her as her short arms would permit.

'These are very good – *very*!'

'Thank you.'

Mrs Burton rested the paper in her lap and squinted slightly. 'Are you a *proper* nanny?'

'Yes,' Lily said, as Mrs Chappell had told her to, speaking slowly in her best, well-spoken English. 'I've had a very good training and considerable experience of looking after five young ones. I don't think I'd have any problem with one little boy.'

'No, quite. And ... What about India? You did realize you'd have to sail the seas? Live quite the other side of the world!'

'Yes. I should welcome the adventure.'

'Well, Susan hates it!' This seemed to slip out by mistake and the colour rose in Mrs Burton's cheeks. 'Lord, I shouldn't have said that. Most indiscreet of me. But she does. All those diseases. Of course, that was what led to ... Oh, dear me, my mouth does run away so ... She tries to make the best of it, though, dear Susan does. But the poor darling does so need help, what with Isadora being so ...' Once again she stopped. 'Cosmo is not Susan's only child. She has a daughter, who is ... rather difficult. But she would not be your responsibility. Do you think you could adjust and be a help to my poor sister?

'Well, I hope so – very much.'

'Well—' Mrs Burton stood up. 'That's very hopeful.

17

I'll be letting you know. But I expect you'll take the post? You look the adventurous sort.'

On the long train ride home, Lily already felt she had indeed begun on an adventure, was discovering in herself a taste for it. She kept saying her new name to herself. *Lily Waters.* That's who I am now. It made her feel strong.

Three days later a letter arrived, saying that her interview had been successful and if she was still willing to accept, the family would book her passage on a P&O liner to India.

Chapter Four

Ambala, India, 1905

Lily's first months in India were full of mixed, sometimes overwhelming, emotions.

There was the journey to begin with, exciting, daunting, setting out to the other side of the world with nothing but hope and excitement, a small tin trunk containing her possessions and no clear idea of what she was going to find. The P&O steamer was an adventure in itself. She made friends with another nanny called Jenny, who was blonde and good-humoured and was on her way back out to a family in Poona after delivering one of the children to relatives in England.

As they progressed east, the temperatures gradually rising, the two young women often walked out on the glaring deck to take the breeze blowing from the sea. Jenny, in a big sisterly way, was able to brief Lily about India.

'You get used to it after a while,' she said cheerfully. 'The summer months can be hellish if you don't go up to the hills, of course, though I expect your family will. And there's a lot of social fun – parties and so on – for the adults and children. Just make sure you drink boiled water and wash your hands a lot. Lots of carbolic soap! It's all right out there, really it is. You'll soon settle in.

Beats living in a backstreet in rainy old England, I can tell you.'

The morning the boat gently nosed its way into the harbour at Bombay was one Lily would never forget. She stood on deck beside Jenny, the sun high, the humid heat alleviated by the breeze over the sea. The ship was rolling gently, the sea was a deep, ruffled green, and gradually the land came more clearly into view.

'Dear old Bombay,' Jenny said, shading her eyes with her hand. 'D'you know, I loathed it all when I first came. But it's grown on me. See the coast there – they call that the Ghats, that part rising from the sea – and then the mountains behind.'

Lily thrilled with excitement at the sight of it. The high land in the distance looked a dull sandy colour, stained with patches of verdure lower down. Jenny had said the monsoon rains were not yet over and all the land was bright and green during the rainy season. As they moved closer, she began to see the city, a wide hotch-potch of white buildings, brilliant in the sun. The breeze dropped and gradually smells began to reach her, strange, alluring, sulphurous and scented. She felt the damp, heavy heat wrap round her. By the time they slid into the dock she was sweating profusely, her clothes limp with moisture, but she barely noticed, so enthralled was she by the sight of the bright colours and seething activity on the quay below, the white-uniformed band playing a toe-tapping marching tune and the busy, brown-skinned, *different* people of India.

She said tearful farewells to Jenny at Victoria Terminus in Bombay as they both went to board different trains, Lily north to Delhi, on another leg of her long journey.

'You'll be all right, Lily, dear,' Jenny assured her as

she kissed her goodbye. The two young women had grown very fond of one another. 'You're one of the ones that will feel at home in India – I can tell.'

It was true. Though it was all new and bewildering, beggars and teeming streets and everything strange, the heat, the food, the temples and mosques, yet amid all that she felt immediately happy and at home, as if this was a place where she was somehow born to be.

The long train journey to Ambala Cantonment, across the great Punjab plain north of Delhi, was exhausting, as were the first days of getting used to the town and its ways. It was half native town, half army cantonment, and riding in a *tonga* that first afternoon, along a wide road through the cantonment, she caught sight, with an astonished gasp, of the huge, elegant residence of Captain Charles Fairford, in whose employment and family she had now placed herself.

'So – you are the nanny they've sent?' Susan Fairford held out her hand.

'Yes,' Lily said, shrinking inside. Her employer seemed as remote and frozen as the Antarctic.

Mrs Fairford was petite in stature, with hair of a pale honey colour and a strikingly pretty face, with Cupid's bow lips and wide blue eyes. She was dressed in a beautiful ivory gown with bows and flounces in the long skirt, the whole outfit nipped in tightly at the waist and showing off a slim, well-proportioned figure. As she spoke, Lily saw that she had little white teeth almost like a child's. What was absent was any sense of warmth. The hand that she took to shake in introduction was small and unresponsive, like a dead thing.

'Do sit down.'

They sat opposite one another and Lily waited, hearing the ticking of the small ormolu clock from the mantelpiece. The room was at least pretty and feminine after the opulent, but creepy, hall, a museum to dead creatures whose heads and skins decorated the walls and floor. From the garden came the sounds of crows cawing.

'My sister wrote to tell me that she thought you had sufficient experience as a nanny for my son. She also said that she liked the look of you. Knowing Audrey, I suppose she meant that you are pretty, though whether that is a qualification remains to be seen. I have had to trust my sister, being so far away. I hope she has made a wise choice.'

All this was said in a distant, rather languid tone. Lily began to feel rather like a cow which has been brought from the market by proxy. Her heart sank further, but she told herself not to get upset. She had only just arrived and she had not met the boy yet. He was what mattered!

'Well, I hope you think so,' she murmured. 'I'm looking forward to meeting your children.'

'You only need to concern yourself with one of the children,' Mrs Fairford said sharply. 'I don't know if my sister explained to you that we need a nanny for our son Cosmo, to prepare him for going home to school in England. Our daughter, Isadora, will not be going home. She is not . . . She . . .'

Lily watched the woman's face. For a moment her composure had slipped and an expression of pained confusion passed over her face.

'Isadora is not fully able to be educated. She has certain – difficulties. Unfortunately she is much attached to her *ayah*, the Indian girl who continues to look after

22

her. We've tried several times to prise her away from the girl, but it's no good.' Now there was bitterness in her voice.

She's jealous, Lily saw. It was a chink in the woman's armour, and even though she found her cold and intimidating, she could see that Mrs Fairford suffered because she thought her daughter loved an Indian girl better than her own mother, that there was much that lay behind this frosty mask.

'Cosmo is to be your charge.' For a second her tone softened a tiny fraction, but immediately grew cool again. 'We don't want him brought up by natives. When he's old enough he'll go home to Eton, like his father, away from this beastly country. He will learn to be an English gentleman. In the meantime we want you to speak with him – in English, of course, always: you must stop his native prattle. Teach him songs and games from home, his letters and numbers and so on. Above all—' suddenly she looked very directly at Lily as she spoke, with a tone of pleading – 'be a friend to him.'

'Yes, Mrs Fairford.' She was not sure what else to say to this odd, naked request. She felt very discouraged by what she had seen so far of this chilly household. What on earth could Captain Fairford be like? She imagined a tight-lipped, forbidding man and wondered if that was the reason why Mrs Fairford seemed so tense and unhappy. Because she could see straight away that she was not looking at a contented woman. She decided to take the woman's plea for her son as a sign of hope.

'When am I to meet your little boy?' she asked.

'He and Isadora are resting at present. I suggest you go and do the same. I'll send one of the servants to bring you to the nursery at teatime.' It was a dismissal.

'Yes, ma'am,' Lily said.

'You may call me Mrs Fairford. I don't enjoy being called "ma'am".'

'Yes, Mrs Fairford.'

Her employer stood up. 'You may go.'

Lily left the room, feeling low and close to tears. Was she wrong to expect Mrs Fairford to ask her a single thing about herself, about her welfare after her long journey, or to give some indication of welcome or gladness?

You've been too used to Mrs Chappell, she told herself as she slipped along the passage to her bedroom. Not everyone's like that. You're going to have to get used to the fact that you're a servant and nothing else.

But as she lay down on her bed, having crawled in under the swathing mosquito net, it was a dispiriting thought, and her heart ached with unshed tears. On the journey to get here she had felt only excitement and expectation, but now she felt chilled and lonely.

Chapter Five

To her surprise she was awoken by a servant in a maroon uniform bringing a cup of very sweet tea which revived her spirits. The sight of his friendly face also made her feel better and he provided a pitcher of warm water with which she washed, then changed her clothes. Some time later the servant returned.

'I am to take you to the nursery – Mrs Fairford sent me to fetch you.'

As she made to leave the room, he added politely, 'Your name is?'

She gave him her name and he said his was Rajinder. His would be the first of many names she had to learn of the family's large retinue of servants.

The nursery consisted of two adjoining rooms, one for each of the children. Mrs Fairford was waiting for her with both the children: Cosmo on the floor, head bent over a box of wooden bricks, and the girl on a big rocking horse at the side of the room. Lily was delighted to see that they had a magnificent array of toys.

Squatting on the floor beside the boy was the young *ayah*, dressed in a deep red sari. Lily was perturbed to see she had a silver ring through her left nostril. Mrs Fairford sat looking very stiff and formal and Lily felt once again intimidated, though at the same time she suddenly saw that their ages were not so very far apart either. Susan Fairford could not have been many years her senior, but it felt as if a great gulf of age and class separated them.

'Ah – Miss Waters,' she said in her clipped, cut-glass voice. 'Your timing is good, at least. These are my children. Isadora, Cosmo – this lady has come to live with us. She has come to be your new nanny, Cosmo, darling!' There was the first real hint of warmth in her voice as she spoke to her little boy.

'Izzy – Isadora! Say hello to Miss Waters.'

The girl stopped rocking for a moment and looked at Lily from beneath a very straight fringe of mole-brown hair. She had a round face with slanting eyes which stared hard at Lily. Then she smiled in a remote, inward-looking way and said something Lily couldn't make any sense of before going back to her rocking.

'In English, please, Izzy,' her mother rebuked her sharply. 'This is the trouble, you see, with children spending all their time with native servants. They pick up all sorts of bad habits.'

Lily glanced at the Indian girl. It seemed very rude of Mrs Fairford to speak like this in front of her, but her face remained expressionless.

'Now – Cosmo, darling,' Mrs Fairford's pretty face softened a fraction. 'Come and meet Miss Waters.'

The boy stood up and came towards them and as he did so, Lily experienced a peculiar pang. Never before had she seen such a beautiful child! He was slender, almost fairy-like, with a head of tumbling, honey-coloured hair. His lavender-blue eyes were widely set and shone with life and energy, with an open affection, utterly winning in its lack of guile. He was wearing a navy and white sailor suit, and his little legs, protruding from the shorts were slim, and fragile-looking.

'Oh!' Lily exclaimed, hardly meaning to. 'Hello, Cosmo, dear! Aren't you lovely!'

She squatted down as he came towards her and to her surprise he ran straight into her arms and cuddled her, clinging on like a baby monkey. She found herself laughing and, caught off balance, almost tumbling over.

'My goodness, well, this is a very nice greeting!'

Looking up as she held the slender form of Cosmo Fairford, she caught sight of his mother's face, alight with a kind of wistful joy. The *ayah* was smiling as well and Lily saw that she was young and sweet-faced.

'Nursie nursie!' Cosmo drew back and chanted into her face. 'My nursie nursie!'

'Yes – I'm your nursie,' Lily agreed, a smile of joy on her face. In that moment she had received the warm welcome for which she had yearned.

'Well – he appears to approve of you, at least,' Mrs Fairford said. As she got to her feet she seemed to close down again, becoming cold and withdrawn. 'The children always spend an hour with myself and their father before bed. Otherwise, *Ayah* will be able to tell you about Cosmo's routine and his likes and dislikes.'

She went over to Isadora who looked round at her with a blank expression, then as she went to pat the girl's head, Isadora fought her off, screeching.

'Oh, Isadora, do you *have* to?' Mrs Fairford withdrew, her voice full of weary distaste, as Isadora cried, '*Ayah*! Want *Ayah*!'

The *ayah* seemed to have more success in soothing the child's strange outburst. Lily could see that Mrs Fairford tried not to show the change in her feelings as

27

she parted with her son, but her smile, the softening of her eyes showed the great love she had for him, which broke through her mask of coldness. She kissed his cheek, stroking his hair.

'You talk to Miss Waters about your little Chip-chip, um, darling?' Aside to Lily, ignoring Isadora's screams, she explained, 'He has a favourite chipmunk in the garden. Goodbye, Cosmo, darling – Pater and I will see you later on.' She left the room with a rustling of skirts.

Isadora's tantrum only lasted a few moments, as the *ayah* stroked her head, and arms, soothing her, then hummed a melancholy, high-pitched tune. She looked young, barely eighteen, Lily guessed, but there was something full-figured and mature about her. As she stroked Isadora's head, the silver bangles on her arm gave off musical little jangling sounds. Now her mistress had left she seemed to feel free to speak. She turned and smiled sweetly at Lily.

'*Missy-baba* is getting upset sometime. She like me to sing to her.'

'You're good with her. She likes you,' Lily said, admiringly. It was clear that the girl's mother had little affection for her and no idea how to behave towards her and it seemed very sad. Instead, Isadora had attached herself to this loving young girl who would give her affection.

'She is good girl,' the *ayah* said. She had warm, friendly eyes and Lily smiled back, feeling she had found a friend in this chilly household. 'What is your name?' she enquired shyly.

With a pretty incline of her head, the girl said, 'I am Srimala. You are Miss Waters?'

'Oh, do call me Lily.'

28

A second later, Cosmo, very emphatically, echoed, 'Lily.'

And the two young women smiled at each other.

When she met Captain Fairford later that day, he came as a surprise. After meeting his wife, she had somehow expected a loud, overbearing man with blond hair like Cosmo's and a stiff, military bearing, like the portraits she had seen hanging in the hall. Instead, when she and the *ayah* took the children down after their tea, she met a lean, slender man with a gentle expression and brown hair, which, though cropped short, threatened to break into curls. He wore a neat little moustache which seemed to smile along with his lips, and his eyes were warm and welcoming.

'How very nice to meet you, Miss Waters.' His tone balanced charm and formality in equal measure.

Her hand was taken in a manly grip for a moment and quickly released, but his eyes lingered on her face with a kind look, so that she was startled to find tears prickling in her eyes. She was tired, she told herself, and more emotional than usual.

'I trust you had a good journey? Quite an experience, first time in India, I should imagine?' His voice was soft and beautifully spoken.

She was nodding a reply, a lump still in her throat at being treated so kindly, but he went on, 'Cosmo, I'm sure, has given you a warm welcome. He likes people, I'm happy to say. Not shy or retiring.'

'He's a lovely boy,' she said carefully.

'Oh yes!' he laughed, bashfully. 'Quite so. Grow up to be a credit, I'm sure. Fine chap . . .'

'Perhaps you'd like to go to your room now,' Mrs Fairford interrupted. 'Your supper will be brought to you.'

Lily nodded obediently. It was a relief to her to learn that, as she fitted neither into the category of family nor one of the large retinue of native servants, she would eat on her own in the evening. At the moment, since she was so used to faring for herself, that felt by far the least nerve-racking solution. That night she was longing to be alone.

One of the servants had brought a tray to her room with chicken stew and vegetables, and afterwards she prepared herself for bed and lay with all the new impressions of the day seething in her mind. She wasn't sure about Susan Fairford at all yet – the woman made her nervous. But the captain was much nicer than she expected, even if she wouldn't have a great deal to do with him. Srimala seemed very easy to get along with. And then there was Cosmo – adorable, loving Cosmo. A smile spread over her face in the darkness. She had done the right thing coming here, she knew.

Chapter Six

Lily found Cosmo blissful from the start. She had never expected to experience such a deep attachment so quickly, but the feeling had been instant and only increased over the following days and weeks. He was quite a precocious child, but much loved and therefore very loving. And he seemed to adore her straight away, unquestioningly, as if she was a gift he had been expecting and longing for.

From that first day he called her nothing but 'Lily', however much they worked for a time on 'Miss Waters'.

'Lily, Lily – come and play!' he cried when she first appeared in the morning. And she found there was nothing she wanted more than to come and play! This instant, loving adoration was something she had never experienced before and she found she could hardly take her eyes off him. Of course he adored Srimala too, since she had cared from him when very young, but he seemed to have a heart that extended wide and fully.

It took her much longer to decide whether or not she liked his mother. One moment Susan Fairford was snobbish and cold; the next she could be vulnerable and, at times, even warm, just in glimpses. One of the first surprises was her coming into the nursery during that first week and saying to Lily, 'I suppose you don't know how to ride a horse?'

'No,' Lily stuttered, astonished. 'I've never even sat on one!'

'Well, I want you to learn,' Susan Fairford announced, perching herself stiffly for a moment on the low wooden nursing chair. A large fly buzzed sleepily across the room. 'We are in the habit of riding in the morning here, but Charles and I don't ride together. He rides with the regiment and I like to take Cozzy out myself – we're teaching him, you see. And I'd like some help.' She swallowed and added, as if the admission pained her, 'And company. Not just natives.'

Lily stared at her. The only horses she had ever seen were the nags which pulled drays on the streets of Birmingham. She hardly knew one end of a horse from another! But she wanted very much to please. And the idea of learning to ride and being able to explore the countryside outside the cantonment seemed immensely exciting.

'I could try,' she said uncertainly.

To her surprise, Susan Fairford softened suddenly.

'Good girl. You can learn quickly, I'm sure. Our *syce* is very good.' Seeing Lily's baffled expression she gave a faint smile. 'That's the groom – he looks after the horses. His name is Arsalan and I must say, for a native he's very able. I'll ask him to teach you on a leading rein until you feel more confident.'

Within days, Lily had her first session seated on a horse, in a pair of riding breeches. Susan Fairford rode side-saddle, clad in a long riding dress, but she said Lily might feel safer straddling the horse and being able to grip on. She had never worn trousers before in her life and the thick breeches made her feel manly but much freer.

The *syce* Arsalan was waiting at the appointed time

on the lawn at the back of the house, holding a sleek chestnut horse on a leading rein. Arsalan was a slender man, dressed in loose white trousers and tunic, a bright white cloth coiled with impressive style round his head, with eyes which danced with mischievous warmth. Lily found it impossible to guess his age, but she liked him immediately, even before he had said a word, and she felt her nerves begin to fade.

'Miss Waters?' He gave a little bow from the waist. 'I am here to give you a riding lesson. This is a good, quiet horse. You can ride her solo when you are ready. She will not be giving you any trouble.'

He had a box for her to stand on and he instructed her how to climb on before teaching her how to sit and hold the reins. Although she was very nervous, she instantly liked the feel of sitting on the horse, and the smells of the warm animal and leather rising to meet her. She learned that the horse was called Blaze, because of the white stripe down her nose.

'Now,' Arsalan said, taking the leading rein. 'We are ready to begin walking.'

Patiently, day after day, he taught her to walk, then trot. She started to look forward to her lessons, and as she grew confident, she found it exhilarating. After the first week, though, her leg muscles were so strained that she could hardly walk. When she limped into the nursery one morning with a woebegone expression, Srimala put her hand over her mouth and broke into irrepressible giggles.

'Horse riding is not good for ladies,' she snorted, her eyes dancing with laughter. 'Not riding legs over, like a man!'

Lily sat down, wincing. 'I'm only following orders.' She squeaked with pain as she tried to move a leg again and then started laughing. 'Oh dear! I like it really. I just hope I can get used to it. I don't want to feel like this forever!'

Srimala just giggled more, shaking her head, but then said, mischievously, 'Arsalan says you are very good pupil.' And she realized the servants had been enjoying the progress of her lessons and that she was a bit of a curiosity in the house. 'And that you are very pretty lady.'

Soon, she began to ride with Susan Fairford, Arsalan beside her, while Susan Fairford rode with Cosmo perched on the front of her saddle.

On these excursions, Lily discovered the beauty of the Indian dawn. She would get up in the dark and go outside into the smell of dew on the ground. In the smoky-grey dawn light the trees were like ghosts which became washed in the pink rays of the rising sun. The air filled with smells of flowers and smoke from dung fires and the special aroma of the Indian earth. And she discovered a sense of freedom and space in the immensity of the Indian landscape which lifted her heart into a state of great joy such as she had never experienced before.

Each day they rode for an hour or more, along the road out of the cantonment and into the countryside, all of them silent for long periods, awed by the scene about them. Lily began to get a sense of Ambala as a tiny dot, like a speck of dust in the immensity of India. Her view of it widened, seeing the vivid green fields round the town, the rising sun glinting on streams and paddies and village tanks, the terracotta temples close to the river and the the wayside shrines and circular haystacks at the edges of the fields. She saw that Ambala was simply one of a myriad of settlements on the great Punjab plain stretching north to the mountains, to the snowy Hima-laya whose meltwater poured down to become the great Ganges on its way to the Bay of Bengal.

It was the first time she had been out, anywhere, into wide countryside, not hemmed in by streets and buildings, and it made her see things afresh. The cantonment was an inward-looking world with its own bazaar, and rit-uals of church and flag-waving military parades and parties, striving to keep as separate as possible from the 'native' town: from India itself. This state of affairs was in fact maintained by a stream of Indian workers whose names Lily was gradually beginning to learn. She liked learning these new words, often from Srimala, who laughed unrestrainedly at the way she pronounced them.

'The man with the donkey – he is the *dhobi*, the laundryman,' she instructed. Lily soon came to recog-nize this man, who peered out through round, pebbly spectacles and carried a flat iron full of heated coals. 'And the *mali* – he is doing the garden.'

The cantonment life seemed to be all-consuming, as if there was nothing else. Yet now, riding through the soft air of these beautiful, roseate dawns, she saw with wonder, with infatuation, that there was so much more; there was all this vast land, and the great arc of the sky, stretching almost unimaginably further than she could see.

During these morning rides, she began to get to know Susan Fairford differently.

Over the weeks Lily had watched the Fairfords and found them confusing. Charles Fairford, when he was at home, behaved like a model husband, ever courteous and charming to his wife, and attentive to his children during his brief times with them. The regiment had a number of animals attached to it as mascots and companions for the men. Some were dogs, but there was also a monkey called Nippy, and sometimes Charles Fairford carried Nippy home on his shoulder to see the children and let them watch his tricks. Lily was as charmed as they were by the tiny brown creature with its shiny, intelligent eyes.

At first Lily envied what seemed to be the idyll of a perfect marriage, lived out in splendour and comfort. But she soon grew to see the loneliness of Susan Fairford's life. Charles was away a great deal. He dined in the Officers' Mess several times a week, leaving Susan to find what friendship she could among the other army wives. Lily saw, and Susan allowed her to see, that Charles was a man married more to the army than to his wife. And though Charles was the picture of strength and health, India did not suit Susan, who was prone to prostrating stomach complaints and fevers which reduced her to a most wretched condition.

She was also forever in a nervous state about the children's health, the hygiene of their clothes and food and who they mixed with, and her anxiety made her constantly irritable. But sometimes, in the gentle light of those morning rides, she relaxed and became more confiding, as if the uncertain light of dawn dissolved also some of the boundaries between mistress and servant. On a horse she became girlish and happy.

Chapter Seven

The burning, muggy months of Indian summer gave way to the pleasant days and chill nights of winter. For Lily, life revolved happily round the little world of the nursery, the children's routine of meals and games and sleep, and its child's rhythm made her feel secure.

One night, towards the end of October, she woke to the sound of knocking.

'Miss Lily!' Srimala hissed through the bedroom door.

Srimala was outside. 'It is Mrs Fairford. She has been taken ill, and is asking for you.'

'For *me*?' Lily said, astonished.

'The captain is not here—'

Captain Fairford had gone up country for a few nights with the regiment and Susan's maid did not sleep in the house but went home to her family every night.

'She has a fever and she wants you to come – quick, hurry!'

The night was cold, and Lily put her dressing gown on and followed Srimala. She had never been in Susan Fairford's bedroom before and she held her gown round her, feeling nervous and as if she were trespassing. A candle was burning on the bedside table and the mosquito nets were lifted back over the bed frame out of the way. Lily could make out the restless form, lying under only a sheet and looking surprisingly small and vulnerable.

With grave eyes, Srimala looked across and beckoned to Lily, who moved nervously, closer to the bed.

'Lily?'

'Yes, Mrs Fairford.'

'Give me a drink of water . . . Please . . . Srimala, you can go.'

Srimala shot an encouraging smile at Lily and disappeared with a gentle clink of bangles.

'You may sit down,' Susan Fairford said, after sipping from the glass of water. As Lily sat on the chair by the bed, she heard Susan murmur, 'I do feel so very unwell.'

Lily was reminded of sitting beside Mrs Chappell's bed in her last weeks.

'Is there anything else you would like?'

Susan was obviously running a high fever. She gave a low moan, her face creasing in distress.

'Oh, I do have such a terrible pain in my head . . . As if it's going to crack open . . . If you could cool my head . . . There, in the drawer – handkerchiefs . . .'

Lily carefully laid a wet handkerchief across Mrs Fairford's forehead, pressing it gently to her temples, the way Mrs Chappell used to ask her to. As she did so, Susan Fairford moaned again.

'Oh, you dear girl . . . Oh, for someone to understand . . .'

She began to sob suddenly, tears rolling out from under her closed lids, her body quivering. Lily was quite unsure what to do, so she took the sodden handkerchief and cooled it again, pressing it gently to her mistress's forehead, wondering what it was that was causing her such distress. But she did not feel it was her place to speak and she stood, gently caressing her temples. She wished Srimala was still there. After a few moments of the shuddering sobbing she said, as she remembered saying to Maud Chappell, 'Is there something else I can do for you?'

'Get me out of this country – that's how you can help!' Susan Fairford cried, in a distraught voice. 'I hate India – it killed my baby and they'll take Cosmo away from me, they'll send him away and there's nothing I can do about it, nothing! Oh God, what can I do? I'm so worthless, sitting about here in pretty clothes doing nothing, being nothing in my life! All I can ever so is sit and watch life go past. And they'll take my beloved little boy away from me and he's all I've got I'll . . . I think I'll go mad . . . !'

She curled in on herself, on her side like a child, and the sobbing became truly heartbroken, though in between she groaned at the extra pressure her crying was inflicting on her head. The sound of her grief reached down into Lily, touching something in her. When the woman had quietened a little, Lily said to her, 'What do you mean, they'll take him away?'

'To school, of course . . .' She spoke slowly, her voice slurred with exhaustion and pain. 'He has to go . . . No choice – Fairford family, traditions and so forth. Eton, the army, India . . . That's Cosmo's life, whether he likes it, or I like it. Charles won't hear of anything else. Boarding school before they're five, get them out of India to prep school or they go native, send them home . . . My family's not of their station . . .' Her voice had been hard and bitter as she spoke but now her face contorted and she was crying again. 'And there's Cranbourne, that wretched place. It's only in the family through Charles's mother: her brother inherited the estate and he was far too odd to marry – and Charles's brother William is just like him . . . Oh, I don't want Cosmo to go. I can't bear it!'

Lily took courage and reached across, taking Susan Fairford's clammy hand in hers as she wept. Feeling the pressure of Lily's hand on hers, she opened her eyes, startled, as if she had almost forgotten she was there.

'Thank you,' she said with such sudden humility that Lily felt tears slide into her own eyes. 'You're a dear. I do believe you are. I do so need someone to be kind to me.'

What about Captain Fairford? Lily thought. He was such a gentle and handsome man and he seemed so kind and polite. Perhaps Mrs Fairford was missing him?

'The captain will be back very soon,' she said, in an attempt to be reassuring.

Susan Fairford opened her eyes again. She looked sad, but also angry. Haltingly, she said, 'The trouble is, you see, Charles was born in India. That makes all the difference. He can't begin to understand how I pine for home, because for him, this is home. But it will never be for me.' Her lips curled in disgust. 'Filthy, stinking place, with all their heathen habits ... D'you know, on winter mornings like now, when we take the horses out, just every so often there's a smell, a whiff of England in winter or spring, that cold air. And just for a second then, I'm back in Sussex, and the orchards, the villages and little churches. I haven't seen it for five years now and I so long to. Sometimes it feels like an illness, like grief ... Can you understand?'

Lily thought about it. Did she know how to feel loss, grief, for a place, or a person? Move on, don't miss anything, anyone, that was her way. After all, who had she ever had in her life who she could really lose or miss? She had barely let herself think of Mrs Chappell or England. She had shut it all away and left with barely a backward glance, had simply transferred herself here. No, to be truthful, she could not really understand.

'I do a bit,' she said, trying to be helpful. 'But I don't have a family at home, you see.'

Susan Fairford's eyelids were drooping with pain and tiredness.

'No?' she said, drifting. 'I suppose I know nothing about you, Lily. You're a strange girl ... But kind. I can see that ...'

Lily sat by her as she drifted off to sleep and stayed with her until the dawn light seeped in at the windows.

Chapter Eight

Ambala, India, 1907

'Ironside? Mr Ironside, the Daimler mechanic? Splendid – it *is* you!'

The round, pink face appeared among the natives who swarmed round Sam the moment he stepped down from the train. Sam was damned glad to see the bloke. He had no idea where to go next or how to deal with all these wogs, not knowing the ropes at all, so he stood looking over their heads and brushing smuts off his sleeve. It wouldn't do to look uncertain of himself.

The fellow was barking commands in Hindustani, shooing all the Indians out of the way, and suddenly the hustle and bustle of coolies and tea vendors shifted away in search of someone else who might be interested. The two of them faced each other in the shade of the platform.

'Corporal Hodgkins – sir.' The fellow clicked his heels and made as if to salute, but as an afterthought, stuck out his hand instead. 'At your service, sir. Welcome to Ambala Cant. The captain sent me to meet you, sir. They're waiting for you at the Fairfords' residence.'

'The car . . . ?'

'Already unloaded, sir, this morning. All ready to go, she is, and looking very nice, if I may say so. Hand me your bag, sir – no, *jao, jao!*' He bawled at another coolie who approached to try and take the luggage. Sam could see the fellow enjoyed shouting about the place like that. 'Let's be going, shall we, sir?' he continued unctuously. 'You'll find it more congenial at the house. Very nice, it is, at the Fairfords'.'

Corporal Hodgkins led the way along the platform, past the whole array of waiting rooms – first, second, third classes, one for ladies with its closed screen doors which immediately made Sam curious about what went on inside, his mind diverting irresistibly to the mysterious bodies of Indian women under those bright, silken clothes which they wore so seductively, and he had to drag himself back to the present. He sized Hodgkins up from behind. Not what you'd think of as a soldier, Sam thought. He reckoned that of the two of them he was the one who looked fitter for soldiering. His frame was trim and muscular. Nothing to be ashamed of there. But following the corporal he saw that the fellow was very robust, despite the schoolboy face. Sam wasn't keen on these army types, expecting them to come on all superior, so he took childish pleasure in seeing that one of Hodgkins's bootlaces had come loose and was trailing in the dust.

As they left the station building, Sam screwed up his eyes against the piercing sunlight. It was February, so the temperatures were pleasant, the sky a wintry blue. At once they were surrounded by more hullaballoo, a teeming crowd of humanity all desperate to scratch a living. Among the crowds he noticed human grotesques from which he averted his eyes – one ghastly figure squatting by the wall with no nose! And all muddled up with them were cows and filthy, skeletal dogs and huge, dusty crows. And the flies and piles of ordure – the stench of the place! God in heaven, what a hole! It was worse even than Delhi, if that were possible. The sights and smells turned his stomach.

But when they reached the goods yard all this was wiped from his mind because, to his astonishment, there was the Daimler! Of course this should not have been any surprise, but it still felt like a miracle.

'Amazing,' he muttered to himself, a delighted grin spreading over his face. 'That anything works in this hellhole!'

He hadn't seen her since the docks when they craned her on to the ship, and hadn't actually seen her taken off when they arrived in Bombay. He'd still been feeling so dicky when they arrived that he hadn't been able to leave the cabin, so a fellow had brought him a docking paper to sign. But now, here she was, paintwork shining, parked up there like a familiar face in all this foreignness, so that he almost wanted to go up and kiss her, as if she was his woman waiting out there for him.

'There we are, sir...' For one second he thought Hodgkins was going to salute the car, but he managed to restrain himself. 'I say, the horseless carriage! I'm looking forward to seeing you start her up!'

Sam was looking forward to it too. He knew that car, every inch of her, like he knew Helen's body. He could show Hodgkins a thing or two. While he was getting the starter handle in place, Hodgkins went to put his bag in the back, but the next thing Sam heard was a strained kind of grunt and when he straightened up he couldn't see Hodgkins anywhere.

'Damn and blast it!' came from the rear somewhere.

Hodgkins had sprawled flat on his face in the dirt, and by the time Sam got round to him he was jumping up quick, brushing himself down, putting his *topi* back on straight. The silly bugger had tripped over his own bootlace.

'All right?' Sam asked, keeping his face straight.

'Yes, of course,' Hodgkins snapped, with puce cheeks.

Sam strolled round to the front again, cool as you like, and cranked the handle. The Daimler started up like a dream.

Until then, he hadn't given much thought to meeting Captain Fairford. The journey itself had been adventure enough: the sea voyage through Suez to Bombay, then the long train ride to Delhi, and north-west to Ambala. He'd had no real idea, until then, of the true size of India. He had to hand it to those engineer boys – building railways here was some feat. The few paper inches the journey had traversed on the map translated into hour upon hour of baked country.

In fact, the notion of seeing the Daimler again and delivering her safely hadn't seemed real, but now it felt marvellous to be behind the wheel. With Hodgkins barking out directions, he drove along the edge of the 'native town' to the cantonment, where Captain Fairford would be waiting for his car. Sam's job was to instruct the captain and his staff in driving and maintaining her.

'The native town is pretty much off-limits,' Hodgkins was saying.

'Many motors here?' Sam was having to watch the road carefully, what with all the carts and bicycles, the dogs, children and cows all gawping as they passed and meandering across the dirt road.

'Just a few. Not all as fine as this one though. The captain is very *pukka*.'

At a glance, in the bright sunlight, Sam saw glimpses of side streets, jumbled messes of hovels heaving with dark-skinned people. He shuddered, but he wasn't going to show Hodgkins. He wanted to be seen taking everything in his stride. But it was the smell that was most overpowering. A pall of foul smoke seemed to lie over the native lines, the air tinted brown.

'Dung.' Hodgkins had seen his grimace. 'The fuel they use. Cow dung. The stink gets right into your nostrils until you don't notice. But you don't want to have anything to do with the natives. The only chaps who take themselves off there are after a bit of . . . well, you know . . .' Sam didn't have to turn and look to see the smutty expression on his face. 'A bit of recreation, let's say. By crikey, you'd have to be desperate – that's all I can say. Oh – and for Christ's sake don't go hitting any of the cows. You'll have every Hindu in the neighbourhood down on you in a pack. Sacred, you see, old man. Top of the pecking order, the cow.'

'I see,' Sam said.

'Now – this is the cantonment,' Hodgkins announced proudly.

He hardly needed to say. They were on broader roads, trees on either side, and larger buildings set back from the road. After the glimpses of the native part it seemed very orderly and quiet. There were a few individuals on the road, in khaki drill, and a horse and trap came trotting towards them, with a jingling of bells. A red stone church tower appeared on their left.

'Just down here,' Hodgkins said.

Blimey, Sam thought as they swung into the drive of the dazzling white residence. He was nervous now. There was serious money here. As they turned in, a native child who'd been squatting by the gate leaped up and dashed towards the house on legs thin as hairpins, shouting and waving his arms. He must have been waiting to pass on the news, Sam realized, because a moment later people started to appear and by the time he'd cut the engine off there was quite a crowd gathering outside the arched frontage of the house. In the sudden quiet, the billowing cloud of dust the car had raised blew in a slow swirl across the lawn.

Hodgkins leaped out of the car, looking immensely important and pleased with himself. Sam just had time to take in that the whole household seemed to have come out and there was quite a gaggle of natives, all staring, with a few white faces scattered among them. One figure pushed through the rest and walked smartly towards them. Sam felt himself tighten inside. Captain Fairford. He had to spend the next six weeks or so at the man's side. He braced himself for all the class and army superiority which would come off him like sweat.

At last Hodgkins had a viable reason to salute, which he did with tremulous gusto, heels clicking.

'At ease,' Captain Fairford said. 'Thank you, Hodgkins.'

Hodgkins lowered his arm, took two steps back, tumbled over one of a row of flowerpots neatly arranged along the front edge of the lawn and lurched backwards, ending up flat on his back on the grass. Titters came from the female members of the party. With an effort, Sam kept his face straight.

'Are you all right, Hodgkins?' Captain Fairford, who had been striding towards Sam, diverted for a second.

'Yes, sir. Quite all right, sir.' Once again, Hodgkins scrambled to the vertical, hat in hand, bending to right the pots of fledgling chrysanthemums.

'Splendid.' Captain Fairford held out his hand, eyes

not quite managing to convert their twinkling amusement at Hodgkins's antics into something more formal. 'Captain Fairford, Twelfth Royal Lancers. You're the Daimler mechanic? So glad you've arrived at last. The house has been on tenterhooks.'

The captain was younger than Sam had expected, lightly built with dark brown, wavy hair and a sensitive face that would have seemed more in place on a scholar than a soldier. And he had a modest, neat 'tache, much like Sam's own. There was keen intelligence, shrewdness, and the dark brown eyes, though still tinged with laughter, took Sam in at a glance. However swift the glance and with whatever upper-class etiquette, Sam knew he was being measured up. But he felt himself relax. He liked the look of Fairford, so far.

'Ironside. Motor mechanic.'

'Well – welcome to Ambala.' He looked properly at the car then. 'I *say*,' he breathed.

The captain circled his new acquisition, making admiring noises and firing questions and the rest of the household edged forward. Most of them seemed to be native servants. Among them, though, Sam's attention was caught by a European woman holding a sleepy-looking boy in her arms. She was dark-haired, her features voluptuous and extraordinarily striking. He thought he had never seen a face with so much life in it, the dark eyes seeming to flash with energy as she looked at the car, and yet there was a closedness in her expression which he found immediately intriguing. She held the boy to her very tenderly, his fair curls bright against the dark stuff of her blouse. After a moment Captain Fairford seemed to remember something and looked round.

'Where's Sus— er, Mrs Fairford?'

'She's with *Ayah* and Isadora,' the dark-haired woman said. Her voice was soft and well-spoken.

Captain Fairford nodded, and turned his attention back to the car. The servants were gathered round now, chattering quietly, inquisitive fingers marking the dust on the hot bonnet.

'Well, Ironside,' the captain said, hands on hips. Sam could see the man was excited and he liked him for it. He was a car man, all right. It just got hold of some men and wouldn't let go. 'We must get you a drink, and as soon as you've had a wash and brush up, we'll take her out for a spin.'

'Why not before?' Sam said, holding his gaze. 'Sir.'

A grin spread across Captain Fairford's face. The fact that the establishment where Fairford was educated would have been far superior to Sam's Coventry Board School was of no account in those seconds. They were like two eager lads in a school yard.

'Well, Ironside, if you're game – why not?'

Chapter Nine

Charles Fairford was a gentleman. From the moment Sam arrived in the cantonment the captain went out of his way to put him at his ease, treating him almost like an equal. The same, however, could not be said of his wife.

Sam disliked Susan Fairford on sight, and it was pretty clear she felt the same about him. Of course, he thought, it was hard to tell with these stuck-up little English misses what their actual feelings might be about anything, but she certainly went out of her way to pull rank and put up every social and class barrier she could get away with.

That first afternoon Sam took the captain out for a quick spin. They weren't alone. From the crowd of servants, Charles Fairford called out a tall, thin native fellow. With everyone else watching – that was something Sam was discovering about India, the way everything seemed to be done to an audience – he introduced the fellow as his *syce*, or groom, Arsalan. He had been chosen to learn about a new 'horse power' they were developing in the modern world of industry.

'I want you to teach me, and Arsalan here, everything you know,' Captain Fairford said. 'He's my right-hand man.'

Sam hadn't expected that, not entrusting the Daimler to a native. The chap had probably never learned to read and write, so it seemed a bit rich to expect him to get to grips with the workings of the internal combustion engine! But it wasn't his place to argue. As they got into the car he caught sight of the dark-haired woman carrying the sleeping boy along the veranda. Something about the way she moved drew him and he had to be careful not to stare.

This Arsalan fellow sat up at the back and Sam drove the two of them out along the cantonment roads, which all looked pretty much the same to him. The sun had sunk low as they made their way back and the light turned bronze, then pink.

'I don't think I've ever seen light quite like this before, sir,' Sam said, very taken by it.

'Best time of day in India,' the captain replied. They had to speak up to be heard over the engine but even so, Sam could still hear the fondness in his voice. 'Nothing like the Indian sunset, except the dawn, of course, which is beautiful almost beyond description. Or at least by me.' He gave a chuckle. 'I'm no poet, I do know that.'

'You must miss home though?' Sam said.

'Ah, but this is home. I was born here, you see. So talking about England as "home" is merely a turn of phrase for me. Though I was at school there, naturally. For my wife, it's quite different, of course. She grew up in Sussex. Where do you come from, Ironside?'

'Coventry, sir.'

'Of course. How ridiculous of me. And you don't have to keep calling me sir.'

When they braked back outside the house, Captain Fairford said something over his shoulder to the *syce*, who leaped from the car and hurried off into the dusk, then turned to Sam.

'Well – it's marvellous: just what I was hoping for! I can hardly wait to find out all about it and take the wheel myself. Now—' He leaped energetically from the car and turned on his heel to say, 'We dine at seven-thirty, and you'll join us, of course. Consider yourself one of the family while you're here, eh? Now – let's get someone to show you your quarters.'

Sam made sure he was dressed and ready by seven-thirty. He'd brought his Sunday suit, thanks to Helen.

'They're bound to dress for dinner,' she'd said. 'You've got to look right. And there'll be church on Sundays.'

He felt pretty intimidated when he first went into the house. This was how the other half lived all right! Posh was hardly an adequate word to describe it. As for his quarters, he had never slept in a room like it before, although by their standards it was probably quite simple. There was a deep red carpet on the floor, a wide bed draped in mozzie netting and an array of dark, polished furniture and a long gilt-framed mirror, all of first-class quality. On the washstand stood a pitcher decorated with pink roses, all ready, full of warm water.

Before leaving the room he checked his appearance. The suit was quite run-of-the-mill and he wondered if he would measure up. Pulling his shoulders back he was at least reassured by his strong, manly stature. Keen as mustard, that was the impression people had. And he didn't come across as some office-*wallah*, that was for sure. Sam knew he was good-looking. Smooth dark brown hair, alert grey eyes, strong brows. And he knew he was good at his job. 'Cocky sod, isn't he?' he'd heard himself described at the works. But he was going places – he knew it. And he wasn't going to be intimidated by the wealth of the Fairford mansion.

Opening the door, he jumped, startled by a small figure peering up at him outside. The corridor was rather dark and Sam was unnerved for a moment. It must be a girl, since she had long, dark hair and was wearing a white frock. And she had some sort of doll tucked under one arm. But she stood in a strange pose, knees and feet turned out and her face was ... well, not *normal*: it was partly the way she stared at him, not smiling or speaking, that was disturbing.

'Izzy? Isadora!' It was a native voice calling along the passage, high pitched and exasperated. 'Naughty girl, where are you? Come here, now!'

At that moment a mellow-sounding gong ran through the house and the male servant appeared to take Sam to dinner, shooing the child away.

'Who was that?' Sam asked, carefully.

'Mr and Mrs Fairford's daughter,' the man said. 'Her name is Isadora.'

'Is she ... well, all right?'

'She is a mongol, sir.' He spoke with a slight inclination of his head, as if to acknowledge this as a personal sorrow.

'I saw another child? How many are there?'

'Only Miss Isadora and Master Cosmo, Sahib. Miss Isadora stays with her *ayah* – Master Cosmo is undertaking his education with Miss Waters.'

Sam immediately thought of the dark-haired woman carrying the child. 'I see. And the boy, Cosmo. Is he ... ?'

The servant's face broke into a broad smile.

53

'Master Cosmo is perfectly all right. Oh yes, very much so, thanking God.'

The Fairfords were already in the dining room, standing each side of a long, shining table laid with silver and glass. A heavy chandelier cast a gentle pool of light on to the table, leaving the edges of the room in shadow. Sam knew he had not imagined that as he came in the two of them stopped talking abruptly. There'd been some disagreement, it was obvious. Sam was a married man, after all: he knew the sort of thing.

After a second's silence, they summoned smiles to their faces, but the atmosphere was strained. Captain Fairford seemed pleased to break away.

'Ironside! Found your way all right? Fancy a Scotch?'

'*Darling*,' Mrs Fairford reproached him. 'We haven't been introduced.' She had one of those pure, cut-glass voices which set Sam on edge to start with. And after all, wasn't it pretty obvious who he was?

'Sorry – remiss of me. Darling – this is Mr Ironside, the mechanic from Daimler. Ironside, this is my wife, Susan.'

She glided closer to shake his hand, and said, 'Yes – Mrs Fairford.' This sounded like a put-down to Sam, after her husband had used her Christian name. 'How d'you do?'

She was wearing a sapphire-blue dress which swept the floor, a long string of pearls swinging sinuously as she moved. In the dim light, Sam saw her as very pretty. Of course, she was a beautiful woman, with that slender, curving figure and the pale hair, swept up and decorated with tiny jewels which caught the light as she moved.

Her face had all the requirements of prettiness: wide blue eyes, even features, with a distinctive sharpness about them and a definite, smiling mouth. Her neck was long and slim, and the overall impression she made was striking. And yet, when she came up close, somehow the prettiness turned to something else, as if there was a wall around her built of defensive snobbery which drew the life from her features and, to his eyes, made her look pinched and calculating.

'So pleasant to meet you,' she purred, without it sounding so at all.

Her smile communicated no warmth and her eyes contained a subtle contempt which did not allow her gaze to meet Sam's for more than a second, in case, it seemed, she might be soiled by even fleeting contact with someone of inferior standing. Trade, of course, was all he was to her. She allowed her hand to touch just the tips of his fingers, then withdrew.

'How d'you do, Mrs Fairford?' Sam said, already knowing that he loathed the stuck-up bitch for looking at him like that. Or, more precisely, for refusing to see him at all.

'I hope you had a safe journey?' she asked, though her attention was turned to the table, which was laid for three. She straightened one of the place settings.

'On the whole,' Sam said, though he directed the answer at the captain, who was handing him a glass of Scotch. 'Though I must say, sea travel doesn't suit me completely.'

'Oh!' To his surprise, Mrs Fairford agreed fervently. 'Isn't it simply awful! I remember feeling so desperately ill on the journey out here! It almost puts one off the idea of going home to dear old England again, if that were not such a terrible thought!'

The two of them gestured towards the table, and as if some signal had been given, though if there was Sam never saw it, a cohort of servants, each dressed in a similar maroon and white livery, began to bring in the food: a tureen of soup, some wide, white dishes and a tray of bread.

Captain Fairford sat at the head of the table and Mrs Fairford and Sam were opposite each other. Mrs Fairford fretted at the servants about details of the meal – could they not have cut the bread more elegantly, and had they remembered to strain the soup properly? Two of them stood silently in the shadows by the wall as they ate. Sam wondered what on earth they should talk about. Had it been just himself and the captain, they could have talked all evening about the car. There was no stopping him on that subject! And it was clearly what the captain would have liked to discuss as well. But of course, that wasn't women's talk. So Sam kept the conversation light, not technical, talking about things which he thought would amuse.

'Tell me, Ironside,' the captain said, as they began on the soup. 'Surely there isn't still the same fierce opposition to the motor car in England now? While I was at Eton I seem to remember there were all sorts of protests going on – outrage about freedom of the roads, terrorizing of neighbourhoods and so on.'

'Well, yes – we haven't lost that yet,' Sam said, trying to get used to the strange, spicy flavour of the soup. 'There's the Highway Protection League, who'd like to ban the motor car altogether. With attitudes like that, no wonder the French and Germans have been quicker off the mark than us! They're always complaining about the dust and noise – and of course there are always those that will complain because they can't afford a motor, so it's sour grapes against anyone who can.'

'And all those with investments in the railway, of course,' Susan Fairford added. 'Like my dear father, who could never say a single good word about the motor car!'

She gave a genuine smile, seeming to relax for a moment, and Sam thawed towards her fractionally.

'I seem to remember they were hardly allowed to get up any speed at all,' Charles Fairford said.

'We've come on a bit since the early days of steam engines. Remember the early vehicles – only go at two miles an hour in town, and don't go out without a stoker and the fellow walking ahead with a red flag to warn everyone! At least we're allowed to get up to twenty miles an hour now . . .'

'Ah yes, thanks to Lord Montagu's bill.'

'A good Daimler customer,' Sam said. The conservative MP Lord Montagu had brought the Motor Car Act onto the statute book in 1903. Montagu was a Daimler driver and motor enthusiast. 'He's brought it home that we're here to stay,' Sam said. 'Even if there are still people jumping into ditches when they hear a motor coming round the bend!'

Charles Fairford laughed and his wife gave a faint smile.

'It's no easier here,' the captain said, chuckling. 'A fellow I know goes up to Mahabaleshwar in the hot season – that's a hill station down near Poona. The whole town is utterly hostile to the motor car and there are signs everywhere. He said his favourite is one that says, "Any motor car found in motion while travelling to its destination will be vigorously dealt with"! I mean, I ask you!'

As they were laughing, the servants came to remove the soup bowls and bring in the next course, which proved to be beef olives.

After this hiatus, Susan Fairford began on Sam, with a battery of questions between mouthfuls of beef and potatoes. She had evidently had enough of talking about motor cars.

'So where is it you come from exactly, Mr Ironside?'

'From Coventry.' He was about to add 'ma'am' but decided against it. He sipped his drink. The meat had a rather more fiery filling than he was used to.

'Ah, the industrial Midlands! Rather like Charles!' She gave a little laugh, as if the idea of Fairford and himself coming from anywhere remotely similar was too ridiculous for words. 'Charles's family have an estate in Warwickshire – Cranbourne – some miles from Rugby.'

'Not that it's anything much to do with me,' Captain Fairford added. He refilled Sam's glass with Scotch. He'd have to watch it and not get tight, Sam realized. He was pretty tired and he wasn't used to much in the way of spirits. A couple of pints of ale was more his style. These colonials all drank a great deal, he had heard, what with the heat and nothing much else doing.

'I spent school holidays up there,' the captain was saying, 'but apart from that, it's a foreign land to me – as I was telling you earlier.'

'And are you married?' Mrs Fairford continued. She was very direct in her questioning, as if she had some right to know everything.

'Yes, I am.'

'Children?'

'Our first child is expected in June.'

He thought he saw a flicker of some emotion cross

her face, but all she said was, 'How nice. I wonder whether it will be a girl or a boy.'

'I couldn't say.'

'No, of course not. How silly of me. And how old are you, Mr Ironside, if you don't mind me asking?'

'Darling!' Her husband reproached her.

'No, it's all right.' He already thought her rude and condescending and this made no difference. 'I'm just twenty-one.'

'And your wife . . . ?'

'Helen? She's twenty.'

She paused, finishing a mouthful.

'And have you always been a mechanic?'

'I've recently completed my apprenticeship with Daimler.' For a moment he was homesick for something familiar: the great machine shops at the works, the lathes turning. It was all part of him. 'I joined the firm at fourteen. So, yes, I suppose I have.'

'And your wife? Presumably she's not a mechanic?' She gave a silly little laugh. Sam just looked back at her. He wasn't going to let her get under his skin.

'Helen was a photographer – before we married, that is.'

That took her aback. 'How extraordinarily exciting! A photographer! However did that come about?'

Sam laid his soup spoon down for a moment. 'Well, she was taken on and trained. A local photographer – portraits and so on. Helen can develop the pictures, tint them and all the tricks. She knows her trade.' He felt proud of her then, his little woman, whom he had left behind in their modest house, beginning to show that she was carrying his child. He hadn't thought about her enough, he realized. Not for a newly married man.

Before Mrs Fairford could ask any more questions,

he said, 'I believe you have two children? Your daughter tried to pay me a visit earlier on.'

'Izzy?' Her voice was sharp. 'What do you mean?'

'Oh, she only peeped in, when the servant was by the door. Someone was calling her . . .'

'*Ayah*,' she sighed, pettishly. 'She just can't seem to keep control of the girl.'

Captain Fairford laid a hand gently on hers for a second. 'But where would we be without her, darling?'

'I know.' She looked up at Sam with a kind of defiance. 'You see, Isadora is a problem of a child. *Ayah* is the only one she really cares for . . .'

'Oh, nonsense,' the captain interrupted. 'Srimala, our *ayah*, is a jewel though, we have to admit. Had Isadora been like other children we would have brought out an English nanny for her, of course, before she went to school. Our son Cosmo has a nanny, a Miss Waters . . .' His brow creased. 'You know, darling, since Mr Ironside is here, we could have invited Miss Waters to dine with us as well. She might have been glad to meet a visitor from England.'

Susan Fairford's face tightened again suddenly and with a languid little laugh she said, 'Oh no – I really think her place is with the children, darling. After all, we don't want to be *outnumbered* by the lower orders, do we?'

Chapter Ten

Coventry, 1906

Helen's hair was the first thing Sam noticed about her. He saw her coming out of Timmins, the photographer's, which he passed on his way home from the Daimler works every day. Once he had plucked up the courage to speak to her, he sometimes walked her home.

The first time he touched her hair properly was last winter when they managed to find half an hour to themselves away from Mrs Gregory, Helen's mother. They were in the Gregorys' house, it was sleeting outside and they were in the back room by the fire. There was a knock on the door and Mrs Gregory was called out to a neighbour who was in some strife or other. Sam gave a great inner cheer at the thought of being able to be alone with Helen. There always seemed to be some obstacle to his being with her! There was that Laurie fellow from the Armstrong works who was forever hanging around her with his daft grin. Helen always laughed off the idea that she had any interest in Laurie.

'Oh, I've known him since we were knee-high,' she'd say. 'He's just old Laurie.'

But there was also the child and today, for once, she wasn't there either.

Mrs Gregory was a woman of good works, many would have said kindness itself. So upright, Sam sometimes thought sourly, that you could hang a lamp from her.

Although a widow herself, she had taken on the upbringing of her dead sister's child. Helen said that the sister had lived in Liverpool and had taken ill and died tragically young, leaving the baby girl, Emma, to a feckless husband who would never be able to care for her. So Ma Gregory stepped in. The child was a sweet enough little thing, but Helen had to take her turn in minding her and from Sam's point of view she was yet another obstacle to his getting anywhere near Helen. Today, though, Emma was round playing at a neighbour's house and his chance had come!

Mrs Gregory said with a meaningful look, 'I won't be long, you know. You might polish the brasses while I'm gone, if you're short of summat to do.' And she set out into the slushy Coventry street in her old brown hat and coat, her sinewy figure bent against the wind.

'Well, there's a miracle, anyway,' Sam said, shuffling closer along the settle towards Helen.

'Sam! You're awful. She'll get drenched out there, and Mrs Nightingale's been taken bad again.'

Helen turned to him, her creamy face dotted with toffee-coloured freckles, tawny eyes twinkling reproachfully while she tried not to look pleased that they were alone. Sam could think of nothing but his urgent desire to hold her.

'I want to kiss you, love,' he said, taking her hand. 'I've been sitting here bursting to kiss you all afternoon!'

'Oh, Sam!' she said again, as if he was a naughty schoolboy.

He felt like anything but a schoolboy. His feelings were much more manly than that! To give her a few token moments to pretend she was resisting him, he caught the end of a thick strand of her hair. She had washed it and was drying it by the fire. To the touch, it was deliciously thick and heavy.

'Caramels and cream, that's you,' he said. He tilted his head and lightly kissed the shadowy part of her neck beneath her ear. 'All sweet. That's my girl.'

She giggled and her face lit up. Helen was nineteen then, Sam twenty. She was so pretty and everyone liked her, though she was quiet and shy. It all felt right to Sam: Helen was the wife he was looking for, because he needed a wife. It was the right thing. He was going to be a successful and respectable professional man and such men had wives and lived in one of the new, nicely-kept-up villas at the edge of town.

And he thought he was in love. What else could these overpowering feelings mean? It was like an itch on him all the time, that powerful longing to know what it would be like to lie with her, to *have* her, even though he was scarcely sure what that meant. He could see why men said women were a torment. He'd sit beside her and they'd be talking, yet all the time, all he could think about was the way her frock pushed out, tightly cover-ing her chest, a tantalizing swell that gave him an almost overwhelming hunger to reach out and touch.

He took Helen in his arms, seeing her smiling eyes turn solemn, and he had his kiss that day. Once a few months of little walks to the park and snatched kisses had passed, he asked her to marry him. He was at such a pitch by then, something had to shift. He had to lie with her and make her his or he was going to go mad. He knew he was a good prospect, with his apprenticeship. He wasn't sure that Mrs Gregory had taken to him, not *fondly*, but she had no good reason to object to him.

Their wedding night was the first time he saw her naked, though she didn't want him to.

After a nice mutton dinner in an old inn a few miles away, they went up to the old oak-beamed room which was their private haven at last. God knew, Sam didn't know what he expected exactly, but that night was a bitter disappointment. Almost as soon as they got through the door he went to take her in his arms, but she pushed him off, frowning.

'Just let me get ready, Sam!'

Stung, he stood watching her go to the door, saw her slip a little on the uneven floor and say, 'Oh, damn it!' as she disappeared out to the bathroom across the passage. He wanted her to *want* him. He told himself she was shy, and waited, taking his boots off and unbuttoning his shirt, hearing the splash of water, and Helen clearing her throat, then a long silence. He sat on the edge of the bed, beginning to wonder if she was all right or had perhaps been taken ill.

At last she came back in, wearing an enveloping white garment, her lovely hair brushed loose and hanging down her shoulders. Sam's heart leaped at the sight of her, seeing the rounded shape of her soft breasts pushing at the white stuff of her nightdress. Full of desire he went to her at once, to take her in his arms again, and found that she was trembling, and seemed close to tears.

'Helen, my lovely?'

Again, she pulled back.

'Hadn't you better get ready, Sam?'

'Ready for what? I am ready, love—' he managed to put his arms around her – 'I've been ready for you for months and months . . .'

Her face was buried in his chest. It was queer, and frustrating.

'Come on, love,' Sam said coaxingly, though he was getting more and more het up. 'I just want to be with you – for a bit of lovemaking. That's what married people do, you know that, don't you?'

She nodded and a tiny voice said, 'Yes' into his shirt.

'Let me look at you,' he said. Reluctantly she drew back and raised her face. The room was quite dark by now, lit by a single candle, and he could only just make out her features.

'What's the matter, dear?' He kept his voice very patient.

'I don't know what it is. Lovemaking, I mean.' She looked up then, like a little girl, ashamed. 'I don't know what we do.'

Her being so innocent like that made him want her all the more.

'Never mind,' he said. 'We'll find out somehow, together, won't we?' He looked lovingly into her eyes and said, 'I want to see you, Helen. See how lovely you are.'

'What d'you mean?' She sounded frightened.

He managed to talk her sweetly into lying down on the bed with him and once he started touching her round, soft body, she began to loosen up a bit and he did see her at last because, gently pulling her shift up high, she let him complete the marital act. She didn't put up any protest, but watched him, wide-eyed, and when he'd finished she made a little sound, of pleasure, he thought and hoped, and clasped her legs round him.

'Oh, Samuel,' she said, and he felt her breath on his ear. He was happier then. She'd get used to it, of course she would. It was always more difficult for a woman, he understood, and at least he didn't seem to have given her any pain.

Married life started with them living with Mrs Gregory. It was bad from the word go. Anything in the bedroom department felt impossible in her house, and it was difficult enough on their own: Helen just about tolerated the physical side of things. There was very little privacy, especially with the child about. Helen was far too patient with her, in Sam's view. After all, Emma was nothing to her really. But if the child came knocking on the door, Helen would say, 'I'll just let her in, just for a few minutes, poor little thing.' And bang would go their time together. He quickly began to think she did it on purpose to avoid him touching her. But he couldn't stop wanting it, and wanting her. He'd waited long enough and he was a passionate man.

As soon as he could, after a couple of months, he found a house. He had a decent wage now and he thought, We'll get out of Coventry, right away from Mrs G and all that stifling set-up. So they took out the rent on a place in Kenilworth. Helen was a bit upset at first as she'd never lived away from home. But she loved the village and the old castle and cleaner air, and she was such a kind girl that she soon made friends. She took a little job in the grocer's shop and got to know people that way. And they settled. They didn't find a great deal to say to one another, but they both worked hard, and got on with it.

That autumn, after they moved into the house, they

realized there was a baby on the way. Helen was poorly to begin with and went to the doctor.

'Dr Small says you shouldn't have relations of an "intimate" kind during the time a child is expected,' she told Sam.

This came as a blow to Sam. It was an important thing in life to him. He even wondered if the doctor had really said that and almost asked his mother if it was true, but shyness prevented him.

'You make it sound like something dirty,' he said resentfully. 'An animal thing.' She talked as if he was disgusting, like a hog. 'It's just the way men are and I don't see why I should have to be ashamed of it!'

'It won't be long,' Helen tried to soothe him. 'You'll just have to be a good boy, Sam – just until the babby arrives.'

And then, after Christmas, Sam was called into the offices at Daimler.

'We want you to go with a delivery,' he was told. 'One of the new models, to be shipped to Bombay and up to a place called Ambala. Big army station. All being well, you should be back end of March or so.'

God, he was excited! Seeing a bit of the world on the job! And the fact that the delivery out here came up while Helen was carrying the child seemed good timing. She could have some peace and he wouldn't be tempted by the feel of her close to him in the bed. She could rest, safe and cosy in the English winter, while he went off adventuring and slept under the Indian stars.

Chapter Eleven

Ambala, India, 1907

His first morning in Ambala, Sam woke to a tremendous racket of crows from the trees round the house. For a second, he thought the room was full of fog, then realized everything was shrouded in white because of the mozzie net round the bed. He'd got used to being on the ship and it was a shock finding himself in this new place, especially as he'd woken from a dream about Helen and expected to find her in the bed beside him. It was one of those times when he wanted her badly.

There was plenty to take his mind off it, though. So far as Charles Fairford was concerned, today was to be devoted to the Daimler, and he was looking forward to showing the Captain all he knew. And that wife of his would be well out of the way, Sam hoped, doing whatever it was such women did in India.

As soon as he set foot out of bed there came a knock on the door. It was only six in the morning, but when he opened up, there was a native chap standing out there with a tray of tea. My goodness, Sam thought, that's service for you. The man came in, very deferentially, and put the tray down. Beside the teapot was a plate on which were arranged several biscuits and two bananas.

'Sahib would like me to pour the tea?'

'Oh – yes, please! Er – is Captain Fairford up already?'

'Captain Sahib has gone for his morning ride.'

'Ah. I see. Thank you.'

Before his morning ablutions he sat to drink his tea in the cane chair by the window. It was rather misty out, all soft greens and greys. There were Indian voices coming from somewhere and he could just see a chap, thin as a railing like most natives, working with a rake in front of the trees. The sound of his coughing carried across the dew-soaked lawn.

Once he'd downed this rather meagre breakfast and dressed it was still early and all the action seemed to be going on outside, so he decided to slip out for a look around. It was then that he saw Lily Waters properly for the first time, though he didn't know her Christian name then.

He was strolling through the cool morning air smelling the mixed scents of a country that was not his own, along the drive to the gate, thinking to walk a little along the road. He had gone very little distance when he heard the sound of hooves behind him and, turning, saw the two women riding towards him. They made a lovely sight. Susan Fairford was in front, her pale hair just visible under her *topi*, riding elegantly side-saddle, the boy tucked in front of her with a rapturous expression on his face. And riding behind was the woman whom they called Miss Waters. Unlike her mistress she was not riding side-saddle, but astride the bay horse, clad in a modest, feminine blouse and jacket and pair of manly breeches. She was managing the animal with apparent confidence and obvious pleasure, a radiant smile playing round her lips.

'Good morning, Mr Ironside!' Susan Fairford greeted him. There was laughter in her voice and she seemed very different from last night. 'I trust you slept well?'

'Very, thank you,' he replied. He nodded at Miss Waters, touching his hat to them both.

'Good morning,' Miss Waters said, and her eyes seemed full of joy as she looked at him, then shyly away.

They passed on towards the stables and Sam watched, his eyes fixed on Miss Waters's curving form above the shining rump of the horse.

God, he found himself thinking. *What a woman.*

The sun was higher when he returned from his stroll, beginning to burn off the mist. Captain Fairford came round from the side of the bungalow where they'd left the car, striding along manfully, still dressed in riding gear, jodhpurs and puttees. While slender, he was a superbly athletic man. Sam pulled his shoulders back, feeling conscious that he had only ever once sat astride a horse and that an old farm nag, to boot. The safety bicycle had been more his sort of ride!

'Morning, Ironside!' The captain sounded very cheerful, now he was free from the domestic realm.

'Good morning,' Sam rubbed his hands together. 'Chillier morning than I expected!'

'Ah yes – winter nights are pretty cold here,' the captain said as they walked round to where the Daimler was parked. 'You've come at the right time, though – gets damnably hot later in the year. Actually, you'll catch the beginning of it. Come March, the temperature starts to creep up, and by May, June time, phoo! But you'll be long gone by then. Course, we get the extremes here on the northern plains. Anyway – got your breakfast all right?'

'Very nice, thank you, sir.'

'No need to "sir" me – I told you. So, if you're set, we can get cracking. Tell me about this car!'

That had Sam straight into his element, of course. The car was a 45 hp, one of the first new 1907 models, and Sam knew it was an excellent choice. So far as he was concerned, you wouldn't find a better on the market anywhere, and he had admired the captain just from his choice of motor without even meeting him!

'Right then . . .' He hesitated. 'Did you not want your groom to learn about the car too, sir?'

'Oh, there'll be plenty of opportunity to teach Arsalan. He's quick as anything. Just give me a once-over first.'

'Right you are, sir.' Sam was already enjoying himself. 'Well, let's start with the chassis. Of course, they're all built on a pressed steel frame now, not like the old models, you know, all flitch plate, channel steel and wood frames . . . This is a strong animal, this one.'

Animated, he pointed out all the special features, like the clearance between rear axle and side frames, *and*, 'Look here.' He ducked down at the back and beckoned to Charles Fairford to do the same. As they squatted side by side the odours of horse and sweat came off the captain, a pungent, manly combination. For a second, Sam found a powerful image of the women he had met earlier on flash into his mind. Miss Waters: as if she had been summoned by the primitive earthiness of smell. Bewildered, Sam banished her from his thoughts.

'D'you see the height of the floorline?' He was full of it now, rattling on at full speed! 'Well, if you look at any of the models that went before, the floor's been lowered considerably so it's easier to get into the seats – especially for the ladies, of course. Now, you might be

71

thinking, well that's no good, because we'll be scraping the car's belly along the road at that rate.'

He looked round at Charles Fairford and saw he had his complete attention.

'Well, yes, so you would think . . .'

'Ah – well, this is the thing. Just take a look underneath her.'

As requested, Captain Fairford knelt and peered under the car. Sam noticed the sallow colour of his skin at the back of his neck, edged by his strong mahogany-coloured hair. From living out here, he thought. Never really goes white like the rest of us

'See? Good clearance off the road, isn't there?'

'Well, I don't have much to compare with . . . But it seems very good.'

'Lower frame, but more road clearance – so, how have we done it? By raising the engine higher up in the frame, that's how! The gearbox is lower because we reversed the position of the gearshaft and countershaft. *So* – the great thing is, you gain more stability *and* reduce the amount of dust raised off the road. Two things which will be of great importance out here. Quite a thing, wouldn't you say?'

The captain looked genuinely impressed. 'Splendid! Thoroughly splendid.'

They spent a very comfortable couple of hours, kneeling, prodding, peering into the engine, like two schoolboys with a Meccano set. Sam took him through every detail of the engine, cooling system, gears and the springing, which was another of Daimler's proudest developments: springs four feet long – marvellous! And he could see the captain was hooked.

'All I can say is, Captain, you've made an excellent choice,' Sam finished. It was ten o'clock by now, the sun was well up and the air pleasantly warm. A sweet smell of flowers drifted from the beds and pots.

'Well.' The captain straightened up. 'If Daimler's good enough for the king I assumed it would be for me. You've painted a damned fine picture of the workings – thank you, Ironside.'

'More than a pleasure, sir.'

'Fancy breakfast?'

'I thought I'd already had that.'

Charles Fairford laughed. He was a handsome so-and-so, Sam had to hand him that.

'Ah – that was just *chota hazri*, a sort of minor breakfast I take before my ride. It's about time for *bari hazri*. Breakfast major, let's say!'

As they stood there, there came a flurry of running feet and the boy, Cosmo, came tearing round from the back of the house.

'Pater! I want to see the car!'

Close behind, looking flustered, there she was again: Miss Waters, no longer in riding gear.

'I'm sorry, Captain Fairford!' She was blushing, though in her eyes Sam saw elements of mischief on the boy's behalf. 'He's been trying to get out here with you all morning. I couldn't hold him any longer.'

'Not at all,' the captain said easily. 'Of course he must see it! Come here, Cosmo, old chap!'

He swung the boy up into his arms, and into the driver's seat. Cosmo laughed with glee, jumping up and down on the seat, holding on to the steering wheel.

'Make it go, Pater! Make it go fast!'

'Not now, Cozzy. You just have a look for the moment. But we'll get Mr Ironside to take us for a spin later on, shall we?'

They all stood watching the boy for a few moments,

with all his four-year-old, full-hearted glee. Miss Waters's eyes were fixed on him with a rapt smile. But for a moment Sam saw her gaze turn towards him with frank curiosity. He looked back, giving a faint smile, but she fixed her eyes on the boy.

Captain Fairford turned to them.

'I don't know if you've met Miss Waters? She's Cosmo's nanny – doing a sterling job too, I might say. Miss Waters, this is Mr Ironside, from the Daimler Motor Company, who has provided us with this splendid machine.'

They turned to one another again and Sam extended his hand.

'How d'you do, Miss Waters?'

'Pleased to meet you, Mr Ironside.'

She gave him that shy, yet somehow vivacious, look. He had never seen eyes contain more energy and depth. Then she looked quickly away again. Her hand was small and soft and he shook it so carelessly then. He had touched her for the first time, simply as a social formality. Sam had no notion that morning of the extent to which, engraved on his future, would be the mark of his longing to touch her again.

Chapter Twelve

One afternoon, when he had not been in Ambala many days, Sam went for a stroll in the garden while he waited for Captain Fairford. The captain was obliged, naturally, to spend parts of each day working with his regiment on administration, parades and so forth. By three-thirty or so he was usually free, and Sam instructed him, and Arsalan, on the workings of the engine.

The hottest part of the day was rather like English summer, and when Sam approached the house, sweating a little in the afternoon sun, there was a commotion going on outside on the veranda. The two children were there with Mrs Fairford and Miss Waters. He lost his stride for a second, as he didn't relish seeing the captain's wife at any time. It was bad enough having to have dinner with her every night. However, the girl, Isadora seemed to be screaming blue murder, so they weren't taking any notice of him.

'*Ayah* – where is *Ayah*?' Susan Fairford's voice was shrill. 'Lily, fetch the wretched girl. Fetch her at once!'

But before Miss Waters had moved more than a step the *ayah* appeared.

'Oh, for goodness sake, take her indoors until she's quietened down. This is unbearable!'

The *ayah* led Isadora screaming into the house and Mrs Fairford flung herself down into one of the chairs.

She was dressed to go out, in a white, lace-trimmed dress and hat.

'Oh, it really is too much. Just when she was ready. That child will be the death of me. I can't bear it!'

Miss Waters was kneeling with her back to Sam, with Cosmo, whose shoelaces she appeared to be fastening, in front of her on a chair. But then Mrs Fairford caught sight of Sam.

'Mr Ironside.' She sat up, only just managing to regain her formal composure. In fact, she sounded annoyed at having another thing to contend with. 'You'll have to forgive us. We are just taking the children out to a party.'

'Not at all,' Sam said. 'Don't let me get in your way.'

'Do come and sit down,' she instructed, distractedly. 'Charles will be back at any moment.'

He went into the shade of the veranda and sat on one of the lounging chairs, with wooden arms long enough to rest one's legs on, though Sam kept his feet on the floor. He was not far from Miss Waters. She stood up, her attention fixed on the boy, who was looking the image of the perfect gentleman child in a sailor suit. Sam saw a faint smile on her lips, as if she was pleased with her handiwork. Not once did she turn and acknowledge him.

'Don't want my shoes on,' Cosmo was saying, petulantly.

'Oh glory – don't you start as well!' Mrs Fairford snapped, exasperated. 'You see, dressing Isadora to go out is the most *awful* ordeal. The child would run around naked all day if we let her. The moment we begin on petticoats and so forth, all hell breaks loose!'

Sam could hear her trying to make light of the problem, but there was a desperate note in her voice.

She had a printed card of some sort in her hand and was fanning herself with it and he noticed she looked pale and unwell.

'As ever, the only person who can make her see any sense is the *ayah*.'

'So what is her secret, do you think?' Sam asked. He didn't really give a damn what the answer was, but he was trying to be civil.

'Heaven knows,' she replied languidly. 'So long as she gets her out here with her party clothes on, I couldn't care less.'

But his question provoked a reaction from Miss Waters.

'The *ayah* sings to her,' she explained, quietly. 'She sings her into her clothes.'

'With her native mumbo-jumbo, no doubt,' Mrs Fairford snapped.

'She just sings about each item of clothing as they put it on,' Miss Waters said. 'And Izzy gets caught up in it, like a game. Srimala is rather clever like that.'

Her face was as calm and inscrutable as ever, but Sam saw a momentary light in her eyes as she looked down at Susan Fairford. *She can't stand the woman either*, was his first thought, because that was what he wanted to think. He felt a complicity with Miss Waters, since they were both bracketed together as the 'lower orders'. But immediately he saw that it was not that. There was something rather tender in her expression and he was puzzled. Sam wanted to catch her eye and smile, but she didn't look at him. The boy was swinging his feet vigorously, kicking the legs of his chair and she laid a hand on his shoulder to still him.

'Well, whatever she does, let's hope it doesn't take too long. I ordered the *tonga* for half past three. And –

oh, my goodness!' Susan Fairford leaped up. 'Have we the milk? Really, Lily, you should have reminded me.'

'Cook's doing it. He said he'd bring it.'

'Well, go round to the cookhouse and ask him to hurry. Quickly! Knowing him, he's probably only just lighting the fire! *Really*,' she exclaimed as Miss Waters obeyed. 'You have to do everything yourself if you want anything done properly. And really, one doesn't keep dogs to have to bark oneself, does one?'

'Indeed not,' Sam agreed, repelled by her attitude. He realized, to his surprise, that he had less respect for her than for the *syce*, Arsalan. Instructing him about the car, he found that the fellow had a mind like greased lightning; you only had to tell him anything once.

'One can't trust anyone else's servants to boil the milk properly, you see. They're all so lazy and heaven knows what we might all go down with. This country's full of filthy diseases. So we always take our own children's milk, to be quite sure.'

Miss Waters appeared then, holding two bottles of milk wrapped in tissue paper, and a moment later came the sound of hooves and a jingling bell as the *tonga* came along the drive, pulled by a scrawny pony. With magical timing, the *ayah* appeared with a tear-stained, but frilly-clad Isadora, and the three women and two children climbed on to the *tonga*. Cosmo perched on the seat facing the front, between his mother and Miss Waters, and the *ayah* took the girl at the back. It was Miss Waters who put her arm round the boy to steady him, though, and Sam found himself thinking, She is the one who looks as if she is his mother.

As the *tonga* moved off, Miss Waters glanced at him. Their eyes met, though he didn't think it intentional on her part. He felt she was sizing him up in some way.

78

But there was something in the look, a momentary nakedness in that usually closed face, which affected him. He sat and watched the *tonga* disappear past all the flowerpots along the Fairfords' drive and on to the road and found that he was staring for quite some time afterwards.

Chapter Thirteen

As March arrived it grew hotter. The *punkah-wallahs* began their work on the verandas, pulling fans to keep the rooms cool. And Charles Fairford decided that he was now enough of a driver to take the family out for a spin and a picnic tea. They readied the car at four, once tiffin was well digested.

The ladies appeared for the jaunt, erupting from the bungalow and across the veranda in a swirl of skirts, parasols, scarves and fidgeting children. But Sam's eye had only interest in one detail. Was *she* coming? He was not disappointed. With a leaping heart he saw her there behind her mistress.

'Are you ready for us, Charles?' Susan Fairford called. 'We can't keep Cozzy at bay any longer!' Isadora, it appeared, refused to get dressed and was staying behind with the *ayah*.

'Yes, darling – all ready.' He stood smiling, relaxed, one hand resting on the bonnet. He was wearing loose, dust-coloured clothing.

The women had dressed up for the occasion, Mrs Fairford in white, with a very wide-brimmed hat tied under her chin with diaphanous lengths of chiffon. She came sweeping across the drive, but Sam had no eyes for her. Miss Waters followed with Cosmo, who was skipping with excitement. She was dressed more or less as usual, in a long dark skirt and white blouse and a straw hat, of a more modest size than her mistress's, with a strip of soft brown cloth tied round it, forming a bow at the back. It suited her. God, she was a beautiful woman, Sam thought. He had to tear his gaze away so as not to stare. She seemed to have taken up occupation in his mind. It was her eyes which he kept seeing, especially when he lay under the mozzie net at night: those deep, brown eyes, sad in repose, but which could change in a second into dancing life. He ached to see her smile directed at him. And then, ashamed, he would think of Helen, waiting at home to give birth to his child. Good old Helen.

Cosmo broke free from her grasp at last and ran to his father.

'Hello there, old chap!' Captain Fairford laughed. 'Ready for the off?'

'Want to go now. Can we go fast, Pater? Can I drive it?'

To begin with, Sam sat up front beside Captain Fairford, and Mrs Fairford and Miss Waters sat behind with the boy on Miss Waters's lap, yelping with excitement.

Sam watched the captain as he released the brake and set off, steering the car through the gate to the road, face tense with concentration; Sam couldn't help a tinge of envy at the first-class competence of the man. He had everything it took: breeding and money, no struggle to work his way into the right position like the rest of the herd. Charles Fairford had told him that the two por- traits hanging either side of the fireplace in the hall were of his father and grandfather, both astride their horses in full military regalia, both also in the 12th Royal Lancers, the same cavalry regiment as himself. His father had been born shortly before the Mutiny began in 1857, to a father who was killed by cannon fire during its suppression, at the Siege of Lucknow. You could hardly compare, Sam thought, his own father, a cycle engineer, and a grandfather who had been a shopkeeper. It didn't lift you so high up in the world's stakes. Yet he felt a stubborn pride in them as well. They had done well, according to their position.

Steering the car along the road was easy enough, except for the erratic traffic of Indian roads, natives scurrying here and there, pedlars, *dhobis* with huge bundles of washing, native children who ran away from the car but turned to wave from a safe distance, bicycles and *tongas*, dogs and cows.

They bowled along for a time, passing some of the military administrative quarters and the parade ground. The air was lovely, and mellow afternoon light shone through the trees edging the road. Sam began to relax. The driving was not going to present any problems, and if trouble of a mechanical nature arose, he knew he could deal with anything. In fact, he half hoped that something would. Cosmo was chattering constantly with the women behind, and Sam enjoyed the sensation of knowing that if he turned his head far enough to the right he could glimpse Lily. He heard her soft replies to the boy's questions.

'No, Cosmo,' he heard her say. 'You can't sit with Pater today. Your father needs to have the mechanic sitting there.'

Being called 'the mechanic' felt somehow chilling, but he reasoned that he and Miss Waters had barely exchanged more than a word. He was determined to change that.

'We'll be on the Grand Trunk Road soon!' the

captain said. 'It goes all the way from Calcutta, across here to Amritsar, Lahore – right up to the Khyber Pass.' Charles Fairford glanced at Sam quickly, then back to the road. 'We call it the "Long Walk". Have you read any Kipling?'

'No,' Sam admitted foolishly. He'd never been much of a reader.

'Read *Kim*. It's a marvellous yarn and he passes right through here. *Um*ballah, he calls it. He writes about the GT Road, says it's "a river of life such as exists nowhere else in the world". You'll see what he means in a moment.'

Once they had turned on to the wide road, elevated a little above the surrounding fields, they were among a busy stream of carts pulled by stoical-looking white bullocks; of horses, of men and women carrying pots and bundles, some of the men stick thin and strangely dressed, faces painted with white and coloured powders.

'Holy men,' the captain said. 'The road leads to Benares, one of the holiest places in India, on the Ganges.'

People working close to the edge of the fields looked up, their relative peace jarred by the roar of the engine. They passed one or two other cars also and waved at them.

No Daimlers, Sam noticed. A Wolseley and a De Dion – both fine models, of course, even if Daimler was the best. He was tuned in to how the car was running, almost as if it was part of his own body, and she was going well, especially now they were on a superior road. And once again, as with the railways, he thought, My goodness, what an achievement of the empire this is, this great road, stretching hundreds, if not thousands, of miles.

'We've done them a great service here!' he shouted to the captain.

'Who?' he frowned, keeping his eyes on the road.

'Our engineer boys – putting this great road in.'

The captain glanced round, seeming amused.

'We didn't build this, you know! It was here long before we arrived. It was built three hundred years ago, or more, by the emperor of the time – fellow called Sher Shah Suri. He wanted to connect up his own provinces. We've made a few improvements, of course, but it wasn't one of ours. There was plenty going on before we got here. British people so often forget that.'

This stung. Sam felt put in his place. But of course he *had* thought of it like that: India as a backward, primitive place that they were civilizing, with engineers and soldiers and missionaries; a blank sheet to be written upon by the British Empire.

He kept being challenged to see things with new eyes, and was beginning to realize why one could become captivated. The fields spread away on either side, flat and patched with varying shades of greens, dotted with mud huts, haystacks and trees and the movement of small, colourful figures, all dwarfed by the pale arc of the sky

'It all looks so big.'

'Takes getting used to,' the captain said. 'You've been bred on a small island! You should come to the mountains.'

'I'd like to,' Sam found himself saying, to his surprise.

He felt the women listening to their loud conversation from the back and hoped he hadn't made too much of a fool of himself.

Chapter Fourteen

They happened on a picnic spot by chance, a charming spot, a clearing shrouded by several gnarled old banyans with a great many of the vine-like shoots hanging from them.

'How lovely!' Sam heard Miss Waters exclaim. 'It feels almost like a church!'

But that Fairford woman had to go and sour the moment. The captain and Miss Waters were pulling out the things they had brought from the back: a modest hamper, a tarpaulin and rug, and Captain Fairford, gentlemanly as ever, began to help spread the tarpaulin on the dry mud. Susan Fairford stood by the car, adjusting her bonnet and complaining that they hadn't thought to bring chairs. Sam was by the car, giving it a look over to check all was well, and she looked across at him and said, 'It's very strange for us, you see, to be out without the *native* servants to do anything!'

That's telling you, Sam thought. God, the insufferable snobbery of the woman! It was bad enough in England, but it seemed fossilized here. One day it would all have to be knocked down, the whole blessed system, he thought furiously. He hurried over to help Miss Waters with the tarpaulin. She was just picking up a green woollen rug to spread over it.

'Let me help.' He spoke rather sharply, because he was still angry.

'Thank you.' She stood back, as if obeying an order, and he felt apologetic then, but said nothing.

'Miss Waters – Lily!' Mrs Fairford cried, shrilly. 'You must watch Cosmo – he's already right over there, and there might be snakes! Oh, hurry up, do!'

Miss Waters looked dismayed. The boy had already toddled off some distance away.

'Don't you worry – I'll go after him.' In moments, Sam was beside Cosmo.

'Hello, old chap,' he coaxed. 'We're going to have cakes and lemonade. And afterwards, you could help me drive the car a little way.'

Cosmo's face lit up. 'Me drive it? Can I? Oh, *can* I?'

'We'll have to ask your father,' Sam said. 'But if I say you can sit on my lap and have a go, I expect you can drive us back to the big road.'

He had Cosmo in the palm of his hand immediately, and warmed to the child for loving something he loved too. By the time they joined the others they were friends.

Both the Fairfords were standing a short distance from the rug. The captain was enjoying the view across the fields and smoking a cheroot. The smell of it wafted pleasantly on the breeze. Mrs Fairford stood, sipping from a cup, quite near her husband, Sam thought, as if she was still preserving her rank and not wanting to sit down with the rest of them. Miss Waters, though, was seated on the rug, unpacking cakes from the hamper. Sam saw his chance and took Cosmo to sit beside her.

'I'm going to drive the motor car!' Cosmo burst out.

The smile which she gave the boy was still on her face when she looked up at Sam and it was the first full, unreserved smile he'd seen her give. Her lovely, though sometimes melancholy, features lifted, the brown eyes shone. That was the moment, he knew later, when he fell, if that's what you could call it. More like being shot through the heart with no mercy or explanation.

'You seem to have a way with children, Mr Ironside.' The smile had faded.

'I'm not sure that's true.' He sat down beside her. 'I think this young one would do almost anything to be put behind the wheel of a motor!'

She looked astonished, but delighted as well. 'You really are going to let him take the wheel! But how?'

'Oh, I can guide him.' Sam eyed the Fairfords to see if they were moving closer, but they were standing a little apart from one another in the leafy shade. Like Helen and me, he thought, startled. Not ever really close. The thought came as a shock. But he did not want to think about that: he wanted more time to talk with Miss Waters alone. Cosmo settled happily beside her and she handed him a cup to drink from.

'How long have you been with the family?' he asked.

Immediately the words were out, he sensed a change in her, as if a veil, which had been lifted just a second, came down again. He did not feel she was unfriendly, but there was guardedness about the way she spoke which puzzled him. He tried to guess her age but it would have been hard to say. Perhaps like himself, just of age?

'I've been here almost two years,' she said, stroking Cosmo's head of curls. 'They wanted a European nanny for the children, but of course, with Isadora being the way she is, they have had to keep Srimala – the *ayah*. She's been so very good with Izzy. She looked after both of them for a time – and the baby . . .' She hesitated, then, to Sam's surprise, glanced round to see if they were overheard, then whispered, 'There was

87

another child. Two years after Izzy. She died at eight months. That's why Mrs Fairford is so ... particular. They think it was water, or some milk she was given. It makes her very nervous about what they eat and drink.' Sam could see this was a plea for Susan Fairford, as if she had seen his dislike and wanted to say, she's not so bad really. 'It has made her nervous about everything.'

'I suppose it would,' he said, looking back into her eyes. God, she was lovely, that was all he could think about. Being a man, and with such slim experience of these things then, he didn't appreciate the impact of such things: childbirth, the death of a baby, or what they can build or destroy between a man and woman.

'And you like it here?'

'Oh *yes*!' She looked up from arranging little cakes on a plate edged with flowers. The way her eyes moved, that flicker of the lashes, captivated him further. 'I *do*. I liked India straight away. And I've been able to do so many things – like being able to ride. I suppose you're riding with the captain? I've never seen you.'

'No,' Sam said ruefully. 'I'm afraid I don't. Truth is, I'm frightened to death of horses. What with those stamping hooves and whipping tails and tombstone teeth – and the way they throw their heads about!' She was laughing at him now, a surprisingly full-hearted gurgle which delighted him and spread a grin across his own face. 'As for climbing on the back of one, I'd rather lie down in the road in front of a motor car. At least they have brakes and you know they'll stop if you press your foot!'

'You would hope so.' She was still laughing. 'Unless the driver has taken very seriously against you!'

'How long will you stay, do you think?' he asked.

Her face clouded. 'I suppose, only until he goes.'

Fondly, she laid her hand on Cosmo's curls again. 'He'll go to England to school, you see. He's just four – they'll send him at five or six.'

As she said the last words, he was moved to see her eyes fill with tears and she looked down, busying herself with the delicate tea plates and knives. Just then, a young brown bullock appeared on the path, followed and goaded by a small boy trailing a stick in his hand. He came upon their gathering with astonishment, turning to stare as he passed. After a few moments the boy and cow disappeared behind the trees. Miss Waters gave a faint smile again.

'There will be nothing more for me to do here.' She sighed, looking in the direction of the young native child. 'Sometimes I think their children are better off than ours.' She nodded towards Cosmo, who was already tucking busily into a cake. 'They live with their families and stay with them. Most of them, anyway. Terrible things happen to some of them, of course. All the diseases and misfortunes of life here. But at least they don't send them away to live with strangers on the other side of the world when they're hardly old enough to dress themselves.'

'It does seem odd,' Sam agreed, hearing the anger in her voice, though until then he'd never thought about it, not having mixed much with that echelon of people. He would have liked to ask her more about herself before the Fairfords came to join them, but suddenly she said, 'You have come from Daimler? There are a good many motor manufacturers in Coventry, I believe?'

'Yes – why, do you know it?'

She hesitated, just for a second, then looked calmly back at him again.

'No. I don't know Coventry. I stayed, for a very short time, in Birmingham – for a lady where I worked.'

'Ah well – of course, there you've got the Wolseley, Siddley and the Austin,' Sam began enthusiastically. 'Plenty going on there.' He was about to start holding forth the way he could when anyone got him going on motors. But he wouldn't learn any more about Lily Waters by boring her half to death, would he?

'Where's your home then? I mean, in England.'

Looking down and smoothing out the rug, she said, 'Oh, I'm from Kent, originally. But I've moved around a little. My father was a clergyman, you see, so we had parishes in various different counties.'

'Had?'

'Both my parents passed away at all too young an age.' Unlike the plight of Cosmo, this statement did not seem to rouse any emotion in her. 'That is why it has been a pleasure to me to become part of another family. I'm afraid I am really rather alone in the world.'

'No brothers or sisters?'

'I had an elder brother, but he had a weak heart. He was dead at fifteen.'

'How sad.'

'Yes, sad,' she agreed, with such melancholy that it made the pistol wound in his heart throb again. He had a terrible desire to reach out and touch her hand.

'I say – this looks good!' The captain approached with boyish glee and rumpled Cosmo's hair. Sam supposed the boy must get very tired of that as everyone seemed to do it. His hair seemed to ask for rumpling. 'I see you've started tucking in already!'

'Pater, the mech— mech-an-ic man says I can drive the car!'

The captain winked at Sam. 'Good for you!' he said

90

to his son, then added, 'Better if he goes with you, I'd say, at this stage!'

'But you drove here like an expert,' Sam said truthfully.

Mrs Fairford was settling herself down in a disdainful way, as if sitting on the ground was a terrible trial.

'What a marvellous spot, eh?' the captain said.

It truly was. The evening air was delicious, the sun sending sidelong rays of orange-pink light through the trees. The shifting shadows of the banyan leaves and its strange, primeval shape fell over them. Beyond, they could looked out upon the green of the paddies and the dusky edge far, far in the distance where, but for a verdant scattering of trees, the warm, flat land met the sky with no obstacle between.

Cosmo got up and skipped about, happily full of cake and not seeming to want to run too far off. The warm evening light had a calming effect on all of them. A group of four young lads passed along the path and the captain called out a greeting. The boys looked frightened at first, before he greeted them in Hindustani. Sam didn't know what he said to them but they all started grinning away like mad and called something back and they went off, laughing and chattering together. They drank tea and Captain Fairford offered Sam one of the cheroots. Even Susan Fairford, once recovered from having to slum it on the ground, seemed to mellow into a more gentle person for the moment and Sam saw her genuinely pretty smile.

It was an evening he'd never forget. There was the motor there under the trees, all shipshape with no problems and looking splendid, and this soft, caressing air, his life of streets and factories and cramped dark houses all opening out into this unexpected and wondrous world.

And beside him, a woman who he scarcely knew, but whose face and voice, whose *being* utterly captivated him. She had got right under his skin. Perhaps he should have been more frightened. Or guilty. But all he could feel was a sense of expectation as if he was fully, abundantly alive.

Chapter Fifteen

Every moment of the day now he was alert to thinking about Lily Waters and whether he might see her. It was as if Helen did not exist. All he could see was this radiant, mysterious woman's face in his mind and know his craving to be near her. He was quietly in a constant state of maddening excitement.

Two days later, something out of the ordinary happened. They had all gone to bed and the dark house was making its usual creaking, scuttling noises. Sam had slept for a time when a great commotion broke out: the sound of crying, and women's voices raised in panic. Cursing the mozzie net, he climbed out quickly and dressed. Opening the door, he heard Susan Fairford shrieking orders to the servants. She sounded quite beside herself.

'Tell the cook to get the fire going to boil water – quickly, you fool! Send for Dr Fothergill!'

Wondering if he could be of help, Sam lit the candle and crossed the main hall to the other side of the house. The sound of fretful crying was coming from the boy's nursery, and he saw Lily Waters run from the room into the neighbouring one and emerge again in seconds carrying a white cloth. She wore a silky green robe, her hair fastened in two plaits and she looked younger like that, and so sweet, to his eyes, but she was obviously frantic.

'What's wrong?' He went to her. 'Is there anything I can do to help?'

'Of course!' Urgently, she caught hold of his arm. 'You can take us to the doctor's – please, will you? He's so slow and Cosmo's so very poorly!'

'Lily, do come!' Mrs Fairford called in a distraught voice from Cosmo's room. She came to the door, her pale hair loose on her shoulders. 'Have you found Arsalan?' She didn't seem to see Sam standing there.

'Mr Ironside is here,' Lily told her. 'He could take Cozzy straight to Dr Fothergill, in the motor.'

'Will it be all right with Captain Fairford?' Sam was saying, as Susan Fairford ran into the room and snatched her son out of his bed. Even in the dim light Sam could see that the child was running a high fever.

'It's of no consequence whether it is or not!' Mrs Fairford snapped. 'He's asleep. I believe he'd still be asleep if the house caved in! Take him – now! Lily, you take him!'

'I need to dress . . .'

'No, you don't! It's dark! Mr Ironside—' For another brief moment Sam saw Susan Fairford in a different light which softened him towards her a fraction. She looked like a young girl in her nightclothes, her hair loose, frightened and vulnerable. 'Please – can you take him safely?' She looked down desperately at her limp son and put her right hand to her mouth for a second, biting on her knuckles. 'Oh God, look at him! I'm so worried. I want him to see Dr Fothergill straight away. He knows us well . . . I don't want to lose him . . .' She began to sob.

'Of course,' Sam said, feeling sorry for her. And it sounded as if Lily Waters would be accompanying him. Would she? Oh God, *please*, his mind begged.

'Do go, quickly!'

Sam ran to fetch his jacket and by the time he got back to the hall, Lily Waters was waiting with Cosmo in her arms, wrapped in a sheet. Sam was surprised to see Susan Fairford wrapping a shawl round Lily's shoulders in an almost motherly gesture.

'I should come with you – but you're better with him. You'll be calm.'

'It's all right, Susan,' Miss Waters said. 'He'll be all right. Don't worry yourself.'

In those fleeting moments Sam took in with surprise the gentle intimacy between the two women.

'Oh, look after him!' Mrs Fairford came to the door, her voice cracking as the tears came again. 'Look after my little darling!'

'You know I will,' Miss Waters said tenderly as they stepped out into the night.

And then, apart from the sick little boy, Sam found himself alone with this woman whose presence had such a powerful effect on him.

The night was a little chill, but not uncomfortable, the sky an immense field of stars. As they moved round the side of the house the *chowkidar*, a stringy fellow with a cloth tied round his head, loomed in front of them and Miss Waters spoke to him immediately so that he nodded and backed away.

'You speak Hindustani?' Sam said, admiringly.

'I've been here for some time now. You pick it up.'

Sam got the Daimler started and jumped into the driver's seat. They set off, the road lit by the clear white light of the acetylene lamps.

'You know the way?'

'Of course,' she snapped. A moment later, thinking perhaps that she had been impolite, Lily said, 'He had a fit, you see. I don't even know if we should be moving him, but Mrs Fairford was in such a panic and Dr Fothergill doesn't reckon to hurry himself too much if you send for him. Sometimes he doesn't ever arrive . . .'

'I'm surprised the captain didn't wake,' Sam said. There'd been enough racket, after all.

Lily's voice came back sharply. 'He's not there.'

'What d'you mean?' The captain had been at home for dinner.

'He goes out sometimes at night.' She almost snapped the words and Sam did not like to ask any more.

The doctor's house was a mile and a half away, and for the rest of the journey Lily Waters spoke only to give terse instructions. Apart from the occasional grizzling cry, Cosmo stayed ominously silent. Once when Sam glanced at them, he thought he saw the child's eyes open, but wasn't sure. He could feel Lily Waters's worry and tension beside him.

Dr Fothergill's bungalow was a simple white building close to the road.

'You stay sitting,' Sam said gently. 'At least until we've got an answer at the door.'

In the gloom he saw her give a faint smile which felt like a huge reward.

The house was all in darkness and as soon as Sam went near the front, the doctor's watchman leaped up and started nattering at him but of course Sam couldn't understand a word and knocked the door anyway. He expected to have to get through a battery of servants before reaching the doctor but, to his surprise, when the door swung open, there stood a very substantial white man with a bushy, grizzled beard, wearing a vast pair of pyjama trousers, his hairy chest and ample belly covered by nothing but a blanket draped round his shoulders.

With one hand he held an oil lamp and with the other he was rubbing his portly abdomen in a soothing manner.

'Yes?' he boomed. 'Who the devil are you?'

'I'm Captain Fairford's mechanic,' Sam blurted, foolishly.

'*What?* Charles Fairford? Well, what the blazes d'you want? Have you come to tinker with my motor car at one o'clock in the morning? What the devil's the matter with you?' A rather abrupt belch took the doctor by surprise as he finished speaking, followed by the groan of a man plagued by dismally acidic innards.

'Their boy's here with me in the car. He's been taken ill – they said he had a fit.'

'What – young Cosmo?' Reluctantly, he was all attention now. 'Well, speak up, man, do. You should have said before...' Pulling the blanket closer round him he held the lamp high and came down to the car.

'So, what's up with this young fellow? Bring him into the house, um?'

He led them into a kind of snuggery, arranged with the rudimentary carelessness of a bachelor, with the usual animal trophies on the walls and very basic furnishings: chair and table, a mess of belongings and papers, a pair of boots slung to one side, a rug thrown on the floor. There was a thick smell of stale tobacco smoke.

'Bit of a pickle,' Dr Fothergill said. 'Not meant for decent company. Put him down on here.'

He swept a few brass objects off the table, and with a laborious grunt picked up a rug from a chair and spread it on the top. Sam moved to help Miss Waters as she laid Cosmo's distressed little body down on the table. Cosmo stirred and moaned, without opening his eyes.

'What's up with you, young fellow?' Dr Fothergill was gentle with him, feeling the boy's head and limbs. 'Fever, obviously . . .' he mused. 'You say he had a fit?'

'He was restless tonight,' Lily Waters told him. 'His temperature went up very fast so I stayed with him. And suddenly he just went rigid, and his eyes were rolling. He was twitching and not himself at all. And Mrs Fairford was worried.' She looked up into the doctor's eyes and saw that they shared knowledge about Susan Fairford.

'Yes,' he sighed. 'I know, poor girl. Thinks she's cursed by nature – even when she's got a fine, healthy boy here.'

Dr Fothergill listened to Cosmo's chest with the stethoscope, asked a few more questions, and seemed satisfied.

'Well, Miss, er . . .'

'Waters.'

'Of course.' He was speaking very kindly now. 'Tell Susan he'll be quite all right if he just has plenty to drink and isn't kept wrapped up too warmly. Some-times, if the temperature shoots up like that, they can have a bit of a turn. Febrile convulsions, we call it. There's nothing else wrong that I can see. But I'll call in tomorrow. Best thing for him now will be a nice ride home to bed in the breeze. Off you go, both of you.'

At the door, he stopped Sam, laying a weighty hand on his shoulder. 'And whose employ are you in?'

'The Daimler Motor Company, sir.'

'Ah – the royal carriages.' He chuckled. 'Trust Charles! Very good, very good! Well, goodnight to you! And don't overheat that child!'

Chapter Sixteen

Things felt quite different now that they knew Cosmo was not seriously ill.

'What a nice doctor,' Sam said, helping Lily Waters into the car, where she settled Cosmo on her lap.

'He is kind really, even if he seems crusty. I think he's rather fond of Sus— of Mrs Fairford.'

Sam shut her door and stood beside her. He was still wondering about her remarks about the captain, but did not want to ask more questions. 'And you are too. You seem to be a very good friend to her.'

'She's all right, really, underneath.' She looked up at him again, and in the dim light he just made out her smile. It made him lurch inside.

He climbed behind the wheel, taken aback to realize that his hands were shaking. Nobody had ever affected him like this before.

'D'you fancy a bit of a drive – cool the little chap down a bit more?' He released the brake, longing to drive for miles on end, just so that he could stay sitting beside her.

She laughed, which made him ridiculously happy. She seemed relaxed being alone with him. Of course, they were more of the same class, he thought. They didn't have to talk up or down to each other. But was it more? he longed to know. Did she feel the way he was feeling?

'You're a funny one, aren't you?' she said. 'Any excuse to be driving this car! But Mrs Fairford will be worried.'

'Just round the block – the main cantonment road,' he persuaded her. 'We can say it was doctor's orders – it was almost.'

'Goodness – I'm in my nightclothes. I don't think Dr Fothergill even noticed!'

'He was hardly in any position to, was he? He was in his as well!'

They both laughed then, and he eased the car forward.

'It's all right, Cozzy,' Lily soothed him. 'You sleep, little love – we'll be home soon.'

Sam headed away from the Fairfords' house.

'I hope you know the way round by now,' he said. 'Or we'll be lost.' Although that would have suited him perfectly, being lost for hours in this soft night, with a thin moon up and all the stars and this bewitching woman close beside him. She was here, actually here beside him! The very air felt charged and crackling with life.

'If you keep turning left we should be all right. We'll know we're near when we see the church.'

He drove slowly, realizing that he couldn't be sure who or what might loom up into the lights. People seemed to keep odd hours in India, up and on the roads day and night. And of course he wanted the journey to last, on and on so that he could see her face lit by the pink Indian dawn. He glanced round at her for a second, but then had to swerve when some scuttling creature tore across the road in front of the car.

'Damn it – what was that?' His heart was pounding.

She laughed. It was the first time he had ever heard

her laugh like that, a carefree, young woman's laughter and, hearing it, he knew he was completely lost to her.

'I think it was a mongoose!'

Further along he said, 'It's pretty warm tonight. I don't know if I could stand the summer here.'

'Yes, from April to June it's stifling,' she said. 'But we go to Simla. Mrs Fairford likes to get Isadora up to the hills early. She suffers terribly from heat. You've seen what she's like with clothes, even in the winter!'

'She's certainly a character,' Sam said carefully.

'Mrs Fairford is ashamed of her. Always ashamed. It seems such a pity – for both of them. But they rent a nice house up there and it's much more comfortable. And when you see the hills, you'll really love India.'

'I don't know that I shall see them!'

'Surely you must, while you're here?' she said seriously. 'The mountains are so grand, and the air is cool and there are lovely woods and flowers. You can walk for miles and it's not dusty and dirty.'

She was speaking more fluently now. It felt easy being with her. As she talked, though, without being so guarded, he heard an occasional lilt in her voice. She was very hard to place.

'Where're you from again – originally?' Again he glanced round in the dark. He cursed having to drive. He wanted just to sit and look at her. They'd already been quite a way round the block and time was running out. He would have loved to pretend to get them lost to give them more time, but the trouble was that before long he would not have been pretending and there was no telling where they might end up.

'I've lived in several places. I suppose I could say I'm from Kent.'

'It's a queer thing, but when you spoke earlier I

thought you sounded – well, more like me. Touch of the Midlands.'

There was a pause. When she spoke it was as if she had closed down on him again.

'I suppose I begin to sound like whoever I'm with. Some people are like that – they take on other people's way of talking.'

'Like those lizard creatures that change colour depending on what colour the branch is they're sitting on.'

From the corner of his eye, he saw her turn to look at him.

'A chameleon?' she said. 'Yes, just like that.'

He was bursting with questions, and with feeling too, but he could see that if he kept on asking her too much she would withdraw completely. She was not an open person. She told you just enough, but no more. They drove in silence for a few moments, seeing flashes of the trees beside the road in their lights and insects swimming towards them in the beams like tiny scraps of paper. Sam's mind was racing. Here he was, alone with this astonishing woman. What did she think of him? And – the thought came as a terrible reproach – did she know he was married? He had certainly never told her, but it was just possible that Mrs Fairford had. None of these things seemed to matter when he was so overwhelmed with need for her.

'Turn left here,' she said suddenly, breaking into his thoughts. A few moments later they turned into the Fairfords' drive and Sam parked in the usual place along the side of the house. He had no idea how long they had been out or what time it was. It felt like a very long time, but must not have been as much as an hour.

He switched off the engine, leaving them in a sudden

102

silence, the air full of aromatic night smells. He thought she would get up to leave immediately, but she still sat.

'He's got himself well settled,' she said, looking tenderly down at Cosmo. 'It seems a pity to move him. The ride seems to have calmed him down.'

Sam reached over and very gently stroked the boy's head. Cosmo still felt hot, but perhaps less than before. Seeing his gesture, Lily Waters looked up at him and smiled. Blood seemed to pound round Sam's body. There was an answer in that smile – he knew it!

'Lily,' he said, impetuously. 'May I call you Lily? At least while we're alone?'

'All right,' she looked down then, shyly. 'And what's your name?'

'Samuel – Sam, my pals call me.'

'Sam,' she said, in a considering way, and stared ahead towards the trees in the dark garden in a way which made her again completely mysterious to him.

But here was this moment. He might never find the chance to be alone with her again. He had to say something!

'We should go inside – Mrs Fairford will be worried,' Lily said. But still she didn't move.

Her left hand was cradling Cosmo's shoulder, keeping him pressed close to her, and Sam reached round and laid his over it, stroking it with all the ardour he felt, finding the courage to look into her eyes. She looked back at him, a wide-eyed, almost frightened look.

'You're such a beautiful woman,' he told her. He wanted to say everything, all that she made him feel, but he was no good with words. 'You just have . . .' He attempted. 'You have a strong effect on me.'

'Do I?' she whispered. And still she didn't look away.

He could feel the blood pumping round his veins as if there was a giant turbine inside him, as if he might burst, or boil over, without some release.

'Dear God,' he said, barely meaning to let the words escape. 'You're so lovely.'

Impetuously he leaned down and let his lips brush hers, and still she didn't move away. She made a tiny sound in her throat, which encouraged him and he kissed her, gently. She did not resist, and as he became more passionate he felt her respond until he was completely inflamed by her. He had to tear himself away, drawing back so as not to lose control.

'God, woman,' he said. 'I love you. Do you realize?'

She was looking up at him. 'I've never—' she began, then looked down at Cosmo in confusion. 'We must take him in.'

'Where can I see you? There's never anywhere to be alone here – always someone watching . . .'

Again she stared ahead with those dark, mysterious eyes, thinking.

'After tiffin, there's often a time when everyone sleeps. The veranda at the side is usually quiet.'

'Tomorrow?' he said. 'Today now, I suppose.' He could hardly stand the thought of being away from her for so long.

Meeting his eyes, she whispered, 'Yes, all right. At three.'

Chapter Seventeen

He was so afraid that she wouldn't come.

She had told him to wait on the back veranda, overlooking the wide lawn, edged by trees which spread fronds of shade along the edge of the grass. The lawn was beautifully cut: Sam had seen the *mali* out there guiding a young white bullock which pulled the heavy mowing machine, with leather mufflers on its hooves to stop them churning up the turf. The pots of plants edging the lawn looked tired in the heat. It was just after the hottest part of the day and even the insects moved sluggishly. Sam caught the scent of the eucalyptus tree close to the house.

The household was miraculously quiet, and Hassan, the *punkah* lad, was fast asleep on his back, the rope wrapped round the toes of his right foot but hanging limp. He looked in a state of delicious comfort and Sam certainly had no intention of disturbing him.

He sat on one of the cane chairs and tried to distract himself from his inner turmoil by watching two chipmunks darting about at the foot of the tree. He was well fed after today's tiffin of cold meat and potatoes with the fieriest of pickles, but he was not in the least ready for sleep. Not when every fibre of him was on full alert to hear *her* step coming towards him!

The chipmunks were replaced by three wrangling

crows, and then he heard the door open and nothing else after could steal his attention. His blood raced.

She came round the house on tiptoe, looking down at her feet almost as if there might be glass underfoot and he saw that this was out of shyness. He stood up to greet her and at last she met his eyes and gave a smile which sent vibrations through him.

'Shall we sit here?' he suggested.

'Yes' – she spoke very quietly. 'I don't know how long I'll be able to stay.'

Sam nodded towards the *punkah-wallah*. 'He's having a good rest, anyway.'

Lily smiled with real amusement. 'Yes – that's why it's taken me some time to get Cosmo to sleep. His room is stifling!' She selected a chair, carefully arranging the folds of her deep green skirt, but sat perched on the edge, obviously not at her ease.

'How is the boy today?'

'Still feverish, but no more alarms in the night. I've put an ice pack in the bed to keep him cool. But I think Dr Fothergill was right – there's nothing more to it than a fever of sorts.'

'Oh, well that *is* good news.'

'Yes.' She looked up for a second and gave him another faint smile, but then dropped her eyes again, seeming filled with confusion. There was a terrible silence in which both of them were at a loss. But then she seemed to collect herself. Looking across at him, she said, 'How long will you be staying with the Fairfords altogether?'

'It was envisaged that I'd be here for up to six weeks. The captain has taken to the driving and looking after the car like a duck to water, so I can't imagine it will be more.' Sam kept talking, out of his own nerves. 'Strictly speaking, we ought to make a longer trip since he is thinking of taking it on tour. It can be a problem here, you see – what the roads do to the tyres, for a start. The good roads, *pukka*, I suppose they'd say here, like the Grand Trunk Road – they're made of laterite. It's a metallic material, lots of iron in it, and if it breaks up – well, you've got trouble: knife-edged bits of road that slash the tyres to pieces. And of course another thing is all those bullock carts. Get a whole train of those going along a laterite road and you've got eight-inch ruts. It's not the rainy season now, but when it comes, the water washes the ruts out and Bob's your uncle – knife edges again! Your tyres go and your inner tubes . . . We need to get out there and try it all out a bit more. And that's only one thing . . .'

He was about to launch into a catalogue of other besetting problems of dust and accumulator leakage but caught himself in time. Why was he prattling on in this crazed fashion about something a woman would have not the least interest in?

'Sorry,' he said foolishly. 'I get a bit carried away when you get me on to cars.'

But she smiled then, seeming more comfortable.

'I've heard. Mrs Fairford says you're like an endlessly babbling stream on the subject. Oh!' She blushed deeply, putting her hand to her mouth. 'How terribly bad mannered of me to repeat that! I'm so sorry!'

'It's all right,' he laughed. 'I'm surprised she didn't say something even worse. I don't think she takes to me very much.'

The look on Lily's face and her lack of denial of this made him laugh more. He didn't need her to tell him of Susan Fairford's snobbish attitude to him!

'Tell you what,' he said impulsively. 'D'you fancy a spin now?'

'You can't, can you?' she looked alarmed. 'Just take the car out as you like?'

'Don't see why not.' He was all for getting to his feet. 'Just round the roads again, maybe?'

'No – really, I can't. I'm supposed to be keeping an eye on Cosmo. Today especially. I really should be in there now.'

'Of course.' Sam sat back. 'How silly of me.'

They sat for a few more moments, talking of day-to-day things about the household, laughing about the sour-faced Mussulman cook, but Sam was in an agony. Time felt as if it was rushing by so fast and he wanted to say things to her, loving, affectionate things, but he could not seem to begin. A few moments later he saw Hassan stirring in his sleep as if he might wake. How difficult it was to be alone!

Leaning forwards he spoke to her urgently. 'Last night, Lily – what I said to you. I meant it, you know. Every word. Ever since I've been here in Ambala I have noticed you and wanted to know you better. If I was here for longer it might be different, but there isn't much time . . .'

She looked pleased, or worried, or both. But her eyes told him: she wanted him too, he knew it! God, he was in a state. It was the very look of her. And it wasn't how it had felt with Helen (whom he kept trying not to think about). Lily had such a full, graceful figure, and my goodness he'd have loved to take her in his arms, but it wasn't the same animal sort of desire he'd had before bedding Helen. That was there too, of course, he couldn't deny it, but it was more like adoration. He wanted to kneel before her, have her take his head and rest it on her full breast.

Breathing in deeply, he said, 'I've never met anyone

like you before, Lily. You must think me very forward, rude, even, but you just . . . You captivate me. I don't know what else to say . . .'

She was watching him intently and her face showed confusion, as if there was a struggle going on, which he could not make sense of in this beautiful woman who was at once so bold and so shy.

'You're very kind,' she said, looking down into her lap, where her hands were tightly clasped. 'You really are, Mr . . . Sam. I don't know what to say. Except that . . .' And she looked very directly at him, her dark eyes intense. 'You don't want to know me. I don't have any background – nothing to offer . . .'

What was this nonsense she was talking? It made him feel abundantly tender towards her.

'If you're not worth knowing,' he teased gently, 'then why have you come out here to see me?'

She sighed, seeming remote. 'I don't know. Because I wanted to . . . Very much.'

Sam felt like a man meeting a roe deer at the edge of a clearing: that he must not move, hardly breathe, because it would leap back at his slightest twitch. He longed to reach out and take her hand, but he held back, full of respect for her and said gently, 'Well, I'm glad of that, at least.'

She was beginning to smile, and said, 'You're not like anyone I've ever . . .' when there came a moaning cry from inside, and she leaped up, murmuring, 'Cosmo! I'm sorry – I must go!' and was away along the veranda.

Her cry roused young Hassan, who sat up blearily and began to pull on the *punkah*, trying to look as if he had been doing precisely that all the time.

Chapter Eighteen

Isadora was writhing on her bed, screaming and tearing at her red, flayed skin.

'*Ayah* – the calamine lotion. Where is it, you silly girl? Oh, Izzy, be quiet, for the love of God!' Susan Fairford was close to tears as she tried to quieten her flailing daughter. '*Stop* it, Isadora! Oh, Lily, what's going to become of her?' she wailed despairingly.

Lily fetched the jar of calamine lotion and handed it to Srimala. Every year Isadora suffered terribly from prickly heat as soon as the winter was over, and these distressing scenes had repeated themselves since she was very young. Lily knew it was the time Susan Fairford dreaded the most.

'It's all right,' Lily soothed her mistress. 'You know how it is – the lotion will help a little.'

'Oh God ... If we could just get up to Simla, away from this godforsaken place...' Susan Fairford sank down on the nursery chair, putting her head in her hands.

'What is it?' Lily knelt down, looking up into her face. She knew Susan well, her despair over not being able to love Isadora, her grief for the little girl whose life had fluttered away in her arms when she was only eight months old, and her sense of never being a good enough mother to Cosmo. Haunting her also was the knowledge that whatever she did or said, once he was five he would be torn away from her. Susan had, over time, allowed Lily to see her at her most emotionally raw – and, as well as the children, there was the pain of her marriage.

'I don't even know where he is!' she sobbed one night, in Lily's arms when Charles had disappeared again after dinner. He had also not visited her room for any intimate contact for a long time. Susan was a woman who hungered for love and for understanding, and weeks could go by without his ever requiring such union with her.

'Charles only married me because he knew it was the form to have a wife. I was really the only girl he knew,' she told Lily when she was a little calmer. 'My brother was at Eton with him – they educated Lewis, of course. They hadn't the funds for Audrey and me. I met Charles when I went to a prize-giving. The first time I saw him he was standing under a pink blossom tree and he looked like a god! I remember I thought he was very handsome and charming, but we hardly knew each other. And I suppose he just thought I was suitable. He was supposed to choose a wife from home and I was the first resort rather than the fishing fleet.'

The 'fishing fleet' consisted of girls who caught the steamers to India for the winter season in search of eligible men to marry, and the love-starved bachelors of the army and police, the trades and civil service were all expected to take their pick. The disappointed fisher girls would have to get back on a boat home at the end of the season, still single and without prospects.

'I don't know if he even likes me, quite honestly,' Susan told Lily despairingly that night.

'Of course he does,' Lily said. She was baffled by the whole situation. 'He's always so nice to you!'

'He's *polite* to me,' Susan retorted. 'Of course, we can both put on a good show. But other than that, he'd rather be in the mess, where he's got the men round him. He needed me to have children, of course. I was his brood mare. But now he's got the son he wanted, he hardly ever comes anywhere near me. And I feel so *useless*. Some days I just can't bear the thought of life going on and on like this . . .'

Lily knew now that so much of Susan Fairford's tense, angry manner arose through her unhappiness and that there was a lonely, girlish person inside. Today she seemed close to despair.

'I'm not much of a mother,' she said flatly, staring at her lap as Srimala struggled with Isadora. 'You'd think I could manage at least to get that part right, wouldn't you?'

'Oh, dear Susan,' Lily said, taking her hand. 'Cozzy, do come and see your mater and cheer her up.'

Cosmo approached, wide-eyed. He was really more used to Lily's company and was slightly in awe of his mother, but he did as Lily bade him and came and took Susan's hand.

'I don't feel well,' Susan admitted.

'You go and have a lie down,' Lily encouraged her.

'Oh, I get so weary with it all,' Susan said, dragging herself to her feet. 'This climate, all these sicknesses. I just ache to be at home so much I think sometimes I'll die of it.'

Lily took Cosmo out on the lawn. She had a big parasol and they sat in the shadow of the tamarind trees, but unlike Susan Fairford, she mostly didn't mind the heat.

She had taken some story books and Cosmo sat

beside her on a rug, looking at pictures of animals. Susan insisted that he learn the names of British birds and flowers, although he was surrounded by an almost completely different flora and fauna. He sat in the crook of her arm saying, 'That's a robin' or 'a blackbird', as if they were wildly exotic species from another world.

Lily listened with less than half her mind to Cosmo's reading. She had come outside because she knew that Sam might appear in the quiet time after tiffin and that sooner or later Cosmo would drift off into a nap and they might be alone. And more than anything she longed to be alone with Sam Ironside.

She had never met anyone like him before, and she had certainly never felt like this before. She could think of nothing else these days: of his intense gaze which seemed to burn into her each time they met. She had felt it even before he spoke to her, the way he watched her. She loved his strong, impatient walk, and his love of the Daimler and expertise when anything went wrong. She loved the fact that he was funny and kind. That night they had taken Cosmo to Dr Fothergill's, she had felt the electric atmosphere between them and found herself more and more affected by him. But she was afraid. Anyone else whom she had even come close to loving had died or disappeared. How could she let herself feel for this man? Yet, when he declared that he loved her, her whole heart and soul longed to answer. Someone loved her! This handsome, interesting man loved her – and she loved him back! Since that night nothing had been the same and, despite her fear, she had fallen more and more deeply in love.

Of course he soon appeared. He knew she would be there, and they could not keep away from each other.

'Motor-car man!' Cosmo enthused, seeing a movement at the side of the house.

'Motor car' had been one of his first words, very precisely pronounced.

'Oh yes!' Lily said, trying not to sound too excited as Sam strode towards them.

'Hello, young fellow!' He sat down on the rug beside them and, with mock formality, he doffed his hat and added, 'Afternoon, Miss Waters.'

'Good afternoon.' She tried to sound sober but could not stop the joyful smile which took full possession of her face. He was here, at last!

They sat talking in the quiet afternoon, but Cosmo was not going to be left out.

'Story! Story!' he demanded. He loved to hear any tales of motoring exploits.

'Oh, all right then,' Sam laughed. 'Let's see now. What about the Thousand Miles Trial, eh? That was a good one! You see, Cozzy, when new cars are built they have to be put through their paces to see how fast they can go and whether they can climb hills and so on. So there are all sorts of races and trials to test them. So to test a car over a thousand miles is a very big test!'

Cosmo listened, rapt. They knew he would only understand a fraction of what Sam was saying, but he listened with absolute attention.

'Just a few years ago – nineteen hundred it was – sixty-five motor cars and motorcycles all met in Hyde Park – that's in London, Cozzy. There were Napiers and MMCs and Daimlers, of course, and all the foreigners, De Dions, Panhards, Benz . . . They all set off to do a thousand miles – west to a big city called Bristol and then north to Birmingham, Manchester . . .' He smiled at Cosmo's fascinated expression. 'And there were all sorts of mishaps, I can tell you! One fellow had the brakes fail and d'you know how he stopped his car? It was a Daimler like your pa's, as well – and he ran it backwards into a wall! And there was another good story about a Daimler: a chap called Grahame-White bust up his steering gear by running into a ditch. So, you'll never guess what he did.'

Lily was laughing as Sam talked excitedly, as much with his hands as his voice.

'Go on, tell us!' Lily said.

'Well, he needed to steer the car somehow, so he stood on the step, stuck his foot out onto the front wheel and steered it all the way to Newcastle with his boot – fifty-two miles! And d'you know what?'

'What?' Cosmo breathed, utterly captivated.

'When he got there, the sole of his boot was completely worn through.'

'No!' Lily cried. 'That can't be true! Surely no one could do that?'

'True as I'm sitting here.' Their eyes met in mutual love and laughter and Lily felt herself turn weak with longing for him to hold her, for them to kiss and while away the whole afternoon together.

'More stories!' Cosmo insisted.

Sam laughed. 'No peace with children around, is there? I suppose I'll soon . . .' But he bit back the rest of what he had been about to say: that he would soon know what it was to have a child of his own.

Chapter Nineteen

Sam knew he was in love in a way he had never experienced before, as if every nerve in his body was alert – more than alert – on fire! And with it came a tenderness which took him by surprise, and a sense of vulnerability that he, cocky, ambitious Sam Ironside felt in this woman's presence. It was like nothing he had known before. It was exhilarating and rather frightening; above all, he knew he could not let it go.

He had made clear his feelings to Lily, or he hoped he had. He gave scarcely a thought to Helen and all that was waiting back in England. It was as if he had walked into another life so very far off and different that neither one had anything to do with the other. Every moment around the Fairfords' house was charged with excitement at the thought that he might see Lily and be able to speak to her. Through the days, like a miracle, ran a refrain in his head, *I love Lily Waters, my Lily, Lily, Lily . . .*

The next few times he saw her after their meeting on the veranda, she was with Cosmo, or Susan Fairford. One morning he met her with Srimala and the children out on the drive with nets and she said they were going out looking for butterflies. She was dressed in pale blue and looked at him from under her hat, her eyes full of dancing life.

'I only wish I could come with you,' he said, as they stood on the drive, out of hearing of the *ayah*.

Lily looked down for a moment, then back. 'So do I,' she said softly. And her gaze sent a spasm of intense longing through him.

'Where can I see you?' he said quickly. 'I can't bear not seeing you alone.'

She hesitated for a moment, and he thought he saw a struggle going on within her.

'Outside, at the back. Late – eleven o'clock. It's the only way. We'll just need to keep out of the watchman's way.'

There was a moon that night. Sam had dinner with the Fairfords then spent the evening in an itch of impatience. At last, when the house was quiet, he slipped out of the back door and stood under one of the trees at the back of the house in the night air. How he loved that smell, he realized, breathing in deeply. Dung smoke and vegetation and the rich smell of the country's earth. He had not expected this, that he would begin to love the place as well. India was changing him into a new man.

The door opened and he heard her coming out to join him. She stopped, in the darkness, uncertain.

'Over here, Lily . . .' He had been about to call her Miss Waters.

She came to him and for a moment they strained to see each other's faces through the darkness.

'Oh God, you're here,' he said. And they couldn't hold back then, but were in each other's arms immediately. He nuzzled her cheek, seeking out her warm, full lips, stroking her face, her hair, overwhelmed by the feel of her.

117

'Sam,' she whispered, when they drew back for a second. 'Sam.'

'I love you.' He kept saying it because it seemed the only thing to say. 'God, Lily, I love you.'

She was silent and he realized she was profoundly moved. 'Do you?' Her voice was full of wonder. 'Do you love me? No one – not one person has ever . . . I've never . . .' She stumbled over the words and he was touched by her difficulty. He saw her looking searchingly into his face. 'I don't know if I know how to love. But the way I feel, Sam, it's something I've never known before . . . I love you, I think. Yes, I'm sure I do!'

'Oh, my Lily,' he said. 'Lily, my sweet darling . . .' And all sorts of soft things spilled from his lips that he'd never said before because he had never felt like this before, so melted and overcome.

And she, though seeming frightened and unsure of it at first, responded, holding and stroking him as if there was a deep reservoir of love in her, never used, that she was pouring out over him.

'Meet me every night, my love,' he begged her, after they had stood talking in the darkness for a long time, so softly that they had not roused the elderly *chowkidar* from his doze on the veranda. 'I can't bear a day without being with you.'

'Of course I will,' she whispered back. 'Oh, Sam – I never, ever believed anything like this could happen to me. And now it has, I never want to let you go!'

That week was the happiest Lily had ever known, like an ecstatic dream. Since Sam Ironside had come into her life, she knew she was not the same person. She had allowed herself to love and to be loved. When, in their meetings in the dark garden, Sam held her and kissed her, she felt she had been reborn. Everything was lit up about her life. India, the beauty of the garden, Cosmo and her work here: all appeared intensely beautiful because of him. Because of love.

She had never talked so much with anyone. After that first night they moved further from the house and found a spot to stand in under the trees, where they held each other close and kissed and talked – of their hopes and dreams, about the Fairfords and Lily's time in India. She teased Sam about his fear of horses.

'You should learn to ride while you're here, and come out with us!' she urged him. 'There's nothing to it!'

'Not on your life!' He seemed to enjoy her teasing, was prepared to laugh at himself over his ineptitude.

He told her about his family, his widowed mother, his brothers, Alfred and Harry, and his Coventry childhood. And she drank this in, hearing about a real family, something which she idealized as the height of human happiness. And she told him about Mrs Chappell and how she came to be her companion, and about all the grandchildren because they were the nearest thing she had to family. But the rest of her past, her vanished parents and her suffering at the hands of the Hornes, she had still locked firmly behind her.

Sam, longing to know her, would say, 'But your family, your mother and father – you must be able to tell me something about them?'

And she would divert him, kissing him playfully and saying, 'Oh, it's all very boring,' or change the subject, saying, 'There's nothing much to tell.' The truth was she knew so little about her own origins that she was a closed book even to herself. And she did not want to admit that they had abandoned her. It felt so shameful. That was all she knew of her parents – that they didn't want her. What did it matter now, anyway? It was the future she wanted to think about, and now she dared to dream that she might have some of the things which she had never allowed to hope for herself: family, marriage, her own children.

After that first meeting in the garden she sat by her dressing table and looked in the glass. Letting her hair down, she brushed its thick, wavy length over her shoulders, then twisted the skein of hair and pinned it up again, smiling to herself. Her eyes glowed back at her. Had her real mother had eyes like that? she wondered. But she dismissed the thought. What was the point in thinking about it? It was now she wanted to hold on to, the sight of Sam's loving face, his passion for her and the longing she felt for him.

'You're so beautiful,' Sam had kept saying to her in wonder. 'You're the most beautiful thing I've ever seen.'

And tonight, miraculous as it seemed, for the first time in her life she felt beautiful and loved and full of hope.

Chapter Twenty

That weekend, Captain Fairford invited Sam to the Guest Night at the Officers' Mess.

'It's the ladies' night,' the captain said. 'Not at all the form for them to go in any other time! I like to go, even though Susan's not keen. I thought you might find it jolly to come along as my guest instead.' Sam couldn't help noticing that he didn't sound disappointed by his wife's lack of enthusiasm.

Captain Fairford assured Sam that he would provide him with clothes for the occasion.

'We're much of a size, you and I, aren't we? I'll get my bearer to look you out the right sort of gear. It'll be very jolly – high jinks and so forth. You should enjoy yourself.'

By teatime on the Saturday, Sam found a very good quality dinner suit laid out on his bed, with a crisp white shirt, its collar and cuffs starched rigid by the expert *dhobi*, and the studs laid carefully with them. His boots had been polished until they shone like metal. Looking in the glass, he trimmed his moustache and combed back his hair. His mind strayed, as it did so often, to Lily Waters, only a few rooms away on the other side of the house, perhaps changing her clothes for dinner also. The most lovely and arousing of pictures came to mind.

'Ready, Ironside?' He heard the captain outside the door, sounding boyishly cheerful.

'Ready!' Sam called. He found he was looking forward to this, though full of nerves, of course, about how to conduct himself. He felt quite abashed to see the captain clad in full regimentals in blue with a red trim and insignia and gold frogging at the front, with knife-edge creases and all very impressive. But as ever, he treated Sam as an equal.

'We'll take a *tonga*,' the captain said as they left the house. 'I know you're a fine driver, but we don't want anything to go amiss with the car.'

Sam concluded from this that they were in for some heavy drinking. In the lights of the house which spilled out over the grass he saw the *tonga* waiting on the drive, its bony horse dozing with drooping head.

'Listen, Ironside,' the captain said as they clopped away into the dusk. 'I haven't filled you in on plans because I hadn't made up my mind. I'd like you to stick around for another few weeks. We've more to learn on the motor car, for a start. But shortly I'm going to transfer the family up to Simla, in the hills. Then we can go on tour – for a fortnight or so. Give the machine a good working over – our own reliability trial, if you like! And I can show you the country then. India isn't the cantonment. It's a queer, artificial life we lead here and you should see something else. Are you game?'

Sam was flattered and excited. If Captain Fairford required his presence here to put the car through its paces, then who was he to argue?

'Well – yes! That'd be marvellous!'

'Splendid. This is a terrific country. We'll take in all we can – just chaps together, eh?'

Sam realized as he said it that he hadn't been imagining his relief that Susan Fairford did not want to come to the dinner.

The Officers' Mess was not as grand as he had expected, and, like the buildings housing other ranks, it looked pretty jerry-built. As they walked in they were assailed by loud, male chatter and the air smelled of smoke and whisky. The crowded foyer inside had the usual array of game heads on the wall, as did the billiard room, which the captain showed him, to one side of the door. The other officers were also in full regimental dress, a sea of blue, red and gold, and he felt conspicuous in civvies.

Other officers greeted the captain with calls of, 'Evening to you, Fairford. Brought your man with you, I see?'

Waiters were circulating with trays of drinks and Sam found himself holding a Scotch. Immediately, a round-faced, ginger-headed chap appeared beside them, all smiles.

'Pelling – this is Ironside, my mechanic,' Captain Fairford said. 'He's teaching me more than a thing or two about the workings of my new Daimler – fine fellow.' He looked at Sam, who took a mouthful of Scotch, which proved to be harsh stuff. 'This is one of my counterparts – Captain Jim Pelling.'

'Evening – Ironside, did you say?' Pelling clicked his heels together. It was like a reflex with these people. Sam braced himself for condescension, but he could see straight away the fellow was halfway genuine, and not just one of those types who looked straight through you because he sees you as socially inferior. 'Wouldn't mind your skills, old chap. Marvellous. You'll have to take me for a spin, Fairford. My goodness, if I had the funds behind me I'd get myself a motor like a shot. Bombay's the place, I gather. That where yours came from?'

'I had it shipped in,' the captain said, modestly. 'Mr Ironside came with it, all the way.'

'I *say*,' Pelling laughed, without apparent envy. 'You're really rather a maharaja, aren't you, Fairford?'

Various bods came and went and before long the signal was given and they all trooped in for the meal in the mess, which looked just as ramshackle as the rest of the building, with long tables and benches and other oddments of furniture. There were the regimental colours hung over the mantelpiece and portraits of military bods all along the walls, gonged up to the nines.

'Commanding officers through the years,' the captain said, nodding at them as they took their place at the table.

There seemed to be a whole lot of protocol attached to where they sat. Sam held on to the general sense that along the table to his left were the superiors, majors and upwards, and the other side the lower ranks, senior subalterns and so on. Some of them looked flaming intimidating, but he was determined to keep calm and not look rattled.

The meal was an extraordinary affair, though in the end Sam only remembered the beginning of it because he was plied with more strong drink than ever in his life before. Later he could only recall the end of the evening as a blur of rapscallion chaos. The meal began with something called the 'first toast', which was, in fact, a sardine on a piece of soggy bread. There followed a small helping of tinned fish, and then a roasted joint with all the trimmings, all served by the liveried native waiters. All through, Sam found he was downing copious amounts of whisky and gin, to the point where he soon scarcely knew what he was eating or drinking in any case.

'There's a rule in the mess,' the captain instructed him, early on, 'that one mustn't mention any woman's name throughout the evening. If you do, the forfeit is buying a round of drinks! Course, it wouldn't be the end of the world, old chap, but it's a matter of red faces, you see!'

Sam realized that the captain was telling him that if he slipped up, he would foot the bill, but Sam was determined not to embarrass himself or the captain. What he did notice, was that although this was ladies' night, looking along the table, noisy with the sounds of clinking cutlery and glass, and raucous, male chatter, there were in fact remarkably few ladies present at all.

'Do the ladies not enjoy the evening?' he asked. 'There aren't many here.'

Charles Fairford gave a mischievous, boyish smile. 'I think they find it rather rowdy.'

By the time they embarked on a mountainous slab of suet pudding, Sam had sat surrounded by talk of polo games and pig-sticking exploits, all of which was growing more riotous as every half-hour passed. Every so often great bellows of laughter broke out round the table, and occasional bursts of singing, and the noise in general grew louder and louder. Sam was not able to join in the conversation a great deal but by then he didn't mind. In fact, he had had so much to drink that he didn't mind anything at all. He was floating somewhere in his own head, and this changed him too. It wasn't the first time he'd been tight, not by a long way, but large quantities of Scotch made him feel more enlarged and set free. It was something also to do with being away from England, from all kinds of narrowness and keeping yourself pressed in on all sides. England, from here, seemed to him a teatime world of aprons and cake knives and small sandwiches in shadowy, velveteen parlours, all of which stopped you expanding as a man. Here, in all this racket, breathing in a miasma of sweat and booze, he was with physical, manly men who had a place in the world that they were sure of. After the pudding they were served the 'second toast', which this time was a half a hardboiled egg on the same sort of soggy bread. By then all the room was an amiable haze and Sam sat revelling in his sense of inner expansion, of becoming the new man he knew he was supposed to be.

And they weren't done then, by a long way. As they were serving the final course, he saw the mess sergeant place three decanters on the table in front of the commanding officer, a thin, moustachioed fellow.

'The toast, in a moment,' the captain told him, leaning aside from a joke he had been sharing with his neighbour with great guffaws of laughter. 'They'll send round port, Madeira and marsala – take your pick.'

Sam stuck to port when the decanters were circulated and they stood, solemnly, many, including Sam, swaying a little.

'Let us drink to the health of the King Emperor, His Majesty, King Edward VII!' And the place was abuzz with 'Hear! hear!' and 'To His Majesty!', and then the commanding officer lit up a cigar and this, apparently, gave the signal that everyone else could do the same. Charles – as Sam thought of him now – lit a cheroot, and was turning to speak to him when everything was drowned out by the most appalling racket. In Sam's sozzled state it made him jump violently. It sounded as if the place was being attacked, whereas it was in fact the military band striking up.

This was where the evening faded into a dim, dreamlike memory. The sprinkling of ladies vanished somewhere and there was a great noise of furniture being moved in the anteroom and riotous laughter. He could remember flashes of it next morning, in his rotten, morning-after state. Never, in a backstreet brawl had he ever seen anything quite like the 'high jinks' in the mess of these officers of the crown that night. It was the most gloriously appalling behaviour he could remember seeing anywhere!

'Come along, Ironside.' Captain Fairford tugged on his arm. They were both tight as ticks already and Sam was swaying like a tree in a storm. 'Can't have you sitting on the sidelines, now, can we? You come and join in, old man – one of the crowd!'

There was some game called High Cockalorum which involved leapfrogging over other men's backs and throwing each other about in a way injurious both to them and to the remaining furniture. In the midst of it, Sam fell and jarred his elbow against something and later could recall yelping with pain. There were contests with pairs of chaps wrestling on the floor, and at some stage one was being thrown about in a blanket, and glass was breaking somewhere, and Sam could remember seeing two chairs smashed to matchwood and laughing until he was sick into an umbrella stand by the door and was too far gone even to feel embarrassed.

God, it was a lark! What he remembered was the *freedom* of it, and even in his drunken state, standing to one side of the room, heady with thinking, *This is what class and money can do.* Having a position. Doing what the hell you damn well liked, like these chaps, not being pressed down by petty, small-town proprieties. It looked a bigger life, and he wanted it. God, he ached with wanting it.

After that he could remember nothing at all until he

found himself draped over the back of a moving *tonga* with someone's arm holding him firmly on board as if he were a sack of coal, the night sky passing above, blurry with stars, though none of this felt especially odd. And he was singing, in ecstasy and crying, 'Lily, my beautiful Lily, oh, how I love you!' And then he lost consciousness.

Chapter Twenty-One

'Where's the motor-car man? Where is he?' Cosmo's voice rang along the corridors where the servants were scurrying about making preparations for the move to the hills.

They were due to set off the next day, and the passages were scattered chaotically with objects that would not fit into the zinc-lined trunks: tennis rackets, a saddle, a japanned tin bath. Susan Fairford was not the most organized of people and her *distrait* approach to life seemed to infect the servants. The heat was also very intense now and everyone was irritable.

Lily led Cosmo out to the garden, narrowly avoiding tripping over a bootjack which had been left by the door.

'I expect Mr Ironside is with your pater,' she said, trying to be patient, but the truth was she was even more impatient to know where Sam was than Cosmo. This was the last whole day in Ambala before they set off for Simla and Sam would go on tour with the captain, and she desperately needed to see him. So far, apart from Sam's declarations of love for her, they had not talked properly about the future. They were about to be torn apart and there was so little time!

For once the heat was really affecting her, since she was already tense and out of sorts and she found herself unable to be patient. Cosmo's constant questions and demands had brought her almost to screaming pitch and she decided to leave the nursery where Srimala was still trying to distract a fractious Izzy from her prickly heat rashes. Even moving through the house was a relief. Perhaps she'd meet him? Dear God, where was he? She was full of doubts. Was he doing this on purpose? Did he not care for her enough to come and find her?

The morning dragged cruelly. She took Cosmo to play ball in the garden until the heat became really unendurable and her clothes were soaked. Every second of not knowing when she might see Sam was a torture to her.

'Come – we'll go in and have *limbopani*,' she said wearily to Cosmo. Homemade lemonade was one of his favourite things, so he would not make a fuss.

Back in the nursery, she at last had news that explained Sam's absence from circulation. One of the other servants had been talking to Srimala.

'Mr Ironside is not feeling at all well today,' she told Lily.

'Oh?' Lily was immediately anxious and sorry for her doubting him. 'What's wrong – it's not serious?'

Srimala was smiling mischievously. 'He is recovering from his visit to the Officers' Mess with the captain last night.'

Lily rolled her eyes. What went on at the mess Guest Nights, and quite a few other nights also, was legendary.

'Ah – that explains it.' She felt loving and peeved at the same time. Just when they had so little time left and she was so longing to see him! How could he have been so silly as to get so tight that it took most of the next day to recover? Captain Fairford always seemed to be on parade the next day however much he had drunk!

'Oh.' Srimala turned to her. 'Mrs Fairford said she

would like a word with you – I think immediately. Leave Cosmo with me.'

Puzzled, Lily gave her face a quick wash and went along to Susan Fairford's sitting room. She very seldom sent for Lily in this way. Perhaps it was something to do with their transition to the hills tomorrow?

Pushing back strands of hair from her damp forehead, she knocked on the door and Susan called to her to come in. She was sitting at her writing desk, trying to augment the effect of the *punkah* by fanning herself with a thin volume of poetry which often served this purpose but which Lily had never actually seen her open and read.

'Shut the door, Lily.' Her face was pale and solemn, unusually so, as if she had bad news to impart. Lily frowned, beginning to feel nervous.

'Is there something wrong?' she asked.

Susan Fairford gestured to her to take the chair close to her, in quite a friendly way, and sat for a moment looking into her eyes.

'Lily – I know I'm your employer, but I think we have lived enough together to be frank with one another at times. Would you agree?'

'I think so,' Lily said rather hesitantly, though she often held back from being completely frank with Susan Fairford since she felt it was not her place.

'Well, I'm speaking to you this afternoon as a friend. Last night Charles took the mechanic, Mr Ironside, to the mess dinner, as I'm sure you know. There was no problem, nothing untoward, though of course they all had rather a lot to drink and Mr Ironside perhaps is less used to it than most of the regiment.'

She stopped and looked pityingly into Lily's face. Lily's insides turned, sickeningly. What was she going to say? It was obviously bad news. Had something happened to Sam – a terrible accident on the way home? Surely if that was the case she would have heard by now?

'I had not realized that you and Mr Ironside had formed an attachment. Is this true?'

Without dropping her gaze, Lily nodded proudly. 'Yes, it is.'

'We hadn't seen it, you see. Charles heard him, on the way home, singing your praises and his own feelings rather immoderately from the back of the *tonga*.' Seeing Lily begin to smile, she leaned forwards.

'Lily, my poor girl, don't throw your heart away on this man. For heaven's sake, I'm begging you!'

Lily felt her temper flare. What business was it of Susan Fairford to tell her what to feel! She may have been her employer, but this was private business.

'I can't just stay here with you forever!' she retorted fierily. 'I love him, and Cosmo will be gone soon and I shall have to make another life . . .'

'But you can't make it with Mr Ironside!' Susan snapped the words out, trying to drum some sense into her. 'For God's sake, Lily. He hasn't even told you, has he? The man's already married – his wife's at home, expecting their first child . . .'

She stopped, seeing the shock, as if from a slap, spread over Lily's face.

'Oh, my dear . . . My poor girl . . . I'm so sorry!' Susan leaned forwards and took Lily's hand which was turning cold, as if her blood supply had been cut off.

'If he is untrustworthy in this respect,' she said gently, 'then how would you ever be able to trust him in any way? Dear Lily, I'm not trying to be selfish about your future. I just couldn't bear to see you in the thrall of a man who can't even tell the truth about the most fundamental things of his life!'

The deep hurt on Lily's face was unmistakable and painful to see. She sat utterly still, unable to speak, as if she had been felled.

Chapter Twenty-Two

'How *could* you? How could you lie to me, tell me you love me, when all the time you've got a wife?'

Sobbing, she stood before Sam in his room late that afternoon. The day had passed in a swirl of pain. Lily could remember nothing of it. And still she had not seen him, until she could stand it no longer, and just ran to his part of the house and hammered on the door, not caring now who heard her.

Sam, though still looking seedy, was up and dressed. At her distraught accusation, she saw his face fall and become stony. He hurried over to shut the door, trying to take her hand to pull her closer.

'Don't touch me!' she stormed at him. 'How could you?' Her outburst ended with a wordless cry of anguish. Her hair was loosely tied, wild strands curling round her face and hers eyes were swollen with tears.

'God, Lily, my love, listen to me. Just listen to me, *please*!' Sam took both of her hands and almost shook her, trying to make her hear him. 'I know I should have told you. I *should*. But it didn't seem real, not while I was here with you. I've never been in love before, not like this, with you. God forgive me, I married Helen not knowing what it was to love a woman, really love . . .'

His face was distraught and she stared at him, wanting to believe, to hear something that would make everything all right so that she could forgive and love him again. All those times they had gazed at each other, all that she had seen in his eyes, it had to be real. She could not bear it all to have been pretence.

'I didn't know love was like this – that it could be like this,' he said helplessly. 'And we can't let it go, Lily. How can we, after this? I'll do anything; I'll stay here in India. Let's just be together, you and me, away from it all . . .'

Just for a moment she was drawn into his persuasion, his saying to her all the things she wanted to hear. How she longed for it all to be all right, to know she could be with him! But she heard Susan Fairford's words in her mind – how could she ever trust him after this, or have any future with him?

'What are you *talking* about?' she raged at him. 'You've lied to me and now you want to lie to your wife. How could I ever be with you if you can't tell the truth?'

She sank down on the bed, her head in her hands. 'I was all right until you came here.' She could not see the misery her words provoked. 'I was settled. I've never expected much of anything because I've never had much. I had a bad start. But I've liked it here – my work and Cosmo. I felt safe and that was all I wanted. And then you . . .' She raised her distraught face to him. 'I've never loved anyone before – not like that. And you've killed it. You've killed trust, and hope, and all my life here.'

'Lily, don't.' He knelt down beside her and she saw that he was weeping. The day before it would have moved her to the core, but now she felt a terrible coldness seeping through her.

'Don't come crying to me.' She pushed him away

and went to the door. 'What on earth do you expect from me now?' She stared at his bowed head, her eyes icy and hard. 'You've broken it – everything, Sam. Keep away from me. I hate you.'

Early the next morning, in the growing heat, the assortment of carts and *tongas* required to transport the family and their belongings to the railway station began to assemble outside the Fairford bungalow. The servants hurried back and forth with the trunks and bags and other assorted objects, and the family readied themselves.

Lily had packed for Cosmo and that morning she washed and dressed him, replying mechanically to his questions. Her heart was so heavy with distress she could hardly think straight. When she had left Sam yesterday, she was in a cold fury. This morning she felt numb, a dead person with no feeling at all. Would this be how it was now, she wondered, this deadness, forever? Was it not easier just to be like this, to feel nothing, risk nothing? She was used to that, after all. Only Mrs Chappell and Cosmo, and above all Sam, had opened up places of light and need in her which she scarcely knew of and now they had been forced back into darkness again like a cell door slamming.

She did not expect to see Sam Ironside again, did not know if she could bear it if he were to appear. She knew that he and the captain would leave on their tour the next day, once the household were safely out of their way. Surely he would not show his face while she was still here?

She led Cosmo out to their waiting *tonga* and the driver was lifting the little boy aboard when she heard a low, urgent voice behind her.

'Lily!' Sam had come running out from the house, not seeming to care who saw them together. His face looked bleached and sick. 'For God's sake, don't leave me like this, woman. I love you – don't you understand? I can't go on without you! I'm sorry for not telling you, but how could I? I fell in love with you almost the moment I saw you, and I'd never have got near you if you'd known about Helen, that I was married . . .'

'Yes – but now I do,' Lily said. She could not let her heart soften even for a second, watching this man she loved in such distress. It was no good. He was married and that was how it was. There could be no argument about that.

She climbed up on to the *tonga* and put her arm around Cosmo.

'Lily, *please* – I'll divorce her. I'll do anything to be with you!'

'Drive!' she ordered the *tonga* driver. '*Chelo!*'

She sat up very straight as the pony trotted away pulling the *tonga* along the drive and out into the broad cantonment road, and she did not look back.

Chapter Twenty-Three

Coventry, 1907

Sam Ironside dismounted from his bicycle to push it through the front gate and along the side of the house. Already, something felt different about the day. He had taken off his canvas bag in which he took his dinner into the works and was going to the back door, when it was opened by Mrs Blewitt, their neighbour.

'Oh, Sam – you've come 'ome just right!' she cried, flustered. 'Things are getting going all right now. She must've started after you left this morning – you're about to be a father any minute!'

'What, today? Now?' Sam pulled off his cap, bewildered. He hadn't expected this. He was hungry and tired and suddenly it all seemed to be happening frighteningly quickly. He wanted to put it all off for another day.

'Look at you, all sixes and sevens!' Mrs Blewitt was in her forties, a motherly woman with five children of her own who seldom stopped talking to draw breath. 'I'll make you a cup of tea, Sam. Mrs Rodgers is here with her. She delivered two of mine. Helen's doing ever so well.'

Sam sat waiting in the back room. Helen had made it into a neat, cosy place, with a maroon velvet drape over

138

the mantel with jugs and horse brasses arranged on it, a pretty fire screen and their chairs facing each other by the fender. As he drank his tea, he could hear Mrs Rodgers moving about on the bare boards upstairs and her voice, speaking quietly and reassuringly to Helen. Every so often there came a moan or a long-drawn-out wail of pain, but not very loud. Good old Helen, he thought, she was never one to make a fuss. He felt out of place here in the middle of this women's business. He half wished he'd stayed later at the works where everything was familiar, then felt ashamed of this thought.

'I'm surprised you don't want a drop of summat stronger,' Mrs Blewitt joked, as she passed through the room. 'My Sid always had a few stiff ones while I was hard at it!'

Eventually, after several especially agonized sounds, they heard the rasping cry of a newborn and Sam was allowed upstairs. Helen was lying back, looking plump and pale, with her hair raked back from her forehead, a broad smile on her face.

'I feel as if I've been run down by a horse and carriage, Sam,' she said with a wan smile. 'But there she is, anyway.'

In a drawer, by the bed, Sam saw the little crumpled shape of his first child. Her face was puckered, and her eyes seemed to him rather oriental.

'Beautiful, isn't she?' Mrs Rodgers said. 'A proper little maid, you should be proud.'

'She's . . . lovely,' Sam stammered, staring in astonishment. He had never seen a newborn before and could scarcely connect her with himself.

'And your wife's done ever so well. A natural, you are, Mrs Ironside.'

139

'I don't know about that. At least it was quick.'

Mrs Rodgers looked down at her, folding a towel. 'Well, it's not your first, is it?' she prattled thoughtlessly. 'I saw the stretch marks on your belly from the last . . . Usually takes longer the first time, of course.'

It took Sam a moment to take in what she had said. Those shiny trails on her skin – he had never known it could be anything to do with that . . . He turned to look at Helen, seeing the horrified look of shock on her face, and her stricken eyes met his.

The next afternoon, instead of cycling home he went from the Daimler works to his mother's. She hadn't heard yet that she was a grandmother, but Sam had more than this news on his mind.

'Oh hello, Sam, boy! I've baked today – come in and have summat!' Mrs Ironside greeted him. 'Can't have you looking so peaky – you don't look right these days. That's what happens if you go off to foreign parts . . . Ooh' – she stopped, noticing his expression – 'you've got summat to tell me, haven't you?'

Sam smiled wanly. 'She's had a little girl, Mom. Born yesterday afternoon.'

'A girl! Oh, now that *is* a blessing!' His mother sank down on the old settle, beaming at him. Her cheeks were moist and pink from standing over the range. 'After all you boys I always longed for a girl to dress. Not that I'm not proud as punch of my boys . . . What weight is she, Sam, and what're you going to call her?'

Sam realized he had no idea how heavy the baby was. When Helen asked him about names he'd not even thought, and said, 'Lily.' It surprised him how it just slipped out like that.

'Not sure I like Lily all that much,' Helen said. 'Couldn't we call her Sarah or Ann – something *sensible*? Not like that actress.'

Sam agreed, though the king's mistress, Lily Langtry, had not been the Lily he had in mind.

'She'll be called Ann,' he said. And then, because he'd been in a fever over it at the works all day and couldn't keep it in any more, he burst out with, 'It wasn't her first – she's had a baby before and she never said!'

His mother's head whipped round. 'What on earth d'you mean, Sam?'

Suddenly he was close to tears, and he felt a proper fool and swallowed them down. He'd sat on the side of the bed last night when at last Mrs Rodgers and Mrs Blewitt had taken themselves off, and looked sternly into Helen's eyes.

'You'd better tell me what she meant.' He had been holding on to his anger, prepared for lies and deceit, prepared to find that his wife was someone quite other than he imagined. The first thing that came to mind was Laurie, that friend of hers who was always hanging about, and he was all set for righteous fury. But what she told him, crying heartbrokenly as she choked out the words, did something unexpected to him. He couldn't sort himself out over it. It had gone round and round in his head all day.

'I'm sorry, Sam. I'm so, so sorry for not telling you.' She struggled to sit up, wincing with pain. 'I was only young. I didn't know what was happening, and he ... Well, I was fourteen, and it was when Auntie Lou asked me to stay out on the farm at Stivichall. It was one of the men on the farm ... He just kept talking to me, all friendly like, and showed me the horses and then one

141

day he just, well, he *jumped* on me ... It was in the barn ...' She stopped for a moment, weeping shamefully. Sam couldn't move to comfort her. He just sat, watching.

'He was so big and heavy and he hurt me, forced himself on me. Made me bleed ...' She was sobbing. 'And I didn't have any thought of what might happen – not 'til months later and my belly was all swollen up. And Mom ... Well, you know what she's like. Considering, she was very good to me and said she knew I was too young to know what was what and I could stay home, so ...'

Sam's eyes widened as his mind raced. 'Emma! She's yours, isn't she?'

Face running with tears, Helen nodded. 'She doesn't know. She thinks she's my cousin – like they told you. From my auntie in Liverpool. She died just before Emma was born so Mom decided that was what she'd tell everyone. She's been very good to me, in her way. Some mothers would've washed their hands of me and put me out on the streets. And I thought if you knew, you'd think ...' She began sobbing again. 'That I was dirty, second-hand goods and you wouldn't want me.'

Sam remembered their wedding night. He had thought all that hesitation was only shyness; her not having any idea what the marital act consisted of because she was so innocent. He knew now, and from how she had been since, that it was something very different. That to her it was associated with force and fear and she didn't like it, had never really liked it with him either, even though he had tried to tell himself it was getting better.

'Mrs Rodgers saw those marks on me, you know, the little snail trails, as you call them ... I never dreamed

142

she'd say anything, not blurt it out like that. I didn't want you to have to know.'

He had sat, numbly, as she told him. He knew he felt things but wasn't sure what they were. But now, here with his mother, he knew he felt let down, cheated, not just by her but by his marriage. It had all been a fake, with secrets and lies in the background. And that he hadn't known what love was until he met Lily Waters and now that was lost to him forever as well.

'You should've told me,' was all he said.

'Would you have married me?' She was so plaintive, her hair all rumpled now, like a little girl's. 'I wanted to marry you so much, Sam.'

'Yes, of course I would.' He forced himself to sound kind, and he wanted it to be true, but secretly he wasn't sure if it was.

When he had spilled out the story to his mother, she sat looking solemnly at him.

'Now, Sam,' she said emphatically. 'What you've got to do, boy, is stick by her and not let this make any difference. She was young – she wasn't the first this has happened to and she won't be the last. Heaven knows, it wasn't her fault, the poor little thing. She didn't do it to hurt your pride, my boy, and you're none the worse off, are you? You've made your vows and even if this has upset you, you've got a lovely new daughter – a family to look after. Now you take yourself home, Sam, and do your best. Life has its ups and downs like this, boy. And it'll all be the same in a hundred years.'

Cycling home along the Kenilworth Road that night in the mellow evening light, Sam's thoughts were in turmoil. It was June, and warm. He had a good cycle, a

Starley, Coventry-made, of course, and pushing down hard on the pedals was an outlet for the strong feelings surging through him. He rode like a fury, batting away the tickling midges that flew into his face. Soon, though, he realized that at this speed he would get home before he really wanted to and he stopped at the Grove, a fork in the road, where he dismounted and sat down in the shade of the trees.

'*Damn* it!' he erupted, banging his fist on the ground in fury. He was too het up to care that he startled a matronly looking woman who was walking past pushing a perambulator. 'Damn and *blast* it!'

It wasn't helped by the fact that sitting there in the Grove reminded him of that picnic with the Fairfords, in the stronger Indian light but also on a still evening like this one, when he had felt so full of hope and such a sense of expansion. And he had sat talking to Lily. God, how could he have sat there so casually when she was close to him? An ache spread right through him. What he wouldn't give for her to be here now.

Pushing his sleeves up, he lay back and looked up into the leafy branches above him. His thoughts rolled over those months in India. It had been like a book in two volumes. First there was Ambala and Lily, the extraordinary miracle of falling in love, he realized, for the first time in his life. But then their leaving for Simla, and the way it happened between them was still an agony to him. Her face, when she discovered that he was married, had snapped shut, enclosing all the pain he had given her, and he had felt completely helpless, and then she was gone, holding tightly to Cosmo, and he could not reach her.

After that he had spent more than two weeks on the road with Captain Fairford and Arsalan, and it was something he would never forget. The car had fared excellently, and they had rolled on through villages and towns, camped, and stayed in cheap lodgings, gone out shooting game, and gradually wound their way to the foothills of the Himalaya with their precarious terraced cultivation, and then higher up, among the bare peaks with their gigantic screes and icy green streams. Sam saw country of a grand scale and awesome wildness that he could never before have imagined. And he felt it change him, as if the shutters of his mind had been flung wide open to let in all the sights. He understood, humbly, that there were places and people very different from what he was used to. And the captain was like a different man. Away from the routines and domestic obligations of Ambala Cantonment, he seemed to come fully alive. He spoke in a more animated way, laughed more, and Sam could see that he was in his element. He wondered if the captain even liked being married and he wondered the same thing about himself.

One evening when they had camped out in the foothills, the three of them built a fire and were sitting round it in the chill darkness. Arsalan was a complete equal to them for the entire journey. Sam's respect for his capabilities and sheer likeableness grew by the day, and he sensed that of everyone he had seen the captain with, he was most comfortable with his *syce*.

'How long have you worked for the captain?' he asked Arsalan, who was squatting on his slim legs, prodding the fire with a stick.

But Charles Fairford answered, 'Oh, Arsalan and I go right back, don't we?' He made some joking comment in Hindustani and both men laughed. 'We grew up together, you see, Ironside. Arsalan's father was *syce* to mine; they each had sons within the same year, so we were playmates, and it went on from there. We've scarcely ever been apart, except when I was at school.'

Sam saw just how much Charles Fairford could never have anything like this close understanding with his nervy, Sussex-born wife.

He looked back upon that journey as sheer heaven, only marred by his aching heart over Lily, and the thought that he might never see her again. When he boarded the liner for home it had felt like being wound in like a kite, the string shorter and shorter as they approached England's shore. Now his life was contracted back between the walls of the factory and those of their little house in Kenilworth with Helen, who, for all her solid sweetness, could never ever arouse in him the feelings he had known with Lily. It felt all the crueller that now even the wife he had left behind was not quite who he had thought.

After a time he sat up, brushing himself down, and looked out soberly across the road. He thought about what his mother had said.

'Well, pal,' he murmured to himself. 'You'd better pull yourself together and knuckle down.' Immediately he thought of the one thing that did not seem to disappoint: the motor car. He was good at his work, he knew it, and it was satisfying. At least there was something he could pour himself into, heart and soul.

Climbing on to his cycle he pedalled on more soberly than before. He had a good job, and now a family. He had responsibilities. Fulfilling those was a way of showing he was a man. He rode home, thinking hard thoughts about life's limitations. He felt doors closing in his mind.

Chapter Twenty-Four

Mussoorie, India, 1909

The night train from Delhi rocked its way across the Dun valley towards the northern railhead at Dehra Dun, which nestled between the toes of the Himalayan foothills.

Lily was travelling during the July monsoon. The rain was tippling down outside as she looked out, in the grey dawn, at the soaked green paddies stretching into the distance. She saw families crouched together under pieces of sacking, under bridges and against haystacks, anywhere they could find shelter from the relentless rainfall. Droplets blew in gusts against the train windows and ran streaming from the roof, spattering down on to the oozing mud.

The rain had brought the summer temperatures down to a manageable balminess, and in the cool of early morning Lily even felt the need to pull her shawl round her. The other passengers in the ladies' compartment were still sleeping.

Yesterday, she had left Ambala and the Fairfords for the last time. The wrench of it was worse even than she had expected. Her heart was like a heavy stone and her eyes kept filling with tears every time she thought about Cosmo on his sea voyage to England, and Susan

Fairford's distraught face when she had kissed Lily goodbye, before the *tonga* pony trotted off, taking her out along the drive for the last time.

'*Chai!*' The insistent voice of a tea vendor rang along the corridor. '*Chai, garam chai!*'

Lily quickly wiped her eyes, fumbled in her purse for a few *annas* and opened the compartment door.

'Yes – one tea, please!'

The man poured a little cup of steaming tea into a clay cup and handed it to her. She thanked him with an inclination of her head and cupped the little pot of fiercely sweet liquor between her hands. That was how she felt, like a child needing comfort.

She had said goodbye to Cosmo a week ago. They had sent him before the summer vacation so that he could spend some weeks acclimatizing on the family estate in Warwickshire, before starting at his prep school in the Michaelmas term. Accompanying him on the long sea voyage was an elderly missionary lady called Miss Spurling, who was returning to England on furlough and had offered to make herself useful on the journey.

Parting with Cosmo was an agony. For several days she had been overwhelmed with grief, as if all the losses in her life so far culminated in this one. She had made Cosmo the centre and solace of her life, especially over the past two years after Sam. Sam Ironside: his name was engraved on her heart however much she tried to cast him out. Her love for him and his betrayal of her stayed deep and raw in her. It was only by turning all her attention and affection, her need, onto Cosmo that she had been able to survive and start to imagine a future.

For these two years she had watched Cosmo develop each day, from a child of four to one of nearly six, and he was her joy. His lively body slimmed down as he grew taller, and he became agile and already a promising horseman. His face was thinner now, but his blue eyes were always full of the loving trust that she had seen in him when he first arrived. And he loved Lily. Loved and trusted her as he did Srimala, both loving, female presences who were always there. And now they had all been snatched away from each other. Lily knew she would miss Srimala very much as well, since the girls had become such friends over the years. What made it even worse was Susan's lack of faith in Uncle William, Charles's brother in England.

'Charles calls him eccentric,' she told Lily bitterly. 'I'd say he was unhinged myself.'

'He won't be unkind, will he?' Lily asked anxiously.

'Not unkind. He'll probably just forget Cosmo's there most of the time, my poor little lamb. The house-keeper will be the one who looks after him and I gather she's kind enough.'

Sipping the last of the warm tea, Lily slid the window up wide enough to throw the little cup out onto the tracks, where it would sink back into dust. From her bag, she slipped her precious pictures. Before he was sent away, Susan Fairford had engaged a photographer to take several portraits of Cosmo – and one of Isadora, which seemed almost an afterthought. And at the end, Susan said generously, 'Perhaps you would like to pose for a portrait with Cosmo, Lily? It would be something for you to keep.'

Lily was touched. She was delighted to have the picture of Cosmo, but it was also the first picture she had ever seen of herself. The two of them had been photographed in a formal pose, with her sitting, her hair arranged prettily. Susan had fastened it up for her and pinned some small white flowers in it with little pearls at their centre. For the first time, Lily had taken out the seed pearls from Mrs Chappell's velvet-lined box and put them on.

'I say,' Susan had said admiringly, feeling their warm lustre. 'Lily, you are a beauty, you know. Now it really is time you stopped looking solemn and put a real smile on your lovely face.'

Startled, Lily smiled dutifully at her. Did Susan have any idea that she still grieved for Sam? She had managed a radiant smile in the photograph, dressed in her high-collared blouse and long, green skirt, with her beloved Cosmo standing at her knee. He wore a favourite sailor suit, his hair a cloud of pale curls. Despite the solemnity of the occasion, there was just the trace of an impishness in his face, with his raised, slanting brows. It captured him excellently and Lily adored the picture. Looking at it now, she smiled, her heart aching, and kissed his face.

'There, my little darling. Your Lily is thinking of you. Oh, I do hope you're all right, my little dear, and that Mrs Spurling is taking good care of you. And you know Lily will never leave you, darling. I'll be thinking of you and I'll write to you, always.' It was the only way she had been able to manage the separation, by making this pledge. She would be there, like his guardian angel, watching over him, if only from a distance.

She sighed, carefully stowing the picture back in her bag. They were coming into the town now and the other three women in the compartment were on the move.

'I say, Minnie,' one of them urged. 'Do hurry up. We're nearly into Dehra Dun.' She pronounced it 'Derra Doon'.

Lily looked out, her stomach clenching with nerves.

She was on the way to a new post in the hills, not as a nanny this time, but as housekeeper to a Dr McBride and his invalid wife. She had applied for the job because she had liked Simla when the family spent the summer up there, the town nestling precariously in the cool of the immense mountain landscape, and she knew she was going to like Mussoorie. When she heard about the job she thought, I'll go there. I don't want to go to another family, not yet. I couldn't ever replace Cosmo. This still felt like the right decision, but she found the change terribly hard, the thought of beginning again, having to make her way so alone in the world.

She straightened her back and positioned her feet together determinedly. How frightening could a middle-aged doctor and a sick woman be, after all? Breathing in deeply, as if to fill herself with courage, she waited until the train eased its way into the tranquil railhead at Dehra Dun.

The bus wheezed laboriously up the mountain road which snaked between the dark trees, all topped with thick swirls of cloud. The rain fell and fell and twice they had to stop while the earth from landslips was cleared from the side of the road. The bus was a very recent newcomer on these mountain tracks.

Lily had eaten a breakfast of poached eggs in the railway station at Dehra Dun and now her stomach turned queasily as they switched back and forth round the bends. As they climbed and climbed, though, and the rain stopped for a brief interval and there were shreds of sunlight, she caught her first glimpses of the hill station of Mussoorie and her spirits lifted excitedly.

It's lovely! she thought, wiping the condensation

151

from the window. She was filled with a sense of exaltation, immediately liking it even more than Simla. She saw Mussoorie's buildings scattered across the hillsides among the trees, the dark peaks of the foothills ringed with cloud, and she felt at home. She found herself sending up a prayer that she would like Dr McBride and his wife and that she could stay on and on here with them in this little paradise in the clouds. But it seemed too much to hope that she could have as happy a situation again as she had found with the Fairfords and she was full of nerves waiting to see her new home. It seemed a good omen, though, that the rain had stopped.

At last the bus jerked to a halt and Lily climbed down, and stood at a loss for a moment before an elderly bearer approached her, a lean man in a *dhoti* with a shawl wrapped round him.

In Hindi she told him what she needed and mentioned Dr McBride's name. Taking her bag, which he swung up on to the pad on his head, he beckoned to her and set off up the steep, narrow street through the town. The path was still running with water after the heavy shower and all the shop awnings were dripping and hanging with sparkling water droplets. Lily caught glimpses of the food stores, chemists and drapers of Mussoorie before they turned into a quieter side street where they had to edge round two cows which stood ruminatively obstructing the path. At the end of the street suddenly they were facing out over the mountain valley and he led her to a steep little flight of steps, from the top of which she could see over the roof of a large bungalow below.

'This Dr McBride house,' the bearer said, setting off down the steps with goat-like agility in his loose sandals.

Like most of the buildings in Mussoorie, as in Simla, the McBrides' house was perched on the edge of the mountainside with a sheer drop below it, looking out over a dark valley flecked with white flags of cloud. Across the valley was a similar hillside dotted with other yellow and white painted dwellings. At the back of the house Lily saw a tiny garden, with well-tended flower-beds. At first glance, the place looking promising.

'Come, Missy,' the bearer called her. Her young, pretty looks evidently did not qualify her as a memsahib.

A moment later, the door opened, and Lily first saw a very large, thin, curving grey dog, and behind it, she glimpsed Dr Ewan McBride.

Chapter Twenty-Five

'Miss Waters, I presume?'

Lily found herself facing a large, powerful-looking man. His body filled the doorway and the main impression she had of his face was of two stone-grey eyes and a thick, grizzled beard.

'It's all right' – he glanced down at the dog – 'this is Cameron. He won't hurt you. Wolfhounds are very gentle creatures.'

The dog did have mild-looking eyes and he seemed quite timid. She could very easily have been intimidated, however, by the imposing presence and deep-voiced Scottish accent of the doctor, but she was determined not to be overawed. She stood up, straight and self-possessed, and looked directly back at him.

'Yes, Dr McBride. I am Lily Waters. I take it you have been expecting me?'

'Expecting you?' He was suddenly irascible. 'We most certainly have! We've been expecting you for the past three days! . . . Yes, yes . . .' He paid the bearer off and the man trotted away, apparently satisfied. 'Come in, come in.'

'Well, I don't know why that would be,' Lily said, following him into the hall. There was a very large oil painting of a waterfall facing the front door. 'I said in my letter that I should be here on the eighteenth, and here I am.'

'So you are,' he admitted. He seemed like someone who was unused to ordinary conversation. It was strange to her after Charles Fairford's easy social manner. 'I had the fifteenth in mind. My mistake. We'll get you settled in your room, let you rest, and then we can talk about things, um? I expect you'd like some tea?'

'That would be very nice, thank you,' Lily said. She smiled, and Dr McBride attempted to smile back, which barely lifted the gloom from his face.

To her surprise, Dr McBride did not summon a servant to take her to her room, but picked up her bag and led her there himself. His portly frame blocked the light along the darkened corridor, so that she had only an impression of alternating surfaces underfoot, floorboards and rugs, and the dark shapes of pictures on the walls. He opened the door right at the end.

'There – this one's for you,' he said rather curtly. 'The tea'll be along in a few moments. Everything you need, I hope?'

Lily gasped when she went into her room. It was simple enough in itself: a wooden bed, with a rich red coverlet, its legs resting on a large bamboo mat, a small writing table and chair, an armchair and stool. Someone, to her surprise, had left a little jug of flowers on the table by the bed and she wondered who in this household would have added such a touch. But it was the view from the window which captivated her. Apart from one other house, nestling into the hillside to the left and a school below, all she could see was a wide panorama of the black mountain peaks, with puffs of white cloud hanging in the valleys between and gathered in heaped piles against the grey sky behind. Dark birds were wheeling across the white cloud. It was one of the most lovely sights she had ever seen. And this was to be the view she looked out on every day!

A shy servant girl brought her some tea and Lily sat on the chair by the window, unable to tear her eyes from the sight. Gradually the cloud thickened and the rain began to fall again until it was rattling hard on the roof. It felt cosy in the room, though it was a strange feeling sitting there wondering who else was in the house. She wondered if it was the young servant who had left her the flowers.

Soon she grew sleepy after the long hours of travel, and lay down on the bed, thinking about the doctor. He seemed a gruff, austere man and she knew she felt nervous of him, but he had not been unpleasant. Wondering what his wife might be like, she fell asleep.

Her first sight of Mrs McBride was later that evening.

The young girl who had brought her tea woke her and said haltingly that Dr McBride wanted her, if she was ready. Lily quickly washed her face and hands and followed her. She was struck by the fact that so far, this girl, who only looked about twelve, was the only servant she had seen. When asked, the girl told Lily her name was Prithvi.

'Thank you for the flowers,' Lily said.

'No, no,' the girl assured her at once. 'That was Miss Brown.'

With no further explanation she led Lily to Dr McBride's dimly lit study, where the walls were lined almost completely with shelves of books. Entering the room, she found him sitting at his desk, a curved pipe in his mouth and surrounded by a haze of sweet-smelling pipe smoke. Cameron the wolfhound was lying

156

close to his feet. The room contained dark furniture, with thick rugs on the floor, and smelled of a combination of pipe smoke and damp dog.

'Ah, Miss Waters.' He stood up with a slight grunt and gestured at a chair in front of the desk. 'Do be seated.'

This was all rather unusual, Lily thought as she obeyed. In most households it was the mistress who dealt with the new staff, but Mrs McBride was evidently not well enough.

'I hope you're rested?' he asked, sinking back into his chair.

'Yes, thank you.' She sat looking demurely at him. She guessed his age to be about fifty. There was a silence and she wondered if she was expected to say more, but she was distracted suddenly by a loud squawk which came from somewhere behind Dr McBride's desk and a strange, chirpy voice said, 'Afternoon!' with a definite Scottish accent. Seeing her astonishment, Dr McBride smiled for the first time.

'Ah – now that's Mimi ... Are you being a cheeky girl, now? Come – see ...'

Lily moved to where she was bidden and found herself looking into the mischievous, beady eyes of a black, yellow-billed bird in a cage which stood on a table in a dark corner of the room.

'She's a mynah,' he told her. 'They like to mimic ...'

'Afternoon!' the bird offered again, with such apparent spirit that Lily laughed.

'Yes, she's good company.' The doctor indicated that she should sit again. He seemed uncomfortable, glancing at her and away. Beneath his austere, clipped exterior, she saw, there was a shy man. She also sensed an odd intensity.

'I'd better tell you a little about us,' he began in his rumbling voice. 'You've come here as a sort of house-keeper, and that's the long and short of it really. Muriel, my wife, has been an invalid for some years now and she doesn't like to be fussed over by a whole gaggle of natives. She has a nurse, from Cambridge, and we have a cook – a Eurasian fellow, Stephen. Other than that, there's the little girl you saw who does some fetching and carrying and an older woman who comes in to clean. We get by, you see. But we felt another face was needed in the house to oversee everyone. The household has become somewhat chaotic and I'm too busy – patients to see to and so forth. Even a bit of cooking might be required – Stephen's family seem to suffer one crisis after another. Could you manage that?'

Lily was surprised by his rather humble expectations of his servants.

'I've done some cooking,' she volunteered. After all, she had looked after a family before she was ten years old – she could take on anything and master it, she knew that! But she wasn't going to tell Dr McBride such a thing. 'Though you'd have to let me know what you prefer. As for the rest, I'm sure I can help you.'

'Your references were exemplary. Done the job before, eh?'

'No, sir.' She looked into his eyes. 'I was a nanny before.'

'Ah.' He made a small coughing sound, glancing down for a moment. 'That is not a service that will be required here, I'm afraid. No, no, indeed. Anyway . . .' He stood up. 'Before we all dine you'd better come and meet my wife, and Miss Brown our nurse.'

Lily followed him along the corridor to one of the doors, on which he gave a tactful knock and opened it only after invitation from a small sound from within. Inside, Lily saw that the room was a larger, grander version of hers, facing outwards with a sweeping view of the hills between the bronze-coloured curtains. In the monsoon gloom she saw the bed, quite close to the window, with a small form lying on it. She quailed inwardly at the sickroom atmosphere.

Standing beside the bed, stirring something into a glass, was a European woman whose age it would have been hard to guess, a task made the more difficult by a nurse's veil which hid her hair, leaving visible a homely face. She looked up warily at Dr McBride, as if she was afraid of being caught doing something wrong. Lily guessed the woman to be a few years older than herself, possibly as much as thirty.

'Ah, Nurse Brown – I've brought Miss Waters to meet Muriel. Miss Waters is our new housekeeper – she's come to help keep us all in order.'

'How d'you do?' she said to Lily, while busily continuing what she had been doing.

'How d'you do?' Lily replied politely. At this, a fleeting smile appeared on Miss Brown's face, and Lily felt a little more hopeful. She wondered whether to thank her for the flowers, but Miss Brown was looking away as if not welcoming more conversation.

'Muriel . . .' The doctor went gently to his wife's bedside, indicating to Lily that she should follow. 'How are you today, dear?'

Lily was horrified by the sight of Mrs McBride. She saw a tiny woman with faded auburn hair, her body in a state of extreme emaciation which made the blue eyes that looked up in greeting appear enormous in her face. She looked fragile and ill enough to snap if she was moved, but she suddenly gave a very sweet smile.

159

'I'm as you see, Ewan, dear. No better, no worse.'

He took her hand and perched beside her on the edge of the bed. 'Well, I'm glad no worse,' he told her. Lily watched the tender exchange between this huge, robust man and his sickly bird of a wife, feeling tears rise in her eyes.

'May I meet Miss Waters?' Muriel McBride asked faintly.

'Of course, my dear.' The doctor got up and made room for Lily to move forwards and take the bird-like hand that was held out to her. As she did so she heard the doctor say quietly to Miss Brown, 'Has she taken anything today?' And she replied, 'A little, Doctor. About like yesterday.'

Lily had never seen anyone quite so thin before. Muriel's McBride's forearms were shockingly wasted and her cheeks was sunken. Yet the eyes contained a life which seemed to beam up at Lily from this pinched-looking face.

'What a pretty girl you are,' Muriel McBride said. Like her husband, she spoke with a Scottish accent: her voice was high and thin but her tone was welcoming. She gazed at Lily for a moment, asked her name again, then said, 'And where have you come from, dear?'

'From Ambala,' Lily found herself smiling back. 'I was with an army family, but now their son has been sent home to school.'

'Ah yes, of course. And how long have you been in India, dear?'

'Four years, ma'am.'

'And you like it?'

'I do, very much.'

'Yes, I can see you do. I've liked it too. People find that hard to believe. They think it has finished me off.

But I love it. This is a wonderful town ... The mountains here ... Most beautiful ...' She trailed off, and Lily could see the nurse hovering as if waiting to end the conversation. She seemed very protective of her patient. Lily stepped back and Mrs McBride added, 'You are most welcome to our home, dear. I hope you will help look after Ewan, as I am unable to.' Then she gave a strange little smile and much more quietly, whispered, 'You'll be strong, dear, won't you?'

'Oh – yes, I hope so,' Lily said, not at all sure what this meant and feeling terribly sorry for the woman. What on earth had brought the poor thing to this terrible plight? She felt as if she had joined a very odd household.

Once they had left the room, Dr McBride commanded her, 'Come with me a moment.'

Lily followed him to the hall.

'Look, I need to tell you about your duties. After all, there isn't really anyone else to do it. Perhaps you'd care to dine with me this evening?'

To her surprise they dined in Dr McBride's study. It seemed that other than sleeping, he did almost everything else in this room. At the other end of the room from the desk were chairs and a card table which had been laid for the meal.

Seven-thirty found Lily sitting, after a wash and change of clothes, at table with Dr McBride, Cameron the hound under the table, being waited on by Prithvi, the young girl, who fetched and carried with great efficiency from the kitchen. Lily realized that she was older than she seemed, as old as eighteen, perhaps.

The food, consisting of a thin soup and some kind of

meat rissoles with barely cooked boiled potatoes, was rather poor, certainly nothing like as impressive as the food she had been used to at the Fairfords' residence, but she was very hungry by now and downed everything that was offered.

For a time they ate in silence. Even Mimi the mynah had gone quiet. Dr McBride sat hunched at the end of the table, eating with some intensity. At last he rested his knife and fork down and said, 'I know we don't run the household like many Europeans, with servants for every jot and tittle. It's not a money problem, you understand, it's just that Muriel feels safer without too many folk around in the house. You'll have to be a bit of a jack of all trades, sorting out the servants we do have, making sure they knuckle down, a bit of cleaning, bit of cooking, giving Nurse Brown a day off now and then. She won't like it, of course, letting someone else nurse Muriel. But there's nothing to nursing Muriel really – it's more a question of company, and making sure she eats a little.' Again he spoke of his wife very solicitously.

'How long has Mrs McBride been ill?' Lily ventured to ask.

'Ah, well now . . .' Dr McBride put his elbows on the table, clasping his hands, and stared at the little silver candelabra in the middle of the table. 'I'd say . . . It wasn't always anything like this bad, not until recently. Muriel is almost ten years my junior. She's forty-four . . .' Lily realized her guess of the doctor's age had been just about right. 'It's been coming on for quite a while. We never had children, you see. Couldn't seem to. And I suppose . . . Well, the beginning of it dates right back to then . . .'

Lily was disconcerted to be given such intimate detail, but the doctor seemed to want to speak.

'There's nothing wrong, you see – not medically.' He sat back, abandoning his watery dish of milk pudding, and lit his pipe. 'It's something that stems from the mind. Hard to understand.' He blew out a cloud of sweet-smelling smoke. 'In the past year she seems to have reached the point of no return. Nothing I seem to be able to do.' A tone of self-pity had crept into his voice. 'She has become like a child, utterly dependent. It does limit my life rather, I must say . . .' He looked appealingly at her then. 'It wasn't what I hoped for in marriage, I must admit . . .' There was a silence, then the dog stirred, making a small sound and the doctor seemed to recover himself.

'Sorry. My problems. Don't want to bore you with all that.'

'No, it's quite all right,' she said, feeling sorry. 'It must be very worrying.'

'Oh yes . . .' He sighed, wearily. 'Worrying – well, you get beyond worry as such. A doctor who can't heal his own wife. It's . . . Well, humiliating wouldn't be a strong enough word.'

'Heartbreaking?' Lily suggested.

Startled, he looked sharply at her. 'It's certainly that, Miss Waters. Oh yes. It's heartbreaking all right.'

Chapter Twenty-Six

Lily spent her first weeks in Mussoorie getting to know the place and people, and establishing her role in the McBride bungalow.

Her first task was to understand the working of the household and to get to meet the servants. She soon got to know Prithvi, who was seventeen and had had a life of hardship, her mother dying when she was young, leaving her to care for her sick father and two younger sisters. When her father died as well she lost hope of having any sort of dowry to marry and came to live with the McBrides. She was not educated as Srimala had been, by the Sisters in Ambala, and she seldom had much to say, but she was sweet and obliging and ready to accept instructions from Lily.

The cook, Stephen Owen, also presented little in the way of difficulty. Stephen was a very thin, anxious-looking man in his late thirties, whose hair was receding rapidly and who lived his life in a condition of spaniel-eyed anxiety. He invested everything, from his wife's evidently petulant demands to the over-boiling of an egg, with an air of tragic melodrama.

'I am not successful with junkets or blancmanges,' he told Lily woefully, the first morning they met. 'They are forever getting the better of me.' This was followed by a sigh which suggested that this was one of his life's deepest regrets.

He arrived late for work almost every day, always sprucely dressed in European clothes. Stephen's father had been an English engineer, he confided to Lily after a few days. Hubert Owen had fallen in love with a Punjabi girl who had been very pretty but not, Stephen said wistfully, of a very high caste. Nor had he been a man of honour: he abandoned the girl and Stephen grew up in Delhi in an orphanage for the illegitimate children of Anglo-Indian liaisons. He had done a series of jobs in service and had been working in the McBrides' long, thin kitchen for three years, during which, it seemed, his cooking had improved scarcely at all.

'The doctor is a man of great kindness and tolerance,' Stephen told Lily, stretching his eyes wide in his long, sensitive face. She could see that this was a plea for her to be the same.

'We'll get along very well, I'm sure,' she told him. 'But I expect there may have to be a bit of reorganization.'

That, in fact, was an understatement and she found herself surprised that the McBride house was functioning at all when she saw the chaotic state of the kitchen, the lack of any sort of order in Stephen's work, including a sheer lack of basic supplies. She knew she could get stuck in straight away and make things better, as well as helping to improve his cooking.

'The trouble is also Mrs Das,' Stephen admitted. 'She is coming and stealing things and I have never been able to stop her.'

Mrs Das was a very stout, dyspeptic widow who came in to clean for the McBrides and moved round the house muttering bad-temperedly, terrorizing Prithvi and letting out ragged-sounding belches so that it was almost impossible to be unaware of where she was at any time.

Her cleaning skills were also questionable and Lily wondered why they didn't find someone else, but realized that Dr McBride was probably easily satisfied in these areas and did not notice much so long as some sort of meal was placed before him at the right times of day.

'Are you sure she's stealing supplies?' Lily quizzed Stephen.

'Sure as eggs is eggs, Miss Lily,' he said earnestly. 'I have seen her with my very eyes.'

'Well, why didn't you stop her?'

Stephen's face dropped into a study of dismay. 'I did try. But she is a very bullying sort of lady.'

'I'll speak to her,' Lily said. And we'll get some locks put on the cupboards.'

Confronting Mrs Das produced nothing but sly smiles and slippery excuses, but the locks, to which Lily kept the keys, rendered Mrs Das daily more grumpy. Lily wondered whether Dr McBride was neglecting to pay his servants sufficiently, but when she checked, tactfully, with some other households in the area, the rupees they were taking home each week seemed generous in comparison with some.

She set to work cleaning and reorganizing the kitchen and took Stephen out to the bazaar to buy supplies, something she enjoyed so much that she said she would do it with him regularly.

'Oh yes, please, Miss Lily!' he said. She felt sorry for his hopeless air.

'And we'll learn to cook some new dishes, shall we?' she suggested.

By the time she had been there a month, the household was running much more smoothly and the meals had improved no end. The one member of the staff whom she took longer to get to know was Jane Brown, Muriel McBride's nurse. This was partly because at first she saw very little of her. Jane Brown's hours were spent mostly in the sickroom or in her own little room opposite, which faced out to the back and so did not share the spectacular view. So far as Lily could see, she had no other life apart from looking after her charge and going out to Christchurch for the Holy Communion service on Sunday mornings. Lily, on the other hand, was off out during any spare time she had, getting to know this beautiful hill town to which she had already given her heart.

When she did encounter Jane Brown, she seemed at first a very reserved person. It began when she came into the kitchen to heat up milk for Mrs McBride.

'I'll do it if you like,' Lily offered. The first time she had been scouring pans and her hands were covered in grimy soap, but she was truly willing to help.

'Oh no!' Miss Brown said. 'No need for that. *I* attend to Mrs McBride's needs.'

All right then, Lily thought, offended by her tone. I was only trying to be helpful.

She bent her head over the big pan she was scouring out. Miss Brown stood waiting for the milk and Lily could sense her watching.

'Well, you're not afraid of hard work, it seems,' Nurse Brown observed.

Lily looked up at her. In the brighter light of the kitchen the nurse seemed a little younger than Lily had guessed. She wore a long black skirt and white blouse with a high, plain collar, with a starched apron over the top. Her figure was sturdy and well proportioned and her face was kindly, but so far she was not very forthcoming.

'No – hard work has never put me off,' Lily agreed carefully.

'A good scrubbing's well overdue in this house.' Miss Brown nodded at the blackened pan Lily was working on, then said wryly, 'I'm surprised *he* hasn't finished us all off by now. Calling himself a cook – he can scarcely boil an egg without some mishap!'

'Yes,' Lily smiled. 'He is a bit accident prone.'

This seemed to break the ice a little and gradually Miss Brown came into the kitchen more and more when Lily was there.

'How is Mrs McBride today?' Lily would ask.

At first Jane Brown gave non-committal replies: 'Much the same,' or, 'One can't expect much, I'm afraid.'

One morning, however, when Lily had been there about three weeks, Jane Brown came in when Lily was just despatching Stephen to buy the daily supplies. The nurse was obviously agitated and once Stephen had left, the room seemed to be filled with her mood. Lily's thoughts were on the next job, sorting laundry for the *dhobi* man, but she took courage and said, 'Is something wrong? Mrs McBride – is she not progressing today?'

Miss Brown whisked round from staring at the pan of milk, a furious look on her face. 'Progressing?' Her voice was full of pent-up emotion. 'Do you seriously imagine that that poor woman is ever going to be well again, you silly?'

Lily was bewildered. She had not considered that Mrs McBride would not get better even after hearing the little she knew.

'Well, I don't know,' she said hesitantly. 'I don't really understand what is the matter with her. Dr

McBride said there was nothing wrong with her, not medically wrong. I'm sure that's what he said.'

'The woman's dying!' Miss Brown cried. 'Slowly, day by day, she's slipping away, and there's nothing any of us can do about it. And what's worse is, she can't do anything about it either!'

Lily stared at her. 'But why?'

'Because she won't *eat*.' A tear escaped and ran down Miss Brown's cheek. There was more life in her face, suddenly, than Lily had ever seen before, a kind of terrible passion. She poured out the ordeal of her daily work. 'This milk – she'll barely manage a sip or two, though I try and try. Have you any idea what it's like to watch over someone closely when they will *not live*? To watch them lose their hold on life and yet still be alive, day after agonizing day? She started starving herself years ago, a gradual thing at first, I think, and it became a habit, a state she couldn't get out of. And now her body knows nothing else. They've tried everything – mental doctors, all sorts of cures, but nothing works. And she's in decline much faster now, day by day, and I don't think she could take food even if she wanted to.' Miss Brown brushed her hands over her apron in a gesture of nervous distress and wiped her wet cheek. 'She was a nurse herself, you know, trained in Edinburgh.' Her tears flowed again and Lily sensed they had been stored up for a long time. 'Nothing works properly ... Her body ... It's like walking to Calvary with her every single day.' She put her face in her hands and for a moment gave way to her grief.

Lily felt deeply affected by what she was hearing. She had seen the starving poor in India, the scrawny beggars in Ambala, but she had never heard of anyone starving themselves to death deliberately. She was also moved by the sight of this reserved woman breaking down in front of her.

'How terrible,' she said, tears in her own eyes. She had been touched by the sight of Mrs McBride, even when she knew nothing. Now she found her plight deeply upsetting.

'Yes, well...' Miss Brown became brisk now, ashamed of her outburst. She wiped her eyes and poured the warm milk into a cup. 'Mustn't give way. Sorry about that.'

'But it's so very sad,' Lily said. 'You have a very difficult job.'

'Yes.' Miss Brown seemed pleased to hear this acknowledged. 'I do. A slow crucifixion, as I say. Such a life they used to have, I've heard, parties, the high life. He lives like a recluse now – they both do. It's a terrible thing. But one doesn't desert one's post. I certainly shan't leave her.'

Without another word she took the milk and left.

After that, Lily found herself thinking a good deal about Muriel McBride.

Whenever she could get out and have some time to herself, she went walking in between the monsoon showers, loving being outside with the immense mountain panorama spread out before her. The weather had a dramatic character all of its own, changing by the moment so that every time she looked out across the mountains there was something different to see. The clouds were constantly on the move. Sometimes the valleys were dotted with diaphanous white, at others filled with grey, boiling heaps of cloud and the rain would come down in an almost solid mass, followed by sunshine, when the colours leaped out from every rock and bush, the blue sky seemed a miracle and every leaf and flower gleamed with drops.

The main centres of Mussoorie were like two lively little towns, Kulri Bazaar and Library Chowk, joined by the Mall, a straight walkway cut along the mountainside. But there was another route between the two, the Camel's Back Road, which made a winding loop from a point not far from the McBride bungalow for roughly two miles to Library Chowk. It was Lily's very favourite walk, quiet and beautiful, the houses perched on the hill to her left and the dark conifers, the mountains and clouds to her right.

One afternoon, when the sun had broken through for a time, she was just about to set out when she met Dr McBride in the hall.

'Ah,' he said, in the rather austere way he usually spoke to her. 'Off out somewhere?'

'I usually go for a walk in the afternoon, sir,' Lily said. She already had her hat on.

'Splendid idea,' he said. 'Good for the constitution.'

The rain held off that afternoon. On a couple of occasions showers had begun when she was far from home and it was too late to go back, but this time she walked out into hazy sunshine. After some minutes the path took her past the Christian cemetery, its gated entrance like a small whitewashed church beside the path, the burial ground falling away down the hillside. Once or twice she had walked in there and read the names of the British dead who had given their lives to India and never returned home. It was such a peaceful place, the straight trunks of the deodars soaring above and the vivid green terraces of the hillside dotted with the gravestones and crosses of an English parish churchyard.

Two monkeys, ghostly grey with black faces, were perched on the fence. She paused at a cautious distance from them to look down. The air smelled fresh, damp and pine-scented. Today, as so often, her thoughts turned to Cosmo. She missed him with an ache that never left. Had he been here she would have helped him perch on the fence and they would have looked down together, he chattering about the monkeys, asking questions which she answered, in an endless conversation that had lasted through those years of his infancy and without which she still felt bereft. Every week without fail, she wrote him a letter, telling him little things she thought he would understand and be interested in and always sending her love, letting him know she was thinking of him. She knew she would tell him about these monkeys.

Looking out along the peaceful valley she thought how lovely it was here compared to the dusty heat and regimented streets of Ambala. She had wanted to come and forget everything, forget her past and the pain of her brief, but overwhelming experience of love for Sam Ironside. Against her will he still came often into her thoughts as she remembered and wondered painfully whether he ever thought about her.

'Oh, Sam,' she whispered to the quiet trees. 'Sometimes I just wish you were here.'

There had never been time to talk properly, to explain things. She had been so hurt by his deception that all she could think of was getting far away from him. It was still so painful when she thought about it now, even though at times she longed for the feelings of love and happiness that Sam had aroused in her.

But that was in the past: it had to be. And she wouldn't make that mistake again, she thought, walking slowly along the Camel's Back Road. Nothing was worth that amount of pain. And no man would ever again have her heart, open and ready to be hurt.

Chapter Twenty-Seven

A few days later Lily was about to set off for her afternoon walk again. Mrs Das had been particularly disgruntled since the cupboards were now locked up and she could not pilfer rice, sugar and other staples from the kitchen. She positively creaked with complaint, like an old cart.

'What *is* the matter, Mrs Das?' Lily was stung into asking, as the corpulent woman flicked her broom ineffectively round the hall, issuing a constant stream of mumbled invective.

'Nothing is matter,' Mrs Das pronounced resentfully. 'I am saying prayers.'

'Well, they sound very cross prayers,' Lily retorted. What with her and Stephen's endless family problems, it would be good to get out of the house.

She was just heading for the door when Dr McBride came out of his study with his dog.

'Are you going for your daily walk, Miss Waters?'

'Yes, sir.' She waited, uncertain if she was needed.

He came closer. 'Have you ever been up Gun Hill?' She knew where he meant because it was from that hill that the big gun fired every day to mark the hour of noon.

'No, Doctor, I haven't.' She did not meet his eyes. 'I usually take my walk along the Camel's Back Road.'

'There's a splendid view from up there,' Dr McBride

said. 'Not so good in the rains, of course – too much cloud. But they'll be over soon and in the winter, my goodness, you'll see how lovely it is up here. From the hill you can see the really high Himalaya.' He hesitated, then said awkwardly, 'Would you care for a stroll up there this afternoon? Cameron and I would benefit from the exercise.'

Lily was startled. She wanted to say no because she enjoyed her solitary walks which gave her time to think and dream, but it would have seemed rude.

'That would be very nice,' she replied, wondering that he didn't mind being seen out in the company of a maid.

'I'll bring my umbrella, in case,' the doctor said, putting on his hat, a comfortable tweed trilby. He opened the door for her and said, 'After you, Miss Waters.'

They passed through the lively streets of Kulri Bazaar, narrow and teeming with life. There were mixed smells of incense and coffee and frying eggs and the shops selling fruit and vegetables and medicines and bolts of colourful cloth. Lily loved to see the English nannies out with children, holding their hands as they dragged along, staring at the shop windows. She knew some of them by sight now and sometimes stopped to talk.

Dr McBride raised his hat to greet people, and he seemed to know very many of them.

'I can't get far without stopping for a conversation, I'm afraid,' the doctor said. 'It's always rather slow progress.'

'Well, you're a doctor,' Lily said, not being sure what else to reply.

Dr McBride said, 'So I am,' and let out a chuckle,

which surprised her as she'd never heard him laugh before and wasn't sure what was funny.

She saw that people responded to him with deference, but also that they felt sorry for him because his wife was so sick. But she also saw, to her surprise, that he seemed to be enjoying it all. She had imagined that he was a recluse by nature, when now he seemed rather sociable. A few people registered surprise at seeing her at his side, someone unknown to most of them, but as it had been his idea she did not feel disturbed by this.

They passed along the Mall, with its ornate railings edging the drop into the valley, and its big, wrought-iron lamps. There were rickshaws moving among the walkers, and vendors selling mangoes and roasted *dal*, and the sound of horses' hooves coming from behind. A group of riders passed, out for a pleasant ride. Suddenly Lily ached to ride a horse again.

'Now – here to the right, look,' the doctor said. 'This is where we begin the climb.'

A steeply sloping path zigzagged up and up so that the Mall receded below them and they were looking down on houses which had been above them before. Soon they passed the long snout of the gun which gave the hill its name. Lily found the climb easy as she was slender and agile. The doctor, however, had to take it more slowly, and stop on some of the bends to catch his breath. The dog, who was rather old, also loped along slowly.

'You're a fit young filly, I must say,' the doctor said, catching Lily up as she waited for him. Until now he had acted towards her with a distant courtesy, but now, in his look she realized that he was seeing her as a person, not just a servant.

176

'I have been used to being active,' she said, feeling her cheeks glowing with the exercise.

'How so?' he asked as they walked on together again.

'Well, until I came here I was looking after a small boy who had a good deal of energy. And we used to ride out every morning. They taught me to ride in Ambala.'

'Did they, indeed? Good sort of family?'

'Yes. Very good.' She told him a little about the Fairfords.

'Not sure the cantonment life would have suited me,' the doctor mused. 'Nor Muriel, for that matter. She was never much of a joiner – clubs, and so on. She only went out really to please me, you know, do her duty. She was always rather shy and unsure of herself. Still – all in the past that, anyway.'

He stopped himself as if he had said too much. Lily was not sure what to say: her quiet presence often seemed to encourage people to talk.

'I don't know anything about you, Miss Waters,' he said suddenly. 'Do tell me about yourself.'

Lily felt her usual uneasiness at being questioned. 'There isn't a great deal to know.'

But he persisted, so she gave him the story about her father being a clergyman and moving around a good deal.

'You must miss your family, being over here alone?'

'I have no living family,' she said. 'Or none that I am close to.' She looked down at her feet as she walked, hoping to discourage any more questions.

'So what brought you to India?'

'I wanted an adventure, I suppose. To see something of the world.'

'You're a courageous young woman,' he said. 'It

takes a certain sort of person to be able to launch out on their own like that. It's something I admire.'

'Thank you,' Lily said, startled at hearing him flatter her.

Round the next bend she saw that they were nearly at the top.

'Let's see now if any of those shy peaks are going to show themselves today.'

They stood side by side at the viewing point, looking out over what would have been a vista of peaks flanked by the lower foothills, had the whole expanse not been swathed in a thick blanket of white cloud.

'Oh dear, dear,' Dr McBride laughed. He seemed unexpectedly light-hearted and she was seeing a new side of him. 'I did say this wasn't the best time of year. But I hope you've enjoyed the climb. We'll have to come back in a few weeks when the rains are over.'

'It's been a lovely walk anyway,' Lily said. The climb had filled her with a sense of well-being.

'If you like,' Dr McBride said hesitantly, 'I could show you some other places around here. I don't suppose you've been able to go very far. And you appear to enjoy a walk.'

Lily was not really sure she wanted his company as it was more relaxing to be on her own. After all, why would he want to be out and about with his servant? But she always felt obliged to please people and she did feel flattered by his attention.

Blushing a little she said, 'Thank you, that would be very nice,' assuming that he was being polite too and would forget about it straight away.

*

But he did not forget. A few days later he asked her to accompany him. Now it was late in September the rains were drying up and the days were more pleasantly warm. Lily found that her grey walking skirt and cream blouse no longer felt oppressively hot, but quite comfortable, her wide-brimmed hat no longer quite so essential.

That afternoon they walked out to Landour, a village perched along the hillside outside Mussoorie. It was a pretty walk and Dr McBride named for her the medlar and tamarind trees and oaks and flowers growing along the path. He was very gentlemanly and correct and Lily relaxed a little. Of course, the man was lonely, she realized. He didn't mean any harm. He just wanted someone to go for a walk with as his wife could not give him her company.

'Look – a redstart!' He pointed as they were standing on a high path, looking down into the green valley. Lily caught a glimpse of the bird as it flashed past.

'Beautiful,' she said politely, though she had barely seen anything.

Dr McBride turned to her suddenly and smiled, the first spontaneous and joyful smile she had ever seen him give.

'There are some beautiful sights to be seen here, indeed,' he said, looking away into the distance again. 'I've shut myself away too much these past years, and almost forgotten. I have you to thank for reminding me, Miss Waters. I had given up hope of anything better.'

Lily gave a faint smile, unsure what to say. There was a silence, until Dr McBride said, 'Your name is Lily, I gather?'

'Yes, sir.' She looked down at her boots.

'My name is Ewan. You don't need to keep calling me Sir or Doctor, you know.'

Lily felt her heart begin to thump nervously harder. Why was Dr McBride being so familiar with her all of a sudden?

'Yes, I know your name,' she said, looking up at him. 'But I am one of your servants. It would not seem right for me to call you anything so informal.'

His eyes looked deeply into hers. 'Only perhaps when we're alone, Lily?'

And his voice held a pleading tone, but it was also a command that she knew she was not expected to refuse.

Chapter Twenty-Eight

Gradually Jane Brown became friendlier. Though she did not have a great deal of spare time as her life was very tied to Muriel McBride's, she invited Lily to her room one afternoon.

'I bought cakes,' she said unexpectedly. 'I thought we might have tea, if you'd like that?'

'Oh yes!' Lily said. 'I'd love to!' She was pleased by the warmth she saw in Jane Brown's eyes. Lily realized that Jane was shy and had needed time before she could issue such an invitation. For herself, she longed to have a friend to talk to. She so missed the companionship that had grown up between herself and Srimala and also with Susan Fairford.

Jane Brown's room surprised Lily. She had imagined her to be a rather austere person, but when she was admitted to the room opposite Muriel McBride's, she was greeted by a very colourful sight. The bed was swathed in a coverlet of red, yellow and blue paisley patterns and nearby on the wall was a silk hanging in iridescent blue and gold. On other walls were small paintings on silk depicting scenes from the Hindu religious stories, one small painting on ivory and along the shelf processed a number of wooden carved elephants arranged in decreasing size. Lily also saw some prints which looked Chinese and close to the bed, on the wall, hung a wooden cross. There was also quite a collection of books.

'How lovely!' Lily exclaimed. 'You've made it look so jolly!'

'I thought I might as well make a home of it,' Jane said. 'And I like a bit of colour around me. Do sit, Lily – that's the most comfortable.'

She indicated a low wooden chair whose arms ended in a scrolling curve of wood. Lily sat and watched as her new friend arranged cakes on a plate. She was not in uniform, and had on a skirt in deep, watery blues and it was the first time Lily had seen her without her nurse's veil. Her hair was a gingery brown and rather frizzy, and she had it tied loosely in a thick ponytail. She was not a pretty woman, but there was a kindness and intelligence to her face that drew Lily to her.

'Here we are – I've got a pot of tea already made,' she said, handing Lily a cup. 'Sugar? And do have one of these cakes. They really are rather good.'

She settled opposite Lily on the bed and the two of them ate the cream cakes and began to get to know one another.

'I was wondering where you came from by your exotic looks,' Jane Brown said, gazing at Lily's face. 'You do look wonderfully unusual.'

'Oh.' Lily smiled. 'I don't know. I've been told I'm like my mother, but she died when I was very young.'

She told Jane Brown a few details of her usual version of things, and then quickly asked her about herself. Jane seemed to see that Lily did not wish to be questioned and she talked quite fluently then about her own background. She had grown up in Cambridge, where her father was a professor of Chinese history.

'Actually, I spent my first six years in China,' she said, smiling as she tussled with a dab of cream which attached itself first to her lips and then her hand. 'Daddy was researching his book – look, I have a copy here.'

She reached over for a book from the shelf and showed Lily a thick, scholarly-looking work by an author called N. E. O. Brown.

'Goodness,' Lily said. 'That looks very clever.'

'Oh, don't imagine I've read the whole thing!' Jane Brown laughed. 'I never got involved in Daddy's work. But I suppose you do get used to living abroad – it gave me my wanderlust. So when I'd done my training I applied to come over here. I was in a nursing home in Calcutta for nearly two years and then I answered the doctor's advertisement. I liked the sound of the hills and I wanted a change. Goodness ... I say, that was *nice* ...' She put her cake plate down, wiping her lips on her handkerchief.

'Yes – I liked the sound of it up here too,' Lily said. She felt comfortable and well fed after the tea and cakes and she began to relax. She told her about Ambala and the Fairfords.

'I don't know that I'd like cantonment life,' Jane said. 'It all seems a bit claustrophobic to my mind. I get the impression there's a sense of shutting out the rest of the country as if it doesn't exist ... That's what they want, I suppose.' She shifted back on the bed, kicked her shoes off and tucked her feet up.

'Yes, it does feel like a world of its own in many ways,' Lily said. 'I must say, I prefer it here.'

'Course, everyone's haunted by the Mutiny,' Jane said. 'They don't say much about it but when you think of it, how can it go on? All of us over here.'

'What d'you mean?' Lily asked.

'Well, they don't want us here really, do they? We're foreigners, trespassers. It's all absurd in a way. And we know it really – what happened back in fifty-seven – if it happened once, the natives getting up and saying "no more", it can happen again. And it will one day. Don't you think?'

Lily thought about it, the strangeness of the British being in this country somehow. She thought of the cemetery on the side of the hill. 'Yes,' she said, feeling foolish that she did not have any strong opinions. 'I suppose you're right.'

Jane Brown poured them more tea and their talk turned to the household. Lily wanted to ask more about Muriel McBride, about what had happened to her, and Jane Brown, though not a gossip, obviously needed to relieve her own feelings. She reclined sideways on the bed, leaning on her elbow, her skirt spread over her legs and talked.

'Sometimes when I look at her when she's asleep, I just boil with rage that anyone should be in the state she's in. Everyone seems to be doing all they can, but I feel as if I come up against it every day – slap!' She clapped her hands together. 'Just like running into a wall. And sometimes I'm *so* angry with her I just want to shake her and say, "Live! *Just get on with it and live! You've been given this life and look what you're doing with it, lying here as if you're in a tomb when you're still alive.*" She's the sweetest person, you know, but she can't do it. She's forgotten even to *want* to live.'

There was a silence in which Lily guessed she was trying not to weep, but when Jane Brown looked up she was dry-eyed.

'I have to get out sometimes or I think I'd go mad. I tend to walk very early in the morning, while she's still asleep. I quite often see the sun come up . . . Sometimes I just . . .' She pushed herself more upright again for a moment, her eyes searching Lily's face. 'I don't know . . . I have these doubts . . .'

'What about?' Lily asked.

'About *him*. The doctor.' She was obviously troubled but could not quite identify why. 'He's such a nice man, and I feel sorry for him. It's just that now and then, the way he comes into her room, things he says . . . I almost wonder if it's him . . .'

Lily frowned, leaning forwards. 'I'm sorry. I really don't . . .'

'No.' Jane lay down again. 'I don't understand what I mean either. It's more of an intuition. But' – she gabbled the words as if they needed to be said – 'it's almost as if he likes her being so ill. As if he likes feeling in command of it all . . .'

Lily sat back, shocked. 'But how could that be? Surely you can't make someone else ill?'

Jane Brown looked thoughtful, and shamefaced. 'No – you're probably right. I'm being fanciful. It's probably being alone with her too much, because it's all so strange and awful, and I start to imagine things.' She smiled, as if shaking the thoughts off. 'Let's talk about something more cheerful.'

Chapter Twenty-Nine

As the days passed, Lily found she saw more and more of Dr McBride. He seemed unable to leave her alone. Before, when he was not out attending to patients, the house had been very quiet with the doctor secluded in his study, but now Lily kept meeting him in the hall, the corridors, walking up and down as if he was going somewhere purposefully. But it soon became clear to her that he was looking for opportunities simply to be in her company.

There were more walks, and his behaviour was always reserved and very correct, he just seemed to want to be with her, until one day, the second time they went back to climb Gun Hill. They had reached the top, able to see the high, snowy peaks of the Himalaya now the monsoon clouds had cleared. Beyond the dark foothills rose the silent white peaks, the sun shining on them.

'Oh!' Lily was enraptured. She was still panting slightly from the climb, her cheeks glowing with good health. And she had never seen anything so mysteriously beautiful.

'I knew you'd feel like that!' Dr McBride said, and she felt him gazing intently at her face. She didn't turn to look back, but a moment later he clasped her hand, holding it in both of his. 'Oh, my dear girl, you really are so exotic – such a rare flower!'

Lily froze and Dr McBride swiftly let go of her hand.

'I'm sorry, my dear. I just ... But you really are lovely.'

'It's very kind of you, Dr McBride,' she said breathlessly. She did not know what to do: she mustn't offend him, she thought. She might lose her job and be sent away! She gave him a careful smile. 'I don't know what to say.'

'I know. I apologize.' Seeming embarrassed, he looked away at the sweeping mountains laid out before them, thoughtfully stroking his thick beard. 'Perhaps it's something to do with being up here. Some of the highest peaks in the world over there – Everest, of course. They call it the roof of the world, Lily . . .' He turned back to her, then away. 'Oh, good God,' she heard him say. Then, with an effort, he said soberly, 'It won't happen again.'

As they walked back, she accompanying his long stride, he seemed restored and talked about the things they could see around them. Lily was relieved. How could he expect that she could feel anything for him? He was twice her age and a married man, and there was a great gulf between them when it came to class and upbringing. He was obviously lonely and suffering a temporary madness!

But that night, he sent for her and asked her, very formally, to have dinner with him. 'I dine alone night after night. It would be very pleasant to have some company. And especially –' he cleared his throat – 'if it were yours.'

As usual, he ate his evening meal in his study, and when Lily was admitted she found the small table near the window laid for two with candles burning on it. Her palms begin to perspire with nerves. But she told herself, He's lonely, he just wants some company, that's all.

'Come in, my dear, do come in.' He welcomed her at the door and once again she was intimidated by his sheer physical bulk. He was not a fat man, but built on a grand scale, and his large head and square, curling beard only increased his appearance of size.

'I'm so glad you have come, Lily. Come and sit down. Can I offer you a sherry?'

She realized then just how nervous he was of her as he ushered her to the table. On her side plate she found a single rose, deep red and still in bud.

'How lovely!' she cried, without thinking.

'For you.' He gazed at her solemnly. 'I saw it and thought of you. Your lovely face is like a mysterious, closed rose.'

'Oh, I don't think so.' She gave a slight giggle. The first sip of sherry, which she was not used to, was already going to her head. Other than the candlelit table, the rest of the room was in shadow and she felt as if she were somewhere strange and primitive, like a cave.

Dr McBride seated himself opposite her. 'Prithvi will bring us our meal in a moment, though I'm afraid it will not be much of a surprise to you. I expect you supervised Stephen in planning it?'

'Yes – we are to have mutton curry and a sweet rice mould,' she told him. 'And I think Stephen has done it all very well today.'

'I'm relieved to hear it,' Dr McBride laughed, sipping from his own glass of whisky. 'His cooking, so far, has been a little erratic. I'm not given to fussing about food, though. One has to eat to live, that's all. Though I must say, now and then it's good to tuck into something that has not been either charred or boiled to death.

Especially,' he leaned forwards, 'when one is in such delightful company.'

Again, Lily felt a sense of panic rise in her for a moment at what all this might mean. She put her sherry glass down, determined to keep a straight head.

A moment later Prithvi came in. She was wearing a shimmering pink sari, and waited on them with her usual demure shyness, keeping her eyes lowered and silently disappearing without any indication that she found it strange seeing Lily dining with the master.

'Can I treat you to a glass of wine?' Dr McBride asked. 'There's fresh *limbopani* as well, but I thought you might enjoy a drop of good French wine from the Rhone.'

'Oh no, thank you!' She felt rather swimmy already, from the sherry. 'I'd like lemonade, please.'

'As you please, my dear.'

They began to eat, and Dr McBride talked. Lily was glad that he did not expect much from her in the way of conversation. She took a mouthful of Stephen's curry and rice and found it to be very good, so she sat and enjoyed her meal while the doctor told her about his childhood in Edinburgh and how he had come to meet Muriel.

'It was a student prank, you see. Arthur's Seat in the dark – all that kind of foolishness.' Seeing her puzzled expression he explained that Arthur's Seat was an old volcano. 'It's in Holyrood Park, in Edinburgh, my dear. Anyway, of course I broke my ankle and when they took me to the infirmary, I met Muriel. I'd never seen her before even though I was training in the same hospital, so it all felt rather destined. Oh, she was lovely! You should have seen her – all that pale red hair, freckles and so much life in her face. Lord God . . .' He shook

189

his head and she could see his emotions surfacing. 'How could I ever have imagined how she'd come to be … Impossible. It's a torment watching her …' He looked across at her, his expression pitiable, and she was touched. But she could also see that he wanted something from her and she was disturbed and flattered all at once.

'What is the matter with Mrs McBride, exactly?' she dared to ask.

'Nothing. And everything.' He sighed and sat back, holding his wine glass and unbuttoning his tweed jacket. He spoke with the creaking slowness of someone unaccustomed to talking about his personal life.

'Muriel and I couldn't have children. I know where the problem lies. Being a medical man and so on, I looked into it more thoroughly than most. There is nothing wrong with Muriel, as I've told her a thousand times. It's me. I'm infertile.' These last words came out awkwardly, as a confession of pain. 'Sometimes that's the way. So together we can't conceive. Of course, with another man she could bear a child, but Muriel is a most honourable woman and she loved me, loves me still, I do believe. But from then on, gradually, everything went wrong. We were only in our twenties when we married. Of course, the attempts at childbearing went on for a time, but then she started to eat less. It took time and no one noticed at first, until the weight began to fall off her. She spent her thirties eating like a bird. She was thin as a stick and her looks left her, I must say. She used to have a bloom to her and it just made her fade. Terrible to watch.' He took another sip of wine. Lily watched his face. She could feel herself being drawn in by him.

'I've never talked to anyone about it before,' he said.

'Or not in more than cold medical terms. It's something about you, Lily ... I seem to be able to say things ...' He gazed emotionally at her for a moment, then looked away.

'Muriel's condition is a sickness of the mind which makes people starve themselves of food, and it's very hard to understand. It's so life-denying, yet Muriel has always said she does not want to die. A year ago things became very bad and we reached the point you see us at now. I suggested we go home to Edinburgh, but Muriel begged me to let her stay here. She is afraid that they might force-feed her and she says if they did that she would hang herself. I've asked myself day and night for months whether there is anywhere else I could take her that would help. She's had help from the psychiatric doctor here – the physicians of the mind, Lily – but nothing seems to give her back the key to life and instead we have to exist in this living death, day after day ...'

For a moment she thought he was going to weep, but he checked himself and wiped his hand emotionally over his eyes.

'For years now I've just closed in on myself. I love the woman – but she doesn't seem to love me, or herself, enough to nourish herself into life. Part of me has been dying with her. And then you come along, Lily, so alive and so beautiful, with your wonderful, living body and your face ... God, the sight of your face. You've given me such joy, did you know? Just the sight of you each day has given me back my life again!'

'Has it?' Lily said. She felt more in command of herself now, and smiled at him. Perhaps that was all he wanted, she hoped, just to see her, if it made him feel better. 'If so, then I'm glad.'

'Glad isn't a strong enough word for what I feel, Lily.'

She jumped as he got to his feet and came round the table. He was becoming more and more passionate and he took her hand and held it to his lips.

'I adore you. I want to make you mine. I'm not just the crusty old doctor you've seen. There's far more to me than that, but it's been shut away more as every year goes by. I'd give anything for you, to be with you even a little of the time . . .'

Goodness, what was he asking her? Lily thought, panic-stricken. Was this respectable man asking her to become his mistress? Did he think she was some woman of easy virtue who would just do anything he asked? She was in turmoil, half wanting to pull her hand away, but not feeling she could because of the look of longing in his eyes, and the longing inside her which answered it.

'Lily—' He spoke urgently, words pouring from him. 'I know what I am saying to you is very shocking. But I'll lay my cards on the table. I am a quite wealthy man with a dying wife and no offspring to spend my money on. I have entombed myself in my house and my medical practice . . . I don't want to live like this any more. I'm asking you to help me find life again. I can give you so much, my dear . . . I worship you, I can make a queen of you . . . You would not lose respect, or not for long. I am very highly thought of in this town, and I am also much pitied. I have had many offers from women who feel sorry for me, but no one has ever been like you.' He paused for a moment, staring at her. 'Tell me what you want of me, darling one – you only have to ask.'

Something inside her responded to this. She was

alone in the world, with no hope of a real love or marriage, and he was offering an arrangement which she could see might be to her advantage. For the first time in her life Lily felt a real sense of strength. A voice in her answered, Why not? You have nothing to lose and a lot to gain. And amid all her calculations there was a simple longing to be loved and held and desired.

'There's one thing...' He sounded bashful now, looking down at his plate. 'I'm being very forward but I did say I wanted to lay my cards on the table. What I said about my inability to father a child – I know for certain that that is the case. I've performed certain tests ... So if you were to agree to ... to offer me love in every way possible there would be no issue. You need not trouble yourself about that.'

Lily had never heard anyone speak so directly, and felt a blush spread all over her body. She looked down, hoping that in the dim light he would not see.

'I feel a little overcome,' she said carefully. 'I wasn't expecting this. You are very kind.'

The doctor drew Lily to her feet and she obeyed. 'Please say yes, Lily. I don't think I could bear it if you turned me down.'

She made her decision in that split second. A yes to something she barely understood. Standing up, in the candlelight she allowed him to pull her close to him. He seemed so very large as he drew her against him and she was a little afraid, but she quelled her fears. She wanted things from life that she could barely name and this seemed to be a way she could get them.

'Oh, my dearest love,' he said breathlessly, and pulled her to him. A moment later she was wrapped in Ewan McBride's arms, his lips hot and ardent on hers.

Chapter Thirty

For a short time Lily thought Dr McBride was going to be satisfied with her company on the afternoon walks and an evening meal with a few kisses at the end of the evening. But as the days went by, he became more and more ardent until one evening, as Lily pulled away from him to leave his candlelit study, he said hurriedly, 'Let me come to you – tonight!'

Lily turned, hand on the door handle. 'What do you mean?'

Dr McBride was at her side again, taking her other hand. 'Let me lie with you, Lily, my darling! I'm burning for you – you can see.' A sweat had broken out on his forehead. 'I want to lie beside you and make you mine, my darling girl.'

'I've never been that kind of person,' Lily said. 'I don't ... know men.' She was trembling and for a moment she could not look at him, then she raised her eyes to see him watching her with a tender expression.

'I can see that.' He reached for her other hand and held both of hers in his, turning her to face him. She saw his face tighten with desire.

'Of course you're not, my dear. And I don't want you to think I'm treating you in a beastly way, that I have no care for you. God, Lily, I'd do anything for you. I shan't deflower you and discard you. I love you. I want to be with you and look after you.' He stared into her eyes. 'Go to your room, darling, and I'll come to you. My own is too close to Muriel. She mustn't hear anything.'

As if in a dream, she found herself obeying. Alone in her room, she lit two candles and sat on the edge of the bed. She could not seem to think properly. Nothing seemed quite real. Should she get undressed, or wait as she was?

There came a discreet knock and the doctor came inside without a word and softly closed the door. He came to her immediately, his breathing fast and heavy and took her in his arms.

'At last. Oh, at last, my dear little girl!'

Lily pressed against his large body, smelling him, sweat and tobacco and old wool, and felt his hands moving over her with increasing intimacy.

'Let's take some of these clothes off, my dear.'

He undressed her and she let him, passive as a doll, until she was standing naked and he was still fully clothed and she felt vulnerable and embarrassed. He knelt, suddenly, as if before an altar and said, 'Oh, my dear, you're so lovely.' Hungrily, he kissed her breasts, and Lily felt sensations pulse through her nipples as his tongue played over them. She felt confused. How could she feel pleasure in this when she had no love for this man?

'Lie on the bed – I must have you,' he ordered, and stood to undress himself, with great impatience, until she was confronted for the first time in her life by the sight of a naked man, fully aroused and kneeling over her. She found the sight of his body disturbing, the shadows round his belly and groin, his thick penis standing up, and she made a small sound of distress.

'Don't worry, my dear – I shall be gentle with you.

I'm not a monster. And remember, Lily, there will be no issue. There's no need to be afraid.'

But she could see that he was very aroused and he reached down so that she felt his fingers moving in the intimate parts between her legs and it was sore and made her gasp. He eased his fingers inside her and she lifted her body, moaning more from pain than pleasure, which excited him all the more.

'Oh, dear God, open up for me, Lily . . .' He moved urgently on top of her, pushing her legs apart and forcing his way into her so that she yelped at the burning pain it caused. The pain ebbed away but he felt so hard and strange moving in her, acutely excited by her. His bulk blocked out most of the light so that he was like a great shadow engulfing her and she was trapped under the weight of him as he groaned and thrust into her. It was soon over and he rolled to the side and took her passionately in his arms and to her surprise she found herself grateful for it. It was something new, to be held like that, as if she was loved and precious. Her chest began to ache, but she pushed any feelings away. It was no good thinking she could have any emotion about this. Look what had happened with Sam. She had been hurt almost beyond enduring and it was not going to happen again.

'Thank you,' Ewan McBride breathed into her hair. 'Thank you, my dearest love. Oh, you're mine now. My very own. You and I will have some times together, Lily, my love. Oh, we shall!'

Lily closed her eyes. She felt sore and stretched down below and all she could think, at that moment was, *I've survived it, then. It wasn't so bad.*

*

From then on, Dr McBride treated Lily as his lover. She dined with him every evening and he came to her room afterwards, almost nightly as well. He liked her to come to the study for dinner at exactly the same time every night and he was always waiting. One evening she was held up and a few minutes late and when she reached the doctor's study room he was standing just inside.

'Where have you been?' he demanded, and he seemed really worked up.

'Nowhere,' she said, puzzled. 'I just had to show Prithvi how to do something, that's all.

'Don't be late for me.' It was a mixture of plea and stern command. 'I don't like it. I can't stand it.'

So long as she did as he wanted, Lily saw this shy, unhappy man blossom in front of her eyes. This gave her a certain amount of satisfaction, that she could have such an effect on someone. And the doctor had quickly grown besotted with her, promising her all the things he would buy for her and places they would visit. He made her feel special, and adored, and Lily drank it in hungrily. Suddenly she felt powerful and excited. Sometimes she woke, alone in her bed, and wondered if she had dreamed the entire thing. How had this come about? And she did not know if it was a secret in the house. No one said anything, even Jane Brown, though they took tea together regularly and talked. Jane would be embarrassed to raise such a subject, of course, but Lily realized, too, that other than Prithvi, no one saw her very much with the doctor. Even so, she felt self-conscious.

One night, over dinner, she said, 'Ewan, whatever must the rest of the servants think, with me eating in here every night? Don't you worry about them telling your wife?'

The doctor sat back, lighting his pipe, looking contented and well fed.

'There's no need to worry, Lily. The only one who has any contact with Muriel is Jane Brown and she won't breathe a word even if she guesses. She'd be far too wary of upsetting her. She's a good woman, Jane is, if rather starchy. And you know,' he sat back, beaming at her across the table, 'apart from the question of Muriel, whom I obviously don't want to hurt, I find myself strangely indifferent to the idea of scandal. There's plenty of all sorts going on in Mussoorie, make no mistake. It's rather that kind of place. And too many people look for my help for them to condemn me. Blind eyes will be turned, you can be sure.' He reached across for her hand, speaking with great energy. 'I just want to *live*, Lily. God, I do. All this time, I feel as if I've been buried alive. And then you came along...' He smiled beatifically at her. 'Say I can come to you tonight, darling! Don't shut me out, will you?'

He had developed some fiction in his mind that Lily was the one who could decide whether to give or withhold her favours, when she felt now that in fact she had no choice.

Chapter Thirty-One

'Whoever's that?' Lily heard the gossip as she and Dr McBride swept in through the airy foyer of Mussoorie's Savoy Hotel. People didn't even trouble to lower their voices.

'It's that creature old McBride's been seen out and about with. Hadn't you heard? She's his housekeeper, I'm told, but my goodness, you can see what he sees in her! Fancy – you wouldn't have thought he had it in him, would you?'

'Well! You'd think he might be more discreet. Positively flaunting her! But she really is rather a looker, isn't she?'

The hotel was buzzing with one of the winter parties, walls festooned with green boughs, bows and baubles and the red glow of poinsettia leaves and holly, fires burning in the hearths, polished cutlery and glasses and crisp white cloths on tables laden with food and drink. Snow had fallen all across the hills outside, blanketing them in magical white and the mornings were bejewelled with icicles hanging from railings and roofs. The air was bitterly cold, breath streaming away white. On bright days the view across the hills was glittering clear, but when the fog came down, filling the valleys, everyone moved along the Mall and through the bazaars like spectres: *jhampanis* and women in saris, bearers with huge loads tied to their backs and mountain people in hats with ear-flaps appearing in silhouette out of the gloom.

It was warm and cosy inside the hotel, and loud with the sound of festive British chatter. Lily took off her wraps and shawls and they were whisked away by a smartly liveried servant.

'Come along, my dear,' Dr McBride said, taking Lily's arm. When they were out together he always seemed to want to be touching her, pulling her arm through his, or holding his hand in close contact with hers. He left no one in any doubt as to what their relationship was. And as they passed through the festive partygoers, soon finding themselves with glasses of sherry in their hands, he was greeted with cordiality but also a certain embarrassed reserve.

'Evening, McBride!' a short, whiskery man boomed at him. 'Nice to see you in circulation again, old man. Been a long time!'

'I say – Dr McBride!' This time a thin woman, with a harsh voice and inquisitive face. 'So glad to see you're still joining us, with your, er, friend! I don't believe we've been introduced?'

'This is Miss Lily Waters,' Dr McBride declared. He gave no other explanation. He knew they had been seen about together already and that the gossip was flying.

'Didn't I see the two of you at Kempty Falls a few weeks ago?' the woman shrilled. 'How very lovely it is there. So marvellous for an outing.' Lily had noticed, in all the time they had been out in public, that no one ever mentioned Muriel McBride, as if she and her condition were some kind of dirty and shameful secret.

'You may indeed have done,' Dr McBride agreed amiably. They had taken an afternoon out together to the waterfall, a beauty spot outside Mussoorie, in the glowing autumn sunshine, not long after Lily had become Dr McBride's lover. Since then they had gradually come to be seen out more and more in public.

'Lovely spot, isn't it?' the woman cooed to Lily. 'And I must congratulate you on your dress, my dear. What a marvellous design. You really are the belle of the ball tonight, I must say!'

Lily could hear the barbed tone of her voice, but she also knew that what the woman said was true. She had seen an entirely different side of the apparently austere doctor emerging. Ewan McBride liked to dress her himself, choosing the highest quality silks and velvets from stores in Mussoorie and Dehra Dun, even ordering items for her from emporia as far away as Bombay and Madras. He did have an eye for colour, and Lily discovered in herself a gift for adorning herself lavishly, flatteringly, which she had never realized before. Among her wardrobe she now had some of the most beautiful handiwork that India could offer, fashioned into European-style gowns: turquoise and gold silk from Benares, rich coloured mirror cloth from Rajasthan for a dress she had worn for the Hindu festival of Diwali – where the doctor had paraded her among the burning lights of scores of oil lamps and the firework display – Kashmiri embroidery and shawls, and dyed raw silks tailored by the best *dirzi* in the area.

Tonight she had on a long, sweeping gown in a rich cranberry and a delicate, cream, hand-embroidered pashmina. She had smoothed her hair up into a pleat and clipped tiny glass beads into it, rather as she had seen Susan Fairford wear hers, and put on Mrs Chappell's lovely brooch and seed pearls. The jewels glowed against her fresh skin. When she looked at herself in the glass she recognized that her pretty, rounded girlishness had matured into a feminine beauty which took even herself by surprise.

'Oh, my dear, you look quite out of this world.' Dr McBride seemed excited when he saw her. He stroked her cheek as if she were a marble statue. 'Oh, my Lily, you are so beautiful, my dearest child. You really have excelled yourself this time. Come now – are you ready?'

Lily realized that more and more people were starting to recognize her and that she and the doctor were becoming the talk of the town. As they went about the place some were scandalized, some kind, and some a mixture of the two. No one could fail to notice the doctor's transformation from a crusty old recluse to a cheerful socialite with the most beautiful and stylish woman in the room on his arm.

They were much less sure how to deal with Lily, though. As his consort, she smiled at the doctor's side, looking gorgeously attractive but being quiet and reserved. All her life she had never welcomed questions about her background or her past. She did not fit into a normal social mould in any case and now they were scandalizing such moulds by her acting blatantly as his mistress. The other women had to decide whether to be envious or to make a friend of her, but the doctor, it seemed, was indifferent.

'You don't need to worry,' he had said one evening as they rode along the moonlit Mall in a rickshaw on the way back from a party. In the distance Lily caught sight of the white peaks, lit by the moon. The doctor was in a relaxed mood after several whiskies. 'I've told you, I have high standing in the town and despite my outraging some of the more, let's say puritanical types, they'll just have to accept me. I've lived like a dead man

202

long enough. And besides, I've attended most of them at their bedsides over the years and they know it. They're grateful. So you don't need to be afraid. Why don't you just tell them about yourself? Come to that, why don't you tell *me*, to start with?'

'Oh, Ewan.' She rested her gloved hand on his and smiled at him. 'I've told you – there's nothing to say of any note. I'm a vicar's daughter who became a nanny and came to India. That's all.'

'Well,' he chuckled. 'You don't *behave* much like a vicar's daughter, I must say. Or perhaps you do.' He nuzzled his face up close to hers, searching out her lips. 'Perhaps they're the naughtiest of the lot!'

After he had kissed her he drew back and in the dim light she saw his face harden. 'You're not *fast*, are you?' His tone was nasty. 'Giving favours to anyone who asks?'

'*No!*' she said, appalled. What on earth made him say that? 'I'm not. You know I'm not!'

'Well, I hope so. Let's keep it that way, hm?' Lily was chilled by the tone of his voice. Every so often he had these little bouts of jealousy over things he imagined she might be doing. They were all in his mind, but she was stung by the way he talked to her.

She stayed at his side throughout the evening, eating some of the Anglo-Indian mix of food: mutton and poached salmon accompanied by chicken pilau and pickles. Lily was the doctor's decoration: the conversations, the decisions about where in the room they moved or sat, were all his. Sometimes one of the young women who had decided to be friendly would come up and talk to her and Lily found she enjoyed the company, but if Ewan McBride decided to move she would have to cut short her conversation. She had to sit with people he wanted to be with, who were usually older, and she was often bored, but she told herself this was the price she had to pay. It was her job. She had a fine life, lovely clothes and status as a beautiful woman to be looked at. The doctor had told her to cut down on her work in the house, to preserve her energy and keep her hands smooth and soft. She was barely more than his mistress now. But at times she felt terribly lonely and went to the kitchen to talk to Stephen and Prithvi. If it was not for them and Jane Brown her life would have been really very solitary.

She followed the doctor round the room, exchanging pleasantries. The party included some singing of Christmas carols round the piano, led by a plump woman in a crimson dress who was an accomplished player and good at jollying everyone along. The doctor steered Lily into the carousing huddle just as 'I Saw Three Ships' was coming to a lusty end with clapping and cries of, 'Encore!' and 'Marvellous. I say, it does make one long for home!' There was a moment of confusion during which someone pushed in and positioned himself somehow between Lily and the doctor, who had to step aside for politeness sake.

'How about "Good King Wenceslas"?' the pianist cried, and everyone joined in enthusiastically, except Lily, who had no idea of the words. She stood among the crowd, the air laced with smoke and whisky fumes, pretending to mouth the carol and hoping no one would notice. But someone did.

'Would one of these be any help?' a voice said close to her ear, and she turned to see a fair-haired young man in a well-cut suit smilingly offering her a sheet with some of the words on it and little drawings of bells and holly printed in the corners.

'Oh – thank you!' she said, startled. 'Is it so obvious I don't know it?'

'Oh no, not at all,' he assured her. 'I suppose I'm just rather good at lip-reading, that's all! What you're mouthing doesn't seem to correspond all that well. Nothing to worry about, though!'

He laughed so merrily that Lily could only join in as the group launched into, *'Hither, page, and stand by me . . .'* 'Thank you – I don't happen to know this one.'

She saw a puzzled expression come into his eyes, but he refrained from further comment at this odd gap in her education. One of so many, Lily thought. She had been skivvying for the Horne family instead of going to school.

'I'm Johnny Barstow,' he said, holding out his hand.

Lily shook hands, and as she did so, saw the doctor's gaze swivel towards them.

'Lily Waters.'

They were almost having to shout above the singing and he drew her aside a little. She saw that he was well built and very sprucely dressed. His jacket fitted beautifully.

'I've seen you about town, I'm sure,' Johnny said. 'Where do you live?'

'Kulri – near the end of Camel's Back.'

'Ah yes – a fine spot.' He was sipping from a glass of something dark and warm and saw her looking. 'Punch – have you not had some? Here – I'll snaffle you a glass.'

The two of them moved over to where a waiter was ladling out the hot punch and he handed her a glass. Lily sipped it and found it strong and fruity. It made her cough and Johnny laughed.

'Not used to that either, eh? Are you long in India?'

She told him a small amount about her time there, about Ambala.

'Ah yes – good old Umbala,' he said, pronouncing it the old way. 'Funny that – I spent a short time there. I'm an engineer – based at Meerut now, though I'm not army. I'm with the railways. But I always like to get up to our lovely Mussoorie whenever I can. Much better than stuffy old Simla. D'you know the place?'

'Yes,' Lily said, glad she knew something for once. 'We used to summer there, from Ambala.'

'Course, yes. Well, I like it here much better. Very jolly. Tell me – where are you from back home?'

Again, the questions, always questions, Lily thought. How inquisitive people were about each other! She did what she had always done and made up a story.

'Kent,' she said firmly. She wasn't sure why she had fixed so firmly on this version of events. After all, she had only been to Kent once, for her interview with Susan Fairford's sister, but it had felt a respectable place, far from Birmingham's industrial grime and her real childhood.

'How very nice – Garden of England,' Johnny smiled. 'I'm from Essex as a matter of fact. It's splendid to meet you, Lily. I should like to get to know you a great deal better.'

Lily decided she liked Johnny Barstow.

'I expect you've made a lot of friends here in Mussoorie?' he was asking, but she was saved from answering by the carol coming to an end and a sozzled cheer going up from the singers. In a second, Dr McBride was at her side.

'Lily?' His tone was civil, but commanding. 'I think it might be time for us to go home, don't you?'

Lily was a bit disappointed. 'Well, if you think . . .

I was just talking to Mr Barstow here. This is Johnny Barstow,' she introduced him. 'Dr McBride.'

'I think I could have managed to introduce myself,' Dr McBride snapped. It was only then that Lily realized he was trembling with barely controlled emotion.

'Good to meet you, Doctor,' Johnny said, holding his hand out. He had not noticed McBride's furious state. 'I was wondering if our friend would fancy a walk one day, out to Happy Valley perhaps? I'm sure I could arrange a chaperone?'

'I don't think that will be possible,' the doctor snapped. 'We need to be going now. Good evening to you.' He left Johnny Barstow staring after them, ushering Lily towards the door, his hand on her back. Lily just managed to shoot Johnny a regretful smile as they left. She had enjoyed talking with someone of her own age and thought him rather fun. She couldn't understand why the doctor had acted so jealously and hustled her away. Soon they were dressed again in their warm hats and shawls for the ride home. It was snowing lightly outside.

No sooner had the *jhampani* begun to haul the rickshaw away through the snow than the doctor began speaking in tones of icy fury.

'I can't imagine what you thought you were doing in there, young lady!' he spat at her. 'Flaunting yourself like that in so unbecoming a way, I was embarrassed to witness it!'

Lily felt as if she had been slapped. Whatever was he talking about? Up until now, Ewan McBride had been possessive of her, it was true, and he liked to dress her and say where they would go and when, but she had never experienced a reaction like this before.

'I'm sorry,' she gasped, careful not to enrage him any

207

further. She remembered what Mr Horne had been like. You had to calm them down, men who were like that. 'I don't think I was flaunting myself, dear, I was just having a polite little conversation.'

'*Dear?*' He said mockingly. 'Calling me *dear* now, are we? Oh, we are the biddable little miss when it suits, aren't we? When it comes to being taken out and about and having the best finery to wear. You certainly know how to use a man, don't you, Lily? How to play with my heart?'

Lily felt disorientated and a little scared. Whatever had come over him?

'I'm sorry,' she said contritely, even though she didn't really know what she was supposed to be sorry about. 'I don't really understand what I've done to offend you, Ewan, dear. But I apologize from the bottom of my heart. There's no need for you to be like this, really there isn't.'

'Isn't there?' His jealous rage was not over yet. 'How do I know I can trust you? I can't be sure you're not going to give yourself to every holidaying officer in town, can I? Not after tonight, the way I saw you carrying on. After all, you're cheap enough to give yourself to me, aren't you? Parading about like a lady when in truth you're nothing but a little whore.'

Lily felt a rage rise up in her so strong that she wanted to slap his face at such an accusation. My God, the injustice of it, after the pressure he'd put her under! But she also felt cheap. Was that it, she was really a cheap whore? Whatever the case, if she lost her temper all would be undone. She took a long, slow breath, soft handfuls of her shawl clenched in her hands and said calmly, 'Ewan, you really have made a mistake. The young man in there only handed me a carol sheet and was fetching me a drink. We had scarcely said more than a few words to each other. And if you think I would throw away all your love and care for me, and mine for you in such a brief time, then you really are jumping to conclusions and giving yourself pain for nothing.'

By the time they got home she had talked him round and he was in a fever of shame and contrition for his outburst.

'Let me come to you tonight,' he breathed, as soon as they were inside the house. 'I've got to have you. To make things right again.'

He made love to her that night in a hurried, frantic way, and when he climaxed he fell on her, weeping.

'I didn't mean it, Lily, my love,' he sobbed, close to her ear. 'I'm sorry. I didn't mean to say those things. It's just that I love you so much. I worship you, my darling, my princess ... I couldn't bear to lose you. And seeing you with a younger man – it makes me feel wild, jealous ...'

He begged her to let him stay all night with her and soon he was sleeping beside her, his limbs and sex limp after the drink and exertion. Lily held up the candle before she blew it out and looked down at his wide, bearded face. It was almost a handsome face, with a grandeur to it. Lily tried to decide what she felt for him. Did she love him, could she? But there was no warm feeling in her, only detachment and a crumb of pity. She had seen him in a frightening new light that night and felt very uneasy, despite his tears and apologies. Perhaps it was the drink, she thought. But he drank most nights and this had never happened before.

Blowing out the candle she lay down to sleep as the snow fell gently outside, blanketing the roof. She felt very alone and a little frightened.

Chapter Thirty-Two

The winter passed in a whirl of social events. Lily found herself at the centre of British Mussoorie's wealthy social life of parties, evenings of singing, dancing and of plays. She even acted in one, persuaded by some of women who were most friendly to her. She did not have many lines, and was dressed in Japanese costume which the other women told her suited her.

'Just right for you, Lily, when you're so silent and *mysterious*! *Do* tell more about yourself. We're all so keen to know you.'

But Lily smiled and blushingly gave her usual reply, that there was nothing very much to tell and she wasn't at all interesting.

There were many late nights in the colourful, warm rooms of hotels and Mussoorie mansions, among the chattering socialites, the colourful gowns and shawls of the women, smoke from the cheroots and pipes of the men, plenty of drink flowing and the aroma of cardamom and cumin from dishes of rice and chicken, the silent servants. Lily learned to drink just a little but never too much. The evenings ended with the late-night rickshaw journeys back along the Mall in the moonlight, and this became, as time passed, the occasion when Dr McBride let loose the recriminations he had been storing up all evening. After the jolly farewells to other guests as they all piled into their rickshaws, Lily and the doctor would perch side by side on the narrow seat, a blanket wrapped round their knees and for a brief time there would be silence. Then, explosively, he would begin. The last time it was, 'I saw you rubbing yourself up against that Barstow lout again. You really do have to go out of your way to make an exhibition of yourself, don't you?' His voice came down on her like a hammer. He never looked at her during these outbursts, but stared icily ahead of him.

As usual, when he started, Lily felt herself go cold and detached inside. Any small beginnings of tenderness for him, the idea that she might even learn to love this man, had been frozen out of her when his jealous behaviour began the night she first met Johnny Barstow. She had had very little to do with Johnny but the doctor behaved as if she was in some way closely involved with Johnny and was trying to provoke him. All she wanted, in her few conversations with Johnny, was friendship with someone closer to her own age. And in any case, Johnny would be gone soon, back to Meerut.

'Your behaviour disgusts me.' The doctor ground out the words. 'I've given you everything, and look at the way you just hurl it back at me. No gratitude or loyalty! But what can you expect from a cheap street girl. That's what you are, isn't it? A cheap bitch who'll go with anyone for her own gain, to get what she wants ...'

'But Ewan, I haven't *done* anything,' Lily protested as calmly as she could. She had learned not to let herself feel anything. 'And you know I haven't really. Why do you keep accusing me like this?' She tried to humour him, to bring him out of this black mood. You know you only get upset when you start like this. Don't do it – just take my hand and we'll be friends again.'

'Don't touch me!' he roared at her. 'Your filthy hand you've touched *him* with!'

'But I never . . .'

'I didn't ask you to argue with me! You're my servant – you will not speak to me like that!'

His voice boomed along the street. He was slipping out of control and Lily was sure the other rickshaw riders along the Mall must hear them. She sank into silence. It was no good arguing. Why did he imagine all these things about her? Was he mad? But she found now that she didn't care what he imagined. She just wanted to keep him calm so that he didn't hurt her. What would come next was becoming familiar. She would go silently to her room, where he would follow, sometimes still angry, sometimes already full of remorse. Tonight when he appeared, his face in the candlelight looked distraught.

'Lily, my love, my darling!' He sounded almost like a child. 'Oh God, I'm so sorry. I don't know why I said those things – I wasn't myself. I must have had too much to drink. Oh, my little girl, don't look at me like that. Let me love you – come here, let me have you, my darling.'

He was urgently aroused and Lily, indifferently, let him take her while she lay looking at the ceiling waiting for it to be over. At first his lovemaking had given her a certain amount of pleasure. Now she had no feeling or openness to him. She let him use her and that was that. And soon he came with an emotional cry and murmured, 'Oh, my little love. Things are well again now. They are, aren't they?' And he sank into sleep.

*

During those winter months, while the town was covered in snow, Muriel McBride still clung somehow to her fragile life, shut away from view. The doctor visited her solicitously at his usual times during the day and occasionally Lily saw her and heard reports through Jane Brown.

Though she and Jane were still friends, Lily felt very distant from her. She had been pulled more and more into Dr McBride's orbit, and he was demanding of her time. And while she did see Jane and spent some cosy times drinking tea in one or other of their rooms, Lily knew there were a great many things she could not speak to Jane about. She wondered what Jane Brown thought of her. It must, she assumed, be very obvious what her position had become in the household, but the young nurse never said a word about it.

One afternoon when Jane invited her in, Lily felt she really must say something.

'Cold, isn't it?' Jane remarked as she let Lily into her colourful room. She had a fire burning in the grate. 'I'll be glad when the snow goes now. Would you like tea?'

'Yes, please,' Lily said.

As ever, they talked about day-to-day things for a time, but when there was a short silence, Lily said, flushing, 'I know you must disapprove.'

Jane raised one of her thick eyebrows. In her calm voice, she said, 'Of what, exactly, Lily?'

'Of me . . . Of this . . . Of my . . .' She wrestled for the words. 'The way Dr McBride . . . behaves towards me.'

Jane Brown looked steadily at her as if considering what to say. Then she looked away and stared into the fire. She was quiet for some time and Lily began to regret speaking. At last, in her quiet way, Jane Brown said, 'What Dr McBride does is not my affair. All I'd say to you, Lily, is be careful. He seems to be in a rather . . . excitable state.'

Lily looked at Jane Brown's solid, quiet figure. *What do you mean?* she was longing to ask. But she could see that Jane Brown was not prepared to say any more.

More and more, it seemed that Ewan McBride could not bear to let Lily out of his sight. On the evenings when they were not going out to some social event, he would demand that she dine with him. In the secluded study, once Prithvi had served them their meal, he talked to her as they ate. He poured out all his memories of his Scottish childhood spent in Currie, about his younger brother Duncan who had drowned in a river. Sometimes he wept as he talked about his school, the church they attended, his father's humiliation there when his mother was caught in a liaison with a man from the town who was not a churchgoer and who already had a wife. Lily listened, night after night, to his talk, to memories and rage and sorrow. She was relieved that he did not ask her to lay out her past. But she also came to see that he didn't need to know about her, not as she really was. He needed her to be a blank, a mirror for him, to give him back everything he needed.

Sometimes he sat beside her just staring at her, stroking her thick, chestnut hair as if she was a statue he had acquired.

'You're the most beautiful thing I've ever seen,' he said and sometimes tears would come into his eyes. 'I just want to be with you always, Lily – to look at you, to know you're mine,' he kept saying. 'Don't ever leave me, will you? I think I'd go mad. I know I would.'

Before, when he stroked her like that and gazed at her, it had made her feel flattered and admired. Now, though, she felt empty. Sometimes it seemed as if he didn't see her at all, but instead something he had created in his own mind.

The evenings invariably ended in her bed and she lay awake long after he had fallen asleep, looking up into the darkness in lonely silence.

Still, she reasoned, she had had worse times in her life. And she could not seem to see out from it any more. She couldn't imagine anything else.

Chapter Thirty-Three

The Mussoorie snows melted at last, the sun grew warmer and delicate flowers appeared in abundant, pale sprays down the hillsides. However, while spring had arrived, the doctor's moods had darkened.

One morning, when icy streams and waterfalls were rushing the last of the mountain snows down the steep slopes, Lily walked along, drinking in the sight of the hillside glittering green after all the snow. Birds called and fluttered among the branches and all nature seemed to smile, reawakened. The air felt warm and hopeful and Lily took in deep breaths, freeing herself from the constrained feeling she now had all the time in the house. She thought of the mighty sweep of the mountain range on whose hem she was walking, its giant ripple of the earth's crust extending across to Kashmir, Nepal, Tibet, the awesome white wilderness she had heard of so often, and it gave her a sense of exhilarating freedom. She realized, as she moved even faster, almost wanting to break into a run, just how much this winter she had become a puppet who had to dance all the time to a tune played by the doctor. And for these precious moments she could be free of it, could regain a sense of herself. These times made it bearable, standing out on the sunny Mussoorie hillside, when she felt free and young again, and as she made her way back into the house she was smiling.

He was standing in a dark corner of the hall. She saw the dog Cameron before she saw him, coming to greet her out of the shadows.

'And where exactly have you been, missy?'

Lily jumped, laying a hand over her thumping heart. 'I . . . I've been out for a little walk.' She used the low, taming voice she had learned to use with Ewan McBride when he was like this. 'It's so lovely now spring's coming.'

He approached her, and she could see he was tense with rage. 'You went out, alone, without asking me?'

Lily could hear Mrs Das moving about further along the corridor, but the doctor seemed too overwrought to care who heard him.

'I'm sorry, dear,' she said softly. 'But you weren't here. It doesn't do any harm, going out to take the air for a few minutes, surely?'

'Who did you meet?' His hands gripped her shoulders and he brought his face close up to hers, breathing his tobacco breath in her face. She could see where the hairs of his beard entered his skin. 'You're going out to meet someone, aren't you? Behaving like a little whore again. *Tell* me!' He squeezed her so hard that she yelped. Here again were all the accusations he was forever throwing at her. She breathed in deeply, quelling her urge to shout at him, *Of course I'm not meeting other people! How do you expect me to when you keep me here like a prisoner!* But she must not shout: it would be a disaster.

'My dear, I . . .'

'Your *dear*!' She thought for a moment he was going to slap her. His nostrils were flaring, his breath fast and shallow. 'You little hypocrite. You don't care for me! You're just after everything you can squeeze out of me

217

while you torture my heart with your wanton behaviour, running after other men, younger men, to make me feel old and of no value to you. That's all you can think about isn't it – showing yourself off to other men while I rot here, all alone . . .'

Very quickly his rages sank him into misery, so that sometimes he wept in her arms, full of remorse and self-pity.

'Shall we go into your study so that the servants don't hear?' Lily suggested and took his hand. 'Come along, dear.' She led him like a child. 'Everything will be all right.'

As they walked along the corridor she calculated that the most dangerous moments were over. He had begun to hit her, just once or twice. Both times he had caught her on the arm, where the bruises did not show, but she was afraid of worse and constantly alert for his more violent moods. And she knew how to pacify him. It was an instinct deep in her from her years with Mr Horne, from trying to be whatever other people needed her to be. Once they were in the study with the door shut, he started to weep in earnest, sinking down on his chair beside the desk.

'Oh God, one day I'm going to hurt you, Lily. I don't know what comes over me!' She tried to quiet him, her hands on his shoulders, looking down at the thinning crescents of hair at the top of his head. She saw that her hands were bonier than they used to be.

'I'm not a violent man – never have been. It's something you do to me. You're like a demon – you've possessed me, body and soul, woman! I can't bear to think of you with anyone else. It would tear me apart – do you understand?' He turned to face her, full of anxiety. 'I don't mean to hurt you, my dear. I wouldn't harm you for the world. But when I think of you leaving me, of you in another man's arms, it's as if I'm blinded . . . Can you forgive me?'

'Of course,' Lily said, mechanically. She tried to make her voice warm and forgiving, though she felt nothing.

'Do you, my dear – really?' Now he was almost like a child.

'Come – sit on my lap, my sweet, and give your foolish old man a kiss.'

Lily slid round on to his lap and he pulled her close, hands moving greedily on her body. Over his shoulder she looked out at the sunlight slanting over the hills, her mind out on the paths and tracks bright with flowers. Dr McBride was already highly aroused and Lily knew she was not going to get away with just a quick embrace to put things right for him. His hard penis was pressing against her and his breathing was fast and urgent.

'God, woman, I need you!' His breath was hot on her neck and he began fumbling to unfasten his clothes. He gestured towards her and she knew he meant her to remove her underclothes and she obeyed, knowing she must be quick or she would summon another of his rages.

He beckoned to her to straddle him, and he groaned and sighed as he found release and afterwards he clung to her.

'Don't ever go away from me, my Lily,' he murmured. 'Don't ever leave me.'

Chapter Thirty-Four

There was a period, in the February, when Muriel McBride revived for a time and was able to sit up. Lily saw the transformation in Jane Brown as well, a lightness and sense of hope, that she was not necessarily party to an inexorable and tragic slide downwards to death. Lily saw her smile more, and she even became rather humorous in her dry way.

'Mrs McBride would like to see you,' she said to Lily one afternoon when they were in the kitchen again. 'That is, of course, if you're not too busy.'

Lily could see the twinkle in Jane Brown's eye.

'I think I could manage to fit it in,' Lily quipped. 'But why on earth does she want to see me?'

'Oh, I expect she'd just like a change from looking at me all day long.'

Both of them laughed, and exchanged an unusually fond look. Whatever Jane Brown knew or thought, Lily realized, she was not one to sit in judgement.

'I'll come and see her today,' she promised.

She went to the sickroom and found Muriel McBride propped up on pillows, looking out at the sunlit view. As Lily came in, she smiled. There was a strange down of fair hair on her cheeks and her skeletal form seemed thin enough to let the light through. She didn't look any more substantial, but she did seem to have a fraction more energy.

'Come and sit by me, Lily,' she said in her reedy voice. She raised one of her stick-like arms to gesture to a chair and Lily saw the blue veins under her skin.

Lily obeyed. Jane Brown hovered in the background tidying up and Lily liked her being there. The room was light this afternoon, seeming more cheerful, and Lily felt her own spirits lift. She only occasionally realized how much the sad presence of this sick woman dampened the atmosphere of the house.

They talked a little about Muriel's health, though she seemed hardly to acknowledge that she was ill. It was almost like something separate from her that she had no interest in.

'I'm quite all right really,' she said, closing down Lily's enquiries. 'Nothing much to say about it. I must say, Lily, you are looking rather thin and tired. Are you all right?'

'Yes, perfectly, thank you,' Lily said, though Mrs McBride was not the first person to comment on her loss of weight. 'I feel very well.'

She tried to think of a few things to say about her work, even though Dr McBride no longer liked to think of her as employed as housekeeper any more. And she said how lovely it was outside now the weather was changing. It was a friendly conversation, but after a time she saw Muriel McBride still looking rather intently at her with her huge blue eyes.

'I wanted to say something to you, Lily.' She paused and Lily could feel Jane Brown listening somewhere behind her. 'Just to mention that my husband is a man who can tend to run to extremes. Over the years I have seen a number of people affected by it. Just be careful.' These last words were spoken very sadly. Then she looked up, sharply. 'By that I don't want you to think I mean myself. What I have done, I have done to myself. I can't help it, not now. But it's no fault of Ewan's. You, though, Lily – you don't have to stay here. You are free.'

For some reason the words brought tears to Lily's eyes. She did not understand why and she looked down for a moment in confusion, her cheeks burning.

After that, they talked about ordinary things again.

You are free. The words stayed with her, like birds fluttering in her head. She did not feel free, not at all. Every part of her day was hedged in by Ewan McBride, by his need to parade her in public in her finery, his demand for her in bed, and by his rages if he thought she was running out of his control, until she felt like a prisoner in the house. One day, when he was out on his rounds, Lily was about to slip out for a walk when Jane Brown came out of the sickroom, looked hurriedly back and forth and beckoned Lily to her. In a low, urgent whisper, she said, 'Lily, I feel terrible saying this, but he's told me not to let you go out.'

Lily, who had been buttoning her blue velvet coat in readiness for a walk, gaped in disbelief. 'Dr McBride? But he hasn't said anything to me.'

'He says he doesn't want you going out unless you're accompanied by either me or himself. He knows perfectly well that I'm not free to accompany you any-way ...' The words were left unspoken. In other words Lily was not allowed out at all without the doctor.

'But I *have* to go out. I can't just stay in here all day!'

'Yes, I know,' Jane Brown said, her eyes troubled. 'But I'm just warning you. I didn't see you go.'

Lily went out anyway, slipping quietly along to her favourite spot along the Camel's Back Road, but she felt very shaken. More and more often she had reason to feel afraid of Ewan McBride. For the first time she thought seriously about leaving, but the idea of having to start in yet another strange place was so wearying, just when she had made friends here and felt, at least in some ways, secure.

So far he had not found out about her morning walks and they were her one piece of real freedom. She could settle for this, she decided, at least for the moment. She had grown to love Mussoorie very much, seeing its beauty in all the seasons.

One day, she thought, I'll get out of here, but not yet. What she was not prepared for was a change that was approaching even as she stood looking out over the valley that day, one which would turn her life upside down all over again.

Lily was in her room that morning, and as it happened she was writing a letter to Cosmo. He wrote to her, very occasionally now, telling her about rugby and cricket and about boys whose faces she would never know. Though she tried to tell herself that Cosmo had not grown into a stranger, in sad moments she wondered if she would even recognize him now he was almost seven. Of course she would, she told herself. She kept the photograph of herself taken with him on her dressing table.

She heard, distantly, the knock at the front of the house but ignored it. Mrs Das or Prithvi could deal with it and she took no notice of the voices in the distance. But in a moment there was a tap on her door.

'Miss Lily?' It was Prithvi, standing outside with her usual air of apology. 'There is a man,' she said. 'He is asking for you.'

Lily frowned. No one ever came calling at the house for her. She did not have that sort of social life.

'Well who is it, Prithvi?'

'I do not know, Miss Lily. But he is asking for you by name.'

She walked along to the hall and saw a man standing, looking down at his feet as she approached, hat in hand. Hearing her step he looked up, and it was only then she knew him. Her walking stopped, abruptly.

'Lily? It *is* you.' His voice was gentle, wondering.

There again, with no warning: Sam Ironside.

Chapter Thirty-Five

'Oh Lord, why are you here?' she heard herself say.

Sam stepped towards her. He looked just the same, as if he had never been away. The three years since she last saw him evaporated and in those seconds she wanted to pour out all the things she had never been able to say to him, but it was impossible. Her chest felt tight, as if she'd been running.

'Lily?' He stood before her, seeming unable to say any more either, his eyes searching her face. And then he retreated into formality. 'I hope you don't mind my calling.'

'We must get away from here.' It was the first thing she could think of. She could not let Dr McBride come home and find her here talking to another man, let alone one who meant so much to her.

'Well, if that's what you'd like,' Sam said, startled by the urgency in her voice. 'Whatever's convenient.'

'We must go – quickly . . .' Frantic, she snatched up her coat and hat and hurriedly put them on, words tumbling from her lips. 'We'll go along the Camel's Back Road. I walk there often and it's fairly quiet. He won't come there but we must be back by midday . . .'

She saw Sam looking strangely at her and when she'd led him, half running, up the steps out of the garden and turned right along the path, he stopped her, putting a hand on her arm, in a way which felt so familiar she almost wanted to weep.

'Lily, what's the matter? You seem in such a state – all nerves, and so pale and thin! Not like before. What are you so frightened about?'

It was only then that she felt how true that was, how overwrought was her constant state living with the McBrides and how frightened she was of the doctor. But she couldn't begin to put this into words.

'I'm not in an easy situation here in some ways,' she said abruptly. She still felt they were too near the house and she wanted to stop him asking difficult questions. 'Let's walk on. Why are you here? To deliver another motor car?'

'Yes – to the Fairfords again. He wanted the latest model ... The thing is, they're here, Lily. Staying in a house about a mile away. It was all rather sudden. I asked after you, of course, and they said you were up here. And it was Mrs Fairford – she suggested that they come here instead of going to Simla. I don't think she's all that keen on Simla and she wanted a change, and she said she'd like to see you. She's very taken with the way you've kept up the contact with young Cosmo all this time. I rather think she misses you.'

'Yes, I hear from her now and then,' Lily said. 'I missed her when I first came here, and Cosmo, of course, but I haven't missed Ambala and the cantonment life much. You can see why they all want to get away from it.'

'It seems very nice here.' Sam looked across at the scene unfolding to their right from the Camel's Back Road. 'This is a beautiful place. My goodness, it is.'

They walked for a moment in silence. Lily was wearing a skirt in dark red wool. She became acutely aware of everything: the movement of her skirt, the sounds of their boots on the path, of the astonishing fact of Sam here beside her after all this time, his left hand at his side, so close, and of the huge, longing ache which rose in her which she knew she must suppress.

'How is your wife?' she asked, sharply.

'She's well, thank you. Yes, going along all right.'

'And children?' She didn't look at him, but ahead, at the gateway to the cemetery which they were approaching, with its monsoon-stained paint.

'Yes. We have two daughters, Ann and Nancy.' Sam's tone was stiff, as if somehow he did not want to give her the information.

'How old?' She wanted to drill him, to make him suffer, yet she knew it would be herself who suffered the most from hearing about his family.

'Ann is two and a half, Nancy just over a year.' He did not look at her, but peered at the plaque inside the cemetery gatehouse: *MDCCCXXVIII – I am the Resurrection and the Life.*

'And do they look like you?' She glanced at him then, those familiar, intent eyes, the dark moustache. How close she had once been to every detail of him. A kind of tremor went through her, remembering the feel of his body as they had held each other. *Stop it*, she raged at herself. *It should never have happened.* They were passing the grounds of the cemetery on their right and both of them instinctively walked towards the fence and leaned on it.

'Ann does, yes. Nancy favours her mother.' They looked down at the stone crosses and angels among the tall conifers, sunlight shining between the branches and white flowers scattered like stars in the grass.

'And what does her mother look like?' Lily was

relentless. She knew she was being hostile, but she couldn't manage the hurt she felt any other way.

'She's . . . Well, her hair is sort of, I suppose you'd call it toffee-coloured . . .' He was tremendously uncomfortable, she could see. For a moment he stared ahead of him, tapping one hand on the fence in an agitated way. Then abruptly he turned to her.

'Lily, for God's sake – I had to come and see you. Don't keep on like this!'

'Like what? I'm asking about your family, that's all. The family you somehow didn't think to tell me about the last time you were here.'

She didn't meet his eyes. A lump had come up in her throat which made it hard to speak and her cheeks were aflame. How humiliating to show this emotion, all the feelings that had erupted back up in her that she hoped she had long ago laid to rest.

'I know,' Sam said wretchedly. The long pent-up words poured out of him. 'It was wrong of me – utterly wrong. But I was in love with you, Lily . . . So in love in a way I'd never been before – and never have been in my life apart from with you. You bring out feelings in me which no one else . . . I *had* to get to know you, had to love you. If I'd told you then you would never have had anything to do with me, would you? It would have been terrible . . .'

'And it's been terrible ever since!' It came out in an anguished wail, and she found she was overtaken by sobs, quite unable to hold back. She put her hands over her face, her shoulders shaking. 'Oh God, Sam, I wish I'd never met you so I didn't know how it was possible to feel . . .'

'Oh, Lily . . . Lily, my sweet love . . .'

She moved her hands away from her cheeks, which

were running with tears, and saw the anguish on his face.

'My lovely Lily. I just ... I didn't know what to do, to say ... You were so angry and I knew I'd done wrong. When you left the house in the *tonga* that day I felt as if I was being torn apart ...' He seemed about to weep too, but controlled himself.

'I married Helen because I thought I loved her. I've tried to be true. I've been a good husband in every other way – we don't go short. We have our children, our house ...' He stopped and drew in a deep breath. 'And not a day goes by when I don't think of you, Lily. I told myself it would wear off, that I'd forget – you know, knuckle down, get on with my work ... But it's been like that ever since I left, and I try ... The thought of you is like an *ache* that I can never seem to lose.' Daring to move closer, he put his hand on her shoulder and said helplessly, 'You're the woman I love. But ... in another way it's all wrong! I'm married, responsibilities ... I just don't know what to do. I just love you – that's all I know.'

'Oh, Sam!' Lily felt her hurt and anger melt away in the face of his sadness and her heart was filled with tenderness. She drank in the sight of him, so full of sorrow and so lovely to her. 'I was so hurt, so sure you'd deceived me just to play with me, as if I was a little diversion while you were away from home. And I didn't want to believe that because I felt so much for you. But you were married – what was I to think?'

'I don't know.' He took his cap off and rubbed his head as if to try and order his thoughts. 'You couldn't have thought any different. How could you know whether to trust me? And why should you have trusted me when I wasn't telling you the truth?' He replaced his hat and looked into her eyes. 'I'm so sorry. You have my heart, Lily. But even now . . .'

'You're still married,' she finished for him, soberly.

'But, my God, I don't *want* to be, not to her.' There was great sadness and regret in his voice. 'Seeing you again . . . Oh, my love, you're really here . . .'

He was looking down at her, seeming about to kiss her when a giggling group of Indian girls from one of the local schools came past, dressed in red and navy-blue uniforms. Lily and Sam turned and looked down over the cemetery again until the children had moved on.

'I mustn't be long,' Lily said, remembering with a jolt of panic. For those moments Dr McBride had seemed like another life. But here she was and he was horribly real.

'You seem so nervous. What's wrong?' Sam was concerned.

'Nothing.' How could she say what her status was in the McBride household? A servant-cum-mistress, to be controlled and used? For that was the truth of it and she saw now how she had let herself slide down and down into it. 'It's just that they're very particular about punctuality.'

He was staring at her, as if he could still scarcely believe she was here. 'God, girl . . .'

'How long are you staying?' she asked. Suddenly she was excited. It would be lovely to see the Fairfords as well! She would hear more of Cosmo.

'I'll be here for two weeks. I expect Mrs Fairford and Isadora will be staying during the heat. That'll be nice for you, won't it? They said to ask you to call in as soon as you can. Can you get away? You have time off, I take it.'

Lily's mind was working fast. The one thing the doctor must not find out on any account was that she was meeting Sam. But she knew that if she said the Fairford family were here in Mussoorie and she would be visiting Mrs Fairford, that would be just about acceptable, unless he was in an especially difficult or demanding mood, when nothing she did except giving him her full and slavish attention would do.

'Oh yes – of course I'll come! I'd like to see Mrs Fairford very much.'

'And me . . . ?'

'Oh, Sam.' Her eyes were full of pain as she looked up at him. 'Have you come to break my heart all over again?'

With great solemnity he said, 'No, Lily. No. I've come to be with the woman I love, and have loved ever since I saw her.'

And uncaring of who might be watching, he took her in his arms and kissed her passionately.

Chapter Thirty-Six

Lily lay awake much of that night. The doctor had left her alone, to her enormous relief, but she felt as if her heart had been broken open and her emotions were raw and strong. Sam Ironside loved her and she loved him, and she was so full of tremulous joy, as well as fear and disquiet about what that might mean, that she could hardly bear even to lie down. All she could think of was his face, his words of love to her. Her body was full of restless energy and in the small hours she got up and walked around the room trying to quiet herself.

The most immediate worry was how she was going to see anything of Sam without the doctor finding out. The very thought of her anywhere near another man would send him into a jealous rage.

And then a miracle happened. Before he went out to his surgery the next morning, Dr McBride said, 'I've had a wire from an old friend, Duncan McCluskie – he trained with me in Edinburgh. He's doing a spot of work in Patna for a few months and he's coming up to pay a visit. He'll be arriving at about tiffin time. So things will be different for a few days, Lily. I shan't be able to spend as much time with you, I'm afraid. You'll have to find ways to amuse yourself.'

Lily felt her eyes widen and had to suppress a grin of astonished delight. She seized her chance immediately.

'I'm sorry to hear that,' she said, trying to look sober

and talking in the quiet, careful way she always used with him now. 'But perhaps it's a happy chance. You see, I heard yesterday that the family I worked for in Ambala are staying here in Mussoorie and I was going to ask you if I might visit and spend some time with them.' She couched the request very humbly. 'Would that be all right, while you have a visitor yourself?'

'This is Captain Fairford's family, I take it?' he asked. There was an edge of suspicion but he seemed in a good humour. 'Who will be there, d'you suppose?'

'So far as I know, just the captain and his wife and daughter and a handful of servants,' Lily said. 'And I should very much like to see Mrs Fairford and Isadora, their daughter. I spent a lot of time with them, you see.'

Dr McBride seemed reassured. He came and gave her a fatherly pat on the shoulder, then kissed her on the lips, forcing his tongue into her mouth. 'That sounds like a nice little holiday for you, my dear, to spend time with your old mistress. And you deserve a little break. You'll be here at nights, of course, if I need you.'

'Of course,' Lily agreed, her heart soaring with excitement. She could hardly believe how easily he seemed to accept the thought of her going out, and realized it was because he saw no threat to his control. 'Things will be just as normal, dear.'

When it came to meeting Sam again later that morning, as she had arranged to do, Lily was full of misgiving. She felt shy of meeting him, as if they would have to break the ice again.

She wore a favourite dress stitched in raw silk of kingfisher blue and a blue hat to match. The costume looked very striking set against her sultry colouring and she saw Sam react to the sight of her. He was waiting just where she had asked him to, at the corner of the road leading up into Kulri Bazaar. There was a strong smell of frying onions and spices in the spring air and she breathed in happily, catching sight of Sam standing, looking rather self-conscious on the corner, beside a cow with sharp horns that was trying to nibble his sleeve.

'I'm glad you've come to rescue me – I think she has taken too much of a shine to me altogether!'

Lily laughed, as the cow moved away with an affronted slouch.

'God, Lily—' Sam looked at her closely then, seeming awed. 'You're so beautiful. You look astonishing.'

Lily felt herself light up at the sight of him. Her eyes met his, and the bustle of the streets around them seemed to disappear. All she could see was him and she was filled with a soaring happiness.

'I can't believe you're here,' she said, feeling her voice catch. 'I keep thinking you'll just disappear again.'

'I've got ten whole days. The captain said we might as well do the necessary with the car while he was in the hills. It's good for putting her through her paces up here.' He paused, then said, 'Are you free to come up to the house?'

As she walked beside him towards the Mall, Lily kept stealing glances at him. *He's here. Sam's really here, walking beside me.* It was a miracle.

The bungalow which the Fairfords had rented nestled into the side of Gun Hill, along a path off the main one up to the top. Lily climbed up the familiar, steep slope, and what joy to have Sam beside her, not Ewan McBride with Cameron plodding along behind! It was quiet this morning, and they passed very few other walkers.

'I've walked up here so many times,' she said, pausing to catch her breath and looking across at the valley, the green hills with a scattering of houses tucked between the trees. 'I never once thought I'd walk up here with you.'

'I know. It's heaven.' He turned to her and took her hand, lifting it to his lips to kiss it. She saw that he was moved, and it brought tears to her eyes.

'I've tried my best with Helen, my very best, but she's not you, Lily. I've tried not to let myself see it, or feel it. I just keep on, work hard every day, don't think about anything deeply. Then, before Christmas, they told me I was doing another delivery to Ambala and it brought it all rushing back, brought *you* back, stronger than ever. I didn't know if you were there any more, but I knew I couldn't come back to India and not try to find out, to see you again if you were here.'

She listened, moved, all the hurt of the past years forgotten.

'When you left, I think I hated you,' she said. 'You lied to me – or at least you didn't tell me all the truth. I'd never loved anyone – not the way I did you. And do still.'

His eyes registered her words. He glanced around to see that they were alone before leaning down, intensely serious, and kissing her, pulling her close. After a time he drew back, smiling down at her.

'I've got the motor parked in a garage up at the other end.' Sam pointed to the Library end of the Mall. 'I think I might be able to take it out one day. We could go somewhere, just us together. Who's going to worry about all the rules up here?'

Lily's immediate thought was the doctor. How would she ever get away for the day? She decided she really didn't care; she'd find a way.

'That sounds like heaven,' she said, as they climbed the path at the front of the Fairfords' yellow holiday bungalow, outside which there were neat flower beds and a wooden sign by the path which said 'Zinnias'.

Srimala, Isadora's *ayah*, opened the door. She seemed just the same, and with a cry of delight she flung her arms round Lily's neck.

'Oh, Miss Lily! I am so happy to see you again!' She stood back in the doorway, wiping tears of joy from her eyes and looked Lily up and down. 'I have missed you very much. I wish you were still with us! But you are looking so very lean and tired – not like the Lily we knew before. Are you sick?'

'No,' Lily laughed. She felt more relaxed now than she had in weeks. 'I am quite well, really I am.'

They were in the hall, a sparsely decorated space with two cane chairs and a table and a coloured rug on the floor. Just then Susan Fairford appeared, her expression set into its customary cool formality which made her seem very distant. Lily felt chilled by it and said politely, 'How do you do, Mrs Fairford?'

'Lily—' Susan Fairford was about to hold out her hand as she would to an acquaintance, but as she came closer her face softened and she smiled prettily. 'It's so very nice to see you again,' she said, and leaned to kiss Lily on the cheek. Then, to Lily's surprise, briefly, she put her arms round her and when she drew back there were tears in her eyes. She wiped them away hurriedly. 'We have missed you, my dear. All of us.'

Lily felt her eyes fill as well. Even when she left Ambala, Susan Fairford had scarcely shown any emotion. Lily had told herself that she was only a servant and of course her leaving would mean nothing.

But now she saw how much feeling Susan Fairford had been holding back at the time and it touched her.

'We'll order some tea and sit out, shall we?' Susan Fairford suggested. 'It's such a good day. I say, how marvellous you look, Lily – what an extraordinary dress.'

Srimala vanished with a regretful smile and Lily reminded herself that she must go and see her later.

'We're all very casual here,' Susan Fairford said, leading them out to the veranda. 'You find us in our holiday mood.'

It was an apology for the simplicity of the house, which was certainly a far less sumptuous dwelling than they were used to in Ambala. There were more cane chairs out on the veranda, which faced over a small rectangle of garden edged by flower beds with roses and phlox and snapdragons and was, at this hour, in the shade. The three of them settled round a table and soon one of the servants, whom Lily recognized and greeted with pleasure, brought out tea and biscuits and a Victoria sandwich cake filled with jam.

'Ah – that looks very nice,' Sam said. 'The air up here seems to give me an appetite.'

'Well, let's carry on,' Susan Fairford said. 'Charles has taken Isadora out to have a pony ride. She is absolutely mad on horses now – quite different from how she used to be. We ride out with her every day now, and she could not do without it here. Mind you, neither can Charles!' She laughed, pouring the tea. 'I think you'll find our Izzy changed a little, Lily. Wouldn't you agree, Mr Ironside?'

'Yes,' Sam said, accepting a slice of the cake with enthusiasm. 'She's older, obviously. But much calmer than I remember.'

'Of course, you were quite a horsewoman yourself, Lily!' Susan said, handing her a cup of tea.

'Yes,' Lily sighed. 'But there's not much chance here.'

'But there are the pony rides! Surely you could go out very occasionally at least?'

Lily was seized by a sudden great hunger to ride. She had not mounted a horse for a long time, but now the memory of those beautiful mornings riding out on the Punjab plains came vividly back to her and she sighed. How could she explain that her freedom here was curtailed not just by her being a servant but by her master's obsessive moods and whims?

'Perhaps we could go for a ride?' She looked round teasingly at Sam who made a face. She had not forgotten his fear of horses.

'I think I'll stick to the motor,' he said ruefully. 'You can go much further in it.'

'So how is life here treating you, Lily?' Susan Fairford said over the rim of her teacup. She looked relaxed, in a pale pink cotton dress. Lily could see that Sam was more at ease with her than he had been on the first visit, and indeed Susan did seem less tense and forbidding.

'Very well, thank you,' Lily said, carefully. 'I'm employed as a sort of housekeeper. The doctor's wife is an invalid. They're all very kind, and of course I love the town. But do tell me – what news is there of Cosmo?' Though she had occasional letters from him they told her very little.

'Oh!' Susan Fairford rolled her eyes humorously, but then she looked pained. 'You might well ask. It seems he is turning into a rebel – he's been in no end of trouble.'

'*Has* he?' Lily cried. This was not the sweet, biddable Cosmo she remembered! 'What's the matter?'

'Well, so far as I can gather, it's mostly just lack of discipline, and any sort of attention in lessons . . .'

'But he used to be so good!' Lily protested.

'I know.' Susan Fairford took a sip of tea, looking upset. 'He was evidently had up for stealing something off another boy recently as well. Nothing very big, I don't think, but they take that sort of thing very seriously there and of course he was caned. Charles's brother got to hear about it and wrote to us.' She looked at Lily with stricken eyes. 'My poor boy. I feel so far away from him, and there doesn't seem to be anything I can do. I'm so grateful that you still keep in touch, Lily dear. We heard that he still receives letters from you.'

'Oh yes – I'll never forget our little man,' she said. Once more she saw her old mistress looking close to tears and realized just how great a toll the separation was taking on her.

'Our little man . . .' Susan Fairford echoed, bitterly. 'Yes, this is how it happens here, that a child spends more time with strangers, or servants, than with his own mother.' She caught herself out then. 'Still – that's how it is, I suppose.'

They spent a happy hour reminiscing about Lily's time in Ambala and Susan gave her news of people she had known, and other children. Later on they heard the front door open and voices.

'Charles?' Susan called. 'Come out here – Lily Waters is here!'

A moment later Charles Fairford appeared, almost seeming to bound out of the bungalow door. He looked a little heavier to Lily, slightly more thickset, but very strong and healthy. He was beaming broadly.

'How very nice to see you!' he cried, and it sounded genuine.

Lily stood up, smiling, and they shook hands.

'You know, we're really up here because of you?' the captain said. 'Everyone wanted to come and see you, and I thought Sam here should see Mussoorie . . .'

'*So* much nicer than stuffy old Simla,' Susan said.

'I hope you'll be able to come on a few jaunts with us while we're here,' the captain continued. 'How's it suiting you?'

'Very well . . .' Lily began, but she then caught sight of Isadora, who walked out confidently on to the veranda carrying a riding crop and switching it at the air behind her as if she was still on a mount. She was taller, and though her long dark hair was just as messy as ever, she seemed calmer and more self-possessed.

'D'you remember Lily?' her father said gently.

Isadora stared hard at Lily and then, to all their surprise, walked up and planted a kiss on her cheek, saying, 'Lily. She's a friend.'

'Oh – thank you!' Lily exclaimed, deeply touched. She hadn't expected Isadora to remember her.

'There you are, you see,' Sam said. 'No one forgets you, Lily.'

And Lily saw Susan Fairford turn to look at them both, sharply, with a slight frown on her face.

Chapter Thirty-Seven

The week turned out to be more wonderful than Lily could ever have imagined.

When she returned home that afternoon, Dr McCluskie had arrived as promised and seemed to have put Ewan McBride in an exceptionally good mood. Duncan McCluskie was a slim, mild-mannered man. On first sight his blue eyes seemed to hold a melancholy seriousness, but this changed, when he smiled, into an impish cheerfulness as he shook Lily's hand.

'Miss Waters!' His Scottish accent was like crisp mountain ice. 'How nice to make your acquaintance.'

'How d'you do?' Lily said, deciding he looked reasonably pleasant. She had no idea of what Dr McBride had told his friend about her, but assumed he had told him that she was the housekeeper. But then Dr McBride said, 'Dr McCluskie will be staying in the middle room, and we'll be dining together. I hope you'll join us one evening, Lily?'

'Yes, Doctor,' she said, obediently, though she felt a blush spread all over her, and she was sure she saw a sudden sharp look of curiosity come into Dr McCluskie's eyes. What on earth must he think! Housekeepers did not dine with the master of the house! She knew Ewan McBride wanted to show her off as his prize as he did in the town. But she told herself it was not important. He would be gone soon, back to Patna,

241

and she would never see him again, whatever he thought. And the fact that he was here meant she could get out to see Sam and that was all that mattered.

There were several jaunts with the Fairfords. Charles Fairford appeared more relaxed than Lily ever remembered seeing him before. He was obviously delighted with his new model of Daimler and, she saw, was enjoying Sam's company again. He had not brought his *syce* Arsalan with him, and when she asked about him Susan Fairford told her that the groom's wife was very ill with a fever and he had not been able to leave her.

What took Lily by surprise was the difference in the way Susan Fairford treated her. Whereas before, when in her employ, Lily had been a servant, although one to whom Susan Fairford often turned for company and in times of distress and loneliness, now they were no longer mistress and servant, and she treated her more like a friend. The first time the five of them set off for a picnic in the car, the two women sat at the back with Isadora, and Lily felt like Susan Fairford's confidante. She talked about some of the other women in Ambala and what was happening in their lives far more openly than she would have done before. After a time she turned to look at Lily, with a little frown.

'Here am I, rattling on about people. You know' – she considered for a moment – 'you've changed, Lily. I mean, look at that marvellous gown you're wearing. It's quite lovely. You've become a good deal more *sophisticated*. Yes, that's it. You're more like one of us. That's why my tongue's running away.'

'Thank you,' Lily said, choosing not to regard this as rude. She knew what Susan Fairford meant, of course. After all these months of acting as a social companion for Dr McBride, she not only had a wardrobe full of beautiful clothes, including the powder-blue woollen outfit she was wearing today, but she had become used to mixing with the socialites of British Mussoorie, who had come to be more accepting of her now the first gossip had died down. For much of that time she had been quietly observing their ways, but she had gradually assumed some of those and become more confident and at home.

That day they drove out of Mussoorie and found a beautiful place to stop and picnic at the foot of a high waterfall. As the captain drove the car along the snaking road up and down the hills, the high ridges afforded them awe-inspiring views across to the white peaks, and the air was crisp and fresh and gave a great feeling of freedom and expansion. Lily had never been out this far before and she breathed in deeply, feeling her spirits soar with the air rushing against her cheeks, the blue ribbons of her hat streaming behind her, and this family, of whom she had become more fond than she realized, here with her and wanting to see her. Most miraculous of all, seated in front of her, exchanging remarks with Captain Fairford over the noise of the engine, was Sam Ironside. She felt full of powerful, melting emotion at the sight of him. *This is now*, she kept saying to herself, *and he's here, he's really, really here.* The feelings were so overpowering that she could not caution herself about his wife or think of anything but how much she loved him. She had to restrain herself from reaching out to stroke Sam's slender neck, with its dark, tapering hairline.

They parked at some distance from the falls and walked along a fern-lined path to find a place to sit and eat their picnic. Isadora had to be cajoled along with descriptions of the tumbling water.

'But I want to go for a ride,' she kept insisting.

Captain Fairford took her hand. 'We'll go riding later, I promise, Izzy, when we get back. We'll always go riding, you and I, won't we? But come and see the falling water. It's very exciting.'

And the falls were beautiful, tumbling down from the rocks in an abundance of meltwater, arced with rainbows in the sunlight. Nearby, all was vivid green, the rocks speckled with ferns and flowers, and they spread the picnic rug in the fronded shade of the deodars. Lily and Susan laid out the food from the hampers. There was the usual sumptuous Fairford assortment of fare: spiced fritters, cold chicken, a game pie and sandwiches filled with egg and mango chutney and anchovy and watercress. There were walnut pickles and cheese and biscuits. To follow there were fruits and jam tarts, chocolates and a fruit cake, and there was a bottle of champagne with a bucket of ice and crystal glasses and lemon and mango juices, which were Isadora's favourites.

For a time the two men leaned over the car, in earnest discussion, while Izzy skipped about, released from the confines of the car and enchanted by the sight and sound of the falling water.

'She seems so happy now,' Lily said as Izzy floated past, dreamily shredding a piece of green plant in her hands. The two women sat luxuriating in the beauty of the place and each other's company.

'Yes.' Susan looked up with a smile. 'I've tried to spend more time with her. She has been badly done by – by me, I mean. I was ashamed of her, I admit. And I didn't know how to manage her at all. But I've tried, very hard . . .' She looked sadly into the far distance for a moment. 'I don't have children easily. I suppose I'd have liked more babies, but not in this beastly country which snatches them away from you so cruelly. But Izzy is all I have here now – she won't leave me, you see. We won't have to send her away. Srimala's helped me to understand her better. I owe that girl a great deal and I think we'll need her for as long as she's prepared to stay. I suppose she'll marry one day, though I must say she's not showing much sign of it so far.' Susan eyed her daughter thoughtfully as Isadora squatted to bend over something that had caught her interest.

'She's older, of course. She doesn't get agitated quite so often – not when it comes to dressing and so on. It all used to be such a battle – every last thing. You remember, of course.' Lily could see that things had changed and she felt a great admiration for Susan Fairford. She still seemed nervy, not happy exactly, but a little more settled in herself.

'After all,' she said, self-mockingly, 'if you can't even get along with your own children it does seem a pretty poor show.'

There came a sudden burst of laughter from the men, both throwing their heads back, and Lily saw Susan watching them in wistful amusement.

'That's where he's always been happiest, of course. Not with me.' And she lowered her head as if she had said too much and arranged the linen napkins in a starched white fan on the rug.

Lily didn't need to ask what she meant and saw that Susan did not want to be asked.

'And our little Cosmo?' she said gently. 'When will you be able to see him again?'

Susan didn't answer for a moment. When she looked up her eyes were very sad.

'He stays every holidays with Charles's elder brother,

on the estate. Charles says it will be good for him, let him get to know England, the English countryside and so on. After all, he looks set to inherit the place. Charles did the same, of course – but then he wasn't alone; he had his brother and there were more relatives around then. Now there's only William . . .' She frowned. Lily realized she was battling tears. 'The man's . . . I don't know, unhinged in some way, I'm sure of it. He's most peculiar. Quite harmless, I would think, but – that's what I can't stand, you see . . .' Her eyes filled. 'There's my poor little Cosmo, every holiday in that great pile of a place with Uncle William, who's mad as a hatter, and the servants . . . No one to love him . . . And no other children except some of the servants' boys who are rough and older than Cosmo, and from what I gather he spends all possible time with them, when he's not wandering about alone. I'm sure they're a ruinous influence, but . . .' She was trying not to get worked up, but Lily could see she was fighting her sobs as she spoke. 'Charles keeps insisting that it will all be terribly good for him and character-building, and that it will stand him in good stead for the army – you know, the rough and tumble and mixing with all sorts . . . I really don't know . . .' She wiped her eyes. 'Sometimes I just can't bear it, not seeing him, having no say at all in what happens to my beautiful little boy. They're turning him into a stranger! He's become so naughty and rough and dishonest and he never used to be like that at all, did he, Lily?'

Lily found what she was hearing very sad and disquieting and her heart ached for Cosmo. But she wanted to try and be reassuring.

'No, of course not. He was always sweet and well behaved when he was little. But boys do go in for a lot more rough and tumble as they get older, don't they? After all, they don't stay tiny and sweet all their lives. Perhaps Captain Fairford is right. Cosmo's education must be rather like he had himself?'

'Yes, it is, exactly like. And that's what makes me wonder if he'll be like Charles . . .' She bit off her words and looked down, a flush appearing on her face. Visibly pulling herself together and wiping her eyes as the men were approaching for tiffin, she said in a different, sober voice, 'And, of course, this is the way of things. One must do one's duty.'

By the time Sam and the captain reached them she was a model of composure.

'My – this looks a good spread,' Charles Fairford said, rubbing his hands together. 'I've worked up quite an appetite even without my morning ride. I say, Susan, I could get jolly fond of this place. What do you think? A little more relaxed than dear old Simla, eh?'

'Yes, much more,' she agreed demurely, 'though I do rather miss our dear house in Simla.'

'But no motors allowed in Simla!' the captain said. 'That's no damn good, is it, Ironside?' As Sam sat down, the captain pointed at the rocks on each side of the falls. 'Fancy climbing up there after tiffin, Ironside?'

But Sam's eyes were fixed on Lily. He looked handsome and invigorated by the fresh air and sunshine, and he was smiling at her so hungrily, so attentively. She looked into his lovely face and for a moment they might have been alone.

'Ironside?'

'Ah – yes. A climb? That sounds a fine idea,' Sam agreed with absent-minded politeness.

The afternoon passed blissfully. The sky was a deep blue and they sat half in the shade of the tall trees, the

247

sound of the white, rushing falls constantly with them, eating their sumptuous picnic. Everything tasted wonderful and Lily sipped the cool champagne, feeling herself growing even more relaxed and muzzy. She felt she was in heaven, in this place with Sam nearby, able to look at him, talk with him whenever she wanted to. She was just drinking in his presence and she could see that he was doing the same. She hummed with happiness like an instrument that had found the right note and could only keep playing it.

And Sam seemed in such happy form. He entertained them with more of his motor-racing stories, which the captain always seemed to be keen to hear and laughed unrestrainedly as he listened to the thrills and spills of attempts at a round-the-world car race.

'And when they got halfway across Russia – Zust, the Italian car, that is – first of all they almost drowned by driving on to what they thought was dry land and finding it was a swamp. And they had to botch together a new crankshaft bearing – and what did they have for the job? Well—' Sam chuckled gleefully – 'some bits of mud and wood and a handful of bullets in a tin which had had cough sweets in it, and that's how they made do! And then, to cap it all, when they finally got to Omsk, they were arrested – they didn't get to Paris for another two months!'

'But *why* on earth?' Susan Fairford was enjoying the story as well. Lily saw Sam cast a surprised glance in her direction.

'They thought they were spies, because they tried to send a cable in Italian. And when they did get to France, long after everyone else, they claimed that they were the winners because everyone else had cheated!'

'Oh really, that's too much!' Charles Fairford

laughed. 'I've heard of some rum carry-on during the reliability trials out of Bombay,' he said, chuckling at Sam's latest tall story. 'But that takes the biscuit, it really does!'

'Ah well, that's not the end of it.' Sam was enjoying himself, the corners of his eyes creasing with laughter. 'After the race, the Zust car was taken back to England – and it was caught up in a fire at a railway station and burned to billy-oh!'

'No – you're having us on, Ironside!'

'I'm not. It's true as I'm sitting here!'

'What a fellow you are,' Captain Fairford said. Lily could see that he genuinely enjoyed Sam's company. After all, the two of them had travelled together and it had created a bond. And she sat in the glow of Sam's presence, feeling that she had never been so happy before.

Chapter Thirty-Eight

'You're starting to get more roses in your cheeks, Lily,' Susan Fairford remarked a couple of days later as they sat looking out over a breathtaking view of peaks and piled clouds, the sun slanting along the steep green valley. For all the outings and trips the Fairfords took that week, they sent invitation to Lily. Taking the Daimler some way out of town, they drank in the beauty of the Himalayan countryside and picnicked surrounded by its icy streams, its trees and flowers.

The men had gone off for a stroll to keep Isadora happy and the two women were sitting after tiffin, relaxing together. 'You looked really pale and under the weather when we first arrived.'

Lily smiled. She *was* feeling better, but the smile was also one of fondness towards Susan Fairford. Remembering the tense, snobbish woman she had first met in Ambala, she could see what a softening there had been. She knew Sam was still not sure about Susan Fairford. She was less relaxed when he was present, of course, and he tended to read class superiority into everything she said and be needled by it, but Lily had grown closer to her and to respect the struggles of her life. Just because the family had money and class, she knew, it did not always mean happiness.

'Yes – all this lovely fresh air. And your picnics. The

McBrides' food is much more basic, though I've done my best to make it at least more tasty.'

'I'm sure you have – you're very capable.' Susan Fairford looked at Lily closely, with a slight frown. 'And, of course, even more lovely to look at than I remembered.'

Lily blushed under this close scrutiny.

'But I worry for you,' her old mistress went on. 'It's him, isn't it – Sam Ironside – who's put the colour in your cheeks?'

Lily looked down, not meeting her eyes, her blush deepening, but she said nothing, hoping Susan could not see her confusion.

'Lily?' Susan persisted gently. 'Oh dear, I do remember you were both a little involved with each other last time he was here, but all that was such a time ago and it must be over now, surely?'

Lily found the courage to look up into Susan's blue eyes and nodded. 'Oh yes,' she said lightly. 'Completely.'

'You were so quiet, so miserable afterwards. I didn't realize, of course. But Lily – he still is married!'

'I know,' Lily said, even more brightly. 'There's nothing to worry about, really!'

'Well, I do hope so!' Susan said urgently. 'I'm going to speak very frankly, Lily: if there was anything between you, you'd have to get over it, both of you. I'd feel so responsible for throwing you together again. You'll only be in a dreadfully unhappy and shameful situation, Lily, dear! I can see he is far from indifferent to you and men can use one terribly falsely! After all, he can't leave a wife and children, can he? So there's no place for you – none at all. And certainly not without scandal and heartbreak.'

Lily hated to lie when she knew Susan was trying to protect her, but she simply could not bear to let Sam go again or to admit to the obstacles in the way of their being together.

'It's all right, I assure you,' she said, looking Susan directly in the eye. 'I'm very touched by your concern, but there's nothing between myself and Sam Ironside. That was all over years ago. I feel quite calm and indifferent about seeing him again.'

'Well,' Susan said. 'I'm immensely relieved to hear it.'

There were brief times when she was alone with Sam, or almost, walking ahead of the Fairfords, or behind, on the way to or from a picnic. And they talked in low, urgent voices. Lily was now aware that they were being watched. That day, after Susan's warning, they stepped ahead along the path.

'She told me to keep away from you,' Lily murmured.

'Does she know?' Sam's voice was tense.

'She guessed. It's not surprising really, is it? She guessed last time as well. I mean look at us now. It must be very obvious. I told her she had nothing to worry about . . .' For the first time she allowed reality to wash cold over the situation. Turning to him, she said, 'Sam, I don't know what to think. Whatever are we going to do?'

Sam stepped round a rock in the path, his face very serious. 'God, I want to see you alone, Lily. To spend time with you somewhere so that we can talk properly.'

Lily felt just as desperate. It was wonderful to see Sam every day, but they had had so little time alone, and the days were rushing past. Only five remained, and he would be snatched away from her again. Until now she had barely allowed herself to think about it.

'But how can we? Everyone is so determined to chaperone us.'

'One evening? Could you get out, d'you think?'

'Not tonight. I have to dine with Dr McBride and his guest. Perhaps tomorrow?'

'Tomorrow,' Sam said. 'Without fail.'

Soon after breakfast that morning, Ewan McBride had ordered her presence for dinner in the evening.

'Make sure you wear something especially nice, won't you, Lily? Perhaps one of your more exotic gowns. Would you like me to come and choose for you?'

Lily felt her hackles rise at the way he had to control everything, and realized that that was new. Before, she had simply grown used to it. But she knew the way to handle him.

'Perhaps the mirror gown?' she suggested compliantly. It was a very striking dress, stitched from rich pink, blue and peacock-green cloth from Rajasthan, with circles of mirror glass embroidered into the skirt and sleeves. Light shimmered and danced off it and it always produced gasps of admiration when she had appeared in it at parties. She often wore it with a strip of raw green mirrored silk wrapped round her smoothly coiffured hair.

'Oh yes, I think so,' Dr McBride almost purred. She could see that she was to be shown off as a trophy to Dr McCluskie. The thought of dining with the two men made her recoil. She knew she would feel the usual sense of being unreal, not herself, like the china doll that Ewan McBride required her to be.

Stephen, the cook, was in a tizzy because the advent of a guest was so unusual.

'There is going to be a misadventure,' he wailed to Lily, who, on return from the picnic with the Fairfords, decided she had better help.

'But everything is going perfectly well,' she told him. 'Look, you've already done nearly all of it.' They were to have a roast duck with trimmings, and apple pie, and Stephen always got himself worked up about pastry. Even Prithvi seemed in a bit of a state, though she only had to serve the food. The household was simply not used to visitors.

By seven-thirty Lily had dressed herself, with a little help from Prithvi with the hooks and eyes, and put her hair up, wrapping the bandanna round it, and applied a thin line of kohl round her lids. Turning her head from side to side she realized that she looked very exotic. The doctor would be pleased. It was her habit to try and please him. It made her life peaceful. Tonight, though, her own spirit was strong in her and she felt a great flare of anger. Who did he think he was, some sort of puppet master, to have her dancing to his every tune?

'You may think you've got me on a string,' she whispered to her reflection, 'but not for much longer, Doctor. Because I love Sam Ironside and he loves me. And you have no power over that.'

And walking tall, haughtily, she went to the doctor's study and rapped on the door.

'Ah Lily, my dear!' Dr McBride said, throwing open the door to enable her to make a triumphal entry, and in so doing made Lily see that Dr McCluskie knew exactly what was her position in the household, and that she was there to be displayed as if part of a harem. She felt deeply shamed and angry, but she knew that coldly, quietly, she would play her part, for the moment.

'I say, how splendid!' Dr McCluskie leaped to his feet. 'What a very beautiful addition you are to the room, Miss Waters.' Unlike the last time she had seen Dr McCluskie, when he had appeared very gentlemanly, this time she sensed a lascivious edge to his speech which repelled her.

'Good evening, Dr McCluskie,' she said coolly, as they shook hands. She saw by the blush rising from his collar that this bashful bachelor was strongly affected by her presence.

Dr McBride handed her a glass of sweet sherry and Lily sipped it, feeling its syrupy warmth in her throat.

'From what part do you hail?' Dr McCluskie asked, and Lily, feeling the usual dread of questions, trotted out her usual version of events very briefly, before quickly diverting the conversation on to himself, a subject on which he appeared ready to elaborate at some length. As Dr McBride ushered them to the table, Dr McCluskie was telling Lily that much of his work from Patna involved travelling the villages, where he lived for weeks at a time, scarcely ever seeing another white face except those of missionaries in the field.

'It can make a man very hungry for a sight or sound of home,' he said, almost apologetically. 'And tonight is a veritable feast.'

Lily smiled faintly. She saw Dr McBride frowning, but Dr McCluskie, who suddenly seemed to have come to life, began to regale Lily with stories of medical oddities he had encountered in his work in remote villages, and as Prithvi carried in the soup, he was in the midst of a descriptive parade of goitres and tumours and birth defects hideous enough to turn the stomach.

'The whole of the foot was infested with white ants,' he said enthusiastically, as Prithvi fled from the room.

'D'you think, Duncan, we could manage to find a less picturesque line of conversation in front of the ladies?' Dr McBride requested in irritation. 'After all, even some medical men are not used to the rigours of rural India.'

'How utterly remiss of me,' Duncan McCluskie said, raising his glass to Lily. There was a twinkle in his eyes, but whereas before he had seemed placid, now there was a hard edge to him, something mocking. He was already well gone for drink. Both men were drinking whisky. 'Ewan and I go back a long way together – and we medical men, you know, we grow accustomed to talking about things which are not usually aired in polite society. My humble apologies, Miss Waters.'

Lily inclined her head graciously. She wasn't having him thinking that she was so easily shocked. 'Not at all. It was most interesting. I haven't had the privilege of visiting the more remote parts of the country.'

'Ah – no place for a lady, that I can tell you,' Dr McCluskie said, and another stream of reminiscences began.

They finished their soup and Prithvi came in, looking terrified, with the duck, which turned out to be excellently done. As they ate the two men exchanged stories and memories of student years in Edinburgh and their work since and Lily became their captive audience, though she was in any case oblivious to most of it, her mind wandering longingly to Sam. From what she did hear, the more they drank, the more competitive the

256

storytelling became, each man trying to cap the other's experiences. Dr McCluskie had worked in some of the poorest parts of Glasgow before arriving in India and he was a fund of extraordinary tales which Dr McBride, who had been in Mussoorie for years, simply could not match.

'I'm sure Miss Waters doesn't want to hear about all this,' he said more than once, leaning forward to replenish Dr McCluskie's glass.

'Ah, but I must just tell you this one,' Duncan McCluskie insisted, and launched into a story about a family he had been involved with in Glasgow with thirteen children and almost every degree of ill health and misfortune that could be imagined. Listening to him talking about the lives of this poor family made Lily very uncomfortable. Little do they know, she thought, that I come from a place not so different. The Horne girls had left her in no ignorance of the fact that she was a poor foundling whose parents had deserted her. She felt a shudder go through her at all that she might have become. Better to put up with Ewan McBride's maulings than be poor like that!

But she was also becoming more aware of the strained atmosphere between the two men and especially when Duncan McCluskie said to her, 'Perhaps you'd like to come with me on one of my jaunts into the countryside, Miss Waters? I'm sure you'd find it highly educational.'

Dr McBride let out a sudden gust of laughter, but Lily could tell there was a dangerous edge to it.

'Really, Duncan – you are a card. Can you imagine this Lily-flower here out in the squalor of the villages?'

'Oh – I rather think Miss Waters has more to her than meets the eye,' Duncan McCluskie said, looking deep into Lily's eyes, before she lowered her gaze. The conversation was making her feel increasingly uncomfortable, these men acting so competitively over her. Fortunately Prithvi came in again then to clear away the plates and bring in the hot apple pie.

'I say – you've done us proud here!' Duncan McCluskie said. 'I haven't enjoyed a splendid meal like this in a very long time!'

'That's also thanks to our Miss Waters here. She has taken responsibility for organizing the household and making us fully shipshape.'

'Well, it's time someone took you to task, if you won't employ the normal number of servants like anyone else, McBride!'

'I don't need servants – I just need Lily here,' the doctor replied unguardedly. In his half-drunken state he gave her a soulful stare, like a lecherous spaniel. Lily felt more and more uncomfortable, and as soon as the pie was eaten she got up quickly from the table.

'I'll leave you gentlemen to your coffee now,' she said.

The two men lurched to their feet in surprise. 'No, Lily – don't leave us yet,' Dr McBride said. Lily knew it was an order, but she decided to treat it as a request.

'It's kind of you, but I'm very tired and I'm sure you would like more time to talk alone. Goodnight, Dr McCluskie. It has been most enjoyable.'

He took her hand in his clammy one and held it for seconds longer than necessary, staring into her eyes.

'Goodnight, Miss Waters. I'm charmed. Utterly charmed.'

At last she was free to leave the room.

*

If he knocked on the door she didn't hear it. The first thing she became aware of was a light in the room and she sat up, pulsing with shock. She had been deeply asleep, but now there was a figure standing by her bed, holding a candle and she knew immediately from his slender build that it was not Dr McBride.

'No need to be frightened,' he whispered. He lifted the mosquito net and sat down on the bed. Lily could see that Duncan McCluskie was very much the worse for drink. His eyes looked glazed and strange.

'What are you doing here?' She was torn between outrage and fear. It must be the small hours and he had seen fit just to wander in here! What was she, some woman of the streets that everyone could use on a whim? But he was a strong-looking man, with a wild look in his eye at this moment and she was frightened of what he might do. Setting the mosquito net alight with the candle seemed a distinct possibility, quite apart from anything else. She eased herself away from him, in readiness to slide off the other side of the bed.

'Don't pretend you don't know, you beautiful, teasing whore.' His voice was low and urgent. 'Flaunting yourself at me like that all evening. This is what you do for him, isn't it? So you can do it for me. That's what you want, isn't it? I can see you looking at me . . . Well, I'm ready for you.'

Without even putting the candle down he lunged at her, grabbing her round the shoulders with his left hand and forcing his lips to hers while he held the candle with the other, perilously close to her hair. Lily struggled, panic-stricken, and managed to get her legs on to the floor the other side of the bed. She struggled away from him, fighting her way out from under the mosquito net.

'For God's sake – you'll set the place alight! Get that candle away from me. How *dare* you come in here and behave like this?'

But he was not easily deterred. He reached over to put the candle down on the washstand and stood up to fling the mosquito net over the wooden frame before lunging at her.

'Don't go all prissy on me. I know you're his mistress. It's obvious. If you go about dressed up like a bitch on heat, what do you expect? I haven't had a woman in months and it's no way for a man to live. I want you, Lily, and I'm going to have you. By God, if you can give yourself to that old dog, you can give yourself to me too . . .'

He seized hold of her, pressing himself against her with frantic urgency, pushing his tongue in her mouth, his hands groping at her breasts. He took hold of her shoulders and tried to force her down on to the bed. Lily found her mind working faster than she had ever known it. Knowing how drunk he was, she leaned her weight against him. Duncan McCluskie took this as being the response he wanted.

'That's it . . .' He breathed whisky fumes into her face. 'I knew you wanted it. Get on the bed, lie down so I can have you . . .'

Lily drew back as if she was about to obey, but then stepped fast towards him again and shoved him as hard as she could. For a moment the doctor wavered, then toppled over backwards on to the bed.

'You scheming bitch!' he growled.

'Get out,' Lily hissed, standing over him. 'Or I'll wake the whole house. Is that what you want? How *dare* you come and behave in this disgusting way? Now you get up and get out of my room!'

He sat up, groggily, seeming stunned, as if coming to his senses.

'All right, I'll go – I'm sorry.' He got up off the bed. 'Don't say anything, will you? I'm sorry – it's just been so long . . . I got it wrong . . .'

Lily opened the door without another word and waited for him to leave.

'You won't tell Ewan?'

Lily had no intention of telling Ewan McBride because she knew far better than Duncan McCluskie what his jealous anger was like. But she said stiffly, 'So long as it doesn't happen again.'

Chapter Thirty-Nine

Lily did not see Dr McCluskie the next morning, but what had happened in the night and the way she had stood up for herself made her feel stronger. In any case, her mind was full of thoughts of Sam.

She spent a pleasant teatime hour at Zinnias with Susan and Srimala, playing with Isadora, and in a snatched moment, she and Sam arranged to meet at the beginning of the Camel's Back that night.

Lily ate her dinner alone. After last night's events she had wondered how Dr McCluskie would be able to face her, and her only sighting of the two men was that evening. As Lily was standing in the hall exchanging a few words with Jane Brown, the doctors came in out of the dusk. Lily saw a shade of emotion pass across Dr McCluskie's face, a reflex of extreme embarrassment, which was then converted into a superior contempt.

'Good evening, Miss Waters,' he said coldly.

She nodded. 'Mr McCluskie.' It had not been deliberate, omitting to call him 'doctor' but she saw the insult register with him.

However, she spent most of the evening fretting in her room about whether she would be able to leave the house without anyone seeing. She thought about trying to climb out of the window, but, like so many Mussoorie houses, it was built clinging to the edge of the hillside and outside, apart from a narrow ledge, was nothing but a steep drop into darkness. She would have to get through the house as best she could.

At five to eleven her heart was beating so fast she could hardly bear it. She had been pacing the room trying to find an outlet for all her pent-up energy, and at last she opened the door of her room very quietly and crept out into the corridor. She had even left the pillows in her bed to look like her sleeping shape. As she crept along the corridor she heard the two doctors' voices in Dr McBride's study, could smell whisky and pipe smoke and hear their drink-laced laughter. They would be carrying on like that for hours to come. She went to the front door and slipped out into the mild, sweet-scented darkness.

Her steps sounded loud out in the street and she realized that she was never out at night unaccompanied and was unused to the deep darkness, lit only by a crescent moon.

'Lily?' His voice came from the shadows and her whole being leaped with happiness at the sound.

'Sam!'

He caught her immediately in his arms and they clung to each other, at last alone and able to express their feelings.

'God, girl, I love you,' he said into her neck. 'I love you so much.'

'And I love you. Oh, Sam, what are we going to do?'

She wanted to pour out all her fears, but this was not the time to talk and for those moments all they wanted was to stand in each other's arms. But then they heard whistling, and footsteps coming from the Camel's Back Road, and they stepped apart.

'Come on – the car's parked below the Kulri Bazaar. We'll get out of town.'

263

'*Can* we?' Lily was amazed. 'Surely we can't just take it?'

'Lily.' His voice came out of the darkness. 'This is something that doesn't happen except once in a lifetime. And terribly soon I'll have to be gone – back on the ship. What could be the harm?'

'I can't believe it – us just being able to be on our own!'

'All week it's been all I've been able to think about. Come on.' He reached for her.

They walked hand in hand through the winding bazaar, all shut up for the night now, and down, past poor native houses, hearing the sounds of families crowded inside, the cry of an infant, voices, a man singing. And all around, the smells of dung fires, incense and spiced food. Lily breathed in the smells of India, and everything was made lovely because Sam was walking beside her, holding her.

The car was parked in a low building which looked and smelled like a stables. When Sam cranked up the engine the noise seemed to explode into the quiet, and he jumped in and released the brake, switching on the bright headlights.

'Right – we'll find a spot just for us.'

She couldn't see much as they drove along except for moving shadows, aware sometimes of the tall trees above, and of their delicious smell, and of the switching bends in the road. They didn't speak much, not then. Sometimes, as he drove, Sam reached across and touched her hand, pressing it gently.

'You're here – you're really here!' she said once, full of love, drinking in the wonder of his presence.

At last he stopped in what appeared to be the edge of a little clearing and as the engine died the silence expanded round them, broken by the high squeak of some woodland creature. The thin moon looked down on them through the trees which moved gently in the breeze.

'We've been here before – d'you remember?' he said. 'The picnic a few days back.'

'Have we? I couldn't tell on the way.'

'The one with the little stream running between the trees. Where Isadora got her clothes sopping wet.'

'Oh yes!' she laughed. 'Yes, of course I remember!'

Sam got out of the car and was foraging in the back for something.

'I've got a surprise for you. Come on. We'll make it nice.'

She could see very little, but followed him over the soft woodland earth and to the place he seemed to have in mind and she heard a small clanking sound as he put something on the ground.

'I've got wood and paper, matches, a lamp – even tea and cake,' he said. 'We'll have a nice little fire and make it cosy. And there's a rug in the car. I'll just nip and get it.'

'Don't leave me here!' Lily said, alarmed. 'I'm coming with you!'

Sam laughed. 'Well, I'd better bring the bag back with me as well, or we might never find it again.'

Holding hands, giggling like two children, they hurried back through the trees to the motor car to collect the rug.

'Like babes in the wood,' Sam said.

'Isn't there supposed to be a gingerbread house?'

'No.' He thought about it. 'I think that's a different story – I couldn't be sure, though!'

In their clearing he laid the fire and got it burning,

and the wood caught gradually, the flames building and glowing in the night, sending off their warm light and dancing shadows. Lily busied herself spreading the rug on the ground, feeling that although they were outside, with no shelter and the most basic of provisions, she had never before experienced such a sense of luxury. She unpacked the bag, the bottles of tea and bananas and slabs of cake wrapped in waxed paper.

'How completely wonderful!' she said, amazed by the careful preparations he had made.

'I picked up quite a bit camping with the captain,' he said. 'I don't think there are too many animals up here to worry about, but they don't like fire anyway.'

She watched it burning, and glowed with happiness herself, smiling at him in the orange light.

Once everything was ready they sat together on the rug, faces and hands warmed by the flames. In the firelight Sam turned to her.

'Lily, I'm so sorry about last time – that I wasn't straight with you from the beginning. I'm not a liar, not as a rule, only I was so keen to get to know you, so set on you, I knew if I said anything about home and Helen ... Well, I wouldn't stand a chance, and I just ... See, even now, I can talk to you the way I can't to anyone else ...'

'It's all right.' She looked into his eyes. 'It was terrible then. Truly, it was. You broke my heart, Sam. And your wife expecting a child – all of it ... I never thought I'd get over it.'

'I never got over you,' he said with great seriousness.

'Even now—' She hated saying it, but it had to be brought out. 'You've children, Sam – your girls.'

Sam stared gravely into the fire and let out a long sigh. 'Children are a blessing but sometimes ... I suppose it's the responsibility, the burden of it, at times. Being a father, I mean. And I wanted to do it well – take care of them. They're lovely, of course – pretty little things. I could never not take responsibility for them, Lily. But my God, I can't go on the way I am. Not while you exist somewhere. I feel as if everything stops when I'm not with you. As if you're what I'm made for.'

Moved, she reached up and kissed his cheek. 'And you're the same for me. You're the only man I've ever loved and it never went away, Sam, even though you did.'

'It's so strange,' he said slowly. 'Because although I love you, I don't know much about you. You were always a mystery. And you know a bit about me – Coventry, cars and Helen, that's my life. Tell me about you, Lily – will you?'

Immediately she felt the old reflex of shame for the past which made her want to hide everything, even from him. Here he was, a man she felt so much for and even so, she found it so difficult. But his eyes looked down into hers with intense love and he leaned down and lightly kissed her lips. And as well as the shame, she found herself full of an ache, a longing to talk and share with him who she was and where she had come from and feel accepted for it instead of having to pretend to be someone she wasn't. And the longing drove her to speak.

'I don't know much about my background,' she began, her heart beating fiercely. It felt like opening a room which had been locked for many years and being afraid of what might be inside. For the first time in her life she started to talk about the things Mary Horne had told her, about them finding her in the street in

Birmingham, alone in the cold outside a dismal slum dwelling, and about the things she could remember, living with the Hornes, and Mrs Chappell.

'I thought I'd never get over it when she died,' she said, sitting wrapped in Sam's arms, looking into the fire as she spoke. 'I thought she was the only person in the world who would ever care for me, and when she'd gone I had no one else. I wanted to get out and start again, to go somewhere new, so that's when I came out to work for the Fairfords. And there was Cosmo – my beautiful little Cosmo . . .'

Leaning against Sam, warm and cherished, Lily found to her surprise that she wanted to cry, and the tears started coming even though she tried to stop them. She rested her head on his chest, quietly shaken by sobs.

Sam stroked her head. 'What's the matter?' he asked, gently.

When she could speak, Lily drew back and looked up at him wet-cheeked, and seeing his face bronzed and gentle in the firelight, gazing down at her so lovingly, more tears came.

'I've never known this. Not being held like this.'

'Oh, Lily, my love . . .' he said, moved by her and her story. He drew her even closer to him again, his hand on her head, rocking her. For a time they sat quietly, hearing the crackle and spit of the fire, and the breeze gently moving the trees. It felt like sitting in a cave, the light a halo around them, and only darkness beyond. Lily felt warm and loved and alive in a way she never had before. She couldn't say to Sam that although she had been clasped in Dr McBride's arms night after night, it had never felt like this. It had been not love, but being used, and this difference, the longing it answered, filled her with emotion. She felt Sam gently

268

kissing the top of her head and she turned and looked up at him with serious eyes.

'I've got to go home,' he said at last. 'My passage is booked. The works will be waiting for me to come back ... But I'll ...' He was struggling with his emotions. 'Lily, I can't be away from you again. We've got to be together. I'll go and ... finish things, somehow. There's Helen, and the work, and then ...'

'I'll come home,' Lily said. 'It's no good, you coming out here, is it? What would you do? And your daughters ...'

'But we'd have to move away. Somewhere where no one knows us ... I'd send Helen money ...'

'We'd have to find somewhere ...'

It all seemed so momentous, so shocking and terrible and wonderful a decision to be having to make that neither of them could take it in or think clearly. Only then had it become fully clear that they had to be together, at all costs, but how on earth?

'I *have* to be with you,' Sam said in the end, holding her tightly. 'I don't know how, not yet, but it's the only thing I've ever known or been so sure about. Whatever it takes, Lily, I've got to get back to you.'

'I can't bear the thought of you going away,' she said, gazing into his eyes. 'I wish we could just go now, keep moving on, and be together, just you and me.'

Sam smiled fondly. 'I think the captain might have something to say if we just make off with his motor car.'

'We'll go in a *tonga* then!'

'And live on air for the rest of our days?' He squeezed her lovingly. 'My Lily, I want to keep you better than that. I want you to be happy and comfortable.'

She looked up at him in wonder. No one had ever told her such things before, or looked at her with such love in their eyes. Even Mrs Chappell's concern for her was a pale shadow of this.

'I love you, Sam,' she said. 'I want to be with you – always.'

She could scarcely believe it was her saying these words. Sam got up for a moment to put more wood on the fire and it blazed brightly, creating more leaping shadows around them.

'Here – let's have the tea before it's cold,' he said. They sipped from the little tin cup, sharing it, and ate the fruit cake he had brought, and then snuggled together on the rug in the heat of the fire, a coat rolled up under their heads.

'D'you think there's anyone else around?' Lily said. It felt as if they were the only people ever to breathe this clear mountain air.

'I doubt it. There were some huts but they were a way away.'

'Tell me about Helen,' she said

He leaned up on his elbow and looked down into her face. 'What about her?'

'Well, you know – what's she like? Is she anything like me?'

'Lily – no one is like you.'

'You must have liked her or why would you marry her?'

Sam lay back and stared up at the starlit sky. He sighed.

'We've been married for four years. Seems like an eternity. She's all right, Helen is. A good sort, and she's a good mother – you know, kind-hearted and steady. She seems to know what to do for them, without anyone telling her, which must be nature, I suppose. That side of it's all right – the children. But when it comes to me she doesn't want me, not really. I think she married the wrong man, and she knows it. She's got a friend, a chap called Laurie. She should have married him.' He stopped and sighed for a second.

'When you first meet someone, and you're young, you don't know anything, do you? You just think, This must be it, because it's happening and you feel *something* – a lot of it just the body when you come down to it – and you think this is *it*. This is love and how it's meant to be. But you don't know how much more it can be. We don't do anything much for each other, Helen and me. We don't light each other up, never have. And I didn't know there *was* lighting up, not like this, until I met you.'

Leaning up on his elbow, he reached down to kiss her and she responded passionately.

'Oh God, girl . . .' He looked down at her, face full of a wistful hunger. 'It's no good. You're my woman and that's how it is. I've tried and tried, but I can't go back now.'

Wide-eyed she looked up at him, moved by the strength of his desire for her.

'Don't go back,' she whispered. 'Please don't leave me again, ever.'

He kissed her forehead, stroking away strands of her hair. 'I shan't leave you, girl. You're mine.'

It came so naturally, their lovemaking. Lily had gone through the motions so many times with Dr McBride, sometimes feeling her body respond a little, in spite of itself, but never her mind. She had never before responded to a man, or opened her whole self, to anyone. Sam's hands moving over her, his face as he touched her body, gave her feelings she had never had before. The sight of his body as they removed some of their clothes moved her, instead of repelling her the way Ewan McBride's portly frame did.

'God, you're so beautiful,' Sam said, gazing on her as they knelt together, their skin rosy in the firelight. His eyes were full of desire for her, and all she longed for was to hold him close and stroke his hair, his back, to pour all her pent-up affections on to him.

'Come here, love,' he said, and they wrapped their arms round each other and she was overcome by sensations, her fingers caressing his back, the supple skin over hard muscle, the long, powerful spine, and his lips first on her lips, then seeking out her breasts, filling her whole body with sensations of longing and then his urgent request for her to lie back on the rug, her head pillowed as he lay over her, looking down into her eyes.

Sam's desire for her and the loving way he stroked her and entered her filled her with tenderness and longing for him and she felt as if this, not the mechanical way she had fulfilled the doctor's demands, was the first time she had ever made love with a man. This first time was so passionate, so intense that it happened urgently and quickly. But they lay together then, close and warm, pulling the rug round them.

'I never knew it could be like this,' Sam said, looking deeply into her eyes. 'I had no idea. God, Lily, I love you so much.'

'Don't leave me, Sam,' she whispered again, fearfully. 'I love you.'

'I won't.' His breath was warm on her ear. 'Even when I'm gone, I shall be here with you, because you're part of me. We belong together.'

'We'll be together – we *will*,' she murmured, tenderly

kissing his cheek, her hands caressing his warm chest and belly. They lay there, pressed close together in the firelight, among the smell of the pines, until they slept, two tiny figures amid the great Himalaya, where the dark flank of the mountain reached up to greet the star-bright sky.

Chapter Forty

Lily woke first. There was already a fringe of light along the eastern sky and she felt the cool breeze on her face, smelled the trees, the dampness of the dew-soaked ground and knew, even before her waking mind confirmed it, that everything was changed. The sight of Sam's upper arm beside her in the dawn light, his slender features and dark moustache gave her a great surge of happiness. He was here, they were together, and however damp and stiff with cold, now the fire was long dead, this was the only place on earth she wanted to be.

'Sam . . . Sam, my lovely . . .'

His eyes opened and after a second's bewilderment, a smile of wonder spread across his face.

'Oh, Lily!' His lips searched immediately for hers. 'I thought I'd dreamed you!' He held her as if she was the most precious thing on earth and she lay with her head on his chest, hearing the confident beat of his heart.

'Lord,' he said suddenly. 'We'd better get back! The sun's coming up!'

Tearing themselves away from one another they carried the rug and picnic things through the heavy dew to the car, only then noticing how cold they were, pulling the rug across their laps to drive back through the dawn. The sun was coating the mountain ridges with pink and gold as they set off, and as they came into

Mussoorie, hurrying back to Kulri and the parking place, the higgledy-piggledy mountain town was bathed in a bronze dawn light. Sam steered the Daimler into the shed and her engine sputtered into quietness.

'There.' Sam turned, smiling at her, though the thought of having to part again was unbearable. 'Will the McBride household be up by now?'

'No – but it won't be long.' She was fluttery with nerves, but also didn't care what happened now. She had Sam, they were together, and nothing else mattered.

'Come round to the bungalow later – can you?' He put his arm round her, in the dark shelter, and they gazed into each other's eyes. Sam kissed her tenderly. 'I don't think I can stand more than a few hours without you, my lovely.'

'I'll come – of course I'll come,' she said. 'Nothing can stop me being with you.'

When she left him, warm with his kisses, it felt like being physically torn away, but strengthened by the knowledge that she would see him again in only a few hours she hurried up the hill to the bungalow. Alone, panic filled her. It must be after five in the morning – would everyone still be asleep? Prithvi started work very early, but at least she could rely on her not to make any trouble.

She had left the front door unlocked and when she turned the iron handle it opened silently. Catching her breath she stepped into the dark hall expecting the doctor, or at least Cameron the dog, who might bark and give her away. Seeing there was no one around, she closed the door quietly behind her.

'And where exactly have you been?'

He must have been waiting there silently in the passage, because when she turned again she was no longer alone. Dr McBride's form seemed to fill the whole doorway. In the gloom she could make out only the outline of his features, but the tone of his voice told her all she needed to know. He was seething with a rage only barely controlled.

'I've just been out for a little walk,' she gabbled brightly. 'I woke early and the light was so lovely I thought I'd go out and watch the dawn – like Miss Brown does. I used to get up very early in Ambala and ride out with Mrs Fairford and it reminded me of how beautiful the early light is—'

'You lying little bitch!' He strode over to her and seized her shoulders. Lily gasped with shock at the enraged force of him. 'You haven't been in your bed all night so don't play the little innocent with me! I went to you last night and you weren't there. You were with *him*, weren't you? Tell me, you overheated little whore!' He shook her terrifyingly hard.

'With who?'

'With that goat McCluskie, of course! Did you go to his room? Couldn't control yourself? Or some little tryst somewhere? My God, after all I've done for you you'd think you could behave in a trustworthy manner, but oh no, one male visitor to the house and I have to watch you every second.' Again, he shook her so abruptly that her head throbbed and she felt tearful. She was tired, and this came with the shock of a slap after Sam's loving embrace. 'Tell me – admit it! And where is he? Where's that bastard gone off to?'

'I've no idea,' Lily gasped, confused. 'I haven't seen Dr McCluskie – not since yesterday morning, I swear to you.' In her fright she grasped the fact that the only way she was going to calm him down was by appeasement. She could see the anguish mixed with his rage and she spoke to that. Taking courage, she laid her hands on his shoulders.

'Ewan, dear . . .' He went to shake her off but she persevered. 'No, listen, please – I need to tell you something. I didn't want to tell you, to upset you or your guest, but it seems I must now.'

He stared at her, face full of hostility, but he was listening.

'Two nights ago Dr McCluskie came to my room and attempted to have . . . relations with me. He was the worse for drink and rather unpleasant, but I managed to make him leave without anything happening. It was all quite horrible and obviously made facing him again very difficult. But I can assure you, Ewan, dear, that nothing happened, I made sure of it, and that I have no interest in such a boor of a man who could approach me in such a way. He's not like you, dear, not gentle and manly. He behaved like a coward and I hoped never to see him again . . .'

'The cad!' Ewan McBride was still breathing heavily, but she could see he believed her and his fury was not directed at her for the moment.

'And I really have no idea at all where he is now,' she said. 'Let's not worry about him, dear.'

She thought she had talked him round, but then his mood switched again, eyes narrowing, his breath quickening in agitation.

'That may be so,' he said. 'But you must have led him on in some way. I know you, the way you prey on men, I've seen you. And where have you been? You can't just shift the blame to McCluskie. You've been with him, or some other man – I know it, I can *smell* it on you!'

He was winding his temper up again and she became

frightened that he was going to hit her. Even in his rage, on this occasion he did not raise his voice above a venomous hiss: it wouldn't do to have anyone hear. He seized hold of her even harder, grabbing her wrists, and pulled her along the corridor.

'An end to this – I'm not having it. You're going to learn how to behave like a lady, the way I've taught you!'

'Ewan – stop it! You're hurting me – please, don't!'

'Inside – and don't think you're coming out until I say so!' Dr McBride threw open the door of Lily's room and forced her in, shoving her so hard that she stumbled and fell half across the bed. For a second she was stunned, but then she found herself full of explosive rage.

'Don't you push me like that!' she shouted as he disappeared. 'Don't you dare treat me like that!' She ran to the door and went furiously to open it but he was holding the handle the other side and she could not turn it.

'Settle down, you little wild cat.' She could only just hear him, sounding smug and powerful, through the thick wood. 'You're not coming out – not until I say so.'

'You can't keep me in here,' Lily spat at the door. There was no lock so how did he think he was going to stop her getting out? 'I'm not your chattel to push around. I'll come out whenever I like!'

'Oh, that's what you think, my pretty little tiger. We'll soon see to it that you don't come out of there except with my express permission.'

'I'm not staying here!' With a supreme effort she quietened her tone, though the anger she felt with him, the filthy old sod, almost choked her. After her night with Sam, after all Sam meant to her and had made her feel, the thought of Ewan McBride and the way she had serviced him sickened her. Never again was she going to let any man treat her like that!

'Ewan – you're being a bit harsh.' She spoke calmly, seductively. 'I told you, I haven't been with any other man. What man would there be, for goodness' sake, when I never see anyone? Just come in here and we'll talk about it. I'll make you feel better.'

'Don't you come that one.' He still had a firm hold on the door and she heard him shouting for Prithvi, whose voice Lily heard a moment later. Dr McBride issued some abrupt order to her in Hindustani and she was gone again.

A quarter of an hour passed while Lily pleaded, struggling every now and then with the handle, and the doctor held the door fast. She heard a voice outside and thought, Surely Jane must be back from her walk now? But she realized it was Stephen.

'Miss Waters has been taken ill,' she heard the doctor say. There came a murmured reply from Stephen and that was all.

Soon she heard another voice, male and native. There was a clink of tools being put down, then a drill. In a moment Lily realized, to her horror, what was happening.

'No!' she screamed through the door. 'You can't! You can't just lock me in here! For God's sake, this is too much, Ewan – let me out! Oh, please, let me out!'

She was sobbing now as he held the door cruelly closed and she could hear bolts being screwed into the door, one top, one bottom, and finally the rasp of them as they were pushed home.

'There!' Ewan McBride called to her. 'Now you're mine all right, my Lily. And don't you forget it!'

And then the footsteps went away and it was all quiet.

Chapter Forty-One

Lily sank down on the edge of the bed, trying to take in what Ewan McBride had done.

He couldn't really mean it! She had known the doctor wanted to have her in his control but she had never dreamed he would go as far as this. Surely he'd let her stew for an hour or so and then come and let her out? She'd still be able to get to Sam this afternoon if she was patient. And if he didn't come and release her, she'd find a way out, of course she would!

At first she was full of hope, almost light-hearted and still not believing. She crept to the door and turned the handle.

'Oh no you don't, Lily, my love. Don't think you're going to get away with it.'

She sprang back, heart pounding. Lord above, was he still out there, guarding her? The house was quiet and she had assumed he had gone away to begin on breakfast and work as on a normal day, when all the time he had been waiting, silently, outside her door. For the first time she felt a cold plunge of fear. Surely, sooner or later he'd have to go and attend to his patients?

In stockinged feet she tiptoed to the window and looked out over the majestic grey hills bathed in early-morning sunshine. In the yard of the school below the children were doing their morning drill and she could hear the slap of their feet as they ran round and the gong beating time. Below the window was the steep drop. What if she really needed to get out, if the doctor kept her in here all afternoon? The mood he was in made her realize that she had no idea what he might do. What if she couldn't see Sam? The thought was too terrible. No – she was going to find a way out.

She thought about knotting the bed sheets. If she tied the sheets to the window frame, would she be able to climb down? But she knew the back of the house. There was nowhere to climb down to, only the drop many feet to the shrubbery surrounding the schoolyard. She prowled the room. What other way out was there? It did not take long to realize that there was only the door and the window. Other than that the room was completely sealed. Suddenly tired, chilly, she sat on the bed again. She'd find a way, she told herself. She was not going to let him defeat her! What she must do was wait until he must surely have to go away and get someone else to let her out. Prithvi would help her, of course she would. In the meantime she would wait quietly. A nap would pass the time. Lying down on the bed, weary from a night with so little sleep, she cuddled her pillow, longing for Sam.

It was half past ten when she woke, cold and low with an insistent ache in her bladder. At least there was a chamber pot in the room, and she was able to relieve herself, but this did not help with the fact that she was now hungry and needed breakfast. The buoyancy of her mood earlier had completely gone and she sat hugging herself, feeling chilly and desperate. Did he want her to beg, was that it? Would he let her out if she went and pleaded pitifully? She hated the thought of having to grovel to him, but she was already humiliated by being locked up in here. She saw everything very starkly now. This was simply an extension of the humiliating way he had used her all along. And why had she let him? In exchange for pretty dresses and security and, if she was honest, for the sense of feminine power it had given her. She felt disgusted with herself. But that time was no more. All that mattered now was that she get out and be able to be with Sam for these precious hours before they were parted again, and Ewan McBride was not going to stop her!

'Ewan – are you still there?' She held her ear against the door, trying to sense his presence. There was no reply. Once again she tried the handle, straining vainly and with increasingly frantic impatience against the bolts, but the door was well and truly secured. There was no reply from outside.

Lily felt a surge of hope. If he'd gone out on his rounds, surely she could get someone else in the house to let her out?

'Help!' she shouted. 'Can someone help me? Prithvi, *Prithvi* – are you there? Mrs Das? Is there anyone there? Let me out, please!'

She shouted until she was hoarse and then stopped to listen, but there was still no response. The doctor really had gone, she realized, and it sounded almost as if everyone else in the house had as well. Her shouting was completely in vain.

'Oh, please, *please* . . .' she finished in a whisper, sinking to her knees by the door. The tears came then, at being locked in and left here, so powerless. She curled up, rocking herself until the emotion had exhausted itself, then got up, draggingly, and went to the bed where she lay down again. She told herself to be calm.

The morning was only half gone. It was hours before she was due to meet Sam and the doctor would come back at tiffin time, calmer and seeing sense. He would have to make sure she was fed at some time, and then, somehow, she would make sure she got out. She *had* to!

Lying on the bed, she strained her ears to hear the sounds of the house. Distantly she heard doors open and close, but no one came near. There was no sound of Mrs Das sweeping, or Prithvi humming. They must have been told to keep away. She lay thinking longingly of Sam. The minutes dragged past with appalling slowness: eleven o'clock, twelve. The gun boomed across from Gun Hill signalling midday. Lily sat up, driven to an agony of impatience. Was Dr McBride intending to starve her to death? Surely someone would come now?

But another half-hour passed, and nothing. She was very thirsty and there was nothing to drink except the remains of some water in her pitcher for washing. She hesitated to drink it. It might make her ill – but her health had been exceptionally good since she had been India. She poured water into the glass on the washstand and drank deeply, then used a little more of the water to have a wash. After this purposeful activity it was almost one o'clock. All she could think of was that in two hours she must set out to go to the Fairfords' house and meet Sam.

At one o'clock she heard the bolts being drawn back and she leaped up from the bed, hoping desperately to see Prithvi, bringing tiffin for her, and she could beg her for help and everything would be all right. She could hurry down the road to Sam, even if too early.

'Glad to see me, are you?' the doctor said.

His voice was low, full of a controlled triumph. He

was carrying a tray on which there was a small pot of tea, a plate of bread and butter and a boiled egg with a white shell. Balancing it on one hand he closed the door, then put the tray down on the small table near the window. In that split second Lily thought of running for the door, getting it open again, but then he had turned to her and it was too late. He saw the direction of her glance.

'You don't want to be running away, do you now, Lily, dear?' He spoke sweetly, affording himself the pleasure of being kindly since he knew he had the upper hand. Making sure he was between the door and Lily, he came towards her until he was intimately close, looking down into her eyes, laying his hands heavily on her shoulders. Lily controlled herself so that she did not recoil. She knew that he was in a state beyond anything she had seen before and that it was vital for her to behave calmly. She'd do anything she could to get herself out of this situation and regain her freedom.

'Why would you want to run away from me?' He sounded genuinely wounded now. 'I've done so much for you, my Lily. I've fed and clothed you, loved you, given you a good life. You're my little Lily and I don't understand why you'd want to go running after other men like Duncan McCluskie. What has Duncan to charm you?'

'Nothing, Ewan.' She looked up earnestly at him. That at least was true. She found Duncan McCluskie even more repellent than Ewan McBride. 'You've made a mistake, really you have. I don't know why you've let this idea grow in your mind when you know I've always been here when you've needed me. You mustn't get so upset about things that are only your imagination and nothing else.'

'You mean I'm yours – that I mean something to you?' Suddenly he sounded pathetic.

'*Yes.*' She forced as much sweet sincerity into her voice as she could muster. 'Of *course* you do. You've always been so kind and generous to me, dear, and I shall always be so grateful to you.' She stood on tiptoe and kissed his cheek. 'I'm your little Lily, aren't I? No one else's.'

The doctor stared down at her in silence and she thought for a second she had won him over, but then his eyes narrowed.

'You're a wily young minx, aren't you?'

'Whatever d'you mean?' she asked, in a tone of injured innocence.

'Where ... did ... you ... go?' As he said each word he squeezed her shoulders painfully hard as if trying to wring the truth out of her. 'You came in this morning with the look of a lover, Lily. I'm no fool – you can't hide it from me. And I'm not going to let you out of here until I get the truth.'

'You're hurting me!' Lily felt like crying but she wasn't going to break down in front of him. 'I've told you, I went for a walk, that's all. The dawn was lovely, and ...'

'You little liar!' He slapped her hard round the face, his own contorting with rage. Lily cried out. The sting of it was very sharp and she felt a jarring all along her jaw. 'You stand there, lying to me grossly, wantonly, like that! I thought if I could get out of you a sweet word of truth and apology I might think about letting you out some time today. But I can see I was fooling myself. You won't be going anywhere – not today, not ever, if you don't learn to stop lying and tell me the truth!'

Dr McBride gave her a contemptuous shove which sent Lily backwards so that she almost fell on to the bed, and he slammed out of the room. She heard the bolts being rammed furiously into place and his footsteps fading along the passage.

Lily sank to her knees by the bed and buried her face in the covers. How was she ever going to get out of here to see Sam? Her whole being was full of urgency, the need to fly to him. It was now the only thing that mattered. And the doctor seemed to be almost unhinged with jealousy and suspicion. Would she even get out of here today? She buried her head in the covers and sobbed with rage and frustration.

Chapter Forty-Two

After her meal, Lily's spirits recovered for a time. She felt more optimistic. Of course he couldn't keep her here! As soon as his own tiffin was over he'd come and insist that she accompany him on one of their walks. At least then she would be out of the house.

Desperate plans hatched in her mind. She would set off with McBride and somehow give him the slip as they passed through the bazaar. Or she would simply run away from him, straight to Zinnias and Sam!

But as the minutes passed, the clock ticking loudly and ringing out the quarter hours, and there was no sound of footsteps out in the passage, once more she was full of desperation. Half past one, two o'clock. The school below on the hill went quiet. How the minutes dragged as she alternately sat and then paced the room, able to think only about Sam expecting her, looking out for her. Two-thirty came and went and when the time arrived when she should have been setting off she was in an agony of need. He would be waiting for her and think she had decided to let him down!

For the first time she lost control of herself. Weeping, she hammered on the door, bruising her fists as she raged at it.

'Let me out! Someone come and get me out, please! Oh, please don't leave me in here any more! Prithvi? Jane? Help me!'

Still no one came. There was only silence from the house. Three o'clock. Sam would be waiting. She knew that kind of expectation he would be feeling, the way she felt every time she waited to see him. And she would not come. The next two hours passed in an agony as she thought of the Fairfords' bungalow, imagining what was happening there and what Sam might be feeling and thinking of her. If only she could get a note delivered to him, but there was no one she could ask! Once more she wept helplessly.

By the late afternoon, as the sunlight faded to coppery pink, she had sunk into a state of lassitude. She had eaten very little that day, she had only been able to relieve herself in the chamber pot, which badly needed emptying, and any hopes for the day had been dashed. She thought about all the violent things she would like to do to Dr McBride. Sam was leaving for Bombay to catch his ship in two days and she had already missed a precious afternoon with him, thanks to the doctor! All she could think of now was seeing Sam before he left.

All night her thoughts span with anxiety. Surely the doctor would come to his senses and let her out in the morning? How was he explaining her absence to the rest of the household? But this was a worry. The title 'doctor' commanded such power! He could give them some trumped-up explanation for her absence and no one would even question it, possibly even Jane Brown. Lily felt panic rise in her. What if Dr McBride had really lost his senses and was planning to keep her here for as long as he liked, to play with her?

The pink dawn brought a new sense of hope and balance. Of course he'd let her out! He came to her with a tray of breakfast, having neglected to give her dinner the night before. Scrambled eggs and toast and a banana fortified her, but he barely spoke, despite her pleas to him to forgive her and let her go, to tell her what he planned to do. Once more the door was closed and the bolts slammed into place.

The day passed in an agony of uncertainty. Lily sat, half in a trance, or paced the room, losing all sense of time. When the doctor next came in, soon after four o'clock, she had a plan.

'Ewan,' she said, very gently as he put the tray of tea down. 'I wonder if you would allow me to do something. As you know, the Fairfords, my employers in Ambala, are here in Mussoorie, but they'll be leaving tomorrow. You've been so kind and generous in letting me spend some time with them but I wonder now if they won't be thinking me awfully rude for just disappearing without a word. I wondered if I might just go out to see them, perhaps, to say goodbye? Their holiday is almost over and they'll be going back. Might I, d'you think, just walk out along towards Gun Hill for a little while?'

He eyed her, as if considering her proposal seriously, and then, as if to a small child, said, 'We'll see. Let's just see how you behave yourself until then, shall we?'

This gave her a chink of light, of hope, and she dared to ask, 'I don't suppose there has been any message for me, has there? A note, perhaps?'

He poured her tea and handed her the cup. She saw that the soft skin under his eyes looked more puckered than usual with tiredness.

'And who might that be from, Lily?' He spoke with that teasing, ominous tone again and she could hear how suspicious he was.

'From the Fairfords, of course,' Lily said brightly.

'Mrs Fairford has been very kind to me and she was expecting to see me yesterday afternoon. She's the sort of person who might worry – she might even come to the house to enquire...'

'No. Nothing has come for you,' he said, going to the door.

'Doctor – the chamber pot needs emptying, badly!' she blurted.

Silently and with distaste, he took it and brought it back empty. Then, abruptly, he left the room again.

The rest of the day passed. At times, Lily grew severely agitated and then at others, simply flat and hopeless. She tried to sleep as much as possible, to pass the time so that she could avoid the agony of feelings that came upon her. Sam was leaving tomorrow. She had not seen him and he had evidently not attempted to contact her. Surely the doctor would have challenged her over it triumphantly if any note had arrived? She could hardly bear to imagine what Sam must think of her. That she had been playing with him and had deserted him? And why had he not come to see her? She racked her brains desperately for a way she could get out to see him tomorrow.

What if, when the doctor came in with a tray of tea, she could throw it over him and escape while he was standing, scalded and shocked? The next time he came in she was almost on the brink of doing it, trembling at the thought, but she could not quite find the nerve. She thought of writing a note for Prithvi or Jane Brown and slipping it under the door, but of course that was no good. The doctor would most likely find it when he next came to bring her food. Again and again she opened the window and stared down, desperately trying to see if there was any ledge, any staging point big enough that she might lower herself down on to it, hoping every time that she had perhaps missed something. Each time all she could see was the sheer drop down the side of the house and the monkeys' playground of the trees and roofs below in the valley, and she knew that to try and climb down would almost certainly lead to her death. There were moments when even that seemed preferable to staying a prisoner here.

The morning of the day Sam was due to leave, she was awake before dawn. She left the bed and as she did so many times in the day, turned the handle of the door, pushing on it and hoping, vainly. Once again the bolts were fastened. There was no way out. That was the moment when she decided that whatever it took, she was going to get past Ewan McBride, even if she had to scald him or knock him unconscious to do so.

Dressing herself in readiness, she waited as the light changed from an uncertain haze of grey to the strong colours of morning. It was a beautiful day, the mountains touched with gold, and tiny wisps of cloud strewn across the valleys. Lily sat on the bed and breathed in deeply, watching the light change, thinking how many times she had seen that sight.

I won't be here soon to see it, she told herself. She had no fixed idea of what was going to happen, except that she felt strong and desperate and somehow she was going to get out of there and never return. How could she stay with Dr McBride now? She would go and find Sam, travel with him, run away with him and somehow beg a passage on the boat back to England . . . In those moments anything seemed possible. She was full of a vibrating energy. All she had to do was to wait for him to come and she would spring at him. Whatever she had to do, she would be free, and she would go to Sam, be with Sam forever . . .

But he did not come. He brought her no breakfast, not even a cup of tea. He must, surely, come with tiffin, she reasoned, beside herself with anxiety. Was he punishing her in some new way? And if so, for what? Hadn't she been punished enough? When the hour of tiffin came and went she became frantic again. Sam would be leaving on an evening train from Dehra Dun. If she didn't leave the house by mid-afternoon there was going to be no chance of seeing him. He would be gone, thinking the very worst of her, and she'd never see him again. Desperately, she hammered on the door, weeping and begging to be let out.

No one came. The day crawled agonizingly past and by the late afternoon she knew with a dull numbness of despair that she had missed him. Sam Ironside would be gone, with the Fairfords, driving away from her down the twisting mountain roads and bearing in his heart feelings of utter betrayal and anger towards her. Perhaps he would think she had been playing with him, that this was her revenge for his leaving her last time. He would be angry that she had not kept her promises to come. And she ached for his suffering. But then she felt angry and betrayed herself. Why had he not come to the house to find her? Not moved heaven and earth to make sure he saw her? All she had now were the torn ends of unanswered questions and she felt a terrible despair. All the future held was life without him, without love or happiness, and it was a future in which she had no interest. Now he had gone for certain, she scarcely cared whether McBride let her out of the room or not. She had nothing to leave for.

She lay on her bed, facing the wall.

Chapter Forty-Three

The days turned into a week, then two weeks.

No one came near her except Dr McBride, who sometimes brought her food at the normal times, and sometimes not. She realized that this was a calculated means of keeping her in uncertainty. Now and then he brought her a jug of fresh water for washing, emptied her chamber pot and even, once, brought fresh sheets for her bed.

'Why does no one else come and see me?' Lily asked him soon after Sam had left. 'Where do they think I am?'

'So far as they're concerned, you have a fever, a highly infectious one, from which they need to keep their distance,' the doctor told her, genially. He seemed happy now, as if convinced Lily's spirit had surrendered to him. She no longer put up much of a fight about any-thing. Now she knew that Sam was gone, that he had not even tried to contact her before leaving again forever, nothing else seemed to matter. She lay for hour after hour, feeling she had no energy to care about anything. Occasionally she would rouse herself to eat, or wash herself, or to sit by the window, looking out over the mountains and hearing the distant children's voices from the school. Every so often, almost absent-mindedly and without hope, she tried the door. But it never gave.

'How long are you going to keep me here?' she asked one day.

'Until you're better,' he said, sitting by her bed and taking her hand. 'You're not very well, are you, my little one?'

Lily sighed. It was true, she didn't feel well. Certainly not the robust health she was used to. She found it hard to eat much and her innards felt sluggish. She had so little energy that sometimes it was hard to rouse herself from the bed.

'Perhaps if I had some fresh air and exercise I'd feel better,' she said.

'Oh, I don't think that would be a good idea,' he said, concerned. 'You mustn't do anything to weaken yourself further, Lily, my dear. We want you back in the best of health as soon as possible, don't we?' He was speaking to her in the wheedling, childlike voice that he had started to use with her all the time.

Lily felt a chill go through her suddenly. Where had she heard that before? In Muriel McBride's bedroom, the day the doctor had come in and sat beside her with such tender concern, looking down in to his wife's eyes as if she was the most important person on earth. Lily stared back at him, at his heavy form leaning over her, and big soulful eyes, full of the same concern. Inside her, there came a surge of revival. Somehow, she saw, the doctor had made Muriel McBride the way she was and now he was starting on her. He *wanted* her to be ill! She felt herself flood with energy.

Calmly she said, 'You're right, of course, Ewan. I do think I'm not myself at the moment. Perhaps the best thing I can do is sleep for an hour or two.'

'Very wise, my darling,' he said, patting her shoulder. 'And I'll sit with you while you sleep. I love to watch you.'

Lily tried not to let her alarm show. 'There's no

need,' she said, forcing a rueful smile on to her face. 'In fact, if you were here I should want to stay awake and be with you. So it might be said you wouldn't be doing your patient much good! Why don't you go and see your wife? She must be missing you.'

'As long as you promise you'll rest, Lily, darling. I don't want you coming to any harm, ever.'

'Of course I shall.' She lay back obediently, as if ready for sleep and he left the room, casting a look back at her as he did so, as if checking on her.

Lily lay still until his footsteps had receded along the passage. Only then, she realized, she had been holding her breath.

From then on she continued to act her part as the feeble invalid, but now, instead of allowing herself to slip into the poorly stupor which Dr McBride seemed to encourage, Lily's mind was working constantly on plans for escape. Her frustration and anger returned multiplied since her renewed determination did not make it any easier to actually find a way out of the room. Then, one afternoon, she heard a timid little tap on the door and leaped up from the bed.

'Miss Lily?'

'Is that you, Prithvi?' Lily ran to the door.

'Yes. Are you sick, Miss Lily? Dr McBride said you are very sick and must not be disturbed. He said we must not come near. But I was feeling so sorry for you and he has gone out. I came to see if there is anything you need.'

'Prithvi, I'm not sick, I'm all right!' Lily cried. She was trembling wtih excitement. At last, a way out! 'Open the door, will you! He won't let me come out. Just pull the bolts back, Prithvi, please!'

There was a pause.

'The doctor is saying that we must not open the door. That you are not to be let out under any circumstance whatsoever.'

'But I'm not ill!' Lily pleaded desperately. 'He just wants me to be, to keep me here, but I'm perfectly all right, honestly. He's the one who's not well!' As she said this, thinking of the controlled face the doctor showed to the rest of the world, she realized how crazed it sounded. 'Oh, please just let me out and you'll see – just for a moment!'

She knew how timid Prithvi was, how she could never seem to take any decision without authority from someone else, and already her hope was fading.

'I cannot disobey the doctor's orders,' Prithvi's soft voice came from behind the door. 'I am sorry, Miss Lily. But I hope you will be better soon. I must go now. He will be coming back soon.'

'Prithvi, no – don't go!' But it was too late. It seemed so long since Lily had seen anyone, a friendly face she could trust, that she sank to her knees, sobbing. How was she ever to get out if everyone thought she was crazy and wouldn't believe anything she said? Curled up, she wept for a time, feeling defeated. She got up to lie on the bed, but then stopped herself. She often fell asleep in the day, as if to escape from the long, dreary hours, but it stopped her from sleeping at night and if she was sleepless the nights seemed even longer than the days.

Instead she calmed herself and sat at her table, taking a piece of writing paper.

'Dear Cosmo...' The idea of writing to him strengthened her. She had been disturbed by all the news she had heard of him from Susan Fairford. What had happened to the sweet little chap she had known in Ambala, to turn him into the ungovernable boy the school was seeing? It made her sad, yet she could sense, somehow, his unhappiness, however little he said in his occasional scrawled notes to her. How he must have loathed England, the cold, grey days, after the brilliance of India, shut behind the dark school walls. And with no family, no Lily or Srimala to give him love and affection. Her heart ached for him and the ache in her today reached out to him. In her grief, he seemed to be the only person she had left. She wanted to send her reassurance to him even if she had no idea whether the letter would ever be posted. Surely the doctor would not deny her that?

'I am still here in Mussoorie, in the hills,' she wrote, 'and it is very pretty here. You would like it. Not long ago your mother and father were staying here with Isadora and Srimala and some of the servants. I expect they told you. Isadora has learned to ride really quite well. Your father has another new Daimler and the same man who brought the first one came again to deliver it to him. Sam Ironside. You were very small last time he came but perhaps you remember that too?'

She stopped, sucking the end of her pen and gazing out over the hills, seeing nothing. All she could see, with a stab of terrible longing, over and over again, was Sam's face that night when they had lain by the fire, the intense love in his eyes. And now, what did he feel or think of her. She wanted to write, *He's the man I love . . . and now I've lost him, lost him forever . . .*

She found a few other cheerful things to say to Cosmo, telling him she hoped he was working hard at his lessons and that he must try and be obedient and not get into trouble again.

'I hope you remember me, Cozzy, and that I'll see you again one day,' she finished. 'This letter comes with much love from your friend, Lily.'

In her neatest copperplate she addressed the envelope to his prep school. Writing the letter steadied her. She must be patient if she was going to get out of here. Sooner or later, her chance would come. He couldn't keep her locked up here forever.

Dr McBride agreed to post Lily's letter to Cosmo without any obstacle, but still more days passed and Lily had to hold on very hard to her hope of escape. Many times in the day she opened the windows and stood breathing in the fresh mountain air, stretching her body to keep supple and strong.

She tried to keep the day and night separate, but often sleep did not come at night. One night, when she had been in the room for three and a half weeks, she was particularly restless and unable to settle. The house was very quiet, something scuttling in the roof above her head, but otherwise, silence. She lost track of the time, but the silence almost seemed to make a sound of its own.

Lying on her back, she was aware that she felt slightly unwell, suddenly rather queasy.

I mustn't give in to this, she thought. Any sign of illness worried her, as if it meant that she was surrendering to Dr McBride's attempts to sicken her. I'm not ill, I'm perfectly well and I shall not let him make me ill ... But the feeling did not go away. Lily plumped the pillow under her head and turned to lie on her side, closing her eyes. She must sleep, that would see it off.

A moment later, she heard a sound and her eyes

snapped open, her heart banging hard. There was a sound outside the door. Someone was out there!

She sat up in the total darkness, listening with every fibre of her being. She wanted to light the candle but she was listening too intensely to move. She held her breath. No, she was not imagining it – someone was easing back the bolts, slowly, carefully, not the rough way the doctor did it, but softly, so as not to be discovered. The top bolt was eased free, then the bottom.

Lily leaped off the bed as the door opened, letting in a warm glow of candlelight. Standing in the doorway in her nightdress was Jane Brown.

'Lily?' She came hurriedly into the room and shut the door, turning to look at Lily with stern, troubled eyes. 'Are you all right? We hear you have been very unwell.'

'No!' Lily went to her, grasping her arm urgently. 'Please, for God's sake, you've got to help me. He's had me locked up in here and I don't know why! I'm not ill – I never have been ill!'

Jane Brown's eyes searched her face. 'No, I can see. Mrs McBride sent me, to tell you the truth. She was quite sure you weren't ill either.'

Chapter Forty-Four

'Miss Waters, are we awake?'

The brisk tap on the door was followed by the appearance of a white-veiled head. Lily's eyes opened and she sat up groggily. Her bewilderment was plain in her face. Where was she? This small, bare room, the iron bedstead, the work-worn but bright-eyed face staring down at her. Of course, the convent!

'Oh – good morning!' Hurriedly she swung her legs over the side of the bed and felt a lurch of nausea as she did so.

'Slept through the bell again – you are exhausted, aren't you, dear!' Sister Fidelis commented. 'I suppose the last few days can't have been easy for you. But you should be down at breakfast, and the laundry won't wait, you know!'

'I don't usually sleep so heavily,' Lily apologized, pulling her nightdress closed at the neck. She felt uncomfortably aware of her full-breasted body compared with Sister Fidelis's, slim in its chaste attire. 'I'm most terribly sorry. I really will try to do better.'

'Not to worry!' Sister Fidelis almost sang, making to depart again. 'Just get yourself up and ready as fast as you can. There's water in the jug.' She turned at the door and peered at Lily. 'Are you all right, dear?'

'Yes!' Lily fibbed. She felt dangerously close to being sick but didn't want to be any more trouble.

'Perfectly, thank you, Sister. I'll be down in a few minutes.'

'Right-oh.'

Immediately she'd gone, Lily ran to retch over the wash bowl and then sank groaning on the bed. She sipped some water, wondering at how deeply she'd been asleep when all around, from outside, came the sounds of the girls occupying St James's School. This was one of Mussoorie's many educational institutions and was run by Church of England sisters originally from an order in Oxfordshire, most of whom spoke in beautifully modulated English and gave off an air of cultured sensitivity, however mundane the tasks with which they were presented. The convent and school sat perched high above the valleys, with breathtaking views from almost every room.

Lily closed her eyes for a moment and breathed in deeply. She felt better now, but what on earth was the matter with her? Sister Fidelis must be right, she realized. She was in a state of nerves after all that had happened over the past weeks. It was only now beginning to hit her how extreme and bizarre Dr McBride's behaviour towards her had been.

That night, when Jane Brown released her from the room where she had been imprisoned for almost a month, she took Lily's hand and led her like a child down the creaking stairs to her own quarters, where she locked the door behind them and hurried to light the lamp. Both of them then stood and smiled, exhaling with relief, then Lily, completely overwrought, burst into tears and was taken into Jane's comforting, shawl-clad arms.

'Oh, thank you for letting me out. I was beginning to think no one would ever come. He's kept me locked in there all this time – he's mad, I swear it . . .' She sobbed for a moment, then drew back. 'I expect I smell terrible . . .'

'Not at all,' Jane Brown said kindly. 'Are you all right, Lily?' Her eyes were wide with concern.

'Yes. I am now. He just . . .' Her tears came again. She realized how lonely and frightened and humiliated she had been.

'We had no idea – not at first,' Jane Brown said, taking Lily to the chair. 'He told us you were ill, something really contagious, but then when it went on and on. And he was so peculiar about it, his behaviour . . . The man's an absolute menace . . .'

The two women talked for a long time, through the night, sitting wrapped up in shawls and blankets near the unlit fire. Jane Brown described her increasing suspicion towards Dr McBride.

'I'd leave tomorrow, if it weren't that I feel for *her*.' She nodded her head towards Muriel McBride's room next door. 'It's taken me a long time to work it out. He's always so gentle, so solicitous towards her. And whatever she's done, she's done it to herself, there's no doubt. But it's *because* of him, I know it!' Her voice grew passionate. 'He's *caused* it somehow – he helped her to destroy herself and it's so tragic to watch. She's even admitted it to me, in a sort of way. But she's too far gone now to do anything about it.' Jane wiped her eyes, wearily.

'She did warn me about you, to take care of you, I mean – several times, now I come to think about it.' Her face darkened. 'She must have sensed something. The man wants locking up himself, but what can we do? He's such a smooth-talker, so well thought of. Mind you . . .' She hesitated, blushing as she looked across at Lily. There was a hint of a smile on her lips.

'What is it?' Lily asked.

'You should have seen him with that other doctor who was here, McCluskie. Two nights before he went back to Patna or wherever it was, he went missing – all night.'

'Yes – he thought McCluskie was with me,' Lily said candidly, and saw Jane Brown look really embarrassed. She realized then that even if the nurse had guessed perfectly well the full extent of Ewan McBride's uses for her, she was certainly not used to talking about such things. 'Where was he, then?' she asked.

'In a brothel.' She brought out the words rather harshly, as if determined not to be coy. 'They had a very loud argument about it when McCluskie came sloping back in the morning. Dr McBride couldn't seem to control himself at all. You could hear him all over the house.' Lily realized she, too, had heard the argument in the distance. 'That's the only time I've ever known the doctor let rip like that. He always likes to be so in command.'

There was a pause, then Jane Brown looked across at Lily with a sad puzzlement in her eyes.

'Why have you let him use you like this, Lily? You seem such a strong person.'

It was Lily's turn to blush, a deep sense of shame seeming to swamp her. How could she explain that in some way she felt this was what she deserved? But for the first time ever she tried to be frank with this woman who had rescued her.

'I don't know. I suppose he gave me a good job, security. My own background was rather poor, you see. I'd never been wanted by anyone much, or taken out and about like that before, and it didn't seem too high a price, not then. I sort of slipped into it without meaning to and couldn't get out again. I suppose that sounds terrible to you.'

When she looked up she saw Jane looking at her with real pity in her eyes.

'Not terrible. Just sad. We must get you away from here, Lily. Even Muriel has asked me to get you away from here. I know where you can go – at least for the short term.'

Before dawn, Jane Brown dressed and they crept back to Lily's room, where she also pulled some clothes on and packed a small bag of belongings before the two of them quietly let themselves out into the dark street.

'It's a good distance,' Jane Brown said. 'Over towards Happy Valley. We'll have to wake one of the *jhampanis* when we get further away from here. But I should be able to get back in good time. Fidelis and I went to school together – only she was called Rosamund then.'

They found a rickshaw to take them some of the way, and climbed the last mile on foot up to St James's, where Jane Brown knocked loudly on the heavy convent door. At last a sleepy looking *chowkidar* appeared and Jane Brown asked for Sister Fidelis.

'Please tell her Miss Brown is here, and it is an emergency.'

Lily stood feeling very nervous at the idea of rousing the nuns in this awesome-looking place at this time in the morning, but Sister Fidelis appeared, already dressed and carrying an oil lamp, in the light of which she looked remarkably cheerful.

'Miss Waters urgently needs a discreet place to stay,' Jane Brown told her. Lily blushed, suspecting that Sister Fidelis would immediately jump to the conclusion that she was carrying an illegitimate baby. But the woman's expression did not change, nor did she ask any questions.

305

'Come in,' she said, with a welcoming sweep of her arm. 'Are you capable of helping with the laundry, d'you think?'

'I'm sure I am,' Lily said.

'Just wait there a moment.' Sister Fidelis indicated a stiff-backed chair and Lily obediently sat down. She felt suddenly very safe. Sister Fidelis and Jane Brown talked in low voices outside, then Jane came in. Lily stood up.

'I must go back.' Jane Brown looked deep into Lily's eyes. 'You'll be all right here, for a while. They'll find you some work. Then you can look for a new appointment somewhere.'

'Thank you so much,' Lily breathed. She felt tearful, as if that night she had discovered a true friend, then lost her again.

'Let me know how you get on. Sister Fidelis can pass a message on to me.'

Tears in her eyes, she held out her arms and embraced Lily. 'I'll miss you, I truly shall. But you'll find something better, dear, I know you will. Just be careful of yourself, won't you?' And with a kiss on Lily's cheek she moved away, leaving Lily still trying to thank her, and disappeared out of the convent door into the waning night.

Sister Fidelis, Lily was to learn, was a continuous ball of energy who ran the school and convent dispensaries and filled in anywhere else she was required on the domestic front. She handed Lily over to a Sister Rosemary, a plump, cheerful woman of about forty who was in charge of the laundry, an immense room with a high, vaulted ceiling at the very back of the convent, where the nuns' habits and clothing of the girls who boarded were all laundered.

'We could just send everything to the *dhobi*,' she told Lily. 'But we think it's a good training for some of our girls – and for the young native girls who come in to work here. Some have gone on to work in some quite distinguished families. Now – what we could do with is some help with ironing. You know how?'

'Yes, of course,' Lily said.

'No of course about it,' Sister Rosemary retorted. 'Let me tell you, there are plenty of young maids in this town who don't know one end of a flat iron from another.'

The laundry room was warmed by a huge range at one end, on which several irons were heating at once, and close to which was a large, square table padded and draped in singe-marked sheets. At the far end were the washtubs, where a number of native girls were pounding away with dollies in the steamy heat. They looked curiously at Lily as she passed but did not say anything, though one girl gave a sweet smile. They all seemed to have great respect for Sister Rosemary. Above their heads, clothing hung on drying racks hoisted up near the ceiling, and there were three poles which reached up to the ceiling, each with arms extending out like tree branches, also with items drying on them.

'We have to dry everything in here during the monsoon, but there is a yard out at the back. Most of the bigger things are out on lines at this time of year. Now,' Sister Rosemary added briskly, 'let's get you started. I'll show you what's needed with these. They've all been starched already.'

Lily found that her days in the convent were spent quite pleasantly, ironing, often with one or two others, usually native girls of about fourteen years of age, who were respectful and friendly to her, and the day was punctuated by the bell summoning the pupils in and out of their lessons, and by services in the simple chapel. Lily was expected to keep the hours with them, going into the chapel early in the morning, and midday and in the evening.

She didn't mind any of this. Though she had never been exposed to religion she found the life a peaceful haven, and liked the flowers and whitewashed walls of the chapel. But as the days went by, the most difficult problem became her getting up in time in the morning. More and more she found herself burdened by an overwhelming sense of exhaustion, which would come over her when she was standing at the ironing table in the oppressive heat. One day she fainted, coming round to find that she had banged her head, and that she was sitting on a chair with her head forced down between her knees. She sat up groggily to find Sister Rosemary standing over her, along with a small crowd of the laundry workers.

'Back to work!' Sister Rosemary urged, clapping her hands and the other girls scattered. Narrowing her eyes appraisingly, she said in a low voice, 'I think you'd better come outside.'

Humbly, Lily obeyed. In the yard, strung with washing which flapped gently in the hillside breeze, Sister Rosemary faced her in her black habit, which somehow looked more severe in the open air. 'It seems you're not very well. Can you tell me what's the matter?'

'I don't know, Sister,' Lily said miserably. 'When I first arrived I just thought I had an acid stomach. I'd been in a bit of a state, you see. But it hasn't gone away. I don't feel well at all sometimes . . .'

'Especially in the mornings?' Sister Rosemary enquired coldly. 'Hence your frequent absence from morning prayer?'

Lily nodded miserably. There was a pause, Lily sensed, of disbelief.

'Well, don't you realize what this might mean? Is there any possibility that you are expecting a child?'

The question was so shaming it felt like being slapped. Lily felt a thick blush spread through her cheeks. Her mind was reeling. Surely it couldn't be? Dr McBride had assured her he was infertile and she had been with him months with no outcome like this. The only other thing was ... It had truly not occurred to her until then, so ignorant was she of women's ways. That night with Sam! Surely it couldn't be from that. You couldn't find yourself expecting after one night, could you? Surely that wasn't possible! But her confused expression must have spoken volumes to Sister Rosemary.

'I see.' She spoke gravely, and Lily could hear the deep disapproval in her tone. 'Well, we weren't told about this, but of course Fidelis has been wondering ... This changes things, certainly.' She spoke with cool detachment. 'You'll have to stay here for a time, live discreetly. We can see if we can find a home for the child – otherwise it'll have to go to an orphanage. Once it's over and done with, you'll be able to apply for another post.' Her eyes seemed to bore into Lily. 'You foolish girl. What a state to get yourself into. I wouldn't go expecting any sympathy. Now go back to work, while you still can.'

Chapter Forty-Five

Lily spent the next few days in a state of shock and anguish. A child! How could she be expecting a child!

She continued with the struggle of getting up and working in the laundry, but her mind was completely elsewhere. A child – and it had to be Sam's! All the pain she had been trying to shut out over the past strange weeks came crashing in on her, all the agony of her unanswered questions about Sam. What had he thought that day when she did not come to the Fairfords? Had he tried to contact her? He must have been hurt and angry. Had he sailed back to England possibly hating her for rejecting him and letting him down, perhaps thinking only the worst of her? She had no address for him, and how could she contact him now when she was in this state? The hard truth of the matter hit her with a crushing force. How could she trust Sam either? He had come to her as a married man, on the other side of the world from his family. Had he used her for his own entertainment? What would his reaction be if she ever told him she was carrying his child? Might he simply laugh at her naivety and walk away, back to Helen and his settled, respectable life?

Pain and anger surged round in her constantly, leaving her exhausted. Yet, at times, especially when she lay at night in the narrow convent bed, she would call to mind Sam's face, his absorbed, loving expression as he had gazed on her, and she wept with longing at the thought. How could she doubt him? He loved her, she knew it! She was the one who had hurt him and let him down, and she ached for him to be here with her, to pour out to him all that had happened. When morning came, though, and she woke sick and feeling as if she had not even slept, all the doubts crowded in again, accompanied by hard and disquieting certainties: that she was disgraced and carrying a child, that there was no love for her and little help and that, once again, as she had been so often, she was utterly alone.

She worked mechanically in the laundry, at least grateful for the shelter offered her by the nuns. She knew that they were aware of her state and most of them left her alone, unsure what to say to her. But the one person who was kind was Sister Fidelis. Now and again she would come up and sit in Lily's room and talk to her. Often she regaled her with stories about her own life and about the order.

'Oh, it was quite a feat getting everything established up here, of course. It was eighty-seven we started up here. The sisters in the early days arrived on bullock carts – you can imagine how long that must have taken, can't you?'

Then, after a few stories, she might say suddenly, 'Now, Lily, don't fret too much. We'll make sure you're all right. And something will come up for you. God always provides – you'll see. Would you like Jane to come and see you?'

Lily shook her head. In one way she would very much have liked to see Jane Brown, but she was too ashamed to face anyone else. 'I just want to be alone,' she said.

As the days passed, punctuated by the bell-ringing

routine of the school, and May arrived, the heat increased, though of course it was a pale shadow of the blistering scorch of the plains. Mussoorie was bathed in sunshine and filling up fast with summer visitors from Delhi and the Punjab. And after a few more weeks had passed, Lily also began to feel better. What was more concerning now was that, instead of feeling ill, she was beginning to notice the swelling of her abdomen. The idea of there being a baby in there didn't seem real at all and she felt no sense of fellow feeling for it. There were no women around her whom she could confide in, or who had had experience of childbirth, and all she could feel was ignorant and very frightened, despite Sister Fidelis's assurances that everything would be all right. All she could wonder was what was to become of her.

Within a few days, however, Sister Fidelis came bouncing into the laundry room in the middle of the morning. Lily, feeling much better now, was able to stand and do the ironing without any sickness or faintness and she was ironing one of the sisters' robust black habits.

'Lily!' Sister Fidelis hailed her in bubbly tones. She was a woman incapable of formality, it seemed, and had never called Lily 'Miss Waters' the way Sister Rosemary insisted on doing. 'Could you come outside with me for a moment?'

Once more, Lily found herself in the drying yard among the lines of washing.

'I have come to offer you an opportunity to go home – if that's what you would like.'

Lily stared stupidly at her. 'Home – what d'you mean?' For a horrible moment she thought Sister Fidelis

312

meant to the McBride house, that the doctor had come looking for her and softened the nuns with his charms.

'To England, of course! Where else would home be, dear?' Sister Fidelis chuckled heartily.

'What . . .' Lily stuttered. 'What d'you mean?'

'A paid passage home on the P&O is what I mean. There's a family called the Bartletts who come up to Mussoorie regularly every summer and they worship with us. They donate sums of money and so forth.' She waved a hand as if this was of little consequence. 'All very good. Their son is almost six years old and they feel it's high time he was back home at school. Mrs Bartlett happened to mention to me this morning that they're very concerned at how late they've left it and how they want to make sure he is safely accompanied. Well, I thought to myself, Lily has worked with children! What could be more fortunate! All you have to do is accompany young Bartlett – the boy's name is Eustace – on the P&O and deliver him to Mrs Bartlett's sister in Leamington Spa. And then you're free to go. How does that sound?'

'But . . .' Lily was almost too astonished to speak. 'That would mean leaving India!' It was India that felt like home now.

'Well, yes, naturally!' Sister Fidelis laughed at her utter confusion. 'You weren't thinking of staying here forever, were you?'

'I don't know,' Lily admitted. 'I suppose I *hadn't* thought. I've always liked it here . . .'

'Well – think about it now,' Sister Fidelis said briskly. 'I told Mrs Bartlett I had someone in mind, but that I'd have to ask around. I can let her know your reply tomorrow.'

Lily was thrown into complete turmoil for the rest

of the day. She stood moving the heavy flat iron over sheets and starched wimples without even seeing them.

Leave India! She had taken to the country straight away, had thrived here, and thought to stay, but now everything was different. If she had her child adopted, of course, she could apply for another post as a nanny and start again, closing the door on the past, pretending. That was the most tempting solution. It was what she had done so far. But now life had thrown this choice in her way. If she went back to England, would she see Sam? Immediately she knew the answer to that. It was impossible. He was there with his family and that was where he had chosen to return to. Common sense whispered in her ear, compounding her doubts. If he had known she was carrying a child, might he not have deserted her anyway? That was the way men behaved, wasn't it? But somehow, even though she couldn't make sense of all her feelings, she was drawn to going home. She would be near him, at least, in the same country. And she could get a new post with glowing references from the Fairfords. It would be a new start, not in a foreign land this time, but back where she had come from. She knew, with suddenly clarity, that it was what she must do.

That evening, she told Sister Fidelis that she would accompany Eustace Bartlett on his sea journey home to England.

Chapter Forty-Six

Birmingham, 1911

Lily knelt over the pail of filthy water, gasping as the pains tore through her back and abdomen. The scrubbing brush hit the floor with a clatter. Though she could see her breath in the freezing air, she broke out in a sweat. Droplets of it ran down inside her frock. Then she felt a rush of wetness between her legs and realized her underclothes were soaked through. All morning these outbreaks of agony had been coming and going.

'Oh!' she breathed, shakily as the pain died away at last. 'Oh God, help me, somebody.' Looking down the ill-lit corridor, she could see no other human face, only the great expanse of floor which it was her job to scrub, as it had been ever since she came to the home. 'Home' certainly did not feel like the right name for the Bethel Home, two miles from the middle of Birmingham, which took in unmarried mothers. It had been a place of dread even before she got here, that and the gory stories of childbirth she had heard from the women in the bedstead factory where she had worked out the last months before her confinement. Their talk had frightened her terribly.

For a moment she slumped over the bucket, resting her head on her arms, too weary to care about the rank smell of the water.

'I should've gone to the workhouse,' she whispered to herself. They might even have been kinder there, she thought, than these so-called Christian Evangelical ladies who ran Bethel.

A door opened somewhere along the corridor and she was half aware of brisk, clicking footsteps.

'What do you think you are *doing*?' Lily heard, in scandalized tones. It was the one she disliked the most, a long-nosed, zealous woman who they referred to as Sister Leigh. She had a pale, waxen face, brown hair taken back severely under her black uniform bonnet, and a thin figure on which her long black frock hung unbecomingly loose.

'Your job is to scrub the floor, you know that, Waters.' She spoke with a harsh Lancashire accent.

Lily raised her head, straining to see the woman's angular form in the poor light. For a moment her eyes were clouded.

'It's idleness that lets the Devil in. Don't let me find you idling again. Get to work.'

Lily's eyes cleared. She focused on the woman's shiny black boots, loathing her with a passion, with all her self-righteous judgements, her certainty of her own rectitude. It was humiliating to have to beg her, but things had become desperate.

'I'm in pain. The baby – I think it's on the way.'

'Nonsense, you look perfectly all right to me. You're not due yet. I know you girls – not that you are a girl, Waters, which makes you even more of a disgrace – any excuse not to do a full day of wholesome work. No thought of the condition of your souls, any of you.' She folded her arms. 'You deserve to burn.'

As she spoke, Lily was gripped by another racking pain. She seized the sides of the pail and pressed down, crying out as the great muscular clasp of her abdomen pressed tighter until she was panting and moaning. In the midst of her distress she became aware of Sister Leigh's lips urgently whispering words close to her ear.

'Does it hurt? Does it tear and rend you? It should hurt, sister, and it should rend, because only through the time of trial, through suffering and repentance, will you find the light of Christ in the darkness of your sin and wantonness. Pray for suffering, to be put harshly to the test . . .'

Lily gave a loud cry at the height of her pain, feeling as if she was being torn in two.

'That's it, feel your punishment for sin, feel it hard . . . Did he do it to you hard, hard inside you? Did he? Did it burn . . .? You'll burn, Waters, for your depravity, you'll burn in the everlasting fires . . .'

'For God's sake, help me!' Lily cried, when she had more command of herself. 'It's coming. Help me!'

Sister Leigh straightened up abruptly and came to her senses. 'Always such a fuss, you women,' she snapped. 'You should deliver the fruits of your fornication in silence, not with all this carry-on. Get up. Your time has come, and you deserve to suffer.'

She grabbed Lily's upper arm and hauled her to her feet.

Standing on Leamington Spa railway station all those months ago, once she had delivered Eustace Bartlett to his relatives, Lily had felt utterly alone. Eustace was a most obnoxious child and she was overjoyed to be rid of him, but now was the first time she really confronted the question she had been avoiding: what could she do next when she had nowhere and no one to go to? Her solitariness in the world and the precariousness of her situation overcame her. For a moment she thought about how near to Coventry she was, to Sam, but she pushed the thought angrily away. She had got this far without him. She had to manage her life alone. But amid the passengers and movement of luggage, the cars and carts coming and going, she felt like a tiny dot, invisible to everyone else and impossibly small.

As she stood, fearfully looking around her, the station tannoy announced the next train north to Birmingham. It was not somewhere she had ever thought she would return to, but at least she knew it a little and she ached for something familiar. She had hurriedly picked up her holdall and made her way to the Birmingham train.

The home, to the east side of Birmingham, had space for twenty women at a time. When Lily walked in through the forbidding front door she had vowed to do what she always did in a new situation: keep herself to herself, not answer questions or give anything away.

It was a terrible trial being back in England, in this drizzly, soot-begrimed city with its filthy streets and pale, threadbare people, but the home was even more of a shock. The girls were all expected to wear the same clothes: coarse grey frocks, baggy as sacks, to accommodate their swollen bodies, and their hair tied in a regulation plait down their backs. They were housed in bleak, splintery-floored dormitories of six or seven beds. At first Lily loathed the idea of sharing with such rough women after all she had been used to, and the lack of privacy. But she quickly saw that most of the girls in the home were so very much younger than herself. At twenty-eight she was almost old enough to be mother to some of them. And far from being nosy, most of them were desperate to find a listening ear to pour out their own woes and stories to. Lily had a bed in the corner, away from the window which looked across on to the frontage of a sheet-metal works, and next to her was a poor, malnourished-looking girl called Rachel, whose belly was the only rounded thing about her otherwise wasted form.

'It was my dad done it,' she whispered to Lily on the second night. 'He and my mom threw me out and told me to go to the workhouse. So I come 'ere instead. But they're cruel 'ard 'ere, that they are. Sometimes I wish I'd gone and finished myself in the cut.'

Lily listened, her sense of horror increasing even more when she learned that Rachel was only fifteen. After Rachel had fallen asleep she lay looking up into the dark. For the first time in a long while she allowed herself to think of Sam, and she ached with longing and sadness. But, she thought, if she had had nothing else in her life she had had those days with him, that night, and those looks of love, or what she had thought was love. It seemed Rachel's life was over when it had barely even begun, ruined by her father's incestuous attention.

As she got to know some of the other girls better she discovered how young many of them were and how sad their stories. Most of them had been taken advantage of in their naive innocence. Only one, Madge, was older, and at twenty-five had been deserted by the man who promised to marry her. Lily found that the younger girls looked to her, and over those days before the baby started coming she had tried to encourage them and be kind to them. Some of them seemed to have had so little warmth or kindness in their lives.

But now she was in one of the two delivery rooms down in the cellar of the big house and there was no one to show warmth or kindness to her. Sister Leigh half dragged her down the stairs, barely allowing her to stop as the pains came over her again. She tore away from the woman's needling fingers and knelt, groaning, on the stone stairs.

'Come along. Stop all this ungodly noise,' Sister Leigh scolded, pulling at her shoulder. She gave Lily a hard slap round the face. 'This is nothing you haven't brought on yourself so you'll have to put up with it.'

Lily threw her off. Nothing would induce her to move in the middle of this terrible agony. At last Sister Leigh led her down into the stone-floored room which contained a sink, a trolley laid out with various implements and a high, flat bed covered by a sheet up against the wall. There was a gaslight hanging from the ceiling close to the bed, which Sister Leigh lit resentfully.

'Loosen your clothes and get up there,' she ordered. 'Someone will come to you.'

She stood watching, arms folded, as Lily removed her sodden bloomers and petticoat and unfastened the buttons on her dress. Lily wanted to ask what was going to happen, longed for some sort of reassurance, but she wasn't going begging to this granite-faced, sanctimonious woman and she held her tongue.

'Get up on the bed and stay there,' Sister Leigh snapped. She turned abruptly and left the room.

What seemed like a very long time passed. Lily lay on the hard bed. There was no pillow and only the grey wall for company. Every few moments there came a terrible onslaught of pain, burning through her, pressing down on her like a weight. Each time she curled convulsively on her side, gasping and sobbing. Once she bent up so abruptly that she banged her head on the wall. She wanted to get off the bed and each time the agony stopped she thought about getting up but never seemed to be able to raise the energy. She had no idea how long had passed but the pains were coming more and more frequently.

'Oh God!' she cried out at the height of one of the worst contractions. 'God, help me, help me!'

'You might well ask God's help,' a voice said. 'He's certainly the only one who can really help you now.'

The woman standing over her was a plump, blunt-faced person, but she did not speak with the vicious unkindness of Sister Leigh, more a matter-of-fact indifference to Lily's pain. She had on a huge white apron over her black dress, and a white nurse's veil.

'Lie on your back,' she ordered. 'It's more seemly and I want to examine you. Legs up and apart!'

To Lily's horror she realized the woman was inserting her fingers up inside her, but she was determined not to cry out and humiliate herself further.

'You're nearly there,' the woman pronounced. 'It'll be here within the hour, I'd say.'

Even in these last days, with the baby kicking vigorously inside her, Lily had shut from her thoughts the reality that there was a living being inside her that was part of her. She did not want to know, could not let herself take in what that might mean. She certainly would not let herself begin to love it, because unless she got rid of it, pretended that it, and Sam, had never happened, she would have no life. She would be condemned to a life of shame and disgrace, trying to bring up a bastard child on her own, pretending she was a widow or one of the tricks such women had to play to live with any ease in society. And now she was too overtaken by the sheer ordeal of birthing to give any thought to the outcome.

Time swam by. She had no idea how long had passed.

Her whole existence was strung between the pains which seemed to arrive so close together that she was riding a sea of agony. She writhed, wanting to get up, to be on her knees, on her side, but each time she tried to move the woman in black forced her down.

'Get on your back! I'm not having you moving about. It's bad for the baby.'

Eventually the pains became overwhelming. Lily leaned back on her elbows, her legs apart and felt the enormous press of the child's head bearing down out of her. She thought she might split right in two. Screams issued from her mouth. In the midst of it there came a sharp slap round her face.

'Be quiet! How dare you make all that noise?'

It seemed to go on forever.

'Push!' the woman commanded her. 'Breathe and push, push it out!'

'I can't,' Lily cried, hoarsely. It felt impossible. She was completely exhausted. There had been no rest in this 'home'. Only work and more work.

Finally, bearing down with every fibre of her being, she managed to deliver the baby's head, and a few moments later she felt the slither of the body. She lay back, finished, panting. *That's it*, was all she could think. *It's over!*

Then, into the silence came the cry, a cracked, desolate sound which seemed to seize her at the centre of her being and draw her towards it. She leaned up on her elbow again to see the nurse unceremoniously wrapping the child in a length of white cloth. All she caught a glimpse of was dark hair. Sam's hair, she thought, filled with a terrible ache.

'Let me see . . .' Lily begged. 'Oh, please, bring it here . . .'

'It's no good. You're not keeping her, are you?'

'No, but . . .'

'Then it's no good. You'll have to feed her, but you're not to see her now. Won't do you any good. You must accept it. She'll soon be gone – and if you've got any sense, so will you, a gentlewoman like you.'

She took the baby from the room and Lily was left alone, hearing again and again in her head that rending, newborn cry, a sound which she knew would stay with her forever.

There was a nursing room, a place of mixed joy and desolation, where the new mothers were expected to go and feed their infants. The occasions of feeds were strictly timed and no extra time was allowed for holding or playing with the babies.

'No good getting a feel for her when you're giving her up.' Sister Jenkins, who was in charge of the nursing room, was a hearty but heartless person who treated both mothers and babies with utter lack of feeling. Lily watched her sometimes, her pink, brawny face bent over one of the young mothers, waiting to snatch the infant from them the second they had finished their allotted time at the breast.

Lily secretly called her little girl Victoria after the old queen. The home didn't allow the giving of names.

'They'll be given a name,' she was told. 'By their new families.'

The first time she saw the little one, once she had been cleaned up after the birth, was in the nursing room. Sister Jenkins carried her in from the nursery next door.

'Now – here you are. Undo your gown.' She had been issued with a thick, rough frock; the front crossed over her chest, with special ties so that it could be loosened for feeding. Lily was so fixed on seeing the child that she forgot to obey.

'I said undo your gown!' Sister Jenkins snapped. Lily found that her breasts were seeping a clear liquid. 'Now – take her and latch her to the breast.'

Lily held out her arms. She stared and stared at the tiny, perfect form that was handed to her. Tears welled up in her eyes and ran down her cheeks. Oh, she was Sam's child all right! She had thick tufts of dark hair and his sallow complexion.

'It's no good looking,' Sister Jenkins bossed her, trying to manoeuvre the baby on her arms to turn her to the breast.

'It's all right.' Lily drew back. 'I'll do it.'

She wanted to scream at the woman to go away. *Don't touch my baby, you cold, heartless woman! Leave me with her. Leave us in peace!* But she knew it was no good. It would only get her into trouble.

The feeling of the child's mouth on her nipple was strange and powerful and she sat wincing at it and the pains it caused in her stomach. Sister Jenkins sat watching her like a hawk and Lily kept her head down, trying to hide the overpowering rush of emotion which filled her. Here was this tiny being, sucking at her breast, so small and so dependent on her. And she was the first person Lily had ever known who was truly hers, who belonged to her. She felt stripped naked by the emotion, by the need she had for this little child. She would look down at her, wrung with tenderness, wanting to hold her in her arms forever.

What if she were to keep her? The idea ran round and round in her head. But she thought of going out again, alone, to the streets. All she had to her name was the payment from Eustace's family, the small remnant of her wages from the factory and Mrs Chappell's jewellery. What could she possibly give her baby? She would be so much better off with a family who could give her a good life. She forced herself to close down any such thoughts in her mind.

Victoria, she thought, looking down at her, willing both herself and the little girl to be strong. It was a strong name, and she would need to be victorious. She stroked her finger gently over the tiny, warm cheek.

'Right – that's long enough,' Sister Jenkins would decree, peering at the fob watch pinned to her ample chest.

Lily felt as if little Victoria was being torn from her as Sister Jenkins took her briskly away. How could she do the work she did, Lily wondered, when there was all this love and grief in front of her, all the powerful instincts of new mothers? She saw that Sister Jenkins had killed all such feelings in herself. And as she left the nursing room that evening, after Victoria's first feed, Lily knew that to survive losing her, she was going to have to do the same.

It was a freezing day in February when she stepped out through the forbidding front door of the home, dressed once more in her own clothes, holdall in her hand, head down against the bitter wind.

In her head were her instructions: the train to Euston, the directions to her new place of work, where, with Susan Fairford's glowing references, she had obtained a new post as nanny to two young girls at a respectable west London address.

Her figure had soon recovered. She was as rounded

and curvaceous as before, and walked with a healthy step, boots clicking along the cobbles. Looking up, she crossed the road, hurrying out of the path of a coalman's dray. She was wearing new clothes, bought with her payment from Eustace's people, a smart green dress, a new black coat and hat, and in every way she looked like a beautiful young woman setting out to embark on a new life. It was only her eyes that gave away her state, the pain locked in her heart. As she looked along the street, working out her route to the railway station, there was a deep sadness, a hardness which had not been there before, which covered up her grief, her bereavement, which she could not let herself feel.

Holding her head high, and with a determined step, she walked quickly away.

Chapter Forty-Seven

France, March 1918

'Oh God, here we go!'

Sam's hands tightened automatically on the truck's steering wheel. His convoy had just set off as the bugle sounded across the wide expanse of hospital huts to summon the nurses for emergency duty. Already they could hear the planes. Should he stop and turn back?

A small convoy of them had been ordered to drive desperately needed supplies to the casualty clearing station at Armentières. The raids had been coming night after night now the stalemate along the front had been broken by the German assault. Things were bad, very bad. The reception huts in the hospital were flooded with wounded, Allied and German, the place was like a scene from hell and all of them knew the war was hanging by a thread. The Germans were coming closer – they had reached Amiens.

Gripping the wheel, Sam eased his shoulders up towards his ears for a moment, a movement which had become so habitual that he no longer noticed it. His body had been forever taut during the three years he'd been in France; now it was pulled tense enough to snap. It was as if, in this endless hell of war, there was nothing but fear and exhaustion, no other state.

'Where are you buggers, then?' He leaned forward to try and see the droning threat in the darkness. He could hear nothing now, over the roar of their own truck engines. The Boche would be after the Étaples railway, which ran between the wide settlement of the hospital and supply depot and the sand dunes of the coast. Ambulance trains moved relentlessly along the tracks day and night, bringing the wounded from the Front, and it was the main artery along which the supplies to service General Haig's vast army were carried from the base depot. Shell that, and others like Calais and Boulogne, and they would paralyse the Allied supply lines. Just what they wanted, of course, Sam thought grimly. His mind slid round the fear: *And they'll win the war, and then what? What will happen?* But he buried the thought immediately.

He fixed his gaze on the lights of the lorry behind him. Bert, the driver, had leaned from the cab before they set off and called chirpily through his Woodbine, 'Don't lose sight of me, Ironside – no kipping on the job!' Act as if nothing was happening, that was Bert. That was all of them, come to think of it. Close down: don't think.

And you had to use every grain of strength to stay on the road. These rural routes were being grossly over-used, bottlenecked with the traffic servicing the vast army, the roaring lorries and ammunition wagons, the horses and carts, the files of khaki-clad men. The area was already low-lying and marshy and the combination of spring rains and constant churning by wheels and hooves and feet had turned the roads into a quagmire of liquid mud, filling the deep holes and ruts. He began the usual lurching trial of strength which driving in these conditions involved, fixing his mind on it, trying not to think of anything beyond . . .

He didn't hear it coming. Afterwards he knew it was a shell, that it had landed in the mist-filled pasture close by, that it had hurled his lorry over on to its side. But all he knew then was instant blackness.

For a long time he passed in and out of consciousness. When he surfaced, groggily, he knew he was lying somewhere hard, that his face felt stretched and tight, he didn't know whether with caked mud or blood or both, that there was something strange about his left eye, that there were pains all round his body and that he was shaking. He was aware of a dimly lit place, of groaning cries, of a ghastly stench. And then he dipped under again into the darkness.

He was aware of being moved, much later, lifted higher on to a bed; of an atmosphere of chaos, and light in his face.

'I don't think there's much wrong, despite the look of him,' a man's voice said. 'He'll lose the eye, that's all. Not urgent – leave him till later, Nurse.'

'What d'you mean?' Sam tried to say. His mouth tasted metallic, of blood, and nothing sensible came out.

A woman's voice came next and with his good eye he caught a glimpse of her in the dim light of the oil lamp: the VAD uniform, a white veil, her face pale and thin beneath, dark circles under the eyes. And she understood what he was asking

'You've got an eyeful of glass and a lot of bruising. But you seem to be all right otherwise. You've been very lucky. I'll come back to you later ... Too many others to see to ...'

He drifted again, but each time he surfaced, his mind snagged on something. *You've been very lucky ... Too many others to see to . . .* Something familiar. That voice, prim and well spoken. He knew that voice from somewhere.

'Water . . . A drink . . .' His mouth was parched, foul-tasting.

His head was lifted and he sipped water. God, water was lovely. He just wanted to keep lapping it, more and more, but the cup was taken away.

Sam opened his good eye. It was that nurse again.

'What time is it?' he said hoarsely.

'Why?' Her voice was flat and exhausted. 'Does it make any difference?' Then her natural good manners took over. 'I suppose it's five in the morning, or so.'

'Thanks. Am I going to be blind?'

'Can't you see out of that one either?' She came a little closer. Yes, he could see out of his right eye, and he knew then. She had changed a good deal. Had it not been for the voice he wouldn't have known her. But with the voice he was sure now. What on earth was she doing here? Would she remember him?

'I'm going to see if I can get some of the glass out of your eye,' she was saying. 'Before another convoy arrives and we're swamped again.' She seemed about to move away, perhaps to fetch instruments, but somehow he couldn't bear it.

'Aren't you . . . I mean . . . I know you, I think . . .' he said, confusedly. He was stunned, disorientated by seeing her again, here of all places.

'No.' Her voice was brimful of sadness. 'I'm sure you don't. I'm not your mother, or your sister, dear. But I'll look after you, all the same, as if I were.' The

330

utter sweetness with which she spoke brought a lump to his throat.

'But you're Mrs Fairford – aren't you?' As he said it he even wondered himself if he was hallucinating. 'Captain Fairford's wife – Ambala Cantonment?'

With only his one blurred eye he could still make out the change in her face. There was shock, and then she began to tremble. He thought she would weep.

'I seem to recognize you as well . . .' Her voice was high and tremulous, just in control. 'I'm not imagining what you're saying, am I?' She put a hand to her forehead. 'Sometimes I start to doubt myself . . . I'm so very tired . . .'

'No – it's all right. I'm Sam Ironside – remember? From Daimler. I brought your husband his cars.'

He saw her staring hard at him. Even now he felt himself tense, waiting for the response he remembered in her when they first met, the class superiority, her cool snobbishness. Her words came out haltingly, the recognition sinking in.

'Your face – you've so much blood on it I can hardly tell . . . Ironside . . . Of course, Charles's driver . . . We had picnics with the children, and Charles . . . Oh!' The last was an uncontrollable cry. 'Oh God!' She put her hands over her face, her shoulders shaking. 'I'm so sorry . . . Oh, forgive me . . .'

For a few anguished moments, Susan Fairford stood sobbing at the side of his bed.

As the dawn light increased through the windows of the hut, she bent over him, the lamp hanging from a hook near her head, and assessed his injuries again. She was quite collected now. He was covered in blood, she told him, because of a large number of cuts from small glass splinters, which had made his injuries seem far more serious on first sight. Sam realized the tightness in his cheeks was because of the dried blood. His eye was the only thing more seriously damaged and he knew he was one of the most fortunate blokes in there. Even losing an eye was as nothing compared with what some of them were going through.

'There's a bit of a lull,' Susan Fairford said. 'Let's see what I can do.'

And she began to try and remove some of the glass. Her only equipment was a small pair of tweezers. As yet, though, there was no pain, or very little, only a numbness, a feeling that his eye had been punched rather than pierced. As she worked, with great care, he did begin to feel the sharpness in his eye and he winced.

'Sorry,' she said, frowning with concentration. 'It's difficult. I can't see terribly well.'

'Am I going to lose it?'

'Hard to say as yet.'

With his good eye, Sam took the opportunity to study her and it helped take his mind off the discomfort of the operation. In the morning light he was very struck by the change in her. He knew he would not immediately have recognized her had she just walked past in the ordinary way of things. With her hair covered by her VAD veil, her face was uncrowned by its pale, curling prettiness and was thinner than he remembered, and sagging with exhaustion. She didn't look tense any more, or at least not in the way he remembered, her seeming to push other people away as if they might contaminate her. Instead, as well as a deep tiredness, he saw something quieter and more vulnerable.

'How is everyone?' he asked. 'The family, Captain Fairford, young Cosmo?'

She had just drawn back with something pinched in the end of the tweezers which she disposed of into a kidney dish.

'Nasty big piece there,' she murmured. Then, staring down in the direction of Sam's chest, she braced herself to say, 'Charles was killed – in 1915, at Neuve Chapelle. I was told he was shot. Isadora died the year before the war. Heart failure, at thirteen. And my dear Cosmo – well, he's fifteen now . . .'

'Oh God,' Sam said. There had been so many deaths, yet this one, of the fit, energetic captain he had known in India, seemed impossible and utterly tragic. 'You poor woman.'

He hadn't expected to say that, not to her. It seemed too presumptuous and intimate, but that was what came out and he was surprised at himself. Once more her face was gripped by a terrible spasm of grief.

'They say he was very brave,' she said heartbrokenly. 'And I know this should matter, should compensate in some way. But it's not true, of course, it doesn't. Nothing does. And now we look as if we'll lose the war as well, after all of it . . .' There was a pause. 'He never loved me, you know, not as I loved him, but . . . All I want . . . I just want him alive . . .' With a convulsive movement she reached into her pocket for a handkerchief. 'Selfish of me, I know, but that's how it is.'

'There can't be a grieving wife who doesn't feel the same,' Sam said, moved. But even as he said it, he thought, Would Helen feel it? Would she? Would he?

Susan Fairford wiped her eyes and set to work with the tweezers again. 'I'm sorry. I'm very tired. And I must get on before I'm called away.'

'How is Cosmo?' Sam asked. 'He was to go to Eton, wasn't he?'

She sighed. 'He was expelled from Eton. He nearly burned his house down – and it was not an accident. They weren't having any more of him. His housemaster said some terrible things about him. He's now in another establishment in Hertfordshire – Charles's brother's paying. Cosmo loathes it there, but what can I do? It was what Charles wanted for him, an education like his. I only pray to God the war will be over before he takes it into his head to join up. He's so reckless and he'd have no qualms about lying about his age. I've seen younger than him in here.'

'Yes,' Sam agreed. Boys as young as fourteen were fighting on the Western Front.

Delicately she fished several more tiny pieces of glass from his eye. He winced, trying not to cry out.

'Sorry . . .' She frowned with concentration. Once she had eased the eye a little, she said, 'Mr Ironside, you have a family? I'm afraid I can't remember.'

'I do. Three daughters. The last time we met I think we only had Ann and Nancy. Now there's Ruth as well.'

'Of course!' Susan stopped to look at him again. 'Mussoorie! My memory is so bad, I don't know what's happened to me! We were there with Lily – and Izzy was riding horses with Charles every moment she could . . . Oh, if I'd known . . .'

The memory was so sharp for Sam, so painful. Lily Waters. God, what he had felt for that woman! And she had played with him: let him down. The burn of it had never left him. It had made him ill for a time after. When he got home, and was so thin and sad and withdrawn, Helen had thought it was some disease he'd picked up in India.

His tone chill, he asked, 'And what news of Miss Waters?'

'Oh, I believe she's doing well – with a family in London. She's invaluable to them, I believe. And she's been so good to Cosmo – never forgotten him. She writes to him and so on.' Another sigh. 'Sometimes I feel she's more like a mother to him than I am. But I'm grateful, I suppose. At the moment. I had to come out here, you see – to be near Charles, close to where . . . I had to *do* something. We had gone home at the beginning of the war . . . I knew I'd go mad staying with my people in Sussex. At home all everyone complains about are the shortages – food, servants and so on, and living on their nerves waiting to hear bad news all the time. You feel stuck, *suffocated*. And of course I wasn't used to England, after all that time away. At least here you can be of use.'

Sam could see now why she had changed, her face scoured by grief.

'I think,' she said, peering into his injured eye, 'that I have taken out everything I can by this method. Not very satisfactory, I agree, but we'll just have to wait and see. I'll bandage you up – then I must go and see to someone else.'

'I'm very grateful,' Sam said, feeling a distance between them again. He didn't know where he was with this woman, though she had moved him in her sadness. The war changed everything, and she seemed a softer person, whom he began to like, though things like class could quickly rear their head again.

But she looked down at him, and amid the exhaustion, there was something kind and genuine.

'It's so good to see a familiar face,' she said. 'In all this madness.'

Chapter Forty-Eight

Brooklands Racetrack, Surrey, 1922

'All right, Ironside? Marks? Have a good ride down?'

Sam saw a cheery, familiar face through the crowd soon after he and his friend Loz Marks arrived at Brooklands, walking stiffly, cheeks air-burned after the long morning's ride from Birmingham. On their way across to the track, Sam bought a race programme from one of the eager young volunteers who sold them, spending the day moving among the excited crowds in order to be close to the racing. Lucky lads, Sam thought. Had he lived close when he was young he'd have done just the same.

Resentfully, he tried to recall the name of the man who had attached himself to them and it came to him: Jack Pye, someone he had known at Daimler before the war. Sam groaned inwardly.

'There're going to be some marvellous outings today. Count Zborowski's Chitty 1's lapping later – highlight of the day for me, of course,' the man was saying. Sam was barely listening. He found Jack Pye irritating, with his chubby, drinker's complexion and his obsession with high society bods, collecting them the way some people did with loco numbers. The bloke was like a flaming walking encyclopaedia of toffs. Course, he was going on about Chitty 1 because she was built by a count's son, not because he really cared about the engineering involved, Sam thought sourly. He knew he had grown sour about a lot of things these days. God, life was a weary business compared to when he was young! The one thing that lifted his spirits was being somewhere like this, anywhere to do with motors, without it being spoilt by some boring sod like Jack Pye. He moved away, morosely, and left Loz to deal with him.

Sam drank in the sight of the race ground, breathing in the clean air laced with cigarette smoke and exhaust fumes, hearing the motors roaring and the excited social chatter all about them. In the distance he could see the steep curve of the track, crowds of spectators in the middle. There was a race about to begin and the roaring of engines thrilled him. Brooklands attracted enthusiastic crowds for every event and the Whitsun bank holiday meeting seemed to mark the real beginning of summer, and visitors sprawled on the grass, luxuriating in the spring sunshine. High society people came from all over the region with sumptuous picnic hampers, the women in splendid gowns and feathered hats, men in sharply tailored clothes and cravats. Some removed the seats from their motors and sat on them to eat their picnics and sip champagne. These were the ones Jack Pye was inexplicably interested in. Then there were the more ordinary types, eager for a day out, coming into Weybridge on the train, or turning up on motorcycles and sidecars, or pushbikes – and there were the real motor enthusiasts with know-how, like Sam and Loz.

Sam kept one hand in his pocket holding his handkerchief and brought it out every so often to dab his watering left eye. The bright light made it worse. He cursed under his breath as a teardrop escaped and began to roll down his cheek.

'Damned thing!' Then he was ashamed. He'd come all through the war with only some minor scars on his body and that dodgy eye. Some of the glass was still in there and its vision was not good but he didn't have much to complain about.

'Family all right, Ironside?' Jack Pye was at his side again, persisting in talking to him. 'How many children've you got now?'

'Four,' Sam said, resigned to conversation. 'All girls.' He wasn't going to mention Joe. They never did mention Joe, of course. Not at home. And Helen's mother had never said a word afterwards. His own mother had tried to bring it up once or twice but Sam had changed the subject. No good digging it up. It was as if Joe had never been, yet his presence, the ghost of his two-month visit into their lives, lay between himself and Helen more emphatically than any living person.

'Blimey – a houseful of women!' Jack Pye chortled. You must be glad to get out of there, pal!'

Sam laughed it off. *Yes, I am*, he could have said. But it was too close to the truth to joke about. He dreaded going home these days, to the resentment which seemed to be Helen's constant expression. He knew that under it her heart ached with grief for Joe, and for Laurie, who was lost somewhere on the Somme, but she could not show it. She had become a hard, discontented woman and all he saw was her anger and disappointment with him.

He had thought a new start would make things better after the war, leaving Daimler, going to live in Birmingham. Racing had been part of the attraction there, of course, the races Austin had taken part in before the war. They'd been one of the very few British entrants in the Grand Prix as early as 1908. And he'd struck lucky, been one of the handful of engineers taken on by the Austin works out at Longbridge. Business was still hanging by a thread, of course, with the slump, but Sam knew he couldn't have gone back to Daimler and taken up his old life as if nothing had happened. It had been bad enough back in '07, after India, trying to settle back into a life that seemed so shrunken and dull after Ambala and all the travelling he'd done with the captain; after Lily. The thought of her sent a spasm of pain through him, as it always did. After the war there was too much change amid the claustrophobic dullness: too many blokes missing from the neighbourhood, and too much change inside him. No, he'd had to move on or he'd have gone mad. He told Helen, 'I can't stay here.' He never gave her a choice. That was another thing she held against him, uprooting her from her friends, miles from her mother. All his fault, of course and she never let him forget it. She'd never liked Birmingham.

He and Loz managed to shed Jack Pye and cut across quickly towards the track. Along the railings there stood the bookies in top hats taking bets at their stalls. A woman stood close to one of them with a male friend, giggling uncontrollably. Sam saw with distaste that she had bad teeth.

'You going in for a flutter, Sam?' Loz asked.

'No,' he snapped. No point in wasting money.

'All right, I only asked,' Loz said.

The first race was about to begin. It was a small car handicap race and the two of them stood loudly discussing the entrants among the excited crowd, as the expectant roaring of the engines grew louder and louder despite the silencers on the cars. One was a 20 hp Austin, a sports model. God, Sam would have liked to be part of the Austin race team, but he hadn't managed to wangle it yet. At least there was some hope of that, more than of he and Loz building their own 'Special', one of the cars put together privately by amateurs for racing. Loz was forever on about it. Old Loz was a dreamer, pie in the sky.

Sam stood breathing in the scent of exhaust fumes, his eyes fixed on the track. This was the only place where he could almost feel happy. Brooklands was the only track for car racing in the country – the first in the world of its kind. The three and a quarter mile outer track had been built in under nine months and there was a purpose-built test hill for putting the cars through their paces on a steep gradient. All around the grounds were a hive of activity also, sheds divided into workshops where cars were maintained and developed, giving off that engine-oil smell which was the breath of life to Sam. Of course, there were areas fenced off where you could only go if you were an Automobile Racing Club member and he had not reached that hallowed position. Like almost everything else, he couldn't afford it, in this land fit for heroes. The members had their own separate bridge over the track for viewing, as well as a clubhouse, and Sam's usual resentment of the upper classes stirred in him when he thought about it. But that was not something he was going to let spoil his day. He looked round and grinned at Loz.

'We'll be here,' Loz shouted to him, his snub-nosed face beaming with enthusiasm. 'One of these days we'll be racing our own!'

'You're a one,' Sam shouted back. 'Not a hope!'

'Course we will!' Loz was forever optimistic.

'What're we going to use for capital, eh? Potato peelings?'

Sam had met Loz soon after moving to the Austin works, in the machine shop where they started Sam off and where Loz had recently completed his own apprenticeship. The two of them sparked off each other, both mad keen on motors and Loz especially on racing. When Sam was moved out to the works test track which ran round the perimeter of the factory site, the two of them stayed friends. Helen and Loz's wife Mary also got on well. In fact, Mary had been a saving grace. Helen tended to keep herself to herself and be even more miserable and defeated otherwise. Loz and Mary were both cheerful types and had two young sons. Loz was forever on about building a Special with Sam. But they both knew that just getting hold of an old racing car and trying to rebuild and maintain it was fraught with problems, even for amateurs as skilled as themselves.

'Go down that road and all you've got is something out of date before you know it,' Sam said. 'It'd give you nothing but problems.'

Their dream was to try something other enthusiasts were doing since the war – building aero-engines into an old chassis. The thought of all the extra power it gave to the vehicle was heady.

'We know all there is to know, don't we?' Loz had said enthusiastically one evening a couple of months ago when the two of them were ensconced in the corner of a Northfield pub on the Bristol Road, not far from where they both lived. 'All we need's a place to get going . . .'

'And money,' Sam said gloomily. 'It's way beyond us, Loz, on our own, you know it is. It's not just building the thing – there's the maintenance and fuel and getting it to the track meetings. It'd cripple us before we'd even got started.'

What was the good of even talking about it? As a qualified engineer he was on a respectable salary, but he was a father of four. It wasn't the same for Loz, with only two to bring up and a wife who was happy. Sam was only three years older than his pal, but sometimes he felt like a burdened old man in comparison, and his funds seemed to disappear down the drain.

Loz took a long swig of his favourite M&B ale, of which he could drink prodigious amounts without any apparent effect other than an increase in his already chirpy optimism.

'We'd manage,' Loz grinned. 'What's got into you, Sam? I thought you were all for it. I mean, we're a good prospect, not like some. We've got our own tools – we know what we're looking for and how to do it, given the chance. Come on, mate – are you for it? I'm game if you are.'

Unfortunately Loz's sparkling optimism was not always rewarded by events and they were no nearer to doing anything except dreaming. Coming to Brooklands, however, was a great opportunity to see other Specials go through their paces on the racetrack, and find out who was using what engines and which parts, as well as to drink in the excitement of the atmosphere.

The day seemed to fly past as Sam and Loz watched the races from the stands. There were the more serious contests, and others to amuse the spectators, like the Old Crocks race. Nearly all of it was utterly absorbing to them, watching the cars from the various big manufacturing stables like Austin and Vauxhall, but above all the privately built Specials which gave them endless amounts to chew over each time – which chassis, which engine, and all the engineering detail that followed from them.

In the afternoon there was a flurry of added excitement over Count Zborowski's motor Chitty Chitty Bang Bang, setting out to beat his own lap record, running on a Maybach airship motor which had been used in Zeppelins. At last year's Easter meeting it had been the star of the show, winning two races and coming second in another. Zborowski had built a second model called Chitty 2 with a Benz aeroplane engine. Loz and Sam took a keen interest in them.

'They drove it right into the Sahara at the beginning of the year,' Sam said wistfully. Never, ever, had he forgotten the sense of freedom and adventure of being out on the road in India with Captain Fairford in the Daimler. He still remembered those weeks in India as the most exciting of his life.

As Chitty 1, with her long, pointed nose, roared round the track at dizzying speed, Sam found himself baying with the rest of the crowd massed along the track, shouting himself hoarse for Zborowski's car to go faster, faster, to exceed what had been possible before. That was the thing about this game, Sam thought, fizzing with excitement. There was always progress, a sense of new possibility. How desperately he needed to feel that when his home life was so stuck, so deadening!

'She's really cutting a hole in the wind!' Loz yelled at Sam, his fist clenched in the air with excitement.

'She is – must be a record-breaker!' Sam could feel himself lit up, as he so seldom was in his life these days. It was only cars and racing that could ever get him truly excited now and give him a sense of adventure. He could feel his pulse racing, his spirits lifting and a delighted grin spreading across his face. Soon it was announced over the tannoy that Chitty Bang Bang 1 had just achieved her fastest ever lap of 113.45 miles per hour.

'God,' Sam said, awed. He looked round at Loz and both their faces were suddenly serious.

'We've got to do it!' Loz said. 'We've got the know-how. We've got to put together something as good as that!'

Sam was on fire as well – thank God! At least he could be on fire about something! He knew, suddenly, that that was where all the energy and passion of his life could now be directed.

The two of them strolled across the grass in a frenzy, talking non-stop amid the milling crowds. Sam was oblivious to them for a time, lost in his vision of what he and Loz might create with their skill and sense of adventure. Hang the money! They'd do it somehow. They had to! He gave an actual groan when he saw Jack Pye hoving into view again, his fat face pink with excitement.

'Did you see her go! What a thing! I bet the count's pleased as punch!'

Sam and Loz were looking for a spot to sit down and open their flask of tea and it seemed inevitable that they were now stuck with Jack Pye again. They walked on together, Sam keeping his distance a little, and it was when he at last glanced ahead that he saw the young man, just a few yards away from them. He often thought later, with a chill, that had he not just looked up then, none of what happened next might have happened.

But he did look up, and saw a very tall, startlingly handsome young man walking towards him with blue eyes, which seemed to hold a defiant arrogance, and a head of wavy, very thick blond hair. He cut such a figure that it would have been difficult not to stare: he was so obviously moneyed, and conscious of his own wealth and good breeding. He exuded confidence and superiority. And Sam recognized him, somehow, yet he was sure he had never seen him before. He was walking just ahead of a couple who were strolling along in a leisurely fashion, the woman holding the hand of a little ginger-haired boy. The young man seemed impatient as if they were all holding him up.

Sam took in the couple: a tall, thin man in his forties dressed in a beautifully tailored navy coat and holding a rolled umbrella, although the day had turned out so fine. Apart from his clothing he was not very distinctive. He had brown wavy hair, was gentle-featured and, Sam sensed, shy. Resting her arm in the crook of his, was a strikingly beautiful woman. At first all he noticed was the bold flair of her clothing, the crimson velvet skirt, an impression of dark, flowing material at the top, almost as if she were an exotic bird with her feathers moving behind her, and a crimson cloche hat, with a dark band and a black feather tucked in jauntily at one side. The women Sam encountered usually had neither the wealth nor the daring to dress with this kind of panache. Certainly Helen didn't. He was captivated by the sight. And then in those few seconds, beneath the brim of the hat he saw the face, the dark, flashing eyes, and he knew her immediately, with a physical shock, and he was rooted to the spot. He knew it was her, with his whole being, and while he stood, stunned, beside him the tedious Jack continued his endless commentary to Loz.

'Now there's a bit of all right – classy, eh? That's

Piers Larstonbury, carrying her on his arm, the lucky bloke! You don't know who Piers Larstonbury is? The architect – oh, he's got a name for himself in London all right – worth a pretty penny! And that's Cosmo Fairford walking ahead there – another family with a pile of loot stashed away – up our way, Warwickshire, although he's a bit of a waster, by all accounts. Any road, Piers Larstonbury . . .' He repeated the name almost as if it was holy, then lowered his voice portentously. *'That's his boy, but that dame he's with certainly isn't his wife!'*

'Come on, Sam,' Loz said impatiently. 'What's up with you?' They had been walking along towards the paddock surrounding the clubhouse, which was where the society types mingled.

Sam had to remind himself to move his feet. He could not begin to explain what was up with him. Jack might not have known the woman's name, but he knew all right. He had thought all that was over, that he had burned her out of him and that he could even have met her again and not felt anything. But even after all this time, in only a second he had known that that beautiful, mysterious woman was Lily Waters, the woman with whom he had spent the happiest, most intense days ever in his life, who had betrayed him so badly that he had thought at one time that he might never recover. And there she was, moving further and further away, taking with her the answer to the question, *Why, Lily, why did you do that to me?*

He knew in that split second that whatever happened, however much of a fool he might be about to make of himself, he *must* speak to her, submit, if necessary, to her scorn and rejection, to set himself free of her. And if he didn't hurry they'd be in the paddock where only

BARC members were allowed, and he would be shut out.

'I'll just be a minute,' he said to Loz distractedly. 'You and Jack go ahead . . . There's just something . . .'

Leaving a baffled Loz staring and calling after him, he turned back and tore towards the racetrack.

Chapter Forty-Nine

For a moment he thought he had lost them.

He ran faster, not caring what anyone thought, colliding at one point with a man in a loud checked sports jacket.

'Sorry!' Sam shouted to the man's curses.

Had it not been for the crimson of Lily's skirt and the child's bright ginger hair he might have had more difficulty in keeping sight of them. He realized that the four of them were almost at the paddock railings and he hurtled towards them. Only as he came really close did he question his sanity. What in heaven's name was he going to say? Suddenly it all felt like a crazed dream. And he could not just let her pass out of his life again, not without speaking to her.

Cosmo was now lagging, apparently sulkily, behind the others and Sam caught up with him first.

'Excuse me!' He blundered into speech before he could lose his nerve.

Cosmo Fairford's penetrating blue gaze was turned on Sam. He must be nineteen years old by now and what an immensely striking fellow he was, with that god-like combination of looks and breeding! Sam felt all his usual class resentments surfacing again, made worse by the fact that the expression in Cosmo Fairford's eyes was cold and supercilious.

'Yes?' The tone was clipped, as if words cost him dearly.

'Are you Cosmo Fairford?'

Cosmo stopped, with an air of dealing with a tiresome tradesman who it would be easier to humour and get shot of quickly.

'I am.'

Sam was not going to defer to him. He held out his hand.

'Samuel Ironside. You won't remember me, but we met when you were a young 'un. I sold your father a car – stayed with you in Ambala.'

The handshake was instinctively, but languidly, returned. 'I see,' Cosmo said. 'I'm afraid I don't—'

'No, well of course you wouldn't,' Sam interrupted him hurriedly. The tiny boy with blond curls who bounced up and down on the seat of the Daimler back then would not have the faintest idea who he was. That child who Sam had first seen cradled in Lily's arms . . . This man he had grown into, Sam thought, was more cold and superior than even his mother had been.

He saw then, in the corner of his eye, that the rest of the party had turned to look for Cosmo and were walking towards them: Piers Larstonbury with Lily on his arm. Sam turned to them, marvelling that he could achieve such cool composure when he was burning, trembling inside.

'Good afternoon.' Piers Larstonbury's tone was enquiring, his voice quiet. It was plummy, of course, but not with that hectoring bellow adopted by many of his class.

'Good afternoon.' Sam decided to speak out with confidence. 'I just stopped to speak to Mr Fairford. I once delivered a car to his father in India.'

'How splendid!' Piers Larstonbury said. Sam felt himself relax a fraction. He could tell he was in the presence of a true gentleman, one who would treat everyone with courtesy no matter what their walk of life. 'And by which company are you employed, if I may ask?'

'Well, at the time I was with Daimler,' Sam said. 'This was a good while ago – before the war. I'm one of the Austin's engineers now, at Longbridge.'

He had the man's attention: he was genuinely interested, Sam could see.

'And your name is?'

'Samuel Ironside.' He spoke very clearly and only then, he looked at Lily.

There was no pretence. In that moment, he felt strangely proud of her. She was not one of these upper-class misses with their feelings buried under deep layers of social propriety, the sort who might now stare icily at him, or turn away, affecting indifference. She was a real woman, that was how he remembered her. *His woman*, he thought, and now he saw that her gaze was fixed on him, utterly, deeply as if there was nothing else to be seen. He remembered with a terrible pang those dark eyes fixed on him with longing and devotion, where now he could see questioning and pain and, not far below the quiet surface, a quivering restraint of emotions.

'A pleasure to meet you,' Piers Larstonbury was saying. 'I must say, Daimler have made some fine motors, very fine. I have yet to experience driving an Austin. But I'm sure I should like to.'

'The Twenty and Twelve have been highly successful,' Sam said. He did feel a personal pride in the models the company had developed since the war. 'What do you drive?' Piers Larstonbury somehow indicated that he should walk with them and he found himself drawn along in front of Cosmo, Lily and the boy.

'A Daimler, in actual fact – a rather old model now. But I must admit to enjoying a Morgan as well. Damn fine cars. I'm not highly knowledgeable at all. It's Cosmo who's the expert there. He's very keen to race – very keen indeed. He's trying to find his way into it.'

As they strolled along the edge of the paddock, Sam told Piers Larstonbury about the new model of Austin being developed at the works – something more afford-able for the ordinary driver. And then he found himself talking about Chitty 1 and Specials and somehow Sam announced that he was in the process of building one himself.

'How absolutely marvellous! Are you a driver yourself?'

'Not a racing driver,' Sam said.

Piers Larstonbury actually stopped, gazing at him. Sam realized the man was not just being polite, he really did not know much about motoring. He was just a social day tripper, one of the ones who went to the Henley Regatta or racing at Ascot for the social scene, and Sam saw that he was eager to learn and prepared to listen with real attention.

'Course,' Piers Larstonbury said, 'a chap like you with all the expertise – it's ideal! I must say, I rather envy you. All rather new to me, this, you see. I've not come to Brooklands before. I came because . . .' He said no more but the tiny tilt of his head towards Lily and Cosmo gave some explanation. Jack Pye had insisted that Lily was not Piers Larstonbury's wife. So what was between them? Did Lily love him? Sam tried to stop himself speculating. He had seen nothing in Lily's eyes which spoke of love for the man, but perhaps that was what he wanted to believe . . .

They had reached the railings round the paddock. Inside, there were a number of cars parked and clusters of members were standing talking.

'I do wish you luck with your vehicle,' Piers Larston-bury said. 'It sounds immensely exciting.'

Sam knew he had given a misleading picture of the situation, but he was still taken aback to hear Piers Larstonbury speak as if the car was already half built. He could hardly admit now that there was no Special – that he had no money and nowhere to work.

'Well – we're definitely going for an aero-engine – chain-driven chassis, of course – a Mercedes.' He found all their dreams pouring out passionately. 'High gear ratios – we can sort that out with countershaft sprockets. It'd be fantastic to be able to test it on the hill climb here . . . My God,' he finished, 'she's going to be good when we've finished. The likes of Chitty 1 will have to look out!'

'Marvellous.' Piers Larstonbury was looking at him intently. Sam could see he had impressed the man with his know-how and enthusiasm, and he turned to include the others in the conversation.

'Cosmo – Mr Ironside here is in the process of building a Special himself – on a Mercedes chassis. I imagine you have ambitions to race her here when she's finished?'

'Oh yes, of course,' Sam said, still full of conviction. Of course that was what they were going to do!

He could see Cosmo Fairford looking at him with a new respect which he found gratifying. But now he was also face to face with Lily again.

'Cosmo is far more knowledgeable on the subject than I. A devotee, one might say. And a demon driver.'

'Well,' Sam said, attempting to overcome his instinctive dislike of Cosmo. 'From what I remember you started very young. Your father had you at the wheel from about the age of four!'

'Yes,' Lily added suddenly. 'And for ever after.'

Piers Larstonbury looked from one to the other of them in puzzlement. Sam's and Lily's eyes met and held each other's gaze steadily, somehow defiantly.

'You two have met before!'

'Yes.' Lily was in command now, cool and detached as any upper-class mistress of the drawing room. 'We have, briefly. A very long time ago.'

Sam felt her words like ice poured into him. They seemed loaded with cruel indifference. And he realized, foolishly, that they were waiting for him to leave. They could see he was not a BARC member and they wanted their tea. Sam felt small and deflated, like a small boy with his nose pressed up against a sweet-shop window. He had been a little diversion in their day of entertainment and now he was holding them up.

'My colleagues are waiting for me over the other side,' he said brusquely. 'I just wanted a quick word with Mr Fairford here – for old times' sake.' He raised his cap with careful courtesy.

'Well, it's been a delight to meet you Mr, er, Ironside,' Piers Larstonbury said, returning the salute. 'And I wish you every success.'

And it was time for Sam to take his leave. It was over. And nothing had even begun.

353

Chapter Fifty

'Damn,' Sam railed to himself, walking away. 'Damn and blast it! And damn *them*!'

He felt like slamming his hat down on the ground, he was so frustrated and humiliated. He had not managed a single proper word with Lily. Unable to stop himself, he turned back at least to watch her walk away, to have a final glimpse of her.

His eyes caught hers, just as she had also turned to look back over her shoulder. Neither of them could pretend they were not looking for the other, and he saw Lily hesitate. She paused to say something to Piers Larstonbury, then turned back, leaving the boy, to hurry towards Sam.

He saw that she was even more beautiful than he remembered. Her face had matured and there was a more chiselled curve to her cheekbones. She seemed more sophisticated and poised, more formidable. The sight of her utterly captivated him. They stood feet apart, in silence, for some moments. He looked into her eyes but her expression was guarded, frightened even. At last, as she said nothing, he could not hold back.

'I saw you – earlier. I knew it was you.' Looking very directly at her he said, 'I'd know you anywhere, Lily.'

There was a moment, a flicker of vulnerability, but then she said coolly, 'Major Larstonbury felt that he had been very remiss in not inviting you to be our guest for tea in the clubhouse.'

So Larstonbury was a major as well, Sam thought. Course, he would be. Officer class and all that.

'I have people waiting,' Sam said with dignity. 'They'll already be wondering where I am.'

Her eyes widened. 'Family?' He was glad she asked, that the question mattered to her.

'No. Just a couple of pals.'

She seemed to decide something, and stepped closer, speaking fast and urgently.

'Sam, you can help – please. I know you can. We've got to do something for Cosmo – set him on the right path. He's been so unhappy. School has been a disaster for him and the family made him go into the bank and he *loathes* it. I'm so very worried for him. Everything has gone wrong for him ... Losing his father the way he did – and Isadora. The one thing he wants to do is race – he's good, *really* good. He drives on the estate, but he's had such bad luck. Please, Sam – come back and talk about it with us. At least join us for tea.'

There was such appeal in her eyes and voice, such passion in her concern for Cosmo that Sam knew he was already being drawn in. For her, not for Cosmo: he'd do anything to be near her. But he had to be honest with her now. He didn't want to make a complete fool of himself.

'You must understand – we're not far on at all,' he said. 'I may have misled Major Larstonbury. You see, we have no money to begin.'

Lily shook her head dismissively. 'Oh, money! Money's not a problem for these people.'

It was that which decided him. The way she spoke of them, distancing herself from Piers Larstonbury's

355

upper-class sort in a way which put her on Sam's side. For all her learned sophistication it was a class alliance. She looked intensely into his eyes. 'If you need money, you're in the right place. And they need you. Come and have tea, Sam. You won't regret it.'

And so he walked into something he had never expected, not in his most fanciful of dreams.

The clubhouse was an airy-looking pavilion, sporting a low turret and a veranda round the sides, with the atmosphere of a seaside resort. They were served tea round a small table in a wide room full of the genteel sounds of conversation and laughter and teaspoons clinking against china and the sweet scents of cake and strawberry jam. Piers Larstonbury behaved with utter courtesy, apologizing to Sam for his oversight in not inviting him the first time.

'Miss Waters is so much better at these things than I,' he said. And he shot a look at Lily which revealed, quite nakedly, his feelings.

He adores her, Sam saw. He watched carefully to try and make sense of it all. Did she feel the same?

'Not at all,' Sam said carefully.

'This is my son, Hubert,' Piers Glastonbury said. The little boy, whom Sam guessed to be about five, had just taken a huge mouthful of jam sponge and he stared round-eyed at Sam, who gave him a smile.

There was a silence and Sam took a sip of tea, then turned to Cosmo. He could swallow his dislike of the fellow for Lily.

'I gather you're keen to race? What have you done so far?'

Cosmo came to life then. 'I've driven always – on my

356

uncle's estate. He's had a few motors, mostly saloon models, of course, but I've hammered those round the track. A couple of friends bring their motors – we have all sorts going round there. One or two Austins, a Mercedes, a Weigel . . .'

Sam frowned. 'You mean you've got a circuit?'

'Oh yes!' Cosmo said proudly and for a second Sam caught a glimpse of the eager young boy. 'I mean, not like here, of course, not banked and all that, but a track Uncle's let me carve out round the grounds. He's plenty of space, after all. There's even rather a good hill for testing uphill speeds . . .'

Sam began to feel a real glimmer of excitement. He didn't like Cosmo, but he could see the passion in him, the real hunger for motors and driving which gave him a sense of kinship. And surely the boy must have some of his father's qualities?

'Why not have a go building your own, then?' he asked. 'Plenty of people give it a go.'

Cosmo's face fell, became almost sulky. 'No idea where to begin, old man. I've had a few thoughts, but I've no expertise and none of my friends are in that line. They sent me to work in a bank . . .' he finished in disgust.

While he was speaking, Sam noticed that Lily and Piers Larstonbury were quietly conferring beside them and he saw, with a dart of deep jealousy, that she had laid her hand on his forearm and was looking into his eyes. Piers Larstonbury gave her a smile of intimate adoration, then he looked at Sam.

'She's a great persuader, this young woman. Tell me, Mr Ironside. Where do most of these vehicles, these Specials, come to be built?'

'Anywhere anyone gets the chance,' Sam said. 'At the

357

back of workshops, in old barns and sheds – I've even heard of one or two being pieced together in people's bedrooms. Course, there are also the workshops here.' He sighed, not realizing how much longing there was in his voice. 'This would be the dream place to do it. There are all those workshops away from the track with all sorts going on in them, and you'd be breathing the air in this place, with the company reps on hand for parts and right by the track and the test hill. A lot of these are company-owned, of course, most of the big firms have sheds here. Most amateurs can only dream of anything like that. They'll work at it every spare moment they've got, hardly sleeping, hardly doing anything else to get it built, get it right. But they'll still be in the shed at the bottom of the garden until what they build is successful. Then, with any luck, they can live on their winnings!'

Piers Larstonbury smiled at his wistful passion. Sam saw him exchange a glance with Lily. Her eyes burned with feeling and she gave the slightest, persuasive nod. Cosmo seemed unaware what was passing between them and sat eating cake, sunk back into his usual sulkiness.

'Mr Ironside.' Piers Larstonbury became business-like, pushing his tea plate to one side and reaching into his breast pocket for a fountain pen and a small note-book. 'I have a proposal to make to you.'

Chapter Fifty-One

Lily sat beside Piers Larstonbury in the front of the Daimler. Little Hubert was so exhausted that he was asleep with his head on Lily's lap before they had even left the race ground. Even so, Lily kept her head bent low, stroking his hair to hide the tumult of feeling going on inside her. Sam . . . *Oh God, seeing Sam again . . .*

After a while she looked out of the window, but it was not the trees and fields of Surrey she was seeing but Sam's face, the way he had looked at her, searching her eyes in pain and bewilderment. Why should *he* be in pain when he had hurt her so badly? She gripped the edge of the seat until her left hand ached. All the agony of those years, of Sam, the baby, she had locked away deep in herself.

Don't ever look back, she had told herself. *Forget. Don't ever think, don't expect anything from life, not of love, of having a real life of your own. Just take what you can wherever you can.* She had never expected to see him again, but suddenly there he had stood, those deep grey eyes staring into hers, filling her with an agonized sorrow and anger and longing. She had loved him – God how she had loved him. And their child, little Victoria. All of it came back, searing through her.

'Are you all right, my darling?' Piers Larstonbury asked.

'Yes – thank you. Just a little tired.' Lily managed a

359

calm voice. 'I think I might have a little doze if you don't mind.'

'Of course, my dear. You rest. It's been a demanding day.'

She was not in the least sleepy but closing her eyes would give her refuge. Before doing so she turned to look at his gentle face, frowning slightly as he steered the motor car. He was a good man, she knew that. An unlikely looking man to have been a soldier, like so many who were thrown into it, but all she had ever heard of him was praise for his complete dedication to his men and his kindly way with them. He had had a reputation for it. And he was utterly besotted with her. But although at times she appreciated his kindness, her gaze held no returning passion. He was another man she allowed to use her. It had become her way of surviving.

Laying her head back, she thought instead of the young person who had been her one enduring passion. She felt a surge of satisfaction. At last today she had managed to achieve something for Cosmo, to please him, set him on the road to a life he really wanted. The thrill of seeing his face when Piers and Sam had shook hands on their agreement to let him race was reward enough. It had been she who had engineered that exchange, who had taken Piers's hand and looked deeply into his eyes, knowing that in those rare moments, when he thought she was truly responding to him, she could ask of him almost anything. Major Piers Larstonbury was an unhappily married man and Lily, as he told her endlessly, was the true light of his life.

'I just don't know what I'd do if you were to leave,' he told her sometimes. 'My darling Lily, I simply couldn't bear it.'

And she remembered almost the same words on Sam's lips, and those of Ewan McBride and Harold Arkwright, in whose household she had worked briefly when she first came back to England: those same old words, she thought, quite empty of meaning, and in the end, so cruel. Never ever would she believe anyone again who said those words to her. But she knew Cosmo would not leave her. He depended on her in a way he had never been able to do with his mother. She had been the one who had held him in her arms for so many days of his childhood. She had written to him faithfully at school, she had been the one to visit him during the war when Susan Fairford was in France, trying to bury her own grief in her work as a VAD. Lily knew Cosmo needed her, even though he was so often rude and disagreeable. And just occasionally she was repaid by him becoming sweet and vulnerable, his buying her bunches of flowers and apologizing for his behaviour.

'You're the only one who's ever really bothered about me, Lily,' he'd say despondently, looking wretched in a way that melted her heart. 'You've been like a mother and sister to me in one.'

Yes, he was her boy. She needed no one else and she would do anything in her power to help him. That was her mission in life, other than her own survival: her devotion to Cosmo. Anything else that might truly have been hers had been cruelly snatched away.

Piers Larstonbury was simply a means to an end. She had gone to his house to earn her living and as the months passed he had become more and more obsessed with her, as men always seemed to. And in her need to earn a living, and seeing his wealth as an opportunity, she had given in to him, becoming his lover, allowing him to quench his loneliness with her. She would not admit to her own loneliness. Her heart was cold and closed now, since Ewan McBride and above all since little Victoria. She was untouchable – and that was how she had intended to remain, and had done. Until today, when Sam Ironside stood in front of her and looked into her eyes, and she was torn open again.

Chapter Fifty-Two

Once she had stepped out of the Bethel Home that day, leaving Birmingham for London, knowing that she would never see her baby Victoria again, Lily had vowed that she would not look back. If she did, she would not be able to go on.

She had secured her job with the Arkwrights, in a comfortable home in Islington. Harold and Letitia Arkwright had three small daughters. Letitia Arkwright informed Lily on her arrival that the last nanny had 'got herself into trouble' and had to depart. She was a thin, wrung-out-looking woman even though still only in her twenties, who looked perpetually anxious, screwing up her face as she spoke as if the sun was too bright, even though they were in a darkened room.

'I must be sure of having someone of good character this time,' she said.

Lily, who had no desire to go near another man ever again, had no difficulty in reassuring her.

A month passed and she and the three girls, who were not too difficult a challenge, all got used to each other. But long after that, things went quickly to the bad when Harold Arkwright started on her. It began with long, lingering stares from his mud-coloured eyes when he met her on the stairs or when she presented the girls to their parents in the evening. Lily soon realized the cause of the last nanny's 'trouble', though

363

poor Letitia Arkwright seemed not to have recognized the rabid womanizer she was married to, even though his attempts at seduction happened quite blatantly under her own roof. Harold Arkwright owned a number of successful millinery businesses in different quarters of London. He also displayed a shrewd ability for making money on stock and shares and the family were certainly comfortable, if not extravagantly, wealthy. He was a short, stocky man with very thick, black hair, an impressive moustache and an air of urgent muscular energy which contrasted rather pitifully with his wife. Letitia spent most of her evenings reclining on the couch exhausted, reading a novel and not inviting company. Harold, as soon as he came home from attending to business, began to spend his evenings in pursuit of Lily. Though she slept in the nursery she had her own tiny sitting room, very simple, with just a couple of easy chairs and a small table, and an old Turkey rug partly covering the dark floorboards. Over the little leaded fireplace was a shadowy oil painting of chrysanthemums. Mr Arkwright started appearing there in the evenings, tapping discreetly on the door. At first she didn't feel she could refuse to open it.

'You are the most beautiful thing I've ever seen,' he would murmur, hovering on the threshold. Bolder, he would then come in and close the door. 'God, what a woman you are, Miss Waters. Come here, my dear. Come and sit beside me.'

'No – I really must go and see if Lizzie has settled,' Lily would say, or some similar excuse, and flee to the nursery. She became frightened and did not answer the door, pushing a chair up against it. Harold Arkwright took to mooning about outside the door. At first he was hesitant, polite. Then, as his ardour for her grew, it became extreme.

Lily endured several very lonely, desperate weeks at the Arkwrights. Though she never once succumbed to Harold Arkwright's advances, she felt under continual sexual threat. Once only he pushed his way into her room one night, begging her to let him lie with her, but she threatened to scream and wake up the children and call his wife. He seemed surprised and very offended at her resistance to him. He never tried it again although she went to bed with a chair pushed under the nursery door handle. But she was not sleeping well, and was jumpy day and night. It felt like revisiting a nightmare.

Though she scarcely knew it, she was not very well. She was still in a raw state after all the grief and shocks she had endured. Also, she was not used to England, to the grey drabness of the city streets after the loveliness of Mussoorie, and she did not know another soul in the place to call a friend.

Worst of all, here she was once again being pursued in this gross way. Why did men behave like this to her? Was she giving them some abnormal signal which she did not recognize? She felt lost and contaminated, and at times like those she could believe all the cruel accusations those religious women had made in the Bethel Home, that she was dirty and shameful. Sometimes she looked in the yellow tinted mirror in the nursery and even though her same wide, dark eyes looked back at her, her strong brows and thick, waving hair, she could barely recognize who she saw. At night she lay in bed and wept until she was so tired that sleep had to come.

At the height of her desperation, one evening, while Harold Arkwright patrolled the carpeted corridor outside the nursery, she sat on a cork-seated stool in the children's bathroom beside the nursery. It was quiet, except for a persistent drip from one of the bath taps, and for the first time she allowed herself to think, to remember.

In the dark winter gloom she often pined for India. Taking leave of it had been so painful and made all the more fraught because she had had the dreadful Eustace in her care. Unless actually asleep he couldn't sit still for more than a few moments at a time and he fidgeted ceaselessly. He needed constant entertaining and, whether entertained or not, was rude and aggressive. The train journey to Bombay had entailed some of the most exhausting and trying hours she had ever experienced. She sat sweating by the window of the train as they chugged for endless hours south-west to the coast, intermittently trying to engage Eustace in games of 'I Spy' or noughts and crosses, or in his story books. It was only when he was actually asleep, in the afternoon, that she had enough time really to look out and think about her own farewell to India, and in doing so, she ached with sadness.

Five years she had been in this country, but England now felt a lifetime away. She thought about all her time with the Fairfords, and with a shudder the strange, dream-like months with the McBride household, yet all amid the loveliness of Mussoorie which had stolen her heart. She thought of Sam with an agonized longing which never left her. But, she reasoned, if he had really loved her and wanted her, he would surely have found some way to let her know. Had things been different, had Sam not changed her, opened her to her feelings, she could have made her life in India. But what would have become of her? She might have floated from post to post in the houses of British families whom she might admire or despise, but she would always be a servant, forever a foreigner, an old maid growing scrawny and strange. And now she was carrying a child and only difficulty and disgrace could follow. She had no fellow feeling, then, for the infant. There was no sign of it except sickness and exhaustion and all she could think of was that she had to be rid of it. She had to survive and struggle to find a new life. Staring out at the endless skies and plains of India, she felt her own aloneness and a surge of determination. She would go back to England; she would not let herself fall prey to maternal feelings – that would lead her only to disaster. She was going to survive and make something of herself, no matter what it took.

But when the P&O steamer pulled majestically away from the port at Bombay, Lily found tears pouring down her face. The hotchpotch of streets of the city, the ghats and hills all faded as they moved away on the deep green water, until the coast with its smells and sounds was lost to her, its colours only a line of blurred umber in the distance.

It all felt like a dream now: India, Birmingham, the bedstead factory. She could have found more genteel work, but she wanted something anonymous, where she'd be one of a crowd, and could disappear again almost without comment. These frightening, lonely months of waiting were something she just had to get through. She took a cheap room with a Miss Spencer, who, while haughty in manner, was also clearly very particular about cleanliness. Lily could not bear the thought of anything less, after all the lovely houses she had lived in. When she went back alone at night to her little attic, her legs and back aching dreadfully, her hands burning sore from handling wire all day, at least it was to an atmosphere of order and cleanliness even though it was poor. Even so, the musty smell of these houses, their dampness, the odour of boiled cabbage and potatoes spoke to her of a familiar poverty and meanness, so that sometimes when her eyes were closed she could believe she was back in Mrs Horne's house, with Ann and Effie about to torment her the moment she moved.

Lily lay on her back and stared despairingly at the crack running along the dingy ceiling.

Dear God, she thought. *What on earth am I doing back here?* All she had tried to be, and here she was, a fallen woman carrying the child of a man who she thought had loved her, but who had left her with no message, or hope of seeing him again. And now she was back where she started in the squalid Birmingham streets. But she pushed these thoughts away. She would not think. She would not feel. If she did, she would go mad.

She allowed herself, now, to remember the horror of the home, and to think of Victoria. Supposing she worked hard and earned herself enough means to try and get Victoria back ... ? Abruptly she stopped this fantasy, leaning against the edge of the bath, shaken by racking sobs. It was far too late. Victoria had been taken away for adoption. They had told her this and at the time Lily had been pleased at the chance of a home for her instead of knowing that she would just be handed over to the orphanage. But that meant Victoria was even more completely lost to her. She couldn't go snatching her from her home even if she could find her. There was no use in thinking about it. Victoria was better off with a family who could give her a proper life. She must think no more about it and look to the future.

368

She let herself weep for a time, then dried her eyes, back in the present with the drip-drip of the tap. What on earth am I reduced to? she thought. Spending my evening hiding in the bathroom from Harold Arkwright? This was madness. She got up, resolved to find another post where she could feel safe.

Such a haven presented itself with a Mrs Jessop and her two little girls, whom Lily had cared for all through the war in a house in Surbiton. Mr Jessop was away for most of the war and Lily found a female household in which to pass the shortages and endless bad news of those years. Daisy Jessop was a kindly, timid, rather dull woman who, unlike some, did not flourish when her husband was away but came to rely more and more on Lily. She became very fond of the two girls, Cissy and Margaret, and Mrs Jessop kept her on longer really than her help was required and after Mr Jessop had returned, looking ill, but otherwise unharmed. But Lily started to feel as if her life was slipping past in this quiet, suburban life, and that there must be more on offer, even for someone like her.

Chapter Fifty-Three

The Larstonburys' house in Hampstead, an imposing brick mansion of four storeys close to the heath, impressed Lily immediately.

When she arrived in June 1921 the walled garden behind was a feast of colour with pots of tobacco plants and daisies and geraniums, the white pom-poms of guelder roses and mauve clusters of wisteria blossoms hanging from the back wall of the house.

Inside, the big, light rooms were richly furnished to exotic taste, with large mirrors giving a sense of space and light, the rich colours of Persian rugs and elegant furniture gleaming with care and smelling of beeswax.

Lily, loving children as she did, became very quickly fond of the two Larstonbury infants, Hubert, aged five, and little Christabel, who was two. Virginia Larstonbury, a willowy, intellectual redhead who spent much of her day buried in books, had named her daughter after the suffragette Christabel Pankhurst. Virginia had also come from a moneyed family. She had a taste for hangings and drapes in rich, eastern colours and Lily felt at home with the silken touches of India, the echoes of Benares and Rajasthan that she saw about the house.

She did not dislike Virginia Larstonbury exactly, but she found her intimidating. Virginia was a woman of 'interests', the chief one apparently being 'theosophy', and she attended a great many meetings, some of them held in the front parlour of the house in the evenings, when a strangely dressed, intense collection of people arrived and sat talking for hours on end. Virginia was twenty-nine, and, as Lily discovered, fifteen years younger than her husband. She was also not his first wife. Piers Larstonbury had been married and widowed before the war, leaving him with his first two children, Elspeth, now seventeen, and Guy, fifteen, who only appeared from their boarding schools in the holidays. Guy, Lily gathered from the servants, was a sensitive, artistic soul rather like his father. Elspeth, on the other hand, was a firebrand who resented Virginia and had an explosive relationship with her.

Hubert was pale, with Virginia's colouring and wide, rabbity blue eyes. He was very delicate and sweet-natured, prone to being set upon by other more robust boys, and Lily felt protective towards him. Though he was not as heart-meltingly beautiful as Cosmo had been, she found him easy to deal with, a child who responded easily to affection. Christabel was more solid, dark-haired like her father, but with a much more temperamental nature than her brother. She was, however, a particular favourite of Virginia's mother, Lady Marston, who adored girls and had very little time for boys, so on the day Lily took Hubert to Brooklands, Christabel was with her grandmother in South Kensington.

Virginia Larstonbury, beautiful in a languid way, with her tresses of straight red hair and pale, freckled skin, was a woman of moods and strong tempers.

'I don't believe in the difference between human beings,' she proclaimed one day from the couch, looking up from her book. Lily caught sight of the book's title: *Married Love* by someone called Marie Stopes. 'We are all equals, no matter what our state in life, and should be treated as such. Do you not agree, Lily?'

Do you mean we *are*, or we *ought to be*? Lily wanted to ask. But she usually found it better to appear to agree with people, so just said quietly, 'Oh yes, I'm sure you're right.'

However, Virginia Larstonbury's ideals of equality did not seem to extend as far as her servants, some of whom she treated arrogantly. And she was sure she was right about almost everything, which was one of the things that made Lily begin to pity Major Larstonbury, wondering why he allowed his wife to speak to him so contemptuously. After all, he was an architect with a successful practice in town, but because he did not share her lofty notions she sometimes treated him as if he never had a thought in his head.

'Oh, it's no good talking to *you*, Piers,' Lily sometimes heard her say. Yet she seemed to like Lily, who was nine years older than her, and who was genuinely fond of the children.

'I don't know how you do it,' Virginia often said, on her rare visits to the nursery. She would throw herself languidly into the cane chair and pick up Christabel to swamp her with a cuddle.

'Hubert never behaves as well as that for me. Oh, but I just couldn't spend all day with them, much as I adore the little darlings. It would drive me quite frantic! One must have a place for learning, for cultivation of the inner life. Or perhaps it's not necessary for everyone. Some of us are very sensitive to *life*. Are you sensitive to life, would you say, Lily? After all – you're very *pretty*,' she finished, rather inconsistently.

'I don't really know,' Lily said, blushing because she really did not know how to conduct such a conversation. 'Not like you, I don't suppose.' Although in some ways she thought Virginia Larstonbury was very *in*sensitive, especially when it came to her husband and children. Almost anything else seemed to matter more, most of the time.

Piers Larstonbury had not behaved to Lily the way most men in her life had – far from it. Months of her employment in his household went by before he did more than pass the time of day with her. He worked a great deal and was not much in the house, but when he was at home, he was always very well-mannered to his wife, however irritable and impatient she could be with him.

For the first five months of Lily's time in Hampstead she scarcely saw the master of the house, except during those after-tea visits each evening with Hubert and Christabel into the cosy drawing room, and even then her task was only to take the children down, well cleaned and dressed for their parents, and to fetch them away again at the appointed time. Her main exchanges with Piers Larstonbury consisted of 'Good evening', 'Goodnight', and little more. He seemed to her a pleasant man, very good mannered, in particular to Virginia, a man who treated his servants with respect and his children with affection during the brief times he was with them. Other than that she had little impression of him, except from some of the servants like Lottie, the tweeny, who always said he was 'ever so nice. Much nicer than *her*.'

That winter, though, Lily had an unexpected visit from Piers Larstonbury in the nursery. It was a miserable November night, bitter outside, with drizzling rain and the wind whipping meanly along the London streets. The children were not well. As the afternoon darkened early into evening, first Christabel and then Hubert began to complain of sore throats and to run a high temperature. It was not long before they both obviously needed to be put to bed and to miss the evening visit to their parents. Lily sent a message down with Lottie to say that the children were ill.

'Lor',' Lottie said, with a frightened face. 'I hope it ain't that influenza! Any rate, *she's* not in, for a start, so I don't know as anyone'll come.'

The thought of the Spanish influenza made Lily even more worried. So many people had died from it and there seemed to be no cure. The fever took a grip on both children quickly. Lily only managed to snatch a quick bite to eat and spent the evening wiping the two feverish infants down with a cool flannel, as she had done for Cosmo when he was poorly in India.

At eight o'clock or so, when she was sitting on Christabel's bed, stroking the child's forehead and worrying about whether they should call the doctor, there came a discreet tap on the door.

'Come in!' Lily called softly. Startled, she saw the master of the house in the dim light of the doorway.

'May I come in?' He spoke softly, thinking the children were asleep.

Hubert was lying in a twitching slumber, but Christabel cried 'Daddy!' and immediately tried to sit up.

'No, Christabel – lie down!' Lily quietened her.

Piers Larstonbury came over to his daughter's bed and stood looking down as she lay with her teddy bear beside her. Lily was touched by the look of tenderness on his face.

'I thought I'd pop up and see my little dears. I don't

like to think of them being ill and Virginia's gone out. I hope I am not causing a disruption?'

'Of course not,' Lily said shyly. She felt a little overwhelmed by his presence so close to her but glad of someone to share her worries with. 'I was wondering whether we need to call the doctor. I'm worried it might be influenza.'

Piers Larstonbury adjusted the tails of his jacket out of the way and sat down on the edge of the bed, opposite Lily.

'Hello, Chrissie. How're you feeling, dear?'

'Feel poorly,' Christabel said.

'Oh dear, well we can't have that, can we? Do we need a special fairy to come and make you feel better?'

He laid his hand across the little girl's head and gently felt around her neck and throat with his long fingers. Christabel winced as he touched her throat.

'Is it sore, darling? Perhaps you're right, Miss Waters. Don't you worry. I'll drive round and ask for Dr Marchant.'

He returned within the hour with the doctor, a very small, serious man who decreed that the children needed to be kept cool and for the fever to 'come to a head'.

'They're two fine, strong children – they'll be right as rain in a few days,' he said, looking at his fob watch as if in a great hurry. Lily thought he could have taken a little bit more trouble, but of course you wouldn't dream of arguing with a doctor.

The two men disappeared and Lily was about to ready herself for bed, when to her astonishment, Piers Larstonbury came back into the nursery.

'I just thought I'd pop up again and say goodnight,' he said softly. Once again he sat himself down, this time on Hubert's bed. Hubert stirred and gave a miserable little moan. 'Poor little things. I thought Dr Marchant was a bit short with us, didn't you?'

'Well, yes,' Lily agreed shyly. She thought how kind Major Larstonbury was. 'He did seem to have other things on his mind.'

Piers Larstonbury looked across at her and smiled suddenly. She had the impression that he had suddenly seen her really as a person, not just a servant.

'How long have you been here now, Miss Waters?'

'Almost six months, sir.'

'And where were you before?'

'Not too far away.' She told him about her post with Mrs Jessop through the war, but did not mention the Arkwrights. 'Before that, I worked in India.'

'Did you, by jove!' He turned fully to look at her. 'Well, you've seen more of the world than I have. I must say, it's a country I'd be most interested to visit. Did you like it there?'

'Very much.' As she sat down on the chair close to the bed, memories flashed across her mind, lovely ones of the Fairfords, Cosmo and the horses. And then followed the wave of pain and longing which came with thoughts of India: Mussoorie and Sam. 'But I thought really I should return to this country at some stage. I did notice that people who had been there for a very long time found it terribly difficult to come back.'

'Yes – I'm sure you're right,' Piers Larstonbury said. 'How very wise.'

There was a pause, during which he looked into her face in a somehow troubled way and she realized that she liked him. She had seen him in a new light that night, realized how much he loved his children, and that he had also come back up here because he was lonely. He lingered, talking of this and that, asking her things about the children, about herself. Soon he had been there almost an hour, seeming to forget the time. At last he stretched and looked round at the clock.

'Goodness me!' He leaped up. 'It's almost half past ten! I suppose Virginia will be home from her meeting any moment. I'm so sorry to have kept you.'

'Not at all!' Lily had been surprised how much she had enjoyed it. She had, as ever, not given too much away about herself, but it was a pleasure to sit and talk to someone. Her job could be a very lonely one.

'Well – goodnight, Miss Waters. I hope the children are not too restless in the small hours.'

'We'll all get on all right,' Lily said.

Before leaving the room he gave her a sweet, grateful smile.

Chapter Fifty-Four

He fell in love with her during the grey chill of that winter.

Piers Larstonbury was not like other men Lily had met and at first she did not recognize his growing devotion to her. She did notice that he was about the house more, and thought the children's illness, from which both of them recovered well within a week, had drawn him close to them and he wanted simply to spend more time with them. Sometimes he came to the nursery and sat quietly looking at a story book with Hubert. But every so often his gentle voice reading the story would become halting and Lily might look up and find his gaze resting on her as she played with Christabel and her doll on the floor.

If she met him anywhere in the house he made a point of speaking to her now, when before he had seemed absent or almost unaware that she existed. And gradually she saw in his eyes something she did recognize: the deep, helpless stare of a man who had become strongly affected by her.

She first realized it at Christmas. There was a very festive atmosphere in the house. Virginia Larstonbury was lavishly hospitable and liked the house to be decked out with a tree and boughs of greenery and holly, streamers and candles and vases of winter blooms. The children were very excited. Piers's two older children,

Elspeth and Guy, were home for the holidays. They did not see a great deal of Guy, who spent much time either visiting his friends or in his room at the top of the house, where he painted in watercolours. Elspeth, however, was much in evidence, particularly in her explosive rows with Virginia. She was small in stature, with long, mousy hair, and looked as if she should be gentle and timid, but she was in fact highly temperamental, especially in the presence of her stepmother.

'I don't know why I bother coming back at all sometimes!' Lily heard Elspeth storming at Virginia one afternoon. Lily and Lottie the maid met on the stairs in the middle of this particular spat as raised voices came from the drawing room. 'When you treat me like some kind of *servant*. You don't want me here! I feel like Cinderella in my own home!'

'Oh, don't talk such utter nonsense, you ridiculous girl!' they heard Virginia snap at her. 'You really are the end, making everything into such a drama, when I'm doing all I can for you – and you making me into some kind of witch in a fairy story.'

'Well, sometimes you are just like a witch!' Elspeth shrieked. '*Just* like! You don't really care – not about Daddy or anyone. You only care about those queer people at your coven, or whatever it is you do . . .'

As Virginia exploded in outrage, Lottie raised her eyebrows comically at Lily. 'I don't know where she gets it from,' Lottie said. 'Miss Elspeth, I mean. They say her mother was the gentlest woman you could meet . . .'

Lily had learned that Piers Larstonbury's marriage before the war had lasted until Cecily Larstonbury died after a long illness in 1912. The couple's children had been brought up by a succession of mother substitutes against whom Elspeth had evidently perfected her skills in verbal combat. Lily kept out of Elspeth's way as much as possible. So far as she was concerned, her job was with Hubert and Christabel and no one else.

The house was full of visitors over the Christmas period, people from various branches of the family, and the children were sleepless with excitement for several nights before. The evening before Christmas Eve there was a party, the house lit up, music and comings and goings, loud laughter and chatter until very late. Lily stayed in the nursery trying to distract the children into sleep. On Christmas Eve there was another row about who would be going to church. Virginia did not hold with Church of England religion any more. Piers Larstonbury, who was more conventional, wanted to go to the midnight Eucharist. Elspeth, it appeared, was also prepared to go, chiefly in order to fall out with Virginia about it, and the evening was punctuated by bad-tempered outbursts between the two women.

In the midst of all this, Lily, having just got the children to sleep, heard a tap on the nursery door. With Christabel's little frock that she had been folding still in her hand, she tiptoed to the door.

'May I come in?' he whispered. Piers Larstonbury was always very polite, almost as if he found Lily intimidating.

Hesitating, she said, 'The children are already asleep,' but she stepped back to let him in.

'I thought they might be by now.'

She closed the door and went to lay Christabel's dress on the little white wicker chair in the corner. Close by, on a table, a dim light was burning.

'Actually, it was you I wanted to speak to.'

From his breast pocket his brought out a small

package and held it out to her, though she stood across the room from him.

'This is for you – a little Christmas gift.'

Lily felt a sense of panic rise in her. She knew that all the servants in the house would be given small gifts in the morning – but all together, by Virginia, not like this.

'Please,' he said, seeing her hesitation. 'Take it. It's just a token, but when I saw it I knew it would suit you.'

Lily was full of confusion, but also of curiosity to see what he had thought would suit her. She took the slender, tissue-wrapped gift from him, her fingers trembling, aware of him watching her intently.

Within the folds of tissue lay a silver object, studded with turquoise stones. Lily gasped.

'Oh – it's so beautiful!' Then, foolishly, 'Is it a hairslide?'

Piers Larstonbury lifted it from the paper. 'Perhaps I can show you. Your hair looks marvellous like that – so modern.'

Just two weeks earlier she had had her hair cut much shorter, into a fashionable pageboy level with her ear lobes. Piers Larstonbury stood on her right and drew the silver slide in past her temple. For a second it felt cold against her scalp.

'Perfect.' His voice was quiet, somehow awed. 'I knew it would be. It's perfect.'

Lily put her hand up and felt it. The clip was so beautiful – she knew somehow without him telling her that it was silver, that he had bought her something expensive and beautiful – and she had no idea what to do next.

'Thank you,' she said, her cheeks burning as she turned to him. 'It's lovely. I don't know why you . . .'

'No – you don't, do you?' They were standing close and his gaze was fixed intently on her. 'You don't know, you don't see – that's one of the things which makes you so extraordinary, my beautiful Lily. You're so lovely, so innocent, somehow.'

Her heart began pounding with panic. *Oh God, no, not this again.* Not another man ... What he saw as innocence was really the fact that she was closed to people, to men especially. She had built a rampart round herself so that she need never feel pain again – or thought she had.

'You've no idea what I feel for you, have you, you lovely, lovely woman?'

From this reserved, gentle man the words began to pour out. He was worked up, his face tight with emotions, 'You captivate me, Lily. You're so very beautiful, so gentle ... I feel as if you've given me life back again ... Your presence in the house has made the difference to everything ... I need to see you, to keep looking at you ...'

She stood under his words as if they were a shower of rain, not knowing what else to do. She knew that she had no feelings of this kind for Piers Larstonbury, but his words filled her with yearning to feel herself loved and to be able to love after these long, lonely years. And they also made her afraid and suspicious, because she knew that men's words of love meant nothing and she must not give way to them.

At last he stopped, and stood looking down at her. 'I couldn't hold back from telling you how I feel any longer. You're all I think about. I'd forgotten it was possible to feel like this, to love like this.' He laid his hands on her shoulders, looking at her with burning longing. 'Oh, Lily, let me kiss you, please do!'

'Major Larstonbury . . .' She struggled for words, and in the difficulty of it all felt anger rising in her. He had given her a gift as a bribe, something to force her to give into him! 'We are in your house, under the same roof as your wife, and your children are asleep here . . .' She waved her hand towards the sleeping children's beds.

'I'm sorry . . .' He lowered his hands to his sides abjectly. 'I've offended you. I've been clumsy and foolish. I'm just so much in love with you, so overwhelmed.'

Lily stood, looking at him. She could hear Ewan McBride: *I love you, I need you, Lily* . . . And Harold Arkwright and Sam. *Samuel Ironside.* She was filled with a bitterness of pain that she had not allowed for a long time. It seemed to rise up behind her throat. Men betrayed, they took what they wanted, without a care for your feelings. Men were liars.

Her expression seemed to freeze him.

'I'll go,' he said, to her astonishment. 'I'm sorry. I've been clumsy . . . A fool.'

Full of anger and of a longing regret, she watched him leave the nursery.

Chapter Fifty-Five

During the excitement of Christmas, she saw very little of him. He was there, in the parlour, standing in the background on Christmas morning when Virginia and Elspeth, in the shelter of a temporary festive truce, distributed little gifts to the servants. Lily received a little case of fine-quality writing paper and envelopes. She wondered who Virginia Larstonbury imagined she might have to write to, but she thanked her politely. She felt Piers Larstonbury watching her but she did not look at him.

He kept away from her for days, and she thought that that was the end of it. Then, gradually, as if nothing had happened, he made excuses to be near her again, to spend time with the children, even accompanying her to Hampstead Heath one Sunday afternoon when she took them out. He behaved with absolute decorum on all occasions and was also very attentive to his children.

'I scarcely saw my own father, growing up,' he said, as they strolled across the winter heath. Lily was pushing Christabel in a little carriage while Hubert trotted happily alongside his father holding his hand, awed by the treat of his being with them. 'He died without me knowing him.' He talked about his school, about having been sent away to board at the age of five.

'It was why Cecily, my first wife, and I decided to send Guy so much later, when he was ten. She was so attached to him, she didn't want him to go at all, but it's the thing to do, of course. Boarding school makes a man of you. Certainly helps you fit in when you're thrown into the army.' As he spoke he didn't sound altogether convinced. 'But I do think they go too young: it breaks some bond with the parents which you can never quite mend again.'

'Yes, I think you're right,' Lily said, thinking of Cosmo. 'Sometimes children seem to be more attached to their nanny than their parents.'

'Exactly so.' He smiled down at her. 'Which is why I want to be with them some of the time. I wasn't with Elspeth and Guy enough. Guy's remote from me, really.'

'Will you send Hubert away?'

'Perhaps.' He sounded miserable suddenly. 'I don't know. That will depend partly on Virginia. She rather favours boarding. I suppose she's not really very maternal. Not like you. You're marvellous with children.'

Lily blushed. 'I suppose I've always felt at home with them.'

She felt more relaxed with him that afternoon, though she could hardly forget his outburst of those weeks ago. And as they walked home along the smart London street, though, she realized she had not had such a long conversation with anyone in a long time, and he didn't speak to her like a servant. As they neared the house again, he said, very politely, 'It's been a real pleasure, this walk, Miss Waters. I've enjoyed our time together a great deal.'

She had to admit to herself that she had enjoyed it too. Above all, it was his kindness which drew her in. But all the time, in his attention she felt an unspoken pressure. Although he was behaving like a gentleman,

385

she knew the strength of his feelings for her and that they had not gone away. She had already become very fond of Hubert and Christabel: supposing she kept refusing to give in to their father's desires and he got rid of her? It was a terribly painful thought. Each time she left a family, the separation from the children almost broke her heart. She was living under his roof and he was being so kind to her. Somehow, as the days passed, it seemed impossible not to repay him by giving him what he wanted.

It happened the first time when Virginia was away, staying with her sister in Hampshire. Very occasionally she took the children with her to be looked after by the sister's nanny, but more often she went alone, in her colourful, drifty clothes, leaving the two infants in Lily's care, seeming content not to see them for days at a time.

She made such a visit in the last week of January, saying she 'simply couldn't bear London and this filthy weather any longer', and after a flurry of case-packing, disappeared in a cab to Paddington without saying when she would be back.

Lily barely noticed when Virginia was not there and the day passed much as usual, trying to keep the children occupied in cold, rainy weather.

But he came to her that night, late in the evening. It was as if she could predict what would happen, that he would come knocking softly on the door of her room, the way Ewan McBride used to come, and Harold Arkwright tried to, as if this was what she was destined for. She was proud of herself for not giving in to Harold Arkwright, whom she found detestable, but this was

386

different. When she heard the soft knocking she was already in her long flannel nightdress, her hair brushed.

She found her thoughts very cold and collected as she pulled round her the red silk dressing gown which Virginia had handed on to her, with a dragon across the back. The situation felt at once very familiar, yet far removed from her as if happening to somebody else.

'Lily?' He stood in the dimly lit passage. In the daytime he called her 'Miss Waters'.

Lily said nothing. She stood looking up at him.

'You know why I'm here.' His tone was soft, almost humble. 'Will you let me in?'

Dreamily she stood back to let him step past her and closed the door, turning to face him.

'I don't want to force myself on you,' he said straightforwardly. His hands were in his trouser pockets. 'I'm not that sort of man and I think you know I'm not. It's just that what I feel for you is so overpowering. I see you day after day and I long for you. I think you know Virginia and I don't have a ... an intimate marriage. Sometimes I don't think she has much regard for me at all. And you ...' He took his hands from his pockets, making a gesture which somehow encompassed her. 'You arrived in this house and at first I scarcely noticed. It seems incredible to me now. This astonishing, beautiful woman, with something ...' He looked at her with his head on one side. 'Something sad in her, which moves me ...'

As he spoke, to her astonishment, she felt a lump rise in her throat and the beginning of tears. She did not know what he had seen in her, nor did she really know what there was to be seen, but it felt a miracle that anyone had tried to see and understand. She lowered her gaze, embarrassed by her emotion.

'Lily?' He came to her and put his hands softly on her shoulders, then, as she did not resist, drew her into his arms. It was as if something broke open in her then, something quite unexpected and long dammed up, his gentle concern reducing her to sobs which shook her whole body, seeming to come from somewhere so deep in her that she was silent for long seconds at a time before they broke over her.

'Oh, my girl,' he said, so lovingly that it made her weep all the more, feeling held, somehow like a child, and being treated kindly. It brought out a deep tenderness in him.

'Oh, darling, little darling,' he said, stroking her hair, and as she grew calmer, he drew her to the bed. 'Come – lie down and let me embrace you . . .' When she was calmer he looked seriously into her face. 'I would marry you, d'you know that? I want you to know, Lily. If I could see a way . . . I feel so very strongly about you.'

She stared back at him, astonished. But he scarcely knew her at all! How could he be so sure? She thought men very strange.

The comforting turned to lovemaking, and she surrendered to him, to being held and cared for. As they lay together he lifted himself on to his elbow, his gentle face looking down at her. 'I shan't leave you with a child,' he told her, adding with a faint smile, 'I have a way to stop it. Of course, Virginia has educated me very thoroughly about this with all her talk about women needing control over their fertility.'

His fingers teased open the front of her nightgown, pulling back the soft cotton until he could see her breasts. He gave a low moan of pleasure and began to lick her nipples, his eyes closed, seeming to lose himself in her. Lily felt flickers of pleasure go through her, knew she was beginning to respond to him, her body seeming to spread and open at his touch, yet her mind was quite detached.

He rolled on to her, needing urgently to be inside her, and he moved in her with absolute pleasure and absorption.

'Oh God,' he gasped, breathless, 'Lily, oh, my Lily . . .' And after a number of urgent movements he climaxed in her with a sob, holding her very tight and close as if she were the most precious thing in the world.

Lily held him as he recovered his breath in her arms, feeling the comforting warmth of him, his hair close to her cheek. She liked the smell of him, a mixture of sweat and something sweet and exotic. Staring up at the shadowy ceiling she knew she was held in the arms of a nice man, a kind enough one for her to have let herself weep. But could she love him? She did not believe so, but in those moments she wished that she could.

Chapter Fifty-Six

At first, Lily had never considered that Piers Larston-bury might be able to help Cosmo.

He conducted his affair with Lily with absolute discretion, so that she was certain no one else knew what was going on. He was very cautious about coming to her at night, choosing times when Virginia was away or when it was so late that she was asleep, so their time together was limited.

The winter passed and Virginia was as preoccupied as ever, going out to her theosophy meetings, lunching with her friends, exploding over political disappointments.

'They've turned down votes for women in the United States!' Lily heard her voice expostulating from somewhere in the house one morning. 'And I thought they were supposed to be an *enlightened* country!' Virginia had been a suffragette in her younger days, marching for the vote before it was granted to women in 1918.

'I suppose that was when I fell in love with her,' Piers told Lily. 'She was so full of conviction, so *fiery*, and of course so lovely to look at as well.' He sighed with great melancholy. 'The trouble is, I'm not sure women like that are meant for marriage.'

'I don't want to hurt her feelings,' he said one night as they lay together. He stroked Lily's back. With a pang, it reminded her of Sam. 'I just need you, Lily, my darling. You came and took me by surprise.'

It was that night that she decided to tell him about Cosmo. Piers had somehow managed to bring a tray of tea up to her room in the small hours, waking her because he longed for her so much and Lily laughed at the picture he painted of him creeping about down in the kitchen once the maids were asleep.

'Anything for you, my darling,' he twinkled at her. Often he sat just staring at her adoringly, as if he could not drink in the sight of her enough. 'Hell, high water . . . Anything for my love!'

Lily smiled in what she hoped was a proper acknowledgement of his words.

'My goodness.' He sat holding his teacup, eyes fixed on her. 'You're such a mysterious woman. I never have any idea what's really going on in your beautiful head. It makes you even more attractive, darling.' He leaned forward and kissed her lips, lingering over it. He drew back and asked, 'And where did you go today?'

It had been Lily's day off, a break she was allowed every fortnight.

'I went to meet a friend.' She hesitated, frowning. Cosmo had worried her that day, more than ever before. 'I say friend – he was the boy I looked after in India – Cosmo Fairford. He's grown up now, of course, and working for Lloyds Bank. I can hardly believe he's already nineteen, and so very handsome, towering above me!'

'Fairford . . .' Piers mused. 'Is he one of the Warwickshire Fairfords?'

'Yes – his uncle oversees the estate. His father Charles stayed on in India – in the army. He was killed in the war. Cosmo came here to school, of course.'

'Oh, well I'm sure he's thriving,' Piers said lightly. She could tell he was not really interested, but listening because he felt he had to. He put his empty teacup down and sat beside her, stroking her. This was always the beginning of lovemaking, the warm movement of his hand on her shoulders, her neck, before his fingers found their way inside her nightdress, seeking out her breasts.

'I'm not sure.' She could not keep the worry from her voice. She wanted him to hear what she was saying, not go off into the trance of lovemaking without taking notice of her worries. Intimate relations had narrowed the social gap between them and she wanted to make this demand on him. 'It's not really what Cozzy's cut out for at all. He's always been rather more of an outdoors sort of boy. I wish I knew how to help him.'

Piers rested his hand on her collarbone, looking down into her eyes and said, 'Tell me more about him.'

She had met Cosmo in the Lyons Corner House in Oxford Street that afternoon. They sat at a table close to one of the grand marbled columns, not too close to the orchestra, and she drank in the sight of him. He was even more handsome than the last time she had seen him. His hair had remained thick and blond, his eyes were a vivid blue, gazing coldly from above a nose which had developed to become prominent and aquiline. Lily was full of pride at the sight of him, though he had come rather more casually dressed than she would have liked, attired as if for summer in white flannels, a grey jacket and rather foppish bow tie. But she passed no comment as she was so pleased and grateful to see him, and his mood was already sombre and off-hand. She felt she must humour him, until he softened and became her boy again.

'Now, let me buy you tea,' he said expansively. He seemed to be putting on a rather lord of the manor attitude which Lily found touching and sad because he also seemed to her so young. He ordered a huge tea of scones and cakes, far more than was really needed, and they sat talking while the orchestra played jaunty waltzes and mazurkas.

'How are you enjoying the work – any better than last time I saw you?' Lily ventured. She saw him about once a month now they were both in London.

Cosmo was spreading copious amounts of butter on a piece of fruit tea bread.

'Oh, it's not so bad,' he said airily. Then he stilled the knife and looked up at her. His face fell into something less posed. 'Actually, I loathe it. Every damned minute of it, to tell you the truth. It's like being buried alive.'

'But you were so fortunate to be taken on,' Lily said encouragingly. She said no more but both of them knew she was talking about his disastrous school record. Lloyds seemed a great career to her. 'And I'm sure you'll be marvellous at it.'

'You know I loathe being stuck indoors all day,' he said, biting ravenously into the tea bread.

'But you could have stayed on the estate, surely?'

'What with Uncle William, that crazed old fool? God in heaven, I've had a lifetime's worth of him, I can tell you. The only reason I go there at all is that it's the only place I can drive. He hardly knows what's going on on the estate any more and he certainly doesn't take any notice of what I do. But I don't want to be running the blasted place. When my turn comes I'll pay a man to do it. I want to be *driving*, Lily – motor racing! That's my thing. I *know* it! If I could just get someone to take me seriously, get a break . . .'

Lily watched him sadly. She wondered how good a driver he really was. And no wonder nobody would take a risk on him with a record like his. When he was twenty-one, perhaps he might have the wealth to buy himself into whatever he desired, but at the moment he did not have the connections or personality to get where he wanted. She knew he put people off by his manner and her heart ached for him when she thought how sweet and trusting he had been as a boy. She watched sadly as she saw him take a little hip flask from his pocket and steal a drink out of it, even while they were taking tea.

'Cosmo,' she reproached him. 'Is that really necessary?'

'Oh, don't *you* start,' he snapped, really unpleasant for a moment and she immediately had to appease him.

'I expect things'll work out: they have a manner of turning out in ways you don't expect,' she said lamely. What else could she say? 'How's your mother? Have you heard from her?'

'Oh, I suppose she's about somewhere,' Cosmo said bitterly. 'I had a birthday letter from her, that's all.'

Perhaps you're not nice enough to her when you do see her, Lily thought. Perhaps you drive her away.

She and Susan were in contact occasionally, short notes which mainly exchanged news of Cosmo. Susan was now living down on the south coast and did not disclose much about her life to Lily. However, she had once mentioned her encounter with Sam Ironside when she was a VAD in 1918 and the thought made Lily ache. There was nothing else she could do except hope that meant that he had safely survived the remainder of the war.

Sitting here with Cosmo, though, she also felt a pang

of possessive pride that once again she was the one seeing him, mothering him, not Susan. She needed Cosmo to need her, for her to be special to him.

But when she parted from him she felt uneasy. He was unhappy, felt thwarted by his work in the bank, which he had in fact chosen to do himself, even though he always made out he had been forced into it. Why had he gone to do the very thing he was going to dislike so much? she wondered. He had succumbed to the pressures of his class and family, it was true, but it seemed more than that. There was a vein of perverse self-destruction in him that she could sense and which worried her deeply.

As the weeks passed, she mentioned Cosmo to Piers Larstonbury quite regularly. She did not tell him that Cosmo had been expelled from Eton, or about any of the other troubles. She painted a picture of an admirable, if frustrated young man who was trying to make his way in the world.

As Piers fell more and more deeply in love with her, he seemed prepared to do anything for her.

'Perhaps we could meet somehow – you and I and Cosmo?' she suggested. It was Cosmo who talked about Brooklands, about how he loved going there. He haunted the racetrack as often as he could. Lily did not think Piers knew much about cars, but she had heard him say many times that he was interested in widening his life, in finding out about new things.

'It's as if I've narrowed things down so that I barely do anything except work,' he said. 'I feel younger with you, Lily. I don't know much about the motor car, but maybe we could find a way to go without it being a problem. I know – we could take Hubert. He might be very taken with it all!'

And so, come the Whit holiday, when she had been Piers Larstonbury's mistress for four months, she found herself at Brooklands with Piers and Cosmo – and Sam Ironside.

Chapter Fifty-Seven

Sam returned to Birmingham from Brooklands that evening after the Whitsun meeting, feeling set on fire.

After the long ride back to Northfield in the dark, once he had dropped Loz off, he had a feeling of bottomless energy, as if he had just been reborn. As he pushed his motorcycle round to the back of the house he knew that whatever happened, there was no going back. In those few hours, everything had changed.

Helen was standing in the back room, heating a pan on the range. She looked a little hunched, her long hair tucked in the back of her checked dressing gown. Her hair was still a caramel colour, but thinner and less abundant now. Her face looked thin and sallow. He realized again with a shock that she was younger than Lily Waters. As he stood at the back door he was able to watch her for a second before she saw him, and he had a bewildering sense of her being utterly strange to him. Although she was the mother of his four daughters, it was as if he did not know who she was and never had. He found it disturbing and reassuring at the same time, as if he knew he did not belong to her, and was sure now that he did not want to and had never truly wanted to.

'You've made good time,' she said, glancing at him, while her attention was still half on the simmering milk. He knew she was resentful of the way he could just take off for the day and she couldn't, even if in truth she did not want to go anywhere herself.

'Yes,' he said, pulling his jacket off. The room felt warm and cosy after the buffeting night air. 'It was a good run.' He flung the jacket over a chair. On the table there was a teapot with a crocheted green and yellow cosy which Helen's mom had given them, and the last of a loaf, lying face down on the board next to the bread knife. There was also a bowl of sugar with a few crumbs in.

'Want some cocoa? Or tea?'

'Stick the kettle on, will you? I'll make the tea.'

She silently did as he asked and brought her own cup of cocoa and spooned sugar into it, tutting.

'Girls've made a mess of the sugar again. I've told 'em and told 'em.'

And then she gave him a long, penetrating look.

'What's up with you?' she said.

He did tell her, but not then. He had to get used to the idea, of all that Major Larstonbury had said that afternoon.

'I am, as I have said, an outsider to the motor trade and motor racing,' the major said. 'However, thanks to ... circumstances' – once more his eye rested on Lily for a second – 'I can see myself becoming quite an enthusiast. Today has been an eye-opener: you've impressed me, Ironside. So – I'm prepared to make available whatever funds are needed to keep you for, let's say a year. I'll rent you the work space to build your motor car and you will have a free hand in all technical aspects, which I know very little about. You will, I know, do the job to the very best of your ability.

There is only one condition I would ask of you: that once you are ready to enter your vehicle in track races, your driver will be' – he gestured – 'Cosmo Fairford.'

Cosmo sat up straight and looked utterly astonished. Sam could not take in what he had just heard either. He looked at Lily, who was watching him, her eyes aglow. Sam stuttered into questions. What did Captain Larstonbury mean – where was he to work? Who with? Did he seriously mean simply to hand over the project to him, trusting a man whom he had met only this afternoon?

'It sounds to me as if the best place you could possibly work is here, at Brooklands,' Piers Larstonbury said. 'If that would be acceptable. And you mentioned that you already have colleagues who are ready to work on developing the vehicle with you? I am offering myself as your patron. My own instincts and those of Miss Waters, who clearly thinks highly of you, point in the direction of a very fruitful partnership. I realize this may mean some personal sacrifices for you and your family. Perhaps you'd like a little time to think about it?'

'No!' Sam was mentally rushing ahead. He could not think straight about the details. He only knew he was being made the most astounding, once-in-a-lifetime offer and all his instincts told him to grab it! He could scarcely take it all in and felt like dancing about on the tables.

'I'd be delighted to accept,' he said as soberly as he could manage. 'Thank you, Major Larstonbury.' All his class niggles were forgotten now. What a great man the major was! 'We'll build a marvellous Special. We won't let you down.'

There were hand shakings and the writing down of addresses in Piers Larstonbury's artistic hand, and he assured Sam that he would make arrangements for him as soon as possible. He would even write a letter to request leave of absence for him from the Austin works. Sam felt as if his fairy godmother had arrived and he was in a daze as they stood up to go. And then he knew he had to part from Lily.

He was beside her as she walked from the clubhouse, holding the boy's hand again. Cosmo, full of life now, was talking animatedly to Piers Larstonbury.

'Lily – this was your doing, wasn't it?'

She turned and looked at him and he could not read her expression. It was triumphant yet amused, as if she were celebrating her own sense of power.

'He'd do anything for me,' she said softly, looking down at the ground.

Sam leaned close to her, with a desperate impulse. 'I've got to see you.'

Lily raised her eyes. 'I expect we shall meet, through all this.' And her gaze left him again.

Hope leaped inside him at what he thought he saw in her eyes. She was still his woman – deep down they both knew it. But there was not time to say anything else. He took his leave of the party, and watched them depart towards their car, and it was only then, once he was alone, that the full impact of what had happened had hit him. He was going to work at Brooklands and build a Special!

'Loz! Where the hell are you? He's never going to believe this ... He's going to think I've been on the bottle all afternoon ...'

Leaping and fizzing with excitement he pulled his hat off and tore across the ground to find his friend.

*

He told Helen, straight out with it, a few days later, after the wire had arrived from Piers Larstonbury, and after he had sorted things out with the Austin.

That had been like a dream as well, going to the old man and telling him what he wanted to do. Herbert Austin stood looking at him in silence for a few moments, considering the situation. Sam knew he was in a strong position. He had been taken on at the Austin as a promising engineer in the years when things were very lean. During the Depression which hit the industry after the war heaps of men had lost their jobs. Who could afford to buy cars then? Come 1919, Austin had had to lay out to re-equip the works for peacetime production and that had set them back; they were installing automated machines to speed production, but the first model, the 3.6-litre Austin Twenty, trying to do something like Ford, had not really taken off. It was too big and clumsy. By last year some of them were doing stints at the works with no wages – Austin was broke. Sam was one of the ones who stuck it out. It had been a hell of a time – living on air almost, Helen keeping on at him to leave and go back to Coventry, and they were still recovering. He didn't really know why he'd stayed – bloody-mindedness mostly. And Austin had promised him a job for life if he wanted it after that. He knew Herbert Austin felt a debt of gratitude to the engineers who stuck by him. They were the ones who had saved the company in its darkest hour.

'I had a cable from this Major Larstonbury,' Herbert Austin said.

Sam stood while Austin sat behind his desk, its surface littered with drawings from the company draughtsmen. There was great excitement at the moment

401

– the new model, known as the Austin Seven, about to be launched. Some thought it was misguided, but Sam was in favour of a car the ordinary man could afford – he might stand a chance himself! He felt a pang of regret.

Austin slipped the end of his pen in his mouth for a moment, then withdrew it. 'He's talking about your being released from us for a year. And he's going to meet your wages?'

'So he says,' Sam said. 'And Loz ... Lawrence Marks.'

'Hmph,' Herbert Austin said. There was a pause, which seemed to imply that the man must have more money than sense, but then he said, 'You wanted to be in the company's racing team, I seem to remember.'

'Oh yes,' Sam said. 'I'd've liked to. There hasn't been an opening.'

'I should have found you one, shouldn't I?' A little smile played on Herbert Austin's rather austere features. 'Then I shouldn't have had to let one of my finest engineers go taking off. You'll come back?'

It was a more of a statement than a question.

'Oh yes. I've a wife and four children.'

'This Piers Larstonbury – is he an engineer?'

'An architect, I believe. He doesn't know much about motors at all.'

'Hmph,' Herbert Austin said again. 'Well, well. I suppose you'll have to do it. Don't you go beating us, though.'

And a moment later Sam was leaving Austin's office, feeling as if he had grown wings. Later, he and Loz sat in the pub and grinned at each other for a long moment before they erupted into yells of delighted laughter. They were going to Brooklands! They had been given

402

the chance of a lifetime, to build their own Special and race it – and the old man had more or less given his blessing!

They downed a pint each at high speed. Loz's round, boyish face was pink and alight with glee.

'By crikey, Sam – we're going to do it! We're going to build the best bloody Special that's ever gone round Brooklands!' Then he put his glass down slowly on the table and his face sobered rapidly. 'Christ – what's Mary going to say?'

Mary Marks evidently had quite a bit to say at the idea of her husband taking off to go down and 'play racing cars' at Brooklands. But Mary and Loz were good pals and Mary had only two children, and two sisters near. In the end she was also proud and grudgingly pleased for Loz even though she desperately didn't want him to be away so much.

Helen was a different matter. As he came out with it, blunt and direct because he couldn't think of another way of doing it, Sam saw her face close up, as if he had frozen something deep in her. But he could do no other, he knew that. The opportunity was irresistible to him. And under and within it also, running like a deep, subterranean river of new life, was the thought of Lily. He tried not to think of Lily, keeping his mind on the practical things, the cars and engineering, his head swarming with ideas and plans. But in quiet moments, in bed at night beside Helen's resentful sleeping form, or at odd moments of the day, the memory of her came to him overwhelmingly. However much she had hurt him, he knew she felt something for him. Her eyes had given it away just in those seconds when they met, and the pull of her now was far too strong. He was going south, could only go south to do the things he burned to do – and to be near her.

'You're leaving me,' Helen stated.

He told her the day he saw Herbert Austin, that teatime. He was astonished by the way she just plunged in like that, as if she could see it all so clearly.

'Don't talk daft!' he said. 'It's for a year – overall. But I'll be back up to see you!'

This was said with a kind of guilty optimism. He knew he probably wouldn't come often. He had been careful to tell her straight away that there would be money – the equivalent of his wages. She wouldn't go short, so she needn't worry on that score. When the wire of confirmation had come through to him so promptly and to Herbert Austin, he knew the man was not fooling him. And he also knew that Lily was behind it. Of course, Lily wanted to get that Fairford boy on to the track. That was part of the deal. But was it not more than that? Was it not seeing him again that had spurred her to use her influence over Piers Larstonbury? He did not think she was in love with the man, though it was hard to tell. A pang of jealous suspicion filled him at the thought. But she had said she would see him ... She wanted to see him.

Over those days Helen rocked between resentment, anger and a pathetic sadness. She had lost him and she knew it. And she was full of rage and grief and at times begged and begged him not to go.

'But I'll be back – very soon,' he assured her. 'It's a great chance – old man Austin even thinks so. I'm doing this for all of us – for the girls and you ...'

'You don't love me – you never have,' she said one evening, perched in utter misery by the range.

And he knew with terrible clarity in that moment that what she said was true. But he said, 'Don't talk daft. You're my wife, aren't you?'

She looked across at him, with tear-stained cheeks.

'But you're still going, aren't you? Whatever I say?'

Quietly, able to do no other, he said, 'Yes, love. I am.'

Chapter Fifty-Eight

July 1922

'So—' Sam stood up from where he had been bending over the open engine as Loz rushed into the shed – 'are we on?'

Loz's hair was standing on end from his habit of running his oily hands through it. Like Sam, he was dressed in an old boiler suit smeared with oil and there was a good helping of it on his face, which was otherwise pink and beaming with excitement.

'Yep – Shelsley Walsh, Saturday! We'll be ready by then, easy!'

Sam grinned, flexing his stiff back. He wiped his left eye, which was watering badly this morning, then gave the car's bodywork a fond pat. She'd held up well on the test hill here at Brooklands. It was a specially built incline where the motor cars could be put through their paces on a gradient as steep as one in four in parts. But now it was time for a new challenge.

'Better send a wire to the major. I expect he'll want to be there.'

And if the major came all the way over to Shelsley, and Cosmo Fairford, surely *she* might come too. The thought made Sam ache.

They had been installed at Brooklands for five weeks

now and he hadn't seen Lily or heard from her. Piers Larstonbury, who seemed to have been infected by huge enthusiasm for the project he had taken on, had been down to visit for four out of five of the weekends since they began. He had learned very fast, soaking up information and learning from their expertise. Sam saw that the man was genuinely humble and lacking in arrogance. He treated Loz and Sam as equals and Sam soon came very much to respect and like Major Larstonbury.

During those earliest days, while the two of them tried to decide on the key specifications for the motor, the major had perched on an upturned crate in the shed listening to all the animated conversations about the ratio between power and weight so that it would be as fast as possible but still hold the road, how rigid the structure should be, what size the brakes. Every so often he asked questions.

'Thing is,' Sam explained enthusiastically, 'we need to keep the frontal area down – the cross section. The size of hole it makes in the wind, in other words. Smaller it is, faster she'll go.'

'Won't that engine – all that power – just destabilize the whole structure?' Piers Larstonbury asked. They had got hold of a Mercedes chain-driven chassis and an airship engine. It had worked for Count Zborowski, they reasoned. All the power in that engine!

'No – that's the beauty of it.' Loz was fizzing with enthusiasm. 'You can put a much more powerful engine in without too much problem. Course, the crankshaft speed is so low in an engine that size that you have to up the gear ratios no end, but it's easy enough.'

Piers Larstonbury joined in hours of conversations and watched Sam and Loz chewing over all the figures and alternatives of what they might do. They saw their

patron become quite boyish and excited about what he
had taken on and the skill of the men carrying it out.

'That's really thoroughly splendid!' he would say and
often he gave a happy laugh as he said it.

And the weekdays Sam and Loz spent in a blissful
state, something Sam celebrated in himself several times
a day, when he thought how grindingly different everything would have been if he had never met the major.
Even if he and Loz had ever got together enough money
to begin building a motor, which was very doubtful,
they would have been incredibly lucky to have found
anywhere that touched this in terms of a place to build
it. And they would have been at it after a day's toil at
the Austin, squatting about in some cramped place God
only knew where, on dark evenings when they were
hardly able to see, and every hour they could spend of
their weekends with their wives nagging them to stop.
But at Brooklands they had their own shed in a row of
others, amid the buzzing hive of activity round the
racetrack, and they could absorb themselves totally in
their passion with monkish single-mindedness.

Race days were only a small part of what went on at
Brooklands. Cars were designed, built, tested, rejigged
... Some chaps went through a great to-do about
covering up the engines of the cars they were working
on if anyone came close, as if guarding highly innovative
secrets. But mostly Brooklands felt like a college or
university. They met engineers from all over the place,
talked, shared problems and ideas, all endlessly fascinated by the same challenges and triumphs of the motor
car. And they could spend all day there, sunshine pouring in through the windows on to the cluttered space:
the plentiful supply of tools which Major Larstonbury
had ensured they were provided with hung all round

408

the walls, and the smells of metal and rubber and oil, meant Sam felt he had found paradise.

'I'll let the major know,' Loz said. He paused, about to go out of the door again. 'Sam – are you sure about that Fairford bloke?'

Cosmo was to undertake his first drive at Shelsley Walsh. Previously they had only seen him on runs round the test track at Brooklands. Loz had taken an instant dislike to Cosmo Fairford. Sam knew it was partly that he was of the class Loz was forever making fun of and he just wasn't comfortable with him. But it was more than that: Loz didn't trust him. He hadn't said outright, but Sam could tell.

'He's a good driver by the look of him,' Sam said. 'We'll give him a try.'

Loz stared at him for a moment as if trying to work something out. *Why are you risking our precious motor to this toff who you've only seen drive a handful of times?* Then he went out again.

Sam stood, hands on waist, watching him through the window as he walked away. There was a slight frown on his face. Loz was right. They hadn't fully got the measure of Cosmo Fairford – they were taking a risk. But they needed a driver. Neither of them was up to it, not at race speeds, and Loz hadn't suggested anyone better, had he? He was not prepared to explain his reasoning to Loz. *Lily loved Cosmo.* And he knew that this was why he and Loz were here at all, because Lily Waters had such influence over Piers Larstonbury, because the major was in love with her. Cosmo was part of the arrangement whether they liked it or not and Sam hoped to God he was as skilled a driver as he claimed to be. He found Cosmo petulant, and arrogant, but none of that mattered so long as he could hold that motor through the wind and take her as fast as she'd go! And out of a sense of loyalty and respect for Cosmo's father, Captain Fairford, and the child he remembered Cosmo to have been, and of gratitude for those weeks in Ambala, he was prepared to give him a chance. And because of Lily. Of course because of Lily.

Sam and Loz motored to Worcestershire separately from the major and Cosmo, towing their racing Special on a trailer. Like most of the racing cars she had been given a name – Piers Larstonbury had insisted that she be called the Heath Flyer, as befitted a vehicle which he had had fantasies of racing round Hampstead Heath.

They set off very early, and after pulling into the race ground at Shelsley Walsh in the late morning, soon found Cosmo Fairford's Morgan and the major's Daimler parked up side by side, evidently having not long arrived themselves. As he braked and shut off the engine, Sam's heart gave a lurch to see that climbing out from the Daimler's passenger seat was Lily.

'You coming?' Loz said impatiently, as Sam stayed at the wheel, staring across at her.

'Yes, all right, just give me a minute,' he said absently.

Loz tutted and went round to unhitch the trailer. Sam sat drinking in the sight of Lily. He just couldn't stop looking at her: she was so beautiful, with those remarkable, sultry looks, her clothes stylish and elegant and all a deep plum-red, except for the white band round her cloche hat. As he gazed at her, she called out lightly to Piers Larstonbury, obviously reminding him that he had forgotten something, and jealousy flared in him.

'God, she's lovely . . .' he murmured, seeing her

410

cherry lips turned up in a gentle smile. He longed with a deep ache just to be able to go over and speak to her in the easy, loving way they had once shared. For her to smile at him, for everything between them to be as it had been for those enchanting days in India, as it should always have continued to be. The hurt which came at the end of those days stabbed at him again like an unhealed scar. She had hurt him, and at times he wanted to hurt her too.

His eye was caught by movements around Cosmo Fairford's sporty vehicle. There seemed to be someone with Cosmo in the car, but Cosmo climbed out first, from the driver's seat. He even managed to do that with a kind of swagger, Sam thought, watching Cosmo smooth back his wayward blond hair. If it wasn't for Lily's obvious devotion to the lad, Sam could have developed a serious dislike for him, even though he had to concede, he was a damned fine driver. He had proved that on some of the latest test runs at Brooklands, and even Loz had had to agree. *You'd better do all right today, Sonny Jim*, he thought, staring fiercely at Cosmo. *You'd better not mess up with this baby of ours . . .*

Then he saw the other figure emerge from the Morgan. It took Sam a few seconds to recognize Susan Fairford. She was dressed to the nines in a fashionable, pale green outfit which shimmered in the sunlight. She wore a green cloche hat jauntily tilted on her head and looked every bit the society lady. Sam thought of her that night in France in the last spring of the war, thin and exhausted, yet somehow more real, much more likeable when the class barrier had come down. He wondered sourly whether she would even give him the time of day now.

Composing himself, he climbed out of the car and,

411

catching up with Loz, went over to greet the rest of their party.

'Ah – Ironside!' Somehow Piers Larstonbury always treated Sam as the senior of the two of them. Sam was not sure if Loz resented this, but if so he didn't show it. 'So – here you are! Journey go all right?'

'Very well,' Sam said. 'All in one piece and ready to go. Are you fit, Fairford?' He always spoke jauntily to Cosmo. He wasn't going to treat him with any kind of deference.

'Oh yes,' Cosmo said. 'Raring to go.'

Sam saw suddenly that the lad was almost tremulous with nerves and he felt for him. He knew he had to prove himself.

'Mother,' Cosmo turned to Susan who was coming up beside him. 'This is Sam Ironside – the chief mechanic. I don't suppose you remember him from Ambala, do you? Says he delivered a car . . . ?'

Sam braced himself for Susan's chill offhandedness. When he looked at her, though, to his surprise, he saw a genuine, warm smile in her china blue eyes and she held her hand out.

'Of course I remember, Cosmo. Mr Ironside and I have met more recently than that.' She explained, briefly, and Sam saw that she was proud of her months as a VAD. She peered at him with a kind of professional concern. There was still the cut-glass voice of course, but in every other way she seemed to have thawed and her manner was more genuine. 'My goodness, you were lucky not to lose the sight in that eye. How is it?'

'Not too bad, thank you,' Sam said. 'Plays me up a bit, but at least I can see out of it.'

'Were you in until the end?' she asked. 'You had other wounds.'

'Nothing too serious. Yes – I made it to the end.'
And he returned her smile.

'And you have given my son the chance he's been craving for a very long time. We're all most grateful.'

'He's a skilled driver,' Sam said carefully.

'Is he?' Seeing her more closely now, Sam realized how anxious she was, and how nervous for Cosmo. 'We do all hope so.' Turning, she said, 'Perhaps you remember Miss Waters – surely you do? She was Cosmo's nanny and she has been a true friend to him.'

Sam was struck by the warmth in her voice, the note of real gratitude.

'Lily – you remember Mr Ironside? He came with that Daimler for Charles?'

Lily had been standing beside Cosmo, her arm in his, smiling proudly up at him as Sam praised his driving.

'Yes, I remember,' Lily said, quite composed. She loosened Cosmo's arm and for a second her hand was in Sam's. 'How d'you do?'

And then she withdrew and a moment later they all moved apart and he had to see to the car. Sam found that the blood was thundering round his body.

I must speak to her soon, he thought, speak to her properly, or I'm going to go mad.

Chapter Fifty-Nine

'Oh goodness, I do hope he'll be all right,' Susan Fairford said. 'I don't know if I can bear to watch!' She had a handkerchief in one hand, gripped to her.

'Of course he will,' Lily said, but her stomach was also knotted up in apprehension at the thought of Cosmo hurtling into view in the Heath Flyer, which Sam and Loz had thrown such passion and energy into building. Supposing it was all a disaster; supposing he crashed the car – ruined it! Lily sensed that Sam did not have a high opinion of Cosmo. He had had to let him drive since it was part of the arrangement if he was to have the patronage of Piers Larstonbury, but imagine what his reaction would be!

Oh, Cosmo, darling, please be careful, her mind called out to him, but she tried to look calm.

They were behind the barrier at the lower S bend of the Shelsley Walsh track, amid the excited atmosphere. Although a lot of hill tests were still done on the public roads, officially there was a speed limit of twenty miles per hour, which put events like this on the wrong side of the law. Shelsley was a private ground, however, the track twisting through beautiful green, hilly country-side. Shelsley was famous for its 1,000-yard steep climb, a stamina challenge for all kinds of motor car.

All day, since they arrived, the air had been full of excitement and the screech and roar of the motors being put through their paces up the hill. Lily and Susan had spent the time together, and it had been a good chance for them to re-establish their friendship while the men were caught up in all the motoring activity.

Susan was now living alone on the south coast outside Eastbourne, and Lily worried for her. She had only once been down to visit Susan, who had seemed very pleased to see her, but that had been almost a year ago, soon after Lily went to work for the Larstonburys. The two of them had walked on the beach on a warm, early summer afternoon and Lily was struck by how much Susan seemed to need her to be there. She put it down to the war and all the bereavements Susan had suffered, and that she was someone who knew Susan's past. Though she had confided in Lily in Ambala, it had been out of desperation, since there was no one else. Now she seemed a sad, more humble woman altogether, and one who was clearly living a lonely life. She evidently saw a few people for bridge afternoons, but no one to whom she could really feel close, and she met Cosmo only occasionally.

When Lily left to catch the train, Susan almost begged, 'Oh do come again, won't you, please?'

Lily had intended to, but weeks had passed and now she was so much in demand from Piers Larstonbury during any of her time off duty that somehow she had never visited again. She was pleased to see, though, that today Susan had dressed up and looked younger and attractive again.

As they had passed the afternoon together waiting for Cosmo's event, Susan poured out her worries about him.

'I can't seem to get near him at all – he's so sullen with me. And he throws himself into such rages. I'm sure he drinks far too much . . . I can't bear to see my boy like that, but he won't listen to me – does he listen to you, Lily?'

Lily smiled, sadly. 'Not so far as I can see. But I know how much he loathes it at the bank. I so much hope that this chance to drive will give him a new lease of life . . .'

From far in the distance came a ripple of sound. Susan's eyes widened.

'He's off! Oh, dear God, please let him be all right!'

They stood amid the excited crowd on the bank behind the track, straining their ears to hear the sound of the engine approaching. Lily pictured Cosmo, face tensed with concentration, eyes narrowed, jaw clenched so that his chin jutted, alive in every nerve. And she thought of Sam who was never far from her mind. She knew she would be seeing him later and her nerves were so jangled at the thought that she could barely stand still. There was the pull of him, the overpowering need to see him and the fear and anger that went with it, and sooner or later she knew she wasn't going to be able to avoid it any longer.

At last they heard the car and within a moment it rounded the bend at the bottom of the S, its slim, streamlined shape coursing fast up the slope with what seemed astonishing speed. It was over in a few seconds, and they could not see Cosmo's face, only his head and hunched shoulders, and the car swung along towards the top of the S in the track and was gone with a receding roar.

'Oh, dear God,' Susan Fairford breathed.

'He looks marvellous,' Lily said, full of pride for him.

'Let's just pray he gets through . . . He's so impulsive

– erratic, somehow . . . We must go and join them at the end!'

Lily hesitated. Being here with Susan, away from the men, she could avoid it all: Piers Larstonbury's gentle face, his eyes always following her with a besotted, admiring gaze, and Sam, who she knew would be trying to catch her eye, trying to draw her in. Somehow she always seemed to be trapped by the gaze of men. And with Sam Ironside it was all so much more disturbing, frightening, since he was the one man for whom she had ever felt anything real.

Chapter Sixty

That evening they all put up in an inn called the Pack Horse in a nearby village, where a sturdy feast of meat pies, mashed potatoes and gravy, with plenty of the local ale, turned into a triumphant celebration. The car had not only held up but made a very respectable time on the 1,000-yard hill and Cosmo had shown that he could handle her beautifully.

There were nine of them seated round a long table in a low-ceilinged room. At the head of the table Piers Larstonbury presided, with Cosmo and Lily on each side of him. Lily found herself seated beside Mary Marks, Loz's wife, whose two boys were beside her and Loz at the other end of the table, with Sam beside him. Susan sat between Cosmo and Sam.

Piers Larstonbury was obviously enjoying the homely food after Virginia's eccentric fare. He lifted his glass of ale and smiled warmly at Cosmo and then down the table towards Sam and Loz, his mechanics.

'Well!' He raised his well-spoken voice. 'I'd say today was a great triumph and a marvellous beginning. I congratulate you all – and thank you all. You've done me proud.'

'Oh, there are still plenty of improvements we can make!' Loz called along the table. His face was rubicund with beer and excitement and Lily could see he was immensely proud to be able to show off his prowess in front of his wife and sons.

'We'll beat Frazer-Nash yet!' Sam joined in excitedly. 'You just wait and see!'

'Oh yes – we certainly shall!' Cosmo's voice was louder than everyone else's.

Captain Archie Frazer-Nash, in his little two-cylinder car, was winning more events than any other driver. He was certainly setting the standard.

'Well, I sincerely hope so – and believe so too, after today!' Piers Larstonbury said.

Lily was astonished to see the difference in him since they had left London. She was used to seeing him as the sober, rather browbeaten husband of Virginia Larstonbury, someone quiet, dutiful and industrious who lived a genteel and cultured Hampstead life. But the racetrack and the company of a different kind of man seemed to have brought out something lively and boyish in him. She saw that he looked animated and happy in a way she had only ever glimpsed before when he was alone with her.

Beside him, Cosmo was smiling and excited as well, though as the evening passed she watched anxiously as he drank more and more. *Stop now*, she kept thinking as Cosmo grew more red-faced and loud. *Don't spoil everything.* She had no idea whether Sam and the others realized how much Cosmo was drinking. She raised her eyebrows warningly at Cosmo several times across the table, but he chose to ignore her as if she was of no consequence, and she felt slighted by it.

It was impossible for her to relax and simply enjoy the evening. Having Piers, Sam and Cosmo there all at once was overwhelming. She wondered what everyone guessed about her relationship with Piers Larstonbury.

It must have been obvious that she was his mistress. She told herself she didn't care. After all, she had done all this before, hadn't she, and what ever came of it? The British social classes of Mussoorie knew what she was to Dr Ewan McBride, but what could they do? Accept or reject her – it was all the same to her, she thought. No one here was in a position to question anything about Piers Larstonbury. But Sam – what did he think? All evening she avoided his eye, but every so often she looked along the table, surprised to see how much time he spent in conversation with Susan Fairford. She knew he had not liked Susan while they were in Ambala, had been quite scathing about her, where now they seemed to be talking easily, almost affectionately. She took the chance to watch Sam while his attention was elsewhere. He did not seem to have changed, she thought. He was still the slender, serious-eyed man she remembered, still with that quiet intensity about him which had drawn her to him in the first place, yet which would suddenly break open into a burst of spontaneous, twinkling laughter, lighting him up with mischief and warmth. She did not see him laugh like that this evening, even though there were glimpses of it in his smiles at Susan or Loz. And she noticed that every so often he took his handkerchief out and wiped his left eye which seemed to be troubling him. She thought she had also noticed a slight limp. So many young men limped these days. Every so often, as she talked to Loz's wife, Mary, beside her, she felt Sam's gaze fixed on her. It made her tremble inside and she did not look back.

She was glad of the company of Mary Marks, who was a homely, cheerful woman with a pink, round face rather like her husband's, and a broad smile. She clearly felt a bit out of her depth in the present company and in her nervousness became very talkative, in between turning to her boys to admonish them to sit still, be quiet or eat up. Lily smiled encouragingly at the boys. They were in fact very well behaved, perhaps a bit overawed by the occasion, and they seemed nice lads.

'I never thought my Loz would get involved with something like this,' Mary chattered to Lily, soon after they sat down. 'I mean, he's only a mechanic, just very ordinary, in a factory, like, and I've never been out of Birmingham before. It's all very new to me.'

Lily, to her own surprise, since she never usually told anyone anything, found herself saying, 'In actual fact, I come from Birmingham myself. I was born there.'

'Really – were you?' Mary's brow furrowed. 'You don't sound like it – if you don't mind me saying,' she added anxiously. 'Which part?'

Lily hesitated, her usual habits of secrecy pressing in on her. But what did it matter if she was honest with this kindly woman?

'Well, I worked in Hall Green for a good many years. But I was born in Sparkbrook, I believe.'

'Sparkbrook – are you sure?' Mary blushed in confusion at having sounded so surprised. 'I mean, I don't mean to be rude, but it's a bit rough round there. Perhaps your family went up in the world after . . . ?' Realizing she was being rather forward she faltered into silence, blushing even more.

'Yes.' Lily closed down the conversation. 'We did soon move away.' She told Mary that she had worked for Susan Fairford and knew Cosmo as a child.

'Oh, I see.' Mary said, but clearly she didn't see and didn't ask any more questions. Instead she spent a good deal of the rest of the evening chattering about her two boys, a subject she never tired of. But it was a relief to Lily.

Several times during the meal, Piers Larstonbury, who was talking with Cosmo, reached for her hand under the table and whispered, 'All right, my love?'

She smiled, and once, glancing at Cosmo, whispered, 'Please – don't let him drink too much . . .'

She was so happy for Cosmo, that the day had been a success. It was all she dreamed for him, her boy, but she worried for him constantly. There was something in him that felt dangerous, and she wanted to take him to her and protect him the way she had when he was very small. Of course, he would never let her.

The men were all in high, celebratory spirits and as the evening wore on, Lily felt she might drown in Mary Marks's chatter and she began to feel very drowsy.

'I'm going to slip out to the ladies' cloakroom,' she whispered to Mary, and smiling at Piers she slipped from the room. In the little privy out at the back she sat on the wooden seat and rested her head in her hands for a moment. Her head was muzzy after drinking ale and now she was in private, her emotions began to course through her. She found she was shaky and close to tears. Sitting so close to Sam all evening was a torment which filled her with longing for a past she knew she could never recapture, and seeing him opened up raw feelings of grief and anger. If only he'd never come into her life again! She had had those few sweet days with him and then he had caused her nothing but agony and distress.

Angry and close to tears, she washed her hands and dried them on the old piece of towelling hanging on a nail, but they were still damp and she waved them gently in the air as she emerged from the privy into the warm gloom, lit only by light shining through the curtains at the back of the inn.

'Lily?'

His voice: she knew it immediately, and froze like a trapped animal. She saw his slender figure emerge from the shadows and he was beside her.

'Lily . . .'

She did not speak, could not.

'Please – I want to talk to you. We've got to talk properly and there's never any time or place to do it. We never had the chance.'

Her silence made him falter.

'God, woman, I'll never understand you. I thought you loved me – the way you acted, the way you looked at me . . .'

Lily felt a pressure inside her of rage and hurt and tears which strangled the words in her throat. *I did love you, I did, I do!* She lowered her head, full of panic, forcing herself to be a fortress. *Don't let him in. He'll hurt you again and again . . .*

'Leave me alone, Sam,' she managed to say in a low, calm voice. 'I don't want to be disturbed. There's nothing we can say to each other. It's all too long ago – past history. I don't want to dig it up.'

'I see.' His voice was low at first, but it grew louder as he let out his hurt resentment. 'Well, if that's how it is. I just thought you might want to tell me who that woman was in Mussoorie who told me she loved me, who promised to meet me and who never damn well turned up or bothered to explain or apologize and who *I loved*, damn it! Who I've never been able to forget since, who I see all over again and she's as cold as a fish and won't even speak to me. God, I've been a proper fool!'

He backed away from her, still talking.

'Love! Huh – there's no such thing, is there? All this time there was me thinking I'd had something, but that wasn't real either, you were just pretending and playing with me until you had a better offer, no doubt. Some classy toff you could sponge off and mess about with his feelings as well. Piers Larstonbury loves you, did you know? It's written all over him, poor sod. Well, good luck to him – and you. I hope you get what you want, Lily – damn you!'

And he was gone, back into the public house with a slam of the back door, leaving her shocked and trembling in the darkness.

Chapter Sixty-One

'Darling – what a wonderful evening! I had to come and at least say goodnight.'

Piers slipped into her room without invitation. He had arranged for them to have separate rooms, trying to be discreet, even if in other respects he was not in the least careful about letting people know she was his mistress.

'But you're not undressed yet! Are you all right, my dear?'

With genuine concern he came and sat beside her on the pink flowery eiderdown. Lily had no idea how long she had been sitting there after she came up from her encounter with Sam. She knew she should have gone back to the table, but she simply could not face it.

'Are you unwell?' Piers's slim hand caressed her forehead and Lily suddenly felt like crying. She did feel almost unwell, but she knew there was nothing wrong but an eruption of shock and grief which she could not explain.

'My dear, you don't look yourself. Is there anything I can do?'

Lily forced herself to look brightly at him. 'No – thank you,' she said quietly. 'I was just having a few moments of quiet. It's been such a busy day.'

Piers smiled, his delicate features lighting up boyishly. A lock of his light brown hair lay across his forehead.

'Hasn't it just! My goodness – truly splendid. I've had my doubts about that Fairford fellow, but he handled the motor marvellously today. And didn't she go once he got her up to speed! I say, it's all awfully jolly. And I have you to thank, darling. I feel as if I've been given a whole new life – with the motor racing, and you . . .' His face softened as he turned to her. 'Above all, you, my dear. You've made my life so very happy.'

He drew her to him and kissed her, laying his hand over her left breast with a sigh of pleasure. For a second Lily wanted to resist, to ask him to leave her alone when she felt so raw and sad. But then, as he kissed her, she felt a surge of defiance, an angry passion. Damn Sam Ironside, damn him! Why was she still letting herself tangle her emotions with him when he could come to her and rant at her the way he had without ever truly asking her for the truth or for her side of it? And when, whatever he had felt, she had had to bear and lose his child and had suffered so much more! When all the time, here was this man who did love her and was so very kind to her. As Piers Larstonbury began making love to her, she responded with an angry vigour which he interpreted as passion.

'Oh, my darling!' He drew back and looked into her eyes, moved. 'My fiery girl – you are truly extra-ordinary.'

He stood up and gently helped her to her feet, removing her diaphanous blouse until she stood in her skirt and camisole. Reverently, Piers lifted the little white garment over her head.

'My God, you're so splendid . . .'

She watched his face, his seeming to fall into a trance as he caressed her breasts and saw him with a certain tenderness. He was kind, good to her. Was that not enough?

He managed to contain himself enough to maintain his natural politeness.

'May I, my dearest? May I stay with you tonight?'

In answer, Lily unfastened her skirt and let it drop to the floor, then pulled back the covers and got into the bed, sitting looking up at him.

'Oh God,' he sighed. 'Those eyes. You beautiful, beautiful girl.'

Lily watched him hurriedly undress until he stood naked, his thin, pale body, for which she always had to overcome a certain revulsion before she could let him touch her. As he came to lie down beside her, she closed her eyes for a second, preparing herself.

'Come to me, my love,' he said with reverence, holding out his arms.

His lovemaking was always gentle, never rough or anything but kindly, yet it left her somehow untouched. As his hands moved over her body, stroking her smooth skin, she kissed the soft flesh of his neck, longing to respond without having to pretend, to be moved by more than his kindness to her.

Tonight she felt choked, as if she was so full to the brim with emotion she could not contain it, after Sam's angry words and all the turbulent feelings she had been pushing down in herself all day. As Piers lay on top of her, moving inside her, speaking gentle endearments to her, without knowing it was going to happen, she began to cry. Soon she could not control it and she was shaking with emotion.

Feeling her moving under him excited Piers further and he thrust into her harder and faster, so aroused that he did not notice at first that she was weeping. It was only after he had cried out as he reached his climax and lay panting on top of her that she began to cry aloud, the sobs tearing out of her, beyond anything she could quieten or even understand. She wept as if for a heart broken long ago, sobbing and mewling like a small child and she could not help herself.

'Lily – oh, Lily, my love, what is it?' Piers leaped up, disturbed by the violence of her crying, his face full of concern. But she could not answer, could only cling to him and weep all the more, feeling she had gone right down into a dark place which she would take time to come back from. Her eyes squeezed tightly closed as she clung to him, wanting to be held tightly herself.

And he did hold her, not knowing what else to do. 'There, there,' he whispered, as if to a small child. 'It's all right, my darling, it's all right.'

When she was calmer he said anxiously, 'Did I hurt you? I should hate to hurt you.'

'No, you didn't, it's not that.' Lily felt suddenly overwhelmed with tiredness.

'Then, for goodness sake, what is it? You sounded in such distress!'

Lily couldn't begin to explain, even to herself, about feelings that seemed to come from somewhere so long ago, from a time when she was tiny and couldn't remember. And she certainly couldn't explain about Sam.

'Just let me sleep,' she murmured.

Piers held her close to him and stroked her hair. 'Yes, my darling, you sleep.'

The last thing she felt was his kiss on her cheek.

Chapter Sixty-Two

Sam stormed back into the Pack Horse after his tirade at Lily, quivering with fury. The passage, where he stood for a time to calm himself, smelled of stale beer and cigarette smoke. A burst of laughter came through a door which opened and closed nearby. His rage soon drained away into misery.

What have I done? Oh God, why on earth did I speak to her like that? All these weeks he'd waited to be able to talk to her and when he did, all he had managed was to insult her. Why would she want to have anything to do with him now, after that? The thought was unbearable. He considered going back out to try again, to pour out the words of hurt and longing and adoration he felt for her, but then her rejection of him ignited his fury again. She had betrayed him in India, and she would only betray him again!

Defiant once more, he went back to the room where they had dined to find that the meal had broken up. Loz and Mary were just shepherding their sons up to bed.

'Night, Sam,' Loz said, pink-cheeked. 'S'been a great day.'

Sam said his goodnights to Loz and Mary. He saw that Cosmo was being helped to his feet by Piers Larstonbury, and was evidently the worse for drink.

Silly sod, Sam thought savagely. *Given every bloody*

chance in the world and look at the state of him. Cosmo seemed to him like a child, spoilt and petulant. But he could handle a motor all right, there was no denying that. It was as if it was in the blood.

Piers and Cosmo disappeared after their goodnights and the one person left in the room, looking unsure what to do, was Susan Fairford.

Sam was reluctant to go up to bed. He couldn't stand the thought of lying there, full of grief and jealousy as he thought of Lily with Piers Larstonbury. He wanted some company and sensed that Susan did as well.

'Would you like a nightcap?'

Susan gave a faint smile, looking relieved. 'That would be very pleasant. I don't feel quite ready to turn in.'

He fetched them each a small brandy, enjoying the sight of the warm-coloured liquid in the globular glasses. The two of them sat at one end of the long table. Somehow, since the war there was an ease between them.

'He did well today,' Sam said.

'Yes.' She smiled, knowing he meant Cosmo, and he could see the pride and relief, though there was always sadness just behind her social face. Sam felt a twinge of tenderness for her.

'He wants you all to go and stay at Cranbourne, you know, and put the motor through its paces there. I suppose he's always wanted someone to play with up there!' She smiled sadly. 'He has all his toys, but no playmates.'

There was a pause, while Susan sat leaning forwards, turning her glass round and round on the table.

'I do so worry about him.' She frowned. 'He's had so little family – and no father now. Charles would have

430

taken him in hand, been able to show him what to do, had he lived. But Cosmo was so anti everything – the army, India ... I mean, he says he was incredibly homesick for India when we first sent him to school, and then it wore off. Of course, he hadn't lived in India since he was five: he certainly didn't want to go back and join the army there like Charles.' She looked up at Sam with tears in her eyes. 'You know, I don't think Cosmo has ever known what it *means* to be happy.'

Sam looked into her pretty, tired face. 'Have you?'

'*Yes* ... Well ...' She hesitated, considering. I've never really thought ... But yes, I have known happiness. When Charles and I were first married. I loved him, you see – far more than he loved me, I realize ...'

Sam thought of the Charles Fairford he had seen on the open roads of India, the adventurer, always seeking the distant horizon, and so very happy in the company of men, and he saw that to correct her would be an untruth, and she would know it to be.

'I did like India at first. It was an adventure and, of course, Charles was so wealthy and so well thought of. And he was always kind to me. It was one of his great qualities. That's something I realize, from the war, I suppose: even with all the awfulness of things, there is a lot of kindness in the world.'

Her face crumpled for a moment, but she held back her tears. Sam resisted an impulse to lay his hand on her shoulder, to give comfort.

'I was married at eighteen and I was truly happy for, let's say, two years. I had gone up in the world: my family are in trade, you see, not like the marvellous Fairfords. But my people sent my brother to Eton and that's how I met Charles, at prize-givings and concerts and so on. Lewis, my brother, and Charles were good friends. They were in the cricket team. Anyway, that's how it happened. I suppose I was just a reasonably suitable, jolly sort of girl . . .'

'And very pretty,' Sam interrupted.

Susan blushed girlishly for a moment. 'Yes, well that always helps. Anyway, Charles's family wanted him to marry so I was sent out after he'd gone to Meerut. I wasn't part of the fishing fleet – we were already engaged, from a distance.'

She took a sip of brandy. 'We were married in Meerut, and at first I found it all exciting. You know what India's like. In some ways we had it so easy out there, our life of luxury. It was rotten for the young BORs* who weren't married – dreadfully lonely. We used to have some of them round for tea and so on. But of course there's all the social life, and the colour and it's all so exotic and different. And I was madly in love with Charles. I thought he was the most amazing man I'd ever met. And he was, I suppose. But then we had Isadora. I felt dreadfully ill through most of the preg- nancy and then she was . . . Well, you remember how she was . . . And it was as if everything went bad on me. I started to loathe the place. I was afraid, I suppose, as if India had cursed me in some way. Even when Cozzy arrived and he was so lovely I couldn't rid myself of a feeling of doom and dread, all the time, that something simply awful would happen to him. Very foolish really. But . . .' Another sip of her drink. 'In the end perhaps not entirely misplaced.'

'You've had a very sad time,' Sam observed. She seemed so different now, from the frosty young woman he had known in Ambala.

* British Other Ranks.

432

'And you?' She turned to look at him and gave a faint smile. 'How odd, that we should be here like this.'

'My life's been all right,' Sam said. He thought guiltily of Helen, of little Joe. His heart ached. There must be more to love, to life. And he knew there was, but it was cut off from him. He thought of Lily, of what he had said to her and for a second he almost felt like weeping. God, he thought, it's been a long day. I'm more tired than I realized.

He felt he should say something. There was an atmosphere of intimacy between them and he did not want to lose it.

'I suppose the war changed everything,' he said.

Susan nodded gravely. He knew what losses she had endured. 'Yes, everything's shifted somehow. We are not who we were before.'

They were sitting close together and she smiled wistfully into his face.

Without knowing he was going to do it, Sam leaned forward and kissed her. At first he kissed her cheek, but she held his gaze, her face turned up to him, and in the privacy of the quiet back room he kissed her on the lips, holding her slender frame briefly in his arms. He felt her gently kiss him back.

When he drew back, there were tears in her eyes.

'I long to love again,' she said. 'To feel something beautiful and true.'

To his surprise, Sam felt a lump rise in his throat, and he nodded.

Chapter Sixty-Three

'Of course you must come – I wouldn't dream of going without you, darling!'

For several days now, Lily and Piers Larstonbury had been discussing the invitation from Cosmo to go and stay at the Cranbourne estate. This time it was very late, a hot August night, with a night breeze stirring the lacy curtains, and they were once more lying together in Lily's bed.

'But what about Virginia . . .' Lily protested, as she so often did.

'Virginia is scarcely ever here,' Piers said, adding bitterly, 'do you seriously think Virginia ever concerns herself with what I do?'

Lily had realized some time ago that Virginia Larstonbury had taken a lover herself and was completely preoccupied, what with that and with her strange spiritual friends. Lily had seen a burly fellow with a beard and colourful, dashing clothes arrive at the house on several occasions and realized that all the hours they spent shut away together upstairs did not consist of praying or whatever it was theosophists did. But she did not know whether Piers knew about his wife's infidelity. Virginia would appear in the evenings looking pink and sated and unusually good-tempered.

'Oh, my little darlings, come and play with your mama!' she would greet Hubert and Christabel, flinging her arms round them extravagantly and playing with them for much longer than the normal time allotted. With her long red hair hanging loose, kneeling on the floor with the children pretending to be a witch or a bear, since she was good at pretend games, she looked like a large child herself and Lily could feel almost affectionate towards her. She often wondered whether Virginia had any idea of Piers's affair with her. Certainly she never showed the least sign of it and he was ever discreet. Lily had come to realize just how deep was Virginia's indifference to her husband, so perhaps even if she had known she would not much have cared.

'What about the children?' Lily said.

'Bring them as well,' Piers said. He laid his hand on her stomach, stroking her. 'Oh, my beauty, how lovely you are.'

'Could we bring them? It would do them good to be out in the country.'

Piers raised himself on one elbow and looked down at her seriously.

'You are more of a mother to them than Virginia ever has been.'

'I'm very fond of them.' It was true, she was fond of timid, sweet-natured little Hubert and fiery Christabel and had become attached to them.

'We can motor up on Saturday morning, have an early start. And Ironside and Marks are coming with our Flyer with her brand-new engine!' Piers immediately sounded keen and boyish as he always did when he talked about the car.

Lily's heart thumped painfully hard for a moment. Sam would be there! She longed to go and see her beloved Cosmo, to look at the estate where he had spent so much of his boyhood and to be out in the country

with the children, but if Sam was to be there too ...
However much she made herself angry with him, it
didn't make it any better. Seeing him filled her with so
many emotions, most of them painful.

'I should stay behind,' she tried to suggest. 'I'll be in
the way – me and the children.'

'Not at all! I want you by my side. I know none of
them say anything because they're too polite and so on
– and they can't do without me, of course – but they
must all realize what you mean to me by now. It's one
place we can go and feel comfortable, not worry about
what people think. What is it, darling? You look
anxious.'

She stared past him, up at the ceiling. It was her own
fault that she and Sam kept being thrown together like
this. She had made it happen, hadn't she? And she also
knew that, as so often in her life, when she had occupied
this strange social territory, somewhere between servant
and confidante as she now did again with Piers Larstonbury, that in the end she never had any choice but to do
as she was asked.

Forcing her lips into a smile, she said, 'Nothing, dear.
I'm quite all right. Of course we'll go.' It was for
Cosmo, all of it, wasn't it? If there was one thing she
could do it was to see him set on a path to success. Of
course – it was all for Cosmo.

They were up at dawn, carrying the children out to the
car into a hazy morning which promised to turn into
the hottest of August days. The journey reminded Lily
of taking Eustace Bartlett to his people in Leamington
Spa and she wondered how he was getting on. What a
handful he had been! She looked fondly down at Hubert

beside her. No child had ever replaced Cosmo in her affections, but she did have a very soft spot for little Hubert.

When, amid the rolling Warwickshire countryside, they turned off the road into the gates of Cranbourne House, Piers and Lily exclaimed with astonishment.

'My goodness me!' Piers Larstonbury cried. 'I wasn't expecting it to be as imposing as this! Young Fairford has always given the impression of it all being a rather crumbling, unmanageable sort of place that's descending into chaos.'

'It's absolutely beautiful,' Lily said, feeling a great swell of pride. All this would be Cosmo's one day since his Uncle William was unmarried. To think her boy would be the master of a place like this!

The house, at the end of a curving drive, was a four-square and symmetrically proportioned brick Regency manor, its grand front door flanked by white columns. In front of the house Lily saw a garden laid out with rose bushes and small shrubs and flowers.

'What a lovely *parterre*!' Piers exclaimed.

Lily smiled. 'Yes, isn't it.' She had never heard the word *parterre* before. The shaped grass cut round the flowers reminded her of a doily.

'And what a house – no wonder young Fairford was keen for me to see it!'

But Hubert was jumping with excitement for another reason. 'Look!' he cried, leaning across Lily's lap to see better. 'Aeroplane – an aeroplane!'

In the distance, on a bright sward of grass, was an aeroplane, tilted to one side and white and delicate as a resting insect.

'Is it going to fly?' Hubert was asking, when from round the side of the house they saw Cosmo appear with a slow, languorous walk, dressed in white flannel trousers and a red and white checked shirt. His golden hair fell, curling over one eye, and he tossed his head back and raised an arm in greeting, squinting in the bright sunlight.

As Piers braked in front of the house, Cosmo leaned down to the window and Lily beamed with joy at the sight of him. He was so lovely, so tall and handsome!

'Well, you've made good time,' he drawled, not looking at Lily and she felt a stab of rejection. It was as if he could never acknowledge her properly or show how much he needed her, especially if there was any other company about. But she knew it was just his way.

'Hello, Cosmo, dear,' she said.

'Oh, hello, Lily,' he said offhandedly. 'I'll get our man to show you all where your quarters are. There's an attic where you can go with the children. Mother wired to say she's on her way up. And you must come and meet Uncle William.'

William Fairford was about as different from his young brother Charles as it would have been possible to imagine. Lily and Piers were introduced to a short, rotund man dressed in very tightly fitting tweeds, his belly thrusting out dangerously hard at the buttons of his waistcoat. He had a red, jowly face and a great many whiskers protruding from his nose and ears. From under a tweed hat he looked at them with narrowed, sludgy-coloured eyes and said, 'Hmmm. I didn't know there were going to be children. Cosmo – you must inform Mrs Rainbow at once. *She* likes children. And don't think I want to know anything about anything because I don't. Good day to you!' He touched the brim of his cap and sauntered off, tapping the floor with a silver-topped walking cane. 'See you at dinner time!' he called over his shoulder.

Lily watched him in astonishment. Was this really the man Cosmo had spent all his school holidays cared for, or rather ignored, by? He seemed most peculiar and certainly not interested in anyone else around him. How could he be Charles Fairford's brother? But then Susan Fairford had told her that he had suffered with his nerves as a young man, that he had taken after his peculiar uncle. She still felt indignant on Cosmo's behalf and exchanged a look with Piers. But then they heard a woman's voice approaching, talking non-stop before she had even come into view.

'. . . there's a room up to the right and you'll find it's very comfortable and I don't know how many of you there are and of course we're not used to visitors here, him being the way he is and no one ever tells me a thing, of course, not a thing . . . Hello, dears – oh, and little ones as well! He never said there'd be children coming! Oh, my word. Well, that's a treat for us!'

All this from a very stout woman as she appeared panting in the doorway. She wore an enormous white apron and a startled expression in her watery grey eyes.

'Deary me, it's a warm one today!' Her cheeks were very red and she was fanning herself with one hand. 'I'm Mrs Rainbow and no doubt Cosmo hasn't done the first thing to make you comfortable, let alone *him*.' She flicked her head in the direction of the departed Uncle William, not even trying to disguise her exasperation.

Within moments they were being shown into rooms where the beds had been made up most efficiently and Mrs Rainbow swiftly settled them in.

'I've six of my own, all grown and gone now,' she said wistfully. 'And my Herb passed on six years ago ... Time of your life when your children are young – you never get it back.' For a moment she looked watery and woeful, but then beamed at Hubert, and Christabel, who was lying on her bed kicking her chubby legs in the air. 'Oh, and look at you two. Oh, I'm going to like having you here!'

Lily had been given a room at the opposite end of the house to Piers Larstonbury, a relief as she was glad of a break from his attentions, but she tried to look disappointed when he mentioned it later.

'Never mind, my love, I'll be with you!' he whispered to her, and she gave him a smile.

'Has Mrs Rainbow been here for a long time?' Lily asked Cosmo when they joined him downstairs in the drawing room, from where there came a strong smell of coffee. On a silver tray were laid a coffee pot and cups and a plate of biscuits and iced cakes decorated with diamonds of angelica.

'No – only five or six years,' Cosmo said, eyeing Hubert and Christabel as they stormed the corridors at high speed in ecstasy at being released from the car. Cosmo looked a bit irritated, but Lily sensed that he also envied them. 'Before that, when I was at school, it was Mrs Saxsby, and she was an *ogre*.'

'Oh yes,' Lily laughed at the face he pulled. 'I remember now. You wrote about her.'

'Mrs Rainbow will love you being here,' Cosmo said. He nodded at the cakes. 'She likes feeding people. That's why Uncle's so stout. Oh!' He looked out, roused by the engine and sound of gravel crunching outside. 'Here's Ironside!'

Lily found every nerve in her body suddenly on

alert, her heart pounding. Any moment, once again, she would have to greet Sam! And now she knew what he thought of her, his anger and disgust with her. Oh, why had she let Piers talk her into coming here?

They all went out into the sunshine from the cool of the house, to find Sam and Loz pulling up outside, the streamlined silver body of the Heath Flyer looking magnificent on the trailer behind the car. Both Sam and Loz were obviously hot, but they grinned broadly at the sign of the reception party. Cosmo ran forward to meet them, excited as a child.

And amid all the greetings, Lily stood to one side with the children while Sam worked his way through the handshakes. Mrs Rainbow had appeared again and was exclaiming over the car, and her mouth ran away with her when she saw Sam as well.

'Ooh, aren't you a good-looking one!' she said and Lily saw Sam's smile in reply.

'I'm glad somebody thinks so,' he quipped.

At last, very formally, he came forward to shake Lily's hand.

'How d'you do, Miss Waters?' he said, his voice cooler than if she had been a stranger he had never met before.

And while, for the seconds his hand was in hers, she couldn't help remembering how that same hand had moved lovingly over her bare skin and, aching for the tenderness of it, she said equally coolly, 'Good morning, Mr Ironside.'

Chapter Sixty-Four

While Sam and Loz took the motor from the trailer and made some adjustments to her, Cosmo said he would give Piers, Lily and the children a tour of the estate in Uncle William's spacious Morris Cowley.

'That's awfully kind of you, old chap,' Piers said, 'but I think I'd like to stay and watch our Flyer being unloaded. I'm most intrigued by the whole thing and I haven't managed to get down to Brooklands to see her in progress nearly as much as I'd hoped lately. And I can be here to greet your mother when she arrives. Why don't you take Lily? She's very keen to see your home.'

Lily sat in the front beside Cosmo, awed by the sheer size of the estate, which seemed to go on and on across the Warwickshire countryside. She felt so proud sitting next to him, looking at the fields of wheat turning golden in the August sunlight, the gardens and farm cottages and the orchards to one side of the house. What Cosmo most wanted to show her, however, was the driving circuit. The dusty track snaked round a wide area at the far end of the estate, cutting along the side of a hill on a sharp incline.

'My goodness!' Lily said as he took her along it at high speed. 'This is steep – oh, do slow down a bit, Cozzy. You're frightening the children!' Hubert was clinging to her skirt, his hands clenched into fists.

'You have to go fast to keep up the momentum,' Cosmo retorted, not slowing down at all. 'Like the track at Brooklands – remember the slope on that?'

'Yes,' Lily said sharply, 'but we're not racing now.'

She had expected that alone with her, Cosmo might soften and become his more boyish self, the sweet Cosmo who she loved. But he seemed even more on edge.

'You've been doing so well,' she said trying to appease him. 'I'm so very proud of you.'

Since the event at Shelsley Walsh, Cosmo had entered various events at Brooklands and come home in a very respectable time – in one case, in second place. He was riding high and very pleased with himself at the time, but now he seemed morose and unsure.

Lily watched him as he drove, his expression grim with concentration. He looked forbidding. His face, which she had thought of as distinguished, with its Grecian nose, now seemed hard, his forehead more enlarged as he grew older. In fact, she recognized with a shock that in profile he looked very slightly like his Uncle William. She had never connected Cosmo with this part of the family before. William Fairford was an unbalanced, melancholic fellow. Surely Cosmo was not taking after him?

'Darling,' she said softly, trying to reach the Cosmo who would respond to her. 'You're doing so awfully well.'

'Oh, don't mumsy me, Lily,' Cosmo snapped. 'I'm not your little boy any more.'

Lily tried not to show how much he had hurt her. She was also trying not to notice how fast he was still driving. She held Hubert's hand, reassuring him.

'All right. But you are doing so very well.'

'We'll see, won't we?' he said grimly.

After that she was silent, trying to understand him, and why, when he was surrounded by so much wealth and now he was doing all the things he had always wanted to and doing them so well, his mood seemed to have such an edge of despair.

Once they got back, Susan Fairford had arrived and she greeted Lily affectionately.

Mrs Rainbow had set out an impressive meal of cheeses and cold meats and pickle on the long, gleaming dining table and Lily felt the weight of silver cutlery in her hands. There was a silver tureen of creamy watercress soup and they all ate ravenously. The men all stuck together, talking motor cars and aeroplanes, and she heard Cosmo promise to take the others up in it over the weekend. Lily stayed at the other end of the table from Sam and the others, but she was acutely aware of his presence as he sat talking with Piers Larstonbury. She could see from the tensed hunch of his shoulders that he was not entirely comfortable in these surroundings. Sam had always had a chip on his shoulder about wealthy people. *Toffs*, she could hear him saying. Another thing they had had in common, not being sure where they fitted in. His eyes met hers along the table, just once, a deep look when he thought she was not aware, but as soon as her gaze met his he looked away.

She spent the afternoon with Susan Fairford, who was very tired, and the children, who had a nap and then were taken off for some of the afternoon by Mrs Rainbow, who seemed to be on pins to get her hands on them.

The two women sat in an exquisitely decorated sitting room which Susan said was barely ever used. The room looked out to the flower garden at the side of the house through long glass doors edged with cream muslin curtains, delicately embroidered with pink and gold flowers. Susan eased the doors open and they sat on comfortable chintz-covered chairs on either side of a marble fireplace, enjoying the faint breeze in an otherwise baking afternoon. Susan kicked off her shoes and at her invitation, Lily did the same, stretching out in the chair and luxuriating in the feel of the thick Chinese rug under her stockinged toes.

They talked idly in the heat, dozing for a while, and at four o'clock Mrs Rainbow brought in a tray of tea, accompanied by Hubert and Christabel, both looking unmistakably floury.

'Look what we made!'

Hubert was proudly holding a plate of jam tarts.

'Oh, how delicious, dear!' Lily cried, smiling at the child's proud face. 'Thank you so much, Mrs Rainbow.'

'Shall I take them out to the garden for a while?' Mrs Rainbow said.

'Well – yes, if you'd like to!' Lily was delighted.

'Ooh – it's a treat. Come along, 'ubert, Christabel! I've got summat to show you.'

Susan smiled wistfully after her. 'She misses her brood.' Then, suddenly, she said, 'Sam Ironside has come a long way since he first arrived in India, hasn't he?'

Startled to hear his name mentioned, Lily found herself blushing.

'Yes,' she agreed, trying to sound neutral. 'I suppose he has.'

'I realize I know so very little about him. I suppose I never cared to ask before.'

Lily could not think of anything safe to say in reply. In the pause which followed, they heard a dove calling from the roof in the hot, sleepy afternoon, accompanied by the distant hum of an engine.

'He was rather sweet on you at one time, wasn't he?' Susan rearranged the skirt of her pretty floral dress. 'I suppose that's all over with by now?'

'Oh – yes,' Lily said lightly.

'And he's not really in the same class as the major, is he?'

Lily blushed, full of confusion. Her relations with Sam Ironside and Piers Larstonbury were both things she felt quite unable to talk about, but as she sought desperately to think of a way of changing the subject, Susan raised a finger and said, 'What's that noise?'

The sound was growing louder and the two of them got up and went to the doors. The scent of honeysuckle and lavender wafted from the warm garden. Against the mellow stone nearby grew a profusion of sweet-smelling yellow climbing roses.

Susan, looking a thin, girlish figure, put a hand to her forehead and squinted upwards.

'Oh Lord – it's Cosmo. He must be taking someone up. Oh dear, I do so worry about him . . . He can fly as well as he can drive, but all the same . . .'

Shading her eyes, Lily looked up into the soaring blue and saw the tiny white plane scratching its way across. Who had Cosmo taken up? Sam? . . . *tell me who that woman was in Mussoorie who told me she loved me* . . . His words throbbed through her.

'They all love machines so much, don't they?' Susan said. 'Come along – let's go and see them land.'

They hurried, shoeless, following the plane with their eyes, out towards the wide hayfield at some distance

446

from the house, where they found Mrs Rainbow and the children all staring upwards at the circling plane. Sam and Loz were nowhere to be seen.

As they reached the place where the children were standing, the plane landed bumpily in one corner of the field and Cosmo and Piers Larstonbury opened up the cockpit, Piers laughing with pleasure. Lily had never seen him so animated.

'My word, it's just astonishing!' he cried, leaping down, running unguardedly to her and flinging his arms round her. 'Darling, it's the most astounding experience!'

Lily looked across to see Susan watching, and knew that whatever Susan had been guessing, she had now had her thoughts confirmed.

Chapter Sixty-Five

By the end of the afternoon, Lily was wishing she had never come to Cranbourne House.

She had wanted to see Cosmo's home, his inheritance, but being near to Sam was a torment. She felt raw and sad, and that she had been wrong in rejecting his attempt to talk to her. But now it felt too late. Sam simply behaved as if she wasn't there.

'I think I'll have an early night,' she told Piers Larstonbury that evening, after Mrs Rainbow had served them a sumptuous meal of roast pork and a huge syrup pudding. Uncle William, it appeared, liked the best of solid, traditional food and nothing fancy, although he did not eat with them but took all his meals on his own.

Piers was about to join the other men in the smoking room and Lily caught him before he disappeared across the panelled hall.

'All right, my dear,' he said, mellowed with drink and the plentiful food. Moving closer to her, he whispered, 'I'll come to you later, darling one.'

Lily nodded, but kept her eyes cast down.

She lay in her bedroom at the top of the house. The children were in the next room, which had once been the nursery, Mrs Rainbow had told her. The window was open but it was stiflingly hot. She had nothing on but her bloomers and a camisole, but it still felt stuffy and unbearable. For a while she managed to doze, but then woke with a start, drenched in perspiration. Sitting up, she looked out at the dark garden. The house was quiet. She hoped that Piers had been well plied with brandy so that he had gone to his room and fallen fast asleep. Please, she thought, don't let him come in here tonight! All she wanted was to be alone.

The night air smelled delicious and she leaned out of the casement window for a while, the air cooling her. Her room was at the back of the house, facing over the lawn, edged with trees. She could smell the sweet scent of cut grass where the men had been scything that evening.

Lighting a candle, she moved restlessly about the room. On the floor to the left of the window was a small wooden trunk and out of curiosity she lifted the lid, wondering if it contained more toys for Hubert and Christabel to entertain themselves with.

The box smelled strongly of wood polish and camphor. On the top, inside, there was a limp rag doll, not a girl doll, but one made to resemble a soldier, with a helmet and faded scarlet jacket. The face had fierce, staring eyes drawn on in ink and a curling moustache of black wool. She thought it didn't look a very comforting sort of toy. Surely it had not been Cosmo's? She did not remember ever having seen it before.

Underneath there were various little boxes and she opened the top one, which was wooden and full of tin soldiers rather like the rag doll soldier. So there were toys! The next was a box made of faded white card decorated with a painted garland of mauve flowers. Inside, she found a collection of old letters, the paper yellowed and barely holding together on some of the folds. Carefully she picked up the top letter and opened it, seeing a short, blotchy note in childish handwriting, with several crossings out. It was addressed from his prep school and dated December 1887.

> Dear Mother and Father,
>   I am doing very well and I hope you are to. I have got better from my cold and also the chilblains on my toes are not hurting eny more. It is still very cold. We are learning to play rugby. Please write and tell me more about Haroon's pups and about Arsalan.
>   We are singing carols and getting ready for Chrismas.
>   I hope you have a happy and holy Chrismas.
>   Your loving son,
>   Charles

There was a large collection of other similar notes, dated over several years, and as Lily read them, seeing the handwriting mature gradually, her eyes filled with tears.

'I felt sick for weeks when they sent me to England,' Cosmo had once told her. 'It was that sort of misery that makes you feel as if you have a stone inside you. I thought about running away constantly. But how do you run away all the way back to India?'

The letters from Cosmo's father, from a homesick little six-year-old, far away from his parents, his friends and pets, seemed to say so much by saying so little, the ache of it seeping between the lines. She felt very tender towards both father and son. And now Charles Fairford, the rather courtly man she remembered, who seemed happier on a horse out in the Indian countryside than anywhere else, had been laid to rest on the battlefields of France.

Closing the chest, she looked at the garden and was filled with a longing to be out in the night air. Slipping her dressing gown round her and her shoes on, she looked in to check that Hubert and Christabel were sleeping soundly, then crept out and down the long flights of stairs. Remembering her way to the little sitting room where she had sat with Susan that afternoon, she let herself out through the glass doors and into the warm, caressing air.

The sense of freedom exhilarated her and in the relative cool outside she felt full of life and energy. Following the path round to the back, she felt the brush of lavender against her nightdress, and smelled its scent mingled with roses, then the smell of the grass as she moved across the lawn and stopped to look back at the house. She could not see a light on in any of the rooms. A little bubble of laughter rose in her and she turned and ran lightly across the soft green expanse, feeling she might run and never stop. It felt exciting and free to be out so late.

At the far end of the long lawn the grass was longer near the trees and she stopped and looked back again. It was a slightly hazy night, but a half moon was visible through a chiffon of cloud. Its faint light showed the lines of the house. She thought she had never been anywhere more beautiful, not since India, and in the warm night she half expected to smell the dung fires and dry earth and scented oils of the Indian darkness. She thought of those sad little children sent away from home, aching for India in the darkness of English winter nights. Cosmo, she realized, knew as little as herself about family life, or how it felt to be loved and secure.

It did not cross her mind to be afraid to move into the deeper darkness of the trees and she wandered

451

into the longer grass, feeling it tickling her calves. The arching branches above felt benign, like an embrace. She reached out and trailed her hand along one of the tree trunks.

It was then she realized she was not alone. She heard a sound which she knew was a human voice, even though she heard no words. It came from her left and she turned her head to hear better, her heart bumping harder, although she was not afraid so much as curious. As soon as she heard the voice again she knew whose it was, and her heartbeat accelerated even more. Something deep in her would have recognized Sam's voice almost anywhere. But who was he talking to? She crept towards the sound.

Almost immediately she heard a long sighing noise, this time from a woman. Lily's mind raced. Susan – it had to be Susan Fairford!

'You've had a very thin time of it,' she heard Sam say.

Lily realized she was quite close to them and she froze, straining to hear, her emotions a mixture of painful jealousy and a kind of triumph. Wasn't it just like Sam Ironside to be declaring his love for her one day then snuggling up to someone else the next – while he still had a wife at home?

'I'm hardly unique in that,' Susan said.

Lily strained to hear. The low, intimate tone to their voices told her that this was more than just a night-time stroll.

'You must have found me very standoffish when we first met,' Susan was saying.

There came a low laugh from Sam. 'I did rather, I'm afraid. But not now.'

'No. I have changed. The war changed me – changed everything. I suppose I was rather insufferable. I was afraid, somehow. I always had the feeling that I was about to be found out in some way. You know – let the side down.'

'Oh, I don't suppose you ever did that.'

There was a silence, then Susan Fairford said, 'Oh, Sam, you've been very kind to me.'

Lily held her breath.

'You lovely, beautiful woman,' she heard Sam say ardently. 'God, I never thought I'd be holding you in my arms. Not in a million years.'

'Dear Sam . . .'

And then there was a silence in which Lily guessed they were kissing, and there came a faint sound, like a sigh of pleasure from Susan.

Unable to bear hearing any more and terribly afraid that they would hear and realize she was there, Lily crept away through the trees, full of a chaos of emotions. The wide lawn, the smell of grass in the night no longer seemed enchanted but soured.

She clenched her fists, almost bursting with anger and jealousy. *You told him to leave you alone!* she raged at herself. *What do you expect him to do? You don't want him, you know you don't. He's let you down badly enough already. Keep away from him!*

But the pain was almost overwhelming. Hurrying along the lavender-scented path and into the house she was fighting her storm of tears which were only released when she got back to her room. She lay face down on the bed letting the sobs of grief and jealousy and longing begin to break out of her. She knew, with terrible helplessness, how much she loved Sam Ironside, how precious the memory of their love was to her. And when she had been given another chance and he had tried to approach her, she had pushed him away. How he must despise her! And now it was too late. He had given his heart to someone else.

Chapter Sixty-Six

The thought of facing them the next morning was terrible. Lily had had no sleep that night and her reflection in the glass was pale and strained.

'I'll stay with Mrs Rainbow and keep the children out of the way,' she told Susan.

There had been much talk of more flying and of putting the Heath Flyer through her paces on the track and Lily knew that at least Sam would be completely absorbed in that.

'Won't you come out and see Cosmo drive?' Susan said. 'Surely the children could come out as well.' She looked at Lily more closely. 'Are you feeling all right? You don't look terribly well.'

'I just seem to be feeling the heat,' Lily said. 'Nothing to worry about.'

Lily spent much of the day with Mrs Rainbow and Christabel, glad of the woman's cheerful company and to be able to do household tasks rather than be out with all the men and the complications of her heart. She felt overwhelmed with mourning for her love of Sam and did not want Piers Larstonbury anywhere near her, although, to her shame, she knew he genuinely loved her. All this time she had been pretending and the one person she had ever truly loved, whose child she had given life to, she had let slip through her hands through

455

cowardice and pride. Seldom had she spent such a bitter few hours.

She was out in the walled garden with Christabel and Mrs Rainbow when they heard the shouting.

Earlier, Cosmo had swept above them, twice, in the little plane.

'Look at that,' Mrs Rainbow tutted, squinting up as the plane disappeared above the house. 'Nearly shaving the roof. That boy's a case, he truly is.'

When the plane did not reappear they realized that the men were out at the track. And that was the direction from which the estate men came running.

Mrs Rainbow heard the shouts.

'Summat's amiss,' she said to Lily, going to the back door of the kitchen where they had been making tea. 'That's Tim and Bernard.'

'Quick!' Lily heard a deep voice shouting. 'Fetch us a blanket. There's been an accident – Master Cosmo!'

Lily filled with cold dread.

'We need to bring 'im in!'

'But there's a stretcher – remember?' Mrs Rainbow had her wits about her. 'In the outhouse – over there.'

'So there is – come on, Tim!'

Lily picked up Christabel, who was eating a jam tart, and she and Mrs Rainbow followed them. The men had hauled the old khaki stretcher and poles out of the shed and taken off again along the track. Neither Mrs Rainbow nor Lily could move as fast as them and they were soon left behind. But Lily still ran faster than she could ever have expected carrying the little girl. The track was almost a mile away, along the edge of a wheat field, and

456

in the distance they could see the hill rising up with the track cut into the edge of it.

'Oh, my Lord, I can't keep this up,' Mrs Rainbow said, bent over and puce in the face. But Lily ran on, Christabel clinging stickily to her.

She saw the wreck of the car before making out who was who, the men all gathered round, the silence as she drew nearer. The Flyer was upside down and she could see it was in a dreadful mess. She saw Sam bend over Cosmo, who was lying on the stretcher, then straighten up and say something to Piers Larstonbury, shaking his head. She thought her heart would burst. She could not see Susan, and how was Cosmo? *Oh, dear God, let him be all right. Don't let him be hurt, don't let him be dead!*

'What's happened?' she shouted. 'Cosmo – is he all right?'

She saw Susan then, behind Sam, squatting down beside the stretcher by the crumpled silver wreckage of the car. Sam's face turned towards her, and Loz's. Both of them looked stunned and grim.

And then, on the stretcher she saw Cosmo struggling to sit up and her whole being leaped with relief.

'Cosmo!' It was as if she was the only person who could speak. Everyone else was shocked into silence. Lily put Christabel down and tore across to him.

'I'm all right,' Cosmo snapped furiously. He had a great discoloured bump on the side of his head. He sat with his knees slightly bent, arms hanging limply and he was shaking uncontrollably.

'What happened?' She turned wildly to Sam.

Sam shrugged, not seeming to trust himself to speak.

Loz was less reserved. 'The stupid bugger turned the

457

car over, that's what. And look at it – weeks of work and he goes and wrecks it . . .' He punched the air in miserable frustration and stormed off. Lily could see he was fighting tears of anger and disappointment.

'Never mind,' Piers Larstonbury was saying soothingly. 'We can get her fixed – improve her, even. Thank heavens you're all right, Cosmo.'

Susan turned to Lily with a stricken expression. 'He was going too fast – far too fast. Oh, darling, why did you have to . . . ?' She was stroking Cosmo's hair as if he were a small child and he shook her off and got groggily to his feet.

'It was an accident,' he shouted, furiously. 'I didn't mean to turn it over. D'you think I meant to make a mess of it? Now just bloody well leave me alone, all of you.'

'You should come back to the house and get some attention, Master Cosmo,' Bernard, the older of the two men, said. He seemed to be the only one Cosmo would listen to. 'Come along now.'

Cosmo was swaying and clearly faint and he agreed then to get back on the stretcher and for the men to carry him to the house. As they set off along the border of the field, Piers came and in front of everyone put his arm protectively round Lily's shoulders. Lily was so caught up in Cosmo, in the simple relief that he was alive, that she burst into tears. Susan put her hands over her face.

'Oh, dear God,' she wept. 'Oh, my boy.'

And through her tears, Lily saw Sam go to her and take her by the arm to lead her back to the house. She stood, with Piers's arm round her, watching them go.

*

458

The doctor was called out to Cosmo, and he was pronounced to have severe bruising to the head and three cracked ribs.

'You obviously have the good fortune of a cat,' the doctor said. 'That's certainly one of your lives crossed off the list, young man.'

After the initial shock, having seen the crushed state of the car, it began to sink into everyone just how lucky Cosmo had been.

'A quite astonishing escape,' Piers said as they sat at teatime, eating Mrs Rainbow's fruit scones.

Lily felt sick, terribly anxious about Cosmo and finding the presence of Susan and Sam almost unbearable. Sam avoided her eyes, talking to anyone but her, and Lily had to struggle with her sense of betrayal by Susan. But she had told Sam to leave her alone, hadn't she? What else was he supposed to think?

Now the weekend was almost over, they were all making preparations to leave, and Lily knew she had to see Cosmo. She asked Mrs Rainbow to show her to his room at the other end of the house. Lily was taken aback by the bleakness of the place, furnished with only the bed, a chair and a chest of drawers on the bare, polished boards. She had expected a room littered with the remains of a childhood spent here, whereas it looked more like the sort of cell one might expect for a monk. But then, she reminded herself, Cosmo was not here permanently and never had been. He had never belonged here.

Cosmo was stretched out in bed looking very pale and limp. His bright hair was plastered to his temples, the bruising was beginning to come out on his face and he was obviously in a lot of pain from his ribs.

'Hello, dear.' She moved some of the clothing from

459

the chair beside the bed, and sat down. 'How are you, Cozzy?'

His eyes were half open and he seemed very sleepy.

'My ribs . . . Hellish . . . Hurts to breathe . . .'

Lily reached out to caress his forehead and Cosmo flinched, giving a gasp which made him moan with pain.

'Don't!'

'Sorry, dear – you know I'd never hurt you. I was trying to make you feel better.' Frowning, she looked at the swollen lump on the left of his forehead, then, unable to help it, burst out with, 'Oh, Cozzy! How could you be so silly and reckless? Think what might have happened! You could have hurt yourself so dread-fully – and you're lucky not to be dead.'

Cosmo's eyes opened wide suddenly, and in bursts of pained speech he said, 'Am I? Ironside . . . I've let him down. All of them. I'm no good to anyone . . .'

'Cozzy!' Anguished by his suffering she went to stroke him again but he turned his head away.

'Don't baby me!'

'I'm sorry, dear. But I hate to see you like this. Don't take everything so badly! It was an accident. You've done everything so well up until now – remember all the other times? All the successes you've had? Don't let this one cloud everything else.'

'But I've wrecked the car! Completely smashed it! Ironside and Marks will never forgive me.'

Lily thought of the expression of utter fury she had seen on Loz Marks's face and was filled with a sense of dread for Cosmo. Perhaps Piers would want to find another driver.

'It'll be all right, darling,' she said, wanting to pour her love over him as she had always done, to make him feel better. 'I'll talk to Piers – we'll see that it's all right.'

460

'Oh God!' Cosmo cried, with such force she thought he was about to launch himself off the bed. 'Can't you stop interfering, Lily? Everything has to come from you, doesn't it? You can't let me do one thing for myself. You swamp me and make me feel completely useless. Oh, just leave me alone, woman. I'm useless to everyone – just let me face the fact on my own!'

He turned away from her and Lily could see that there was nothing she could say to bring him back to her. She stood up, knowing that he was in one of his dramatic moods, but she was very hurt nevertheless.

'Well, I hope you feel better soon,' she said, trying to keep her pain and anger from her voice. 'Next time I see you perhaps you'll be feeling a little more forthcoming – and grateful for everything that's been done for you.'

Cosmo did not respond or open his eyes, and angry as she was with him, she was frightened by the expression of utter wretchedness on his face.

Chapter Sixty-Seven

'We've got to get shot of him – he's a drunk and a fool and there's no telling what he'll do next!'

There was silence. The two of them were in the work shed at Brooklands and Sam was bent over the engine of the Heath Flyer.

'Sam!'

Sam straightened up, his expression grim. They had come back from Cranbourne the day before, very late, and he knew Loz had been working up to this.

'You know I'm right. You're all pandering to that spoilt brat because you're afraid to say no. He's no good – he's a bloody menace. That Larstonbury fellow can afford to hire any driver he wants, we've built him a bloody good motor and here we are risking it with that *halfwit* Fairford, who can't get through a morning without sucking at a Scotch bottle like a ... a *baby*. Christ, what a shower! I've never seen anything so ridiculous. And you just take it all. "Yes, Major Larstonbury, no, Major Larstonbury, three bags full, Major Larstonbury."'

'No, I don't!' Sam's temper began to flare now. 'But he's the one with the money. If he pulls out on us we've nothing!'

Sam found he was shouting. He knew this was only part of the story, but he couldn't put into words the confusion of emotions he felt. He had to put up with

Cosmo because of the money, it was true, but if he had gone to Piers Larstonbury and suggested they take on a different driver, he knew Piers would listen, even despite the fact the man was clearly helping Cosmo to please Lily. But there was also his old loyalty to Cosmo's father Charles, to the new, tender emotions he felt towards Susan Fairford, and because . . . Lily, there was always Lily, and her devotion to Cosmo – and because he felt as if he was going to explode with all the conflict and muddle inside him. He was still haunted by the wail he had heard Lily let out when she saw Cosmo lying on the stretcher. Her anguish had pierced deep into his heart and his first impulse had been to run and take her in his arms.

They had brought the car back on the trailer to Brooklands with full encouragement from Piers Larstonbury to get her roadworthy again.

'D'you think you'll be ready by the September meeting?' he asked. 'She's in a dreadful mess, I can see.'

'Oh, I think so,' Sam said. It was terrible to see the Flyer in that crushed state but already he was making mental notes of what needed doing. The bodywork would need replacing completely. Cosmo had taken the curve of the hill far too fast, showing off, of course. She'd turned over and rolled. God alone knew how Cosmo had got out with barely a scratch. Must've had the patron saint of drunkards on his side, Sam thought bitterly. Types like that always seemed to get out of trouble and inflict it on everyone else.

He had known Loz would explode sooner or later, and this was only the first of an increasing number of rows that started with Loz over Cosmo. The arrival of Cosmo a week later, still wincing in pain from his ribs, infuriated Loz even more.

'He's a liability,' he ranted to Sam after Cosmo had come into the shed to see the work on the car, the unmistakable aroma of Scotch hanging round him like a mist. 'We've given him a chance and he was all right to start with, I grant you. But he's shown his true colours now. He's hardly ever bloody sober! For God's sake, Sam, we've only got this year and we'll be back to square one if we don't get somewhere with this. In fact . . .' He wiped his oily hands on a rag and flung it over on to the bench. 'I'm wondering whether I want anything more to do with it!'

Sam knew that Loz was in a different position from him. He had no emotional entanglements with this project and he was also missing Mary and his boys.

'Well, you make up your bloody mind whether you're staying or going,' Sam said, 'and stop keeping on.'

He was furious himself. He didn't want to fall out with his old friend Loz. He didn't want Cosmo Fairford as his driver. But without Cosmo there might be no Piers Larstonbury, no car . . . And, still such a strong factor, yet one which he could hardly admit, no Lily.

Chapter Sixty-Eight

'They're ready! It's time for the off!'

Once again Lily stood in the crowd of spectators beside Susan Fairford, but this time they were at Brooklands for the September race meeting. The Heath Flyer, newly restored, was entered in the first handicap race.

Lily thought of Sam down beside the finishing straight with Piers and Loz, of all the passion they had poured into the Flyer. And Cosmo was in the driver's seat. *Oh, keep him calm – let him drive his very best. At his best he's so brilliant, has so much nerve and skill . . .*

'How did he seem this morning?' Susan had come up from the south coast, arriving late so that she had not seen Cosmo before he was marshalled for the race. Lily could see that Susan was even more nervous than she was. She tried to push from her mind what she had heard between Susan and Sam at Cranbourne last month, all her hurt and jealousy. After all, had she not pushed Sam away?

'Oh, he was in fine form,' Lily said. 'Absolutely full of beans. Talking nineteen to the dozen.' In fact, she had not seen Cosmo so talkative or full of energy for a very long time. 'He said he felt ready, and his ribs are healed now.'

Once again Susan was chewing at her fingers, her blue eyes troubled. 'I'll be so glad when all this is over.'

There was a roar in the distance from the crowd,

accompanied immediately by the acceleration of all the engines as the race began. Lily and Susan craned their necks to see the cars approach in a loud, buzzing mass like a swarm of giant bees.

'There he is – oh, Lord God!' Susan gasped. 'Oh, Cozzy, be careful!'

Lily found herself holding her breath as the scattering of cars roared past them along the alarming tilt of the steep Brooklands track. The Flyer looked like a sleek silver teardrop whizzing past, so fast that she could not catch a proper glimpse of Cosmo's face under his leather flying helmet, but only his shape, braced as he grasped the wheel of the rushing car, and then they were gone round the bend, the buzzing roar fading.

'Imagine how it would be without the silencers!' Lily said, rubbing her ears. Silencers were compulsory at Brooklands races.

'Oh, this is awful,' Susan said tremulously. 'I worry so about him. He'll kill himself doing it, I'm sure he will. So many of them have . . .' She craned her neck looking along the track, head topped by a snug green hat, just showing the ends of her pale hair. Lily saw she had lately had her hair cut like her own, in a neat bob.

With each lap they relaxed fractionally. It felt as if Cosmo was in command, was holding on well among the other vehicles, many of them company-built ones.

'There's the Austin,' Lily pointed as they rushed past. She was about to say how pleased Sam would be to beat them on lap times, but she decided not to mention Sam.

Round and round they sped, burning along the tilted outer circuit of track. By the end of the race two cars had had to drop out with mechanical troubles but otherwise all went well and during the last lap Lily found herself almost shaking with relief. He had done it – and he had done it well!

There was another swell of sound from the crowd as the cars tore along the finishing straight and at last the air quietened to a lull, filled with excited chatter and the bookies calling out from their stalls along the track.

'Oh – I feel as if I've just lived a hundred years!' Susan said, shakily.

Lily felt drained as well.

'Sometimes I think it's worse watching than doing it,' she laughed. She wondered how Sam was feeling. Was he pleased with the result?

They did not get to the men until some time later, when they had agreed to meet for lunch, and they could immediately see that everyone was in glowing form. Piers was the first person they saw, waiting for them at the edge of the paddock as they had agreed so that they could come in as his guests for the meal. He beamed as he saw them approaching.

'What a morning, eh?' he cried, his pale, rather donnish face crinkled with enthusiasm. 'Your son has done us proud, Mrs Fairford. We're all delighted. A very respectable lap time – averaged 83.7 miles per hour! He was in marvellous form – come along and join us all for luncheon! Over here.' He indicated their picnic spot on the grass. 'As you see, we're dining *al fresco*!'

For the first time in a long time, as Lily sat down on the warm rug, she saw Sam turn to her and smile, a smile which she realized may not have been particularly directed at her, but somehow also encompassed her in the jubilation of the moment. Those seconds lifted her even more than Cosmo's success and she smiled back happily. For those few seconds his eyes rested on her face and they were caught in each other's gaze.

'Oh, well done, my darling! What a marvellous morning you've had!' Susan went to kiss Cosmo on the top of the head, and for once he did not react with resentment. He was very flushed in the face, eyes bright, and seemed high-wired and taut with success.

They had a light luncheon of cold meats and salad and a crisp white wine and the men all talked excitedly.

'What about going for a land speed record?' Cosmo said. His voice seemed raised a little too loudly. Lily could sense the vibrations of excitement coming from him. He was electric with it, though his moods seem to shift from moment to moment. 'We could go to Pendine Sands – I could take her faster than today if we were on the flat. She can go like the wind . . .'

'What's the current record?' Piers Larstonbury asked.

'It's a hundred and thirty-three point seven over the mile,' Sam said. 'That was here – back in May. Fellow called Guinness.'

'Well, what do you think, Ironside?'

Lily watched as Sam considered the idea, his face serious. In that moment, watching him, she knew he would always affect her by his presence.

'It'd certainly be interesting to try. I doubt she's up to that. It'd test our ratios all right – a new engine possibly . . .'

He and Loz began a technical conversation about what might be needed for more speed, to which Piers listened avidly. Cosmo ate his plateful of food ravenously.

'That's right,' Susan said to him. 'You need to keep your strength up for this afternoon.'

The Flyer had been entered, daringly, for one of the International Class races, competing against models from all over the world.

'I'm flying, Mater,' Cosmo told her, fizzily. 'You wait and see. There's nothing can stop me.'

'Here we go!' Susan cried. All eyes were turned in the same direction and once again the posse of cars came careering round the bend into view at frightening speed. The Heath Flyer was there among them, in the middle, and the two women gasped with relief.

'Go on, Cosmo – drive her!' Susan yelled, in a way quite out of character. 'Go on, go on!'

'He's doing fine!' Lily shouted in excitement.

There was a lull as they waited for the next lap. Cosmo was so full of it he would probably have over-taken a few of them by the time they next saw him. The first cars appeared, screaming their way round the track. Lily narrowed her eyes. Where was the Flyer? To her surprise, Cosmo had slipped back a little, was not holding his own as they might have expected.

'Oh dear!' Susan said.

There seemed nothing else to say and they watched dismally, waiting and hoping that during the next lap he would pick up and overtake.

But the next lap brought an even more worrying picture. As the cars spun round into view there was not a sign of Cosmo, not at first.

'He must be in trouble,' Lily said. 'Perhaps the engine's packed up . . .'

But then, there he was, second from the back, and by the next lap he was trailing way behind everyone else, to the point where there rose a joking kind of jeer from the crowd, seeing Cosmo moving along the track at an apparently leisurely speed.

'That one's out for a Sunday afternoon pleasure

cruise!' a man joked near then, and everyone around laughed. 'Looks as if he's dozed off at the wheel!'

Anguished, Lily strained her eyes to try and see Cosmo. He looked quite composed, very still as he drove, but he was losing speed all the time, the car following a more and more erratic course along the track.

'Looks as if he's had a few as well,' the man next to them suggested. 'Well, that's a bit of a joke – look at that!'

By the time the lap came round again, they stood on tiptoe, straining to see if he was trailing in their wake, but this time there was no sign of Cosmo at all.

'Dear God,' Susan said uneasily. 'Something's gone badly wrong this time. Oh, I do hope he's all right . . .'

'He could be anywhere,' Lily said miserably.

Not knowing what else to do, they waited among the crowd, willing Cosmo to appear. The race still had a couple more laps to go and they heard them coming round again, roaring and then receding, and still no Flyer. Then, moments later, Susan cried, 'Oh, look – there!'

On the near side of the track at the very bottom of the slope they caught sight of the silver gleam of Flyer's bodywork. Moving closer they saw that she had ground to a standstill alongside the bottom edge of the track.

'She looks all right!' Lily said, from the little she could see as they pushed their way across to her. The crowd close to the edge were all peering over at her, talking, speculating and calling out to Cosmo.

Looking down over the barrier, Lily saw that the car was slewed sideways into it, and all they could see was the back of Cosmo's head, encased in brown leather, as he sat, slumped unconscious, over the wheel.

470

Chapter Sixty-Nine

Once the race was finished and the car could be dragged to safety from the track, Cosmo remained slumped over the wheel and did not surface until they had reached a place to stop at the side of the finishing straight.

Piers, Sam and Loz gathered round, then hurried beside the motor as it was trailed along. Lily and Susan went tearing down to them. There was another great to-do going on, as one car had smashed through the railings on the finishing straight and hit a spectator, but they were far too worried about Cosmo to take in fully what had happened or that a good number of people were staring at them.

Cosmo came round, fighting furiously.

'Get off me, woman!' he bawled at Susan. 'Stop fussing over me! Oh, God in heaven . . .'

As he tried to get up and leave the car he seemed overcome by dizziness and sat quickly back down again, looking sick and drained.

Lily was frightened by the sight of Cosmo's flushed face and glazed look. She realized, though, that she had seen him like this before, that perhaps there had been something terribly wrong for a long time and that he had not told them.

'He looks terribly ill,' Susan said, white with worry.

'Just let me go to bed,' Cosmo was saying, his voice full of aggression.

'The doctor'll come,' Sam said, 'but he's seeing to the other smash . . .'

Eventually the doctor appeared, a serious-faced young man.

'Get these people away from me!' Cosmo roared.

'Perhaps you could all stand back and let me examine Mr Fairford,' the doctor said quietly. He measured Cosmo's blood pressure, apparently asking questions. Lily could see Cosmo's face, serious but mutinous. After some time the doctor stood up abruptly and walked over to them, his black bag in hand.

'You're his party?' His voice was curt. 'I should take him back to wherever you're staying and let him rest. There's no point in troubling the hospital.'

'But what's wrong?' Susan asked.

'Nothing that I can remedy,' the doctor snapped. 'You'd better ask him that yourself. Are you his . . . ?'

'Mother.' Susan's brow was crinkled with dismay. 'I don't understand, Doctor. Is he seriously ill?'

'No, he's not. I can't discuss a patient's symptoms when he has expressly asked me not to. Just put him to bed and quiz him yourself. He's a lucky man. That race could have been fatal for him or for several others.'

'Oh yes,' Cosmo shouted from where he was now sitting on the ground, his back against a front wheel of the Flyer. 'Aren't I always the lucky one?'

They all travelled back to the Pack Horse, the cosy public house where they had rooms once more, and Sam and Loz made sure Cosmo was put to bed. Lily's room was next to his, and she told them she would keep a lookout to see that he was all right. Cosmo said he wanted to sleep, but when she looked into the room, she saw him moving restlessly, looking flushed and uncomfortable. His bed was positioned under a low, sloping roof and she was worried that he might hit his head on the beam.

Daring to go closer, she sat beside him, placing her cool palm on his forehead. He looked so young and helpless suddenly and she wanted to mother him as she had when he was tiny.

'Darling Cozzy,' she whispered. 'What is the matter with you, my love?'

Cosmo opened his eyes, which filled with tears suddenly at the sight of her.

'Oh, what is it, dear?' Lily was really dismayed. It was so seldom that he showed any gentle emotions these days.

'I've disgraced us all . . .' He turned his head restlessly. 'I feel so rotten . . . I can't help it, Lily, believe me. I've tried . . . I've tried so hard . . .'

'Tried to do what, darling?' She took his hand, which felt very hot and dry, and leaned over to look down into his eyes.

Cosmo stared at her, and the tears began to run down his cheeks.

'Oh, Lily, you're the only one . . . You're the only one I've ever been able to turn to. You've been so loyal, so patient with me . . . I've let everyone down.'

'No, darling, of course you haven't!' She caressed his hand, as if trying to warm him and thaw the icy coldness of his self-loathing. 'You did marvellously this morning. I know Sam and Piers were absolutely delighted with the time you made. It can't always go right. You know you can do it, and no one's angry with you – you were just taken poorly. It'll be all right next time. Here, love, you look so hot – have a drink of water.'

He lifted his head to accept the glass of water, and she wiped his eyes with her handkerchief, feeling such great tenderness for him.

'You sleep a bit more, dear. I expect you'll wake feeling calmer.'

Once more she stroked his head and he stared up at her. Afterwards, she always blamed herself for not recognizing the utter desperation in his eyes.

'How is he? Shall I go up?' Susan half got to her feet when Lily went downstairs to find her. 'I looked in earlier but he seemed to be asleep. I could take him up his food.'

It was almost time for the evening meal and the smell of roasting beef filled the lower rooms and corridors.

Lily was touched by the way Susan deferred to her over Cosmo, as if she still felt that Lily had a better understanding of how to deal with him.

'He's upset,' she said, sitting beside Susan at a table. 'About the race, I mean. He feels in the doghouse.'

'Well, it was a shame, but if you're ill, you're ill.' Susan put away her leather writing case. Lily couldn't help wondering who she could be writing to. Susan had few people left in the world now, but for her elderly mother and her sister. 'Does he want food?' she asked.

'Perhaps a bit later,' Lily suggested. She did not think it a good moment for Susan to go up there and talk to Cosmo.

The men soon came down and they all ate a good dinner of roast beef. Though there was a subdued atmosphere round the table, Piers rallied them.

'Come along now, do cheer up. We had a marvellous result this morning – quite a cause for celebration! Let's raise a glass to our Flyer and to many more successes! Don't you agree, Ironside?

Sam raised his glass. 'The Heath Flyer. Onwards and upwards.'

Lily wondered what he thought, but he seemed surprisingly calm, almost detached from the situation, and she suddenly realized he was a man of great patience, whereas Loz was sitting at the table with a thunderous expression. Lily's eyes met Sam's. Both of them knew what Loz thought of Cosmo, and how angry and resentful he was about this afternoon's race.

'Well, I'm with you for as long as it takes,' Piers Larstonbury said happily. 'This has been a great adventure for me, thanks to your skill, the two of you.' And he raised his glass again, face breaking into a boyish smile. 'There'll be setbacks, of course, but it's all part of the process – eh, Marks?'

Looking at Piers, sitting there drinking beer with them all in his well-cut clothing, and seeing his kind, courteous way of trying to cheer them all, Lily felt a burst of great gratitude and affection for him. He was a good man, she thought. Such a good man, and she knew he would leave his wife for her in a moment, so devoted was he to her, if she ever showed any inclination to ask. She longed, in that moment, for his goodness to be enough.

'We'd better organize some food for Cozzy,' Susan said as the meal ended. 'I'm sure they'll do a tray or something. Lily, perhaps you'd better take it to him.'

Sam leaned gently towards her. 'Perhaps I should go up as well. I haven't had a chance for a chat with him and I'd like to stop him tearing himself up about it. I know what he's like.'

'All right,' Susan said gratefully.

Sam followed Lily up the stairs with the tray of beef and delicious treacle tart and she was conscious of his presence behind her all the way up. Despite these occasional meetings in the company of others they were still very awkward with each other, as if the air between them vibrated with unspoken emotions that they could not seem to begin on.

'I think it will help if you to talk to him,' she whispered outside Cosmo's room. 'He looks up to you a lot. And he was feeling very wretched about what happened today.'

'He shouldn't,' Sam said. 'It's all part of it. He was taken bad, that's all there is to it.'

Lily gave him a faint smile and went into her own room, whispering, 'Good luck!'

She heard Sam's voice speaking quietly from next door as she folded her clothes away on to the chair and looked for her night things, and she hoped Sam would be able to make a difference to Cosmo's state of mind. Poor Cozzy, he did get so cast down. So often he still seemed like a little boy to her, except that the saddest thing was that he had somehow seemed more happy and complete when he was four than ever he did now.

She was about to undress when she heard a tapping on the door, soft but insistent. Sam was outside, his face very grave. For a second he hesitated, then, inclining his head towards the next-door room, he said, 'I think you'd better come.'

To her astonishment he took her hand, leading her into Cosmo's room where he carefully closed the door.

'Prepare yourself, dear,' he said to her tenderly, and his face was terribly concerned.

'Cozzy?' Wild with dread, she ran to the bed. He was lying just as she had left him, eyes closed, seemingly asleep. The only thing she saw as different was the glass of water which he had somehow tipped over. Then she saw other things: the paper crumpled in one hand, the white dusting of powder on his upper lip, the blueness of both his lips and the stillness of him that was beyond waking. All these things she took in during those seconds which shook inside her like an earthquake invisible to anyone else.

She reached out, trembling, to touch Cosmo's neck, feeling for a pulse of life and hope, but there was nothing. Looking up, her fingertips still pressed to his lifeless flesh, her eyes met Sam's.

'What's happened? Oh my God, Sam, what's he done?'

Sam looked to Cosmo, then helplessly back at her again. There seemed nothing to say.

Chapter Seventy

'Cocaine hydrochloride?' You mean to say that my son has been ... inhaling this ... this powder like some sort of *poet*?'

They were gathered with the doctor and a policeman in the back room of the Pack Horse. Susan, in her shock and grief, had retreated back into the glassy, commanding woman Sam remembered so disliking in Ambala. She sat up very straight, hands clasped in her lap, giving off an air of superior frostiness. Loz and Piers stood tactfully nearby, as did the owner of the public house, who kept repeating that there had never been a death at the Pack Horse before, not while he was landlord.

'I'm afraid to say, Mrs Fairford,' the doctor said, 'that your son appears to have quite a lengthy history of drug addiction, judging by the condition of him.'

They were all frozen with shock and as yet Susan was too forbidding to accept comfort. Lily stood next to Sam, who seemed suddenly to be always at her side. She was also too shocked yet to weep. The doctor said that Cosmo must have known that he was taking a huge overdose of cocaine, that he had taken his own life, and she knew that she must have been the last person to speak to him. The memory of Cosmo's face suddenly made her tremble so that she thought her legs might give way. She groped for a chair and found Sam's arm holding her up.

'Thank you,' she whispered, sinking down on to a wooden bench. She looked up at him and then her eyes filled with tears.

Cosmo's funeral was held ten days later at the church at Lapsley, the village closest to the Cranbourne estate. There had been an inquest, which confirmed that Cosmo had died by his own hand.

There were not many at the funeral. Susan's mother and sister came, as well as Uncle William and some of the estate workers. Lily saw Bernard and Tim there, in their best Sunday suits. Piers Larstonbury drove up with Lily, and Sam came on his own. Loz, he said, regretted that he could not be there: he was needed in Birmingham with his family. Uncle William, no doubt through the prompting of Mrs Rainbow, had invited all who needed to, to sleep overnight at Cranbourne House.

They all stood in the village church amid the smells of old hymn books and candlewax and sang 'Abide with Me' and 'Lead Us, Heavenly Father, Lead Us'. Lily wept, unable to help herself as she thought of Cosmo's life, of his little face as she knew him in India, the eager, loving little boy he had been and all that he had become. Piers stood beside her, gently touching her arm at times when her tearfulness overwhelmed her. He understood that her loss of Cosmo in this tragic way was like losing her own son.

Susan, between her mother and sister, was dry-eyed and brittle, determined, as she said, not to 'lay all my emotions out in public'. She stood very straight, in her black coat and a wide-brimmed hat with a feather trailing gracefully down to the side, and elegant, high-

479

heeled shoes. No one could get close to her: she had closed off from them all.

She's burying the last remaining member of her family, Lily thought. And the memory came to her of them all that day in Mussoorie when they picnicked under the deodars amid the sweeping mountain peaks with their waterfalls and meadows of flowers, when Isadora had been in love with horses and Charles and Susan seemed relaxed together and Cosmo ... But of course by then the circle had already been broken. Cosmo had been sent away: banished from the family, as it had always felt to him. Her eyes filled with tears again. The poor little mite, she thought. He had never really recovered from that.

Piers held her arm as they processed out of the church after the coffin. Cosmo was to be buried on the estate, close to the track where he had so loved to drive. Lily and Piers walked behind Susan and her family and Lily knew Sam and some of the other men were walking behind her. She knew with great clarity then that she needed to be walking on Sam's arm, that that was what was right and that nothing else ever had been or ever would be.

Once they had left the church she turned, looking for Sam with a sudden desperate need, but he had peeled off and was some distance away among the old graves, as if he needed to be alone. He stood looking across at the elms bordering the field beyond the churchyard, a slender, lonely figure in his dark overcoat, and in that glimpse, amid the desperate sorrow of the day which had somehow made everything clear, Lily knew how much she loved him. She longed to go to him, to pour out everything she felt to him.

Instead she walked obediently on Piers's arm to the

convoy of cars which would follow the black-plumed horses carrying Cosmo's body to its resting place at the edge of the fields where he had reluctantly spent so much of his boyhood.

Chapter Seventy-One

It was only once she was in the privacy of her room at Cranbourne that Susan allowed her grief to surface, and then it seemed to come over her with the impact of a heavy blow. Lily was with her as she wept, becoming utterly distraught, and in the end Lily was frightened by the force it. Not knowing what else to do, she went to Mrs Rainbow.

'I've been with her for an hour or more,' she said shakily, 'and she's more and more hysterical.'

'I'll send out for the doctor,' the housekeeper said. 'I expect 'e'll give her a little summat to sedate her.'

Whatever it was they gave Susan worked very effectively and by nine o'clock that evening she was in a deep sleep. Waiting by her bedside, Lily felt waves of exhaustion rolling over her, but she was not sleepy. She felt as if she needed hours to unwind and to think before she could relax enough.

Once she was certain Susan would not stir for some time, she crept from the room, closing the door very softly. She had barely got any distance away when she met Piers in the passage and realized that he had been on his way to her room. Immediately she felt resentful and hemmed in. Poor Piers, how kind and thoughtful he was! But just at present she ached to be alone in order to let the great void of Cosmo's death open within her. She did not want Piers's sexual advances, however much they were dressed up as offering comfort.

'Darling,' he said gently. 'Oh, my poor little girl, what a tragic time it has been. Come to me, my love.'

He went to take her in his arms in his kindly way but Lily, though not wanting to hurt him, found she simply could not bear it.

'Piers.' She stood her ground, resisting him. 'Dear, would you mind letting me be alone for a time, please? It's been such a terrible day.'

'Let me come with you, darling girl. I won't talk, I'll just be beside you . . .'

'No!' she said, more adamantly than she really meant to. Trying to soften the message she said, 'No, Piers. Do go and get some rest. It's been a very tiring day, but I do just need some time alone tonight. Please don't worry about me.'

'Of course, my dear.' She could not tell if his feelings were hurt. He was always so courteous. He kissed her and she watched him go towards his room, turning to raise a hand in affectionate parting to her.

Lily slipped down the stairs and let herself out into the enclosed garden at the side of the house. It was still warm and that lovely space between the walls seemed to distil the early autumn scents: the velvet sweetness of the last roses on the darkening air mixed with the more pungent smells from the herb garden. It was the time of night when the light is so uncertain that she began to imagine she was seeing shapes moving the other side of the garden, then realized that the dark, moving shadow she had seen was a tabby cat which lived in the wake of Mrs Rainbow, and it came up and miaowed at her.

'I haven't anything for you,' she said, bending to stroke it. 'It isn't any use carrying on at me like that.'

She left the walled part of the garden, remembering the loveliness of the smooth expanse of lawn beyond, its scent and the sense of space and freedom it gave her. For the time being her emotion was spent. The day had focused so intensely on Cosmo, on loss and tragedy, that now it was as if her mind had closed down and she could not think, or feel, any more about it. She felt scoured out and blank, needing simply to be quiet and be cradled by the gentle greenness of the place. She bent down and unbuttoned her shoes, slipping them off to feel the cool grass between her toes.

As she walked she saw another shadow moving where the edge of the lawn met the long grass and margin of trees. This time it was far too big to be a cat and she assumed it was one of the gardeners. She prepared herself to say a polite goodnight, but in a moment she knew who it was and that he had seen her.

'Lily?'

Sam stepped forward a few paces, then waited as she moved towards him. The memory of hearing him, here in the clearing with Susan, hardened her towards him, made her try to hold aloof from her need of him. Would this be another fight? she wondered. Another time when they just could not say what needed to be said? She stood barely more than a yard away, hardly able to see his expression.

'Last time we were here,' she said, hardly knowing what would come from her lips, 'I heard you down here with Susan. You were kissing her, were you not?'

There was a silence in which the gaze of each of them met somewhere in the dark space between them.

'Lily . . .' His voice was low and she knew immediately that now nothing would be hidden. 'You can't have forgotten. Please tell me you haven't. I don't know why you decided not to meet me in Mussoorie. I've wondered and agonized about it ever since, about your silence, even after I wrote and wrote. It was so cruel, so impossible to understand . . .'

'You wrote?' she burst out. 'You never wrote! I never heard a word from you. And I was . . .' She stumbled over how to explain about Ewan McBride and the crazed strangeness of those weeks.

'My employer wouldn't let me out. I couldn't get to you, I didn't hear from you . . . I thought you had left without saying goodbye, without trying . . .'

'But you never came! Not a word! I sent notes to the house – nothing back! What was I supposed to think? Lily . . .' He moved closer, but she stepped back, still terribly afraid of him.

'What about your wife? And what about Susan? What *were* you doing out here that night, Sam?'

'Oh God, Lily . . .' Sam made a despairing sound. 'Susan was . . . We just . . . I don't know. We were both lonely, taking comfort in each other for a few moments. It was no more than that. I like her – I never thought I'd say that, for a start! And I feel for her. She's had a rough ride. But we don't want each other, not really – you must know that! I'm not her sort – wrong sort of class altogether. When we came across each other in France, in that hospital, after the captain had been killed, it sort of ironed things out, made us more equal, and I liked her better . . . But that night here – it was just a thing of the moment . . .'

'And your wife?'

Sam sighed. 'I married Helen when we were far too young. Even back then I knew I'd made a dreadful

485

mistake, that first time in Ambala, when I'd met you . . .
I didn't know, not before then, what it could be like. I
got married, thinking that was the done thing, and soon
there was a baby on the way. But that second time, in
the hills – God help me, if you'd turned up that night, I
would have left her and stayed with you. I'm not proud
of that, but that was how it was – how it is. You're the
one, Lily. There's never been anyone anything like you
– nothing's touched it. That week in Mussoorie . . .' He
paused, shaking his head.

'God, woman, I was ill when I got home to England,
just being without you, thinking I'd never see you again
and never understanding why you . . . I suppose I was
pining for you. I was thin as a railing . . .' He looked up
at her. 'But you weren't there, you didn't want me.
You'd made that clear enough. And I had to go on and
do the decent thing for Helen and find other things to
occupy me – to *console* me . . .'

Lily stood quite still, letting the wonder of his words
sink into her.

'What about Piers?' he said miserably. 'He's married
as well.'

'They're only married under the law,' Lily said.
'There doesn't seem to be anything else left.'

'He's a thoroughly decent man, Lily, and a wealthy
one. Do you love him?'

'No,' she said simply. 'I don't.'

He waited a long interval for her to find words, until
at last she spoke into the darkness.

'Sam, I've been and I've done a lot of things I'm
ashamed of. I've been what people – what men,
especially – have wanted me to be. You've probably
heard things about me which must disgust you. I've
been Piers's mistress – for a living, yes, for money when

486

you come down to it, almost like a woman of the streets only more respectable, of course – because I couldn't seem to find any other way to be. I forced myself not to remember you and how it was in Ambala and in Mussoorie because I didn't think I could ever have that again, not with anyone. It frightens me even saying anything now . . . And after you'd gone . . . Oh, Sam . . .'

As the memories came she started to weep, but he did not dare move forward to touch her yet.

'You left me your child . . . When you left I was . . . I was . . .' The sobs interrupted. 'I was expecting and I didn't know what to do. I knew you didn't want me. I went to the nuns on the mountain . . .'

She told him then, about the laundry and the Bethel Home and about walking out that winter morning and shutting away any thoughts of their baby, of closing her heart down and training it to be a cool, calculating place where there were exchanges and bartering of services but no love. As she talked she realized gradually that he was weeping as well.

'Our child,' he said, wiping his eyes. 'Was it a boy or a girl?'

'A little girl,' Lily told him. 'I called her Victoria.'

The tears came then, a crying like none she had ever managed for the grief of Mussoorie, for Victoria, or now for Cosmo, the pain of it all tearing at her inside until she was on her knees, felled by it. Moments later she realized that Sam had come to kneel beside her, holding her head close to his warm chest, saying soft, loving words of comfort while he cried with her.

When she was a little calmer they stood up and held each other close, not speaking for a long time, as the darkness thickened and a night bird shrieked somewhere in the distance. And his body felt so familiar, so lovely against her and she breathed in the smell of him. Their lips found each other's and she remembered the feel of his kisses and the tears ran down her cheeks again at the joy of the memory.

'God,' Sam said, awed, 'I've found you again. Lily – my Lily.' He looked down into her eyes. 'I thought life was going to be the same now until I died, or Helen did. That there'd be nothing, no love. Nothing real that I could call mine.'

'And I thought I'd always look after other people's children, their houses and marriages – that I'd never have my own.' She gazed seriously at him. 'I love you, Sam and I always loved you and I wanted to come to you that afternoon, I honestly did, and I couldn't ... I'll explain to you properly what happened, but I want to know that you believe me.'

'I do,' he said seriously. 'And I always wanted to. I didn't want to doubt you but I didn't know what else to think. Oh, Lily – there's no one like you, my dearest love. No one in this world.'

They stayed in the garden a long time, walking arm in arm round the margin of the lawn, Lily carrying her shoes in one hand, beginning to tell each other what had happened in these years of separation and all that they had felt and done. Sam told her about Joe, the words pouring out.

'We managed to rub along until he happened to us, Helen and me and the girls. I had my work, of course, kept busy and tried to keep on the straight and narrow. And then Joe came ... when he died, well, that was truly the end of it. Helen and I just couldn't seem to get on after that, not even on the surface, the way we'd managed before ...' He gave a deep sigh. 'You keep telling yourself things will be all right. They have to be because you're married, children, responsibility, and that's that. And I do feel responsible – I'll see she's all right. But, oh God, Lily . . .'

He stopped to hold her, kiss her again and she closed her eyes, her head pressed to his chest. She loved this man, how she loved him! It was such a relief, a miracle to know she had not imagined it, all those years ago, that she could love like this and be loved in return.

The moon was high in the sky when they crept up to Lily's room, arms round each other, the stair carpet feeling dry and rough under her feet after the night grass. They knew without saying anything that they could not be separated tonight, or ever again, and closed the door of her room behind them with a sigh of relief and a feeling of complete rightness. They had found each other again.

Chapter Seventy-Two

Bombay, India, 1924

Lily sat on the veranda at the back of the bungalow, smiling across the garden at the sight of a slim Indian girl dressed in a deep crimson sari, leading a little European boy across the shady strip of grass between the flower beds. The boy's grey eyes were fixed solemnly on his feet as he accompanied his *ayah* with his first tottering steps.

'I will sit here for half an hour or so, Lakshmi,' Lily called to the girl. She always made a point of calling her by her name, not just *ayah*, the way so many of the British women did in that imperious way. 'I shall take a little while to write my letter, and then he can come to me.'

'Yes, Memsahib.' The girl smiled shyly. She seemed almost always on the point of giggling whenever addressed, showing a row of strong, widely spaced teeth, and Lily liked her for her happy disposition.

She sat looking out for a moment, watching a clutter of crows wrangling around the birdbath, a little stone pool of water which the *mali* kept topped up. Somewhere nearby there were parrots in the trees. It was very hot and for a few moments Lily sat fanning herself with a few sheets of writing paper before opening the ink bottle and settling down to write.

14 Napier Road,
Bombay

May 10th, 1924

Dear Susan,

It was such a pleasure to receive your postcard telling us the likely day of your arrival. I am so happy at the thought of you coming to the hills with us and your being here. Though the people around here are pleasant enough, I shall so enjoy having a real friend and I'm longing for you to see our darling little Edward again. He will no doubt have grown up a lot since we left – I can scarcely believe we celebrated his first birthday three days ago!

So, we are settling in. We have an airy bungalow, which is very simply furnished and suits our needs perfectly well, and the cook is a good deal better tempered than some! Sam's agenting job for the Austin Company has worked out well so far. Imports are increasing like anything, of course, and, more importantly, he can also work more at what he really loves – dealing with the actual motor cars. He's such a good mechanic that now the word has got round he is much in demand and is happy as anything, off here and there and is already talking about entering the reliability trials here later in the year for the Motor Union of Western India. They have to drive to Mahableshwar and back, and you know Sam – if there's one thing he loves it's being out on the road! Last week we were invited out to one of the villages and while we were there, a man went round with a tom-tom and gathered a crowd together for a lecture on hookworm disease. I didn't understand the local language, but the lecturer used lantern pictures and the effect was very vivid.

As for my Edward – well, I could write pages. He seems to have settled well and I feel very much at home being back here myself. Back to the old mixed feelings of affection and exasperation towards the place! With a child now myself, though, I am anxious about all the illnesses he might pick up and am a bit more jumpy – I know I don't need to explain to you. But so far Edward has kept remarkably well, and even though the great summer heat has arrived, he still seems very happy and lively. He has half adopted a mongoose which lives at the bottom of the garden, and calls it Oose!

I shall leave all else to catch up on once you arrive – and look forward to it with great happiness. We shall come to meet you as soon as we hear!

Wishing you a safe and pleasant voyage and so looking forward to see you.

My love and good wishes,
Lily

Chapter Seventy-Three

Mussoorie, India, 1924

'We should be able to see the mountains today – although it's hard to tell with this cloud,' Lily said.

She and Susan were toiling up the steep path to Gun Hill, both dressed in light frocks, for although they were in the mountains it was still the hottest time of the year. The monsoon rains were due to arrive at any time.

'Phew – I need to get in better condition,' Susan said, pausing on the path, close to a small Hindu shrine which had been cut into the rock since they were last here, containing a small, stumpy Siva *lingam* draped with marigolds.

'Does it upset you, being here?' Lily asked anxiously. They were not all that far from Zinnias, the house Susan and Charles Fairford had rented for those weeks in 1910.

Susan smiled wistfully, wiping her forehead with her handkerchief. Her face, if anything, was even more attractive now she was older. Though more lined, it was more giving, not like the closed young woman she had been.

'Not upset, no. It feels very strange, and brings it all back ... So much of it, especially before the war, feels so very long ago. And, of course, we weren't here with Cozzy ...'

Her eyes filled and she looked away. Lily felt her own throat ache with tears. There was no need for either of them to say any more.

They walked on and reached the top, catching a sight of the great peaks of Banderpunch, Pithwara and the Gangotri in bright sunlight, though a pall of deep mauve cloud was massing to obscure its light. They were buffeted by sudden powerful gusts of wind.

'It's changing fast,' Lily said, shading her eyes. 'The rain's coming.'

'It's astonishing, isn't it?' Susan said. She sighed. 'I so loathed living here, yet it's wonderful to be back.'

She had docked in Bombay the week before, while the plains were gripped by the great heat, and travelled with Lily, Sam and little Edward, the *ayah* and servants, first by rail to Dehra Dun, then road, up to this simple bungalow in Mussoorie.

After a silence, while they watched the cloud edge its way over, blanketing the high Himalaya, Susan turned to her.

'It must be strange for you too?'

'Yes – it is a little bit,' Lily said.

Lily had never told Susan all that had happened to her in Mussoorie, not about the way she had let Ewan McBride use her, or about little Victoria. It felt too private and shameful. Sam was the only person she had told, or would ever tell about all that. The first afternoon after they arrived in Mussoorie, she slipped out while the others were resting, delighting in being in the lovely mountain town again, but with a mission that she wanted to fulfil on her own. She suddenly felt very uncomfortable, wondering if there were people still living here who would remember her, and she pulled the brim of her straw hat well down.

She walked towards the beginning of the Camel's Back Road feeling more and more on edge as the McBrides' bungalow came into view. Her heart pounded at the recollection of how she had had to escape with Jane Brown that night, of the desperation of those days imprisoned inside. The house did not look the same, though. It was painted yellow now, and there were many more pots of flowers in the front garden. She sensed already this was no longer a house belonging to Dr McBride. They must have gone.

Even so, she did not have the courage to knock at that door. Instead, she called at the next house, where she was greeted by a young, slender servant who cocked his head in an enquiring way.

'This bungalow next door,' she pointed, 'whose house is it?'

'That is house of Mr Jenkins,' he said.

'Ah. Not Dr McBride, then?'

This was met with another small inclination of the head. He probably knew nothing about the former occupants, Lily thought, but in case, she asked, 'Where is Dr McBride?'

'He is dead, long time,' the young man said. 'Wife die, then he die soon after.'

Lily was surprised. 'You knew him?'

He nodded. 'I have been here a long time.'

Lily dimly remembered a child of the servants who worked in this house when she was here before and guessed this must be the same boy.

'Thank you.' She smiled at him. 'You have been very helpful.'

She walked away, feeling released. She could walk the streets of the town without coming face to face with the doctor. That part of her past would not come back to pursue her. She revelled in being back, walking the sloping streets, seeing the houses perched along the edge of the hills, all the school children, the bazaars and the awesome sights of the mountains which met her at every turn. It was like a homecoming.

'You seem so very happy,' Susan said, as they walked back down the path. It became easier to talk about personal things, out here in the hills.

'Yes.' Lily darted a smile at her. 'I am. Very. Even though things are irregular. I don't know if we'll ever be able to marry properly . . .'

'People assume you're married, I suppose?' Susan instinctively lowered her voice, even though there was no one else around. The sky was fast turning a threatening, inky colour and they walked faster.

'Yes,' Lily said. 'There might be a divorce. Helen, Sam's wife, is not keen and we'll have to wait for a time. And of course we're a family.' She blushed. 'I'm not young, and I'd still like one more child . . .' For Susan, the old Susan, the whole situation would have seemed a deep disgrace. But Susan had suffered and changed. And, Lily realized, she and Sam were of the same spirit: they were adventurers. He longed to escape from what he felt to be stifling suburban life, and Lily was happy outside social convention so long as she could be with him and with her boy. So much in her life had been irregular right from the start, far more than Susan really knew, that she simply lived with it and rejoiced in finding love.

'No one has said anything to us,' she said with a wry smile. 'But you are not staying in a house that is in the least respectable!'

'Oh,' Susan smiled wanly. 'I think I can learn to live with it.'

'And you? Tell me more about him.' 'Him' was someone who had been given a faint but increasing mention in Susan's letters.

'Well, he's gentle and kind, not wealthy but comfortable enough. His name is Edmund Reardon and he's an antiquarian bookseller, in Brighton . . .' She looked at Lily and laughed wholeheartedly. 'You see, I should really rather like a quiet suburban life, dear, just for a change. I've had more than enough of loss and change and shifting from place to place carrying my garden about in flowerpots!'

'And is he a bachelor?'

'A widower,' Susan said. Lily could hear the affection in her voice as she talked about him. 'He's ten years my senior and his wife died of TB, very sadly – not so very long after they were married. There's one grown-up son. And Edmund is just utterly, utterly sweet, Lily . . .' She looked bashfully at her friend and both of them laughed.

Lily dared to say, 'You know, there was a time when I thought you might find some happiness with the major – Piers Larstonbury.'

'Oh no! Nice fellow, of course, but even if I'd been keen, I don't think he'll ever leave that dreadful wife of his, even if she does run rings round him. And now he and Mr Marks and the rest of the team are so embroiled at Brooklands building all these motors, I should never have seen anything of him anyway!'

Lily wondered whether Susan was right, whether Piers would in the end have ever left Virginia for her. All she could feel for him now, though, was a tender gratitude for his sorrow and generosity when she told him her true feelings for Sam.

497

'I can't keep you here if your heart is somewhere else,' he said, his face pale with shock and hurt. 'But I shall never forget you, Lily. You're a beautiful woman and he's the luckiest man alive.' He was a gentleman, Piers Larstonbury, a kind and rather lonely one.

Susan was telling Lily about her gentle courtship with Edmund Reardon when the first drops began to come down. They were close to the bottom of the zigzag path from Gun Hill and the sky was creaking with thunder, the first drops seeming like the overspill from a vast store of water just waiting to release itself.

'Oh, here it comes!' Lily cried. It was impossible not to feel a sense of exaltation at the beginning of the monsoon, so that the thought of a drenching was glori-ous after all the dust and heat. As they hurried along the Mall, the vendors were quickly pulling scraps of tarpaulin over their wares and everyone who had some-where to go was running for cover, putting up umbrellas as they did so.

And then down it came, the water seeming to gush from the sky in a great, hissing, splashing fall of giant drops which were soon bouncing from awnings and roofs, pouring out from the end of guttering, forming a stream which ran down the sloping streets. Children ran out in it, laughing and catching handfuls of water, the cows took cover under overhanging roofs and everyone seemed to be smiling and shrieking and running or just standing, turning their faces up to catch its cool rush on their cheeks and letting it soak all through their clothing. By the time Lily and Susan reached the gate of the bungalow they were wading, ankle-deep in water.

'Wait for me!' Sam was striding along the road, laughing as water streamed down his hair.

Lily opened the door and ushered Susan inside as Sam reached them, gasping.

'I was looking for you, dear – where've you been?'

'Gun Hill . . .'

She was about to step into the house after Susan, but he caught her hand and they stood for a moment in the little front garden with their hands linked, letting the rain come down and down over them, drinking it in like flowers and loving it.

'That's my girl – God, I love you, Lily . . .' His smiling eyes met hers and he pulled her close and kissed and kissed her in the rain.

For a time, that evening, the great force of the rainstorm had passed and there was a calm lull before a gathering of the next. The air felt washed and clear, and full of the new smell of soaked earth and all the plants and trees looked washed and vivid.

Lily, Sam and Susan sat on the veranda, sipping whisky and water after their evening meal. Edward was settled in bed and as they enjoyed the calm of the evening, comfortable in wicker chairs, every so often, Lily felt Sam take her hand privately, between their chairs, and hold it, giving it a loving squeeze.

A deep quietness seemed to fill the valley. From far away an occasional cry, human or animal, broke into the silence, a peace which had also come upon the three of them. The sun sank behind the dark peaks far over to their left and every now and then they saw the black outlines of birds wheeling against the changing colours as the newly washed sky altered with the sun's retiring. It passed through white-gold to orange and pink, the mountains edged with purple shadows which sank into the smoke-grey of dusk, and they could just distinguish the outline of the peaks. Still they sat on without lighting candles, not wanting to break into the gradual eclipse of the day but let things be, watching the darkness gather, until the hour when there are no more edges to the land, and sky and rock are one.